TENDER SEDUCTION

"The only thing I ask of you is to let me do as I will," Jervais said. His voice had a rare gentleness to it. "Give yourself to me now; don't be frightened. I swear you will have naught to fear ever in my bed."

He gathered Norah in his arms. She'd been cold, even under the bedclothes, but he was very warm. Hot.

He let her lie in his embrace for a while, holding her with no more purpose than to let her get accustomed to the feel of him; then he found her mouth and kissed her deeply.

Norah melted. She grew dreamy and drugged with his kisses, so much so that when he lifted his mouth, hers followed, seeking more. She pressed her lips to his hair as he nuzzled her throat. Excitement surged through her even as she wondered if such pleasure could be entirely sinless . . .

ROMANCE REIGNS
WITH ZEBRA BOOKS!

SILVER ROSE (2275, $3.95)
by Penelope Neri

Fleeing her lecherous boss, Silver Dupres disguised herself as a boy and joined an expedition to chart the wild Colorado River. But with one glance at Jesse Wilder, the explorers' rugged, towering scout, Silver knew she'd have to abandon her protective masquerade or else be consumed by her raging unfulfilled desire!

STARLIT ECSTASY (2134, $3.95)
by Phoebe Conn

Cold-hearted heiress Alicia Caldwell swore that Rafael Ramirez, San Francisco's most successful attorney, would never win her money . . . or her love. But before she could refuse him, she was shamelessly clasped against Rafael's muscular chest and hungrily matching his relentless ardor!

LOVING LIES (2034, $3.95)
by Penelope Neri

When she agreed to wed Joel McCaleb, Seraphina wanted nothing more than to gain her best friend's inheritance. But then she saw the virile stranger . . . and the green-eyed beauty knew she'd never be able to escape the rapture of his kiss and the sweet agony of his caress.

EMERALD FIRE (3193, $4.50)
by Phoebe Conn

When his brother died for loving gorgeous Bianca Antonelli, Evan Sinclair swore to find the killer by seducing the tempress who lured him to his death. But once the blond witch willingly surrendered all he sought, Evan's lust for revenge gave way to the desire for unrestrained rapture.

SEA JEWEL (3013, $4.50)
by Penelope Neri

Hot-tempered Alaric had long planned the humiliation of Freya, the daughter of the most hated foe. He'd make the wench from across the ocean his lowly bedchamber slave—but he never suspected she would become the mistress of his heart, his treasured SEA JEWEL.

Available wherever paperbacks are sold, or order direct from the Publisher. Send cover price plus 50¢ per copy for mailing and handling to Zebra Books, Dept. 3207, 475 Park Avenue South, New York, N.Y. 10016. Residents of New York, New Jersey and Pennsylvania must include sales tax. DO NOT SEND CASH.

SPELLBOUND
NADINE CRENSHAW

ZEBRA BOOKS
KENSINGTON PUBLISHING CORP.

For my sister,
Nancy Paul.

ZEBRA BOOKS

are published by

Kensington Publishing Corp.
475 Park Avenue South
New York, NY 10016

Copyright © 1990 by Nadine Crenshaw

First printing: November, 1990

Printed in the United States of America

Part One: 1155

"The wrath of a woman is much to dread."

—*Tristram and Ysolt*

Chapter 1

Coxgrave Priory stood all but hidden under a low roof of grey mist in the dark forests of England. Within its stout enclosure door, a long, stone-flagged passage led to the chapel. There the nuns gathered to pray seven times a day—matins and lauds, prime, terce, sext, none, vespers, and compline—the *Opus Dei*, God's Work.

The day after Candlemas was Norah of Ramsay's sixteenth birthday. She passed with the other nuns through the antechoir to kneel for the first silent hour of worship. The predawn chapel was shadowy, cold, and empty. Its only furniture was a relict cupboard, which held a treasured piece of the true cross. The grille that divided the choir from the altar had an opening through which the nuns took communion from their priest during his infrequent visits.

Norah swallowed a yawn as she took her place at the end of a correct line of figures all plainly and humbly dressed as she was, in long, monkish brown robes. A white wimple was wound about her head and throat, and over that was her brown veil. The wool of the habit was thick, yet the chill of winter penetrated it. Even in the coldest months no fire ever burned in the priory, except for cooking.

Since she'd been brought here and made a postulant, this chapel had become the hub of her life. Hushed to naught but the slip of sandaled feet, it was simple to the point of austerity, and as functional as a workroom. That in fact was very much its nature. The nuns who prayed here were as calm about it as women in a kitchen. Enclosed for life in these shadowy rooms, they did nothing for the world but commune with God. They sacrificed themselves to prayer in the belief that in doing so they could coax His love down into the world. A very mysterious thing.

Norah thought of them as the women that God kept to himself. At fourteen or fifteen years of age they vowed their virginity and were received into this place that felt so fearfully like a tomb.

She schooled her eyes to her folded hands and sought a better position for her knees. The movement caused her stomach to growl. The sound earned her a glance from Mother Fae, whose eyes were so close-set, so drawn into the center of her face, that they made her expression melancholy. She shook her head, a gesture that said, *Two months of instruction and you are no more fit now than in the beginning*. She went grimly back to her prayer, confident in her belief that each nun received the same amount of food and that a slight hunger was good for the soul.

Two months of this prioress's austere monastic wisdom had reduced Norah, who had always been a

8

slender child, to a skinny, half-starved one. Her skin was wan, her body all bones—and her spirit was almost broken.

But not quite. She'd not yet resigned herself to this entombment, this premature burial. She sneaked a glance down the line of nuns stretched to her left, each one looking like the others, not one proclaiming any particular uniqueness. Their faces, surrounded by the white frames of their wimples, were composed into inward, listening expressions, every one blank, every one unmarked by any experience of real living. And they were trying to make Norah into one of them. Soon they were going to make her take the vows that would put any dream of happiness forever beyond her reach.

A feeling of being caged and suffocated came over her. She had to struggle not to writhe against it, not to invite more censure by giving into this almost unbearable urge to rise up and run into the garden, to the high enclosure wall, and scramble over it, somehow! and be free. The image came to her with unnatural power, and with it came an odor of fear as plain as the metallic tang in the air before a rainstorm. She recognized this uncanny sensation as one of her "visions." It was akin to *déjà vu,* yet subtly different, for instead of seeming like something that had happened to her in the past, it came as a vivid glimpse of the future.

Oh Lord God! I don't believe these visions come to me from the devil. I don't believe what Father said, that I'm Satan's spawn. Accept this prayer, I beg you, consider me with mercy. Please, Lord, don't let them make me one of them!

She clenched her stomach again.

9

And please don't let Mother Fae hear my stomach growl!

The leper had lost most of his hearing. Rattling the bones with which he was required to signal his approach, he didn't hear the three horsemen coming toward him through the weeping grey twilight. The horses appeared before him suddenly on the narrow road. The lead rider, seeing him, yanked back on his reins so hard that his hackney reared and neighed. His companions' horses whinnied. He cursed: "Get off the road, you scourge!" The unfortunate leper, nearly naked, barefoot, and full of sores, scrambled into the forest, carrying his begging tin and his rattling bones with him.

Jervais Le Strand looked back over his shoulder and said to his escort, "Does it seem these wretched are more common down here? I swear, we've seen naught but lepers and sodden peasants for days."

He rode on without waiting for an answer. No answer was needed. The three were in accord most of the time. And they needed to keep their minds on the road, which was no worse than anywhere else, yet was abominable.

They crossed a crude wooden bridge, and few huts stood by the way now. They were approaching the town of Benley, which lay under the king's castle of the same name. Outside the gate were several taverns and alehouses, available for those who preferred to carouse or sleep outside the walls. Beyond a variety of small shops, the riders found the Counsil Tavern. A light flickered in an iron socket beneath the weathered wood of its sign.

The Counsil was locally famous for its fattened partridges and the bream and pike from its fish pond. Jervais rode into the courtyard as if seeking nothing else but refreshment after his long journey on the highroad. Fashion interested him little at any time, but he was dressed even more plainly than usual tonight. He wished to be taken for a simple knight errant. Hence he was accompanied only by his young squire, Charles of Silda, and by his liegeman, Sir Gian of Lesterhouse. They had left their shields, blazoned with the earl of Conniebrook's bear-and-lion devise, with the rest of their company at a camp to the north.

A pair of stringy boys ran forward, slithering on the muddy cobblestones, to take the three horses. Jervais's breath made clouds in front of him as he dismounted and flipped each boy a coin from his wallet.

The tavernkeep, bald and merry, welcomed the men out of the night-numbed air into the warmth and light of his establishment: "By Saint Julian! Come in, come in, Sir Knights!" He showed them the best bench in the room, shewing away an uncouth yeoman clad in hartskin and at the same time waving over his prettiest serving wench.

Jervais said, "Ale for three."

The woman poured out three brimming horns. "My lords?" she murmured in a husky, breathless voice, holding up a spice box. Jervais nodded and she added a pinch of fennel to each horn.

Jervais threw off his cloak, laying bare his hauberk. Beneath it, his thick, quilted tunic of green fustian was sadly discolored. All the oiling and care in the world could not keep iron mail from rusting in

11

this weather. Servants brought meat and bread while he pulled off his helm, the nasal of which had partially masked his face. Though his mail hood still covered his head, now his eyes were exposed. The ale wench paused to stare. "Them's pretty eyes, my lord."

Charles sniggered.

"Well, they are," she protested. "Silver, like a frozen pond."

Jervais waved her away. He'd heard women make every comparison imaginable about his eyes. They were a family trait, however, and he felt no vanity beyond family pride in them.

He spread butter from a crock onto a chunk of bread. At another table, a local ditch-digger tossed a bone he'd gnawed clean to the rushes on the floor. Two dogs scrambled to claim it, a third barked, then all three were fighting. While they were being kicked into silence, Gian cuffed Charles, saying, "Carve your lord's meat, squire."

Charles hastened to do as he was told, bending over Jervais's shoulder. Jervais, leaning back, said, "Gian, you are so endearing. Isn't he, Charles? All good manners."

Gian grinned and dipped his bread into the juice of the meat on his plate. He said in a confidential tone, "If you'd keep more than one squire the boy would have some leisure. Most men in your place would have three."

"Do you need more leisure, Charles?"

"No, my lord," the boy answered fervently.

"You see, Gian, he doesn't want leisure. His poor uncle sent him to the 'gentle' earl of Conniebrook to be 'nourished,' and nourish him I will."

Gian grunted good-naturedly. It was he who answered the first question from the tavern swill-bowls: "What brings three men-at-arms out this time o' night?" He made up a glib lie, speaking the English dialect instead of his own Norman French. His story got a laugh, and he told another. The crowd of tipplers grew jolly, plied with drinks by the tavernkeep. The yeoman asked if they had ever taken a castle by seige, and Gian obligingly started on a third tale: "Seiges incline a man toward corpulence. Now there was a time . . ."

Charles, a solemn youth, remained standing behind Jervais with his arms folded while his lord finished his meal. His stance was possessive.

Jervais lifted his cup often in order to seem to drink as much as anyone, yet he swallowed little. He felt like a hawk amidst dab-chicks.

A tonsured monk was among the gathering, though not a part of it. The man sat alone, as monks usually did, the dislike of clergy being so widespread. Gian muttered privately between stories, "There's no decency about him. Think of all the good beef and ale needed to keep such a broad carcass alive."

"He's in the prime of his manhood," Jervais said, careful to keep a straight face.

Charles couldn't repress a laugh.

Without needing a sign, his companions knew when the time was right to break the group into smaller segments. Charles moved into a corner to dine with the chronic sharp appetite of his nineteen years. For company, he gathered a young shoemaker and a warner and his wife. Jervais could just see the top of his cropped head and his sun-browned, earnest brow. Charles was fortunate in his appearance:

13

blond, strong-featured, with sky-colored eyes. He had a tendency to strike the heroic pose, yet there was nothing about him of the sly or suspect. That he tended to idolize Jervais was only natural. He would get over that.

Gian gathered about him a tinker and his two apprentices, a hackneyman, and a needleseller named Humbert. He set to entertaining them with stories of fighting, hunting, horses, and hawks.

Jervais was left free to join the monk.

Brother Ignatius was a Benedictine outrider, meaning he was privileged to travel abroad on the business of his order rather than remain within the monastery's walls. His religious calling, according to what was said, was not worth an oyster. He was a man who preferred to exercise his own religious rules. And he seemed to do quite well for himself. In the surrounding towns he was known in every tavern—and by every ale wench, as well. He could be hard of heart. This was said by the begging lepers and the widows who had no shoes, all of whom he apparently shunned. Yet wherever personal profit arose, it seemed he could be ever so courteous and humble.

These reports sounded likely to Jervais, for the man sitting opposite him across the small corner table wore a black cassock with sleeves purfled with fur. His hood was fastened to his breast with a heavy, wrought-gold pin. Even his boots were soft. And there was an odd luminosity to his eyes—that implacable glittering quality that said, *Greed.*

He'd just finished eating a whole chicken and a round loaf of bread with his short, stubby fingers when Jervais offered to fill his horn. "Many thanks,

Sir Knight." His charm was like a cloying scent he emitted into the air. He put the brimming horn to his lips carefully and managed to smile even as he downed a goodly portion of its contents; meanwhile his double chin lifted, showing a throat as white as a May lily. Above it, his face was pink. His bulging eyes rolled a little in the wallows of his cheeks. Jervais was reminded of a fat Martinmas hog.

Not given to meaching phrases, Jervais placed a small purse on the table between them. "I'm in need of some information."

The monk hove himself into a more comfortable position on his stool. His eyes on the purse twinkled as brightly as two stars.

"Are you in communication with Coxgrave Priory?"

"Now and then. I know the nuns' priest, a humble man, the servant of the brides of God, more faithful than a dog."

"Do you recall him mentioning a new woman admitted into the nunnery recently? A young woman?"

"Perchance." As his dimpled hand crept toward the purse, Jervais's own hand reached, as if idly, to finger the strings. The monk hesitated, then answered more specifically. "A girl arrived two months or more ago, evidently from afar. She's known as Sister Norah. Of course, that will change as soon as she takes the vows."

For the first time in weeks, a smile pulled at Jervais's mouth. Norah. The name made his veins and nerves tremble. His hand slid away from the purse. In an instant the purse disappeared into the monk's robe.

The monk said, "Coxgrave offers the women solid discipline. There is no coddling, no time for them to brew trouble."

Jervais only nodded and rose. He didn't care a farthing about the discipline of the nunnery. But once he got his hands on little Sister Norah . . .He only dimly heard the monk's next words, yet they stopped him as surely as would a poisoned lance: "I believe she's to take the vows any day."

Jervais gave the man a long look. If she took the vows, it would need a papal intercession to free her of them. A most unlikely thing. Meanwhile, her fief would go to the church. He began to sweat under his tunic.

Gian lifted a questioning brow as Jervais rejoined him. Jervais nodded and ordered another ale. Gian leaned toward him and asked, "What do you think of this wench?"

Jervais looked the woman over. She was perhaps twenty-two years old, somewhat broad-shouldered for her very slender body, with hair of a rich autumnal brown. "She seems a good prospect to me, amateur that I am in such matters." He noticed for the first time that there was a second woman. "But now that one—by St. Aidan, there's a dumpling-breasted trollop. Look at the generous width of her hips." He winked at Gian, though he kept his tone completely matter-of-fact. "When seeking woman-flesh, a man mustn't be foolish. He wants value for his money."

Gian rubbed his chin and made a considering sound. "Maybe you're right." At length, he whispered into the tavernkeep's ear, and the bald man called, "Helaine!" The plump-bottomed girl glanced over her shoulder. She smiled broadly in Gian's direction as she realized what was wanted of her. She sauntered toward the stairs leading to the rooms above. As Gian rose from the bench, Jervais clapped him on the back. "A good choice."

Gian laughed and followed the woman up the stairs. The gathering fell to unrestrained gestures and loose buffoonery and shouts of encouragement. Through the ribald laughter, Jervais saw that the thinner girl was looking at him with her eyes closed to mere slits. The invitation was clear. For a moment he let himself consider her rich rusty hair. The bawdy talk had had its effect; there was that familiar lightning in his blood, and certain thoughts pushed themselves forward. But in the end he was too fastidious to take a woman so low-born.

It was not that he was unneedful, for he'd not had a leman at his disposal for several seasons. And it was not that he was celibate. Though he remained a bachelor, over the years several beautiful and demure ladies had moved into and through and out of his life.

It was simply a matter of dignity. How could a man who loved a queen bring himself to lie on a flea-infested straw mattress with a peasant woman's dirty feet wagging above his back?

He had two rings on his left hand, a plain band that he wore on his little finger, and on his middle finger a stone that twinkled with red fire. It had been a gift from Eleanor, Countess of Anjou, Duchess of Normandy and Aquitaine, and Queen of England. His own Eleanor. She was at Castle Benley right now. And the king was said to be gone for the night.

Castle Benley soared up from wall to wall to massive towers with battlements, a huge bastion of stone hanging over the landscape, seeming—as it was meant to seem—heavy and menacing. When Jervais and Charles arrived at the postern gatehouse, the two stern military men on watch reminded them that it was late to bespeak lodging for the night. But Jervais gave his name and they were admitted.

The strike of their horses' hooves and the jingling of their harness brasses sounded loud in the restricted corridor that was the outer ward. Their mounts were taken, and a page appeared, a meager boy of thirteen bearing a resinous, flaming torch almost as tall as he was. He would show lord and squire to sleeping quarters.

Jervais was interested in castle architecture; hence his glances were sharp. Benley was tunneled with dim passages, and hollow stairways, and somber chambers that seemed cut from solid stone. He glimpsed the great stone-walled kitchen, its tables empty, the cooks and scullions asleep on the rushes before the still-glowing fireplace. The last spiraling stairwell was filled with gigantic shifting shapes that fled before the page and his torch.

Jervais's rank assured him of not having to make do with the garrison, yet the private tower chamber he was given was not large. From the deep embrasure of its single tall, narrow window only a little slit of the misty nightsky could be seen. The furnishings were sparse, though of the highest quality. There was a table and a handsomely carved wooden chair near the fireplace. Unbuckling his belt, he threw his scabbarded sword onto the bed.

By the light of the small fire and one large, wax candle, Charles unlaced the back of his lord's mail. Jervais turned, bent, and took hold of Charles's waist so the squire could pull the hauberk off his back. He swore in gutteral French and bared his teeth when the aventail caught on his chin, then made a sound of relief as Charles at last got the thing off. The armor, which covered him from the top of his head to mid-thigh, weighed more than twenty pounds; he felt light-bodied when it was removed.

The page brought fresh water and towels. The boy had soft raisin eyes. Jervais had been a page once, a seven-year-old boy fencing with a blunted sword. Those had been happy years, when he was given his first horse and hawks and dogs, when he was allowed long rides alone into the dense forest to develop his resourcefulness and his knowledge of woodcraft. He also recalled long lectures for his improvement, however, and sympathized with the boy. He asked him his name.

"Nigel of Stanmar, my lord."

"I know your father. We fought together. Listen to me, Nigel, I want you to take a message to the queen. Can you do that discreetly?"

The boy left with a message that was deceptively simple: "Jervais Le Strand is here."

19

Chapter 2

Jervais let Charles remove his tunic. He washed away the dust of the road in the cold water and put the tunic back on. He felt tired, not a bit refreshed. He wished he had clean clothing, but his traveling chest was at his camp. He must live out of his saddlebags tonight.

The king's court existed wherever Henry Plantagenet was in official residence. For the moment that was Castle Benley, though Henry was gone for the night to Rusmorgan, one of his hunting lodges nearby. Rarely did the court stay two weeks in a place, and while in residence, rarely did Henry keep to the royal castle. Crowned just last October, he already had a reputation for riding fast and far to surprise the stewards and keepers of his manors and estates in untoward moments. Sudden as pestilence he might appear, here, there, anywhere, always when least expected.

Jervais supposed this moving about could be no simple feat. The royal household, from chamberlain to scullion, must number at least two hundred souls, equipped with chapel, beds, kitchen utensils, plate, treasure, clothing, vestments, documents, and all the services pertaining thereto. It must be a life of infernal clamor and commotion.

Nonetheless, Eleanor usually traveled with Henry, riding apace of him, or, if the weather was inclement, borne in a painted litter with the curtains drawn. Jervais supposed her experience on crusade had prepared her for these unseasonable *chevauchées*. She had stayed behind in Benley tonight, however.

He wondered how she fared as Henry's wife. The king was just twenty-two, but a man of pith and action. He had an extraordinary rag bag of an intellect. He'd studied extensively, ransacked the lore of the ancients, and his senses were always at the ready to seize any experience.

Jervais thought all this while trying not to think about little Nigel of Stanmar taking his message to Eleanor, or what possible response it might gain. Even so, consciousness of her nearness slammed through his mind, opening all sorts of doors and banging them shut again before memories could rush out.

When an almost imperceptible knock came at the door, he answered it himself, expecting the page. Instead, a cloaked and hooded woman rustled past him into the room.

His lips fell a little apart. He felt as stunned as if he'd just been drenched with Greek fire. She'd come here. To his room. To his bedchamber. A hope lifted in his mind, unformed but huge. He signaled Charles. The squire, all agog, bowed himself from the chamber.

Charles stood outside his lord's door for a moment,

still caught in awe. The queen and his own Lord Conniebrook! Clearly it was true then.

Since he'd been enrolled as a squire to the earl last summer, Charles had learned to look at his master as a kind of father. His own father was dead, so he welcomed the earl's attention. Lord Jervais rebuked and corrected him with bluntness, but also assumed a father's accountability for his training. In return, Charles attended him as a constant companion and was responsible for generally attending to his comfort. The sense of loyalty he'd developed was so absolute that if his lord loved the queen, then Charles also loved her, without question.

Within the chamber, Jervais realized he was holding an intaken breath; he let it out. "My lady, I had no idea you would come here. You shouldn't have. Someone might have seen you."

She was already shrugging off her mantle. He stepped forward to take the fur-lined blue silk from her. Eleanor. Here. It couldn't be true. His desires and his demands had created this dream.

She was wearing a chemise of white linen. Its long, wrinkled sleeves and long skirt showed fashionably beneath her light blue gown. Without her cloak he saw plainly that she was near to term with Henry's second child. He thought, *This is why she didn't go to Rusmorgan.*

And his unformed hope aborted itself, leaving a white silence behind.

Even pregnant, there was no doubt about it, she was lovely. Though she was thirty-three, the years had not broken the sheath of her youth. About her was that air of belonging to some other, better world. Her thin, high-nosed face shaded from the cream of

22

her brow to the soft redness of her lips to the white skin of her throat. Her fair hair was parted and laced into plaits.

She watched him as he hung her mantle from a peg near the door. They met rarely, and always in such great stealth, that he understood when she took the time now to note what changes were wrought in him. He knew the boyishness was gone from his features. But he kept his hair cut fairly short, and his body was still hard and muscular.

She said, "Jervais, it's been so long."

"A year."

"I should have thought it longer than a year. It has been longer since we've been able to speak alone. Oh my darling, I have so often yearned to see you alone again." She offered him her hands, soft and smooth and fine and white—and cold.

"Your hands are cold," he said, stupidly, unable to think of anything else.

"All of me is cold. This great pile," she lifted her chin to indicate Benley, "is no palace in Antioch."

Antioch, their own personal, leaf-fringed legend.

He led her to the fireside and seated her in the chamber's one chair. He took a stool for himself. It was low and placed his head not too far above hers. He sat staring at her, his hands on his knees. He couldn't believe she was here, actually here with him, just the two of them. He felt so marvelously dazzled by her that he was tongue-tied. His gaze possessed and penetrated her. His body's thirst had never been quenched by mere gazes, but it was all he could have.

She said, her voice tinged with a false pout, "My darling, you neglect me. Your eyes look as blind as a statue's. I come to you at the snap of your fingers, and you sit like a stone staring at me."

"Eleanor," he said, shaking his head a little, "my beautiful Eleanor." His eyes caressed her. The Greeks called love *theia mania*, the madness from the gods. This was madness, he knew it, yet he was helpless against it. "Forgive me," he said. "If I knew of a way, I would repent of all my sins against you."

She smiled like a coquette. "Are they many?" She reached for his nearest hand and touched her fingertip to the ring she had given him. The gesture spoke reams. His large hand folded easily over her cool wrist: he brought her fingers to his lips.

"Ah, my knight, your touch is a magnet almost too powerful to resist—but resist I must." She gently pulled her hand free. "I must take all the pleasure I can in looking at you since I can have no more."

He felt a sudden blast of melancholy. He could never know her intimately, however much he loved her. However great the swell of his need. He might touch her hand, kiss her fingertips, but she was far beyond the reach of his full desire. Her reminder left him feeling empty, devastated.

"Why so sad-looking, my lord? Are you not still my servitor?"

"You know I am and always will be."

She tilted her head a little to one side. "But you shouldn't be here. You should be in the north getting married. Wasn't this the day?"

It touched him that she knew the exact date of his wedding. He drew his mouth into a thin smile. "Old Roger of Ramsay took ill last autumn, and it seems that while he was on his deathbed his daughter got a sudden revelation," he gave the word a twist, "that she should devote her life to praying for his soul.

24

Even before he died, the girl ran off to enter a nunnery. I've traced her to Coxgrave Priory, south of here. I have to collect her before she takes any serious vows."

Eleanor laughed softly. "Are you sure she wants to be a nun—or perchance she's a woman who simply doesn't wish to be subdued to a man's convenience?"

He shifted on his stool. He didn't wish to discuss this with Eleanor.

"But such a fool as to shut herself up in a nunnery! I hope she isn't going to be a nuisance to you, Jervais."

He smiled with just the left side of his mouth. "She will soon learn not to be."

Eleanor's eyebrows were small works of art, elegant, thin curves. She lifted one gracefully. "She is—what? In the bloom of fifteen? And no doubt pretty."

He shrugged. "Sixteen today. I've never seen her, though, nor heard any particular beauty remarked. That usually means a man must assume the worst."

Eleanor shook her head, looking at him bemusedly. Her long braids, intertwined with ribbons and bound with silk the same blue of her gown, moved on her shoulders. "She's young. She will grow up and demand your heart away. I've seen it happen; ugly ducklings blossom into swans."

"My heart has already been given."

It was given in Antioch, during the ill-starred Second Crusade. In his mind, he saw the maps he had studied, the flat Earth with Jerusalem at its center. In his mind, Antioch still possessed that otherness of time and place essential to romance.

He'd been a young paladin, tall and leggy, dressed

25

cap-a-pie in all the chivalric virtues and proclaiming his holy calling with a cross painted on his steel helm. Newly arrived from the West and filled with crusading zeal, ready to pour out his blood in the name of the Holy Church, he didn't doubt he was doing God's will in making war against the Saracen. A crusade was a pious exercise, a penance, a way to Heaven. How could he go wrong?

What he found in the Holy Land, however, was both more and less than the sacred battles he'd expected. His hardest battle had been fought in Antioch.

Antioch, through which the caravans of three continents poured, where turbaned Saracen merchants weighed the treasures of Baghdad and Isfahan against the monies of Venice, Pisa, Alexandria, and France. The babel of languages, the easy commingling of races, the bewildering strangeness of costume. That vague Eastern perfume, musky and charged with spice. The mosques blooming thickly among the cypresses, and the summons of the *muezzin* falling musically through the evening air.

Antioch, where he had fallen in love with Eleanor, wife of Louis VII, Queen of France.

Jervais first met her the day he was mysteriously called into her presence from his company of Crusader knights encamped outside the palace of her uncle, Raymond, Prince of Antioch. He found her amidst her ladies, more elegantly attired than any of the others. She'd been wearing blue then, too, a pale blue gown caught at her tiny waist with a girdle of glittering jewels. Her luxuriant hair hung over her arms, and a jewelled band graced her forehead. She was twenty-five, seven years his senior, yet that detracted not one whit from her allure.

She had a letter in her hand; he recalled the sound of the parchment whispering as she unfolded it and folded it again without reading. "Sir Jervais," she said at last, "we have received this missive from England, and I thought it only compassionate to tell you myself. . . . My lord, I'm afraid the earl of Conniebrook, your father, has passed from his generation."

Her voice was as pure as gold, as sweet as a zither, and it was a moment before he realized the meaning of her words. His father was dead. He stood absolutely still, afraid that if he moved, his body would crack open with anguish. He couldn't allow that to happen before all these ladies.

Eleanor drew nearer and placed her hand on his arm. "I am so sorry, my lord."

She took him into a garden—he scarcely realized he was being led—and wisely left him to his grief. Later, when he had himself under control, she joined him and encouraged him to talk. She talked, too, of the loss of her own father when she was but fifteen. She understood his feeling that his life had been turned upside down and emptied out.

A sympathy grew up between them. That first meeting led to a second, and then a third. She helped him over his initial mourning; he learned to laugh once more. She invited him back again and again. They conversed long hours together. They even made merry—in low tones, so that King Louis's bishops and *abbés* could not overhear. He loved to listen to her singing, to watch her long white fingers plucking at a lute or harp. She sang her own compositions, songs of her longing for love.

27

Occasionally she played chess with him, and won. And then soothed his pride by saying it was only because she was better practiced. He accepted this, knowing she'd been brought up in court accomplishments. Still, whenever she checkmated him she laughed and was delighted; he sensed it was a symbol to her.

Ah, Antioch! The sky was golden, the earth lay open-breasted under the gentle touch of spring, and Antioch was the essence of balladry.

One day, as they sat on a stone bench in one of the palace gardens, Jervais with his long legs outstretched, and Eleanor with her face turned up to the sun, she confided her discontent with her role as Queen of France.

"Louis was trained from his youth to be a monk, you know. His tendencies are still . . . quite monkish. His endless chaplains think me flawed because I give them no future king, but what am I to do when Louis finds being a husband distasteful?" she sighed. "My thoughts can't help but stray sometimes to alternatives."

Jervais turned a face of astonishment upon her. Her words were like a blare of brass. Did any of her alternatives include him? He had no admiration for the austerities of Louis, who as far as he could determine was a monarch in the custody of eunuchs and celibates. If there was any chance Jervais could become her lover—his mind flew to all sorts of possibilities, including a midnight flight with her riding behind him, her arms wrapped about his waist, the soft comfort of her pressed against his back.

He began to ransack the bazaars for the prizes of the East. He plied her with extraordinary and splendid gifts, none of which she would accept. He employed all the seductions and all his eloquence, until one day he simply proclaimed: "I love you."

"And I love you," she answered—magically, unbelievably, touching a previously unplucked harpstring within him.

He pulled her into his arms, crushed her to him, and tried to kiss her. She turned her cheek, "Jervais, Jervais." He recalled himself, but could not seem to let her go. He buried his face in her hair. She kissed his cheek, stroked his shoulder, and finally pushed away from him. On her face was a bright, rather curious expression. Even with his new animal alertness to her heart, he could not fathom that expression.

He stood shaking with the intensity of his love. He said in a whisper, "You are to me as my soul and as my body. Can we never be together?"

"That we must leave to the gods."

"The gods have forever!"

"Jervais, my darling, I am a queen. It brings me little pleasure—and little liberty. It is a great exacting claim upon me, something that chooses me out and calls me to vast things. But it is my destiny."

The effect of that answer was sobering. He felt himself begin to die by inches, from the ankles upward. His wild fancies suddenly seemed foolish. She was a *queen*. The word vibrated in his head like a bell with an ancient voice. And what was he? A youthful earl of a minor fief in the wild northlands of England.

The next time they met, she again took him into the prince's gardens, where the day's light gleamed on the walls of the palace. There she presented him with a gift. "Though I can take naught of you, yet will you take this of me?" She reached for his hand and placed on his third finger a rich ring of silver with a gleaming red stone standing high, blushing in the bright sun.

"I can't—"

She closed his fingers over it. "Take it, I beg you. Let it be quit-claim against all debt I owe you for these past weeks."

"You owe me nothing."

"I do, for you have reminded me that there are still men among men, and that being a woman is not without hope."

He was without hope. It seemed she was cutting him out of her life. He searched desperately for some way to remain connected to her. He said, "I'll take the ring only if you will take at least one thing from me in return—not an object," he rushed to say before she could protest; "I ask you to take my heart as your vassal to serve you always. You shall be my liegelove, and my heart shall always be at your command."

He didn't return to the palace again. While still in the Holy Land he learned that she'd raised the topic of divorce to Louis. Meanwhile, the Second Crusade met with disaster. Jervais turned for England to take up his position as the new earl of Conniebrook amid the chaos of civil war.

Under weak Stephen, effective government had collapsed altogether in England. Anarchy reigned. Jervais chose the side of the Empress Matilda, and later her son, the great grandson of William the Conqueror, Henry Plantagenet. Jervais gained repute for being an ambitious and aggressive warrior, bold and sometimes grasping, a powerful man who could wield a sword with either hand.

He became known for his skills in other arenas as well, as his fame attracted the occasional woman of rank willing to let him vent the excesses of his youthful ardor.

Privately, however, he became increasingly filled with a sense of desolation. It seemed with each season left behind he enjoyed less the delights that flow from routine days. He heard when Eleanor's marriage to Louis was finally, mercifully, dissolved by the vicar of Rome in 1152. She, then thirty-one, promptly wed Jervais's own leigelord, Henry II, nineteen and brimming over with life, truly destined to become a man among men. Henry and Eleanor now ruled most of France and all of England.

She'd found her destiny. Once, when watching a spider drop off a twig and unwind a thread, and then another, until it had built a thin, predevised net, he'd thought of his beloved Eleanor. He'd felt disloyal and immediately banished the comparison. Yet in his deep heart's center he knew the likeness to be true.

She stirred in her chair and began absently to play with one of her braids. Jervais realized he'd fallen into staring at her again as though she were a ghost. He straightened and reoriented himself to the little chamber, where the wax candle had burned low.

Eleanor said, "You have plans for your castle, I understand."

"The refurbishing of the old structure, then a new outer ward. I'm playing with plumb-lines and set squares these days, architect's tools. I've brought a drawing for the king's approval. I've employed a skillful architect, a Norman. The plans he's drawn up are elaborate. Henry should be able to see that what I'm proposing is worthwhile."

"I hope it won't be just another pile of chill stones like this one."

"It won't be stone at all unless I marry my little betrothed." Looking around his shoulder at the fire, he added wryly, "The nearest quarry sizable enough to meet my needs is on Ramsay land."

"A dowry of stone—for a possibly ugly heiress. Is that truly the best you can do?"

He shrugged, leaving unsaid the fact that, except for her, one woman was much the same as another to him. "Ramsay has always cut into Conniebrook at an awkward angle. It was my father's wish to round out our boundary. He arranged the marriage when I was but a boy and the girl no more than a child. But it *was* agreed upon, and now she will deliver what was promised."

"Ah, yes. You men all favor the employment of us members of 'the meaner sex' as instruments to quiet your uneasy borders and prevent bloodshed over your properties. I can almost sympathize with the girl's desire to run away from you." Eleanor took his chin between her fingers and turned his face toward hers. "Such a tender lamb for a ravening wolf. Don't be too harsh with her."

He laughed without a trace of humor. "Sometimes it's necessary to scare people. Sometimes terror is all that stops them from doing stupid things."

Eleanor shook her head. "You have changed, my love."

"I have given up boyish dreams of chivalry and glorious feats, if that's what you mean. I've lived a crowded, stormy life since Antioch, and done things I can't afford to examine too closely, things to secure your husband his crown as well as to secure my own future."

"You have much plaguing you," she replied in the gentle, soothing voice that charmed so many.

"'Tis true. I apologize that you find me in such an ill mood."

"You have proven yourself a good friend, to me as well as to your country. I believe I can forgive an occasional ill mood."

She rose; her gown flowed sinuously around her fertile body. He followed her to the door. Her silken cloak made a sound like a willow swept by wind as he slipped it about her shoulders. She offered her hand for his kiss, and he went down on one knee, transforming the courtesy into an act of renewed fealty. She gazed down at him for a long moment, her expression mysterious. At last she said, "Methinks I was not wrong to fall in love with you in Antioch. Though you have a head hard enough to break a door, you are indeed a handsome man, my Jervais."

He managed a wry smile. "And you are a most impossible woman. You're like a chameleon, a being of a thousand forms, multiple and ungraspable. I've wondered oft how so many aspects could be cunningly wrought into the fiber of one woman." Her brow lowered at what he realized sounded like a complaint. "Even so," he added, "know that my heart is always eager and longing to serve you."

Adjusting her hood over her head, she went out. Beyond the door was a chill recess lit by the leaping fire of a torch. Charles was there playing a silent game of conkers with the raisin-eyed pageboy, Nigel. Both leapt to their feet and bowed at the sight of Eleanor.

There was another cowled figure watching their game. This person stepped forward and proved to be a woman, a servant or a sympathetic lady-in-waiting who had not liked to let her queen travel the dark passages of the old castle alone at night. Jervais hoped she was discreet. Despite Eleanor's advanced pregnancy, this meeting looked as respectable as moat water. Whispers of it could do her no good.

In his concern for her, he didn't consider what such whispers could do to him, and far from his mind at the moment was the fact that Henry had the Conqueror's family temper.

The women started away quickly, down the dark and darker passageway. Eleanor's disappearing image was replaced on Jervais's brain with something like the after-image of a terribly bright object. It was the face of the lovely, young, high-spirited queen of France, her long, fair hair falling to her waist and her deep-set eyes flickering with mischief and gaiety, poignantly beautiful and rare. What cruel blow of fate had made her a queen and him just an earl?

He turned back to his chamber, feeling alone and tired and ready for bed. Through his slit of a window, he heard the mist outside hardening to real rain. Charles came in to undress him. The squire approached him with that solicitous tact which is so difficult for a proud man to bear.

Chapter 3

It was still raining when Jervais rose and left the shelter of the castle. Though the cocks had not yet crowed, his big bay saddle horse was waiting for him, milling with Gian's and Charles's. Gian was keeping his face protected by his hood. Bundled he was, like a monk, from chin to croup. Jervais assumed he was feeling the effects of too little sleep and too much woman.

Jervais's horse blew air through its nostrils in greeting. At the last minute, Charles whisked a cloth from the bay's saddle. Jervais took the reins and a handful of mane in his fist and swung up, stabbing his feet into the stirrups. The saddle was dry. Charles was a good squire.

When Jervais had been a squire, he remembered unending sessions with tedious men expounding on some point or other while he had to nod and ask polite questions. He remembered being made to brush a horse three times in one afternoon, although each time no hair was out of place. Before he was fifteen he had learned to read and write, ride and hawk, play chess and backgammon, thrum a harp and fence with skill. He could also handle a light lance and shield on horseback. From his earliest youth he had accomplishment in arms held up as the one thing most worthy of a man.

His bay snorted and shook its mane while Charles mounted his own horse. The three men started out, leaving the castle by way of the main gate. Jervais was wearing full battle regalia beneath a heavy but finely made cloak of royal red. His intention today was to make a sudden and stunning appearance on Cox-grave Priory.

They headed down the narrow street, between the huts that grew up beneath the castle. Anon they came out the southern end of the town at a trot. Here they were joined by Jervais's full escort, mounted on saddle horses with destriers in tow. Their gear was trussed up in sacks or stowed in the panniers on each flank of the sumpter mules.

They continued south in a motley, unmilitary procession. The thick mud sucked the horse's hoofs so that they had to keep to the edge of the road where the ruts were shallower and hence collected less rain-water.

They rode deeper into the forest, meeting no one. In this weather, few would choose to travel. It was not yet the season for pilgrims and palmers. Jervais was not sorry to see no sick lepers and the sort of poverty-stricken wretches that lined every road come summer.

Their route wound downhill and became slippery with mud and stones. Birch and pine gave way to oaks. The road pinched down and became a trail littered with half-buried stones like uneven steps. The horses slowed to a cautious walk. On either side, the woods that covered half of England stretched out into darkness. The seethe of water through all that foliage filled the air with sound.

Now and then one or another of the men cursed, without real heart: "God's bones," or "God of angels." The "road" continued no wider than a bridle path now. The cavalcade was obliged to string out single-file. Jervais kept his eyes sharp. The forests were tenanted by strange people, sometimes hostile, sometimes fey. As they passed a cairn of lichened rock, he imagined eyes watching him.

What foolish mood is this, Le Strand?

The wet morning seemed infinitely long. At the end of it, just before noon, Coxgrave Priory came into view through the watery daylight. The place was solid and four-square, built high, surrounded by wild-growing rhododendrons. The road was nothing but a narrow grass footpath now, showing how seldom the nunnery was visited.

The number of nuns in England was not great, and most nunneries were cramped. He didn't believe Brother Ignatius's claim that Coxgrave offered discipline to the women. There were a few severe prioresses, but by and large they were known to be easy-going. Jervais had heard of widespread jollity in many priories. There was the story of the nun who had run away with a harpist. And Gian told a good dirty story about some carpenters in a nunnery. And there was a rumor about a priorty where the nuns habitually took their pet hounds into church with them.

Still, this didn't look like a house of pleasure. Perhaps the women here really did live "under the glance of the Lord," in austerity, imprisoning their bodies in order to free their souls.

He approached the wet grey walls with a calm attitude, his mind working smoothly and without rush. After they had clattered up to the outer gate, he sat perfectly still on his horse for a moment. Not even his eyes moved or blinked.

As a warrior, he'd learned to take a moment before each battle to imagine his ultimate victory. It wasn't Norah of Ramsay he imagined now. The girl wasn't that important to him, except that she was his lawful marriage prize. No, it was Ramsay itself he saw. The fief of Ramsay, thrust like a wedge into Conniebrook, a triangle that sharply indented her borders, marking her narrowest breadth and therefore her weakest point. The honor of Ramsay, with its four hundred and eight knights' fees. The stone of Ramsay, waiting to be quarried for the enrichment of Conniebrook. He saw it all as his. He saw it clearly.

A single fang of lightning lit the scene with a flash. Jervais saw a frozen, monochromatic image of his men-at-arms, and he recalled himself. The rain had increased to a deluge that might well cost his entire escort a week in bed. He called out crisply, "I won't be long," and left them wrapped like upright sausages in their cloaks.

He rang the bell of the outer door. No one came, so he pushed through it. The foyer within was bare. Opposite him stood a second door. Beside it was a "turn," a revolving cupboard which was the only communication the enclosed sisters were supposed to have with the outside world. Supplies and letters for them were put on it, and the nuns swung it around, never even glimpsing the faces of those who lived beyond their walls.

A panel in the inner door quietly slid back, revealing a tiny grille. Jervais approached it, stooping and squinting, trying to see through the finely pierced wood. The voice of a woman came to him muffled: "God bless you." That disembodied voice made him shiver. It seemed to come from someone who had once been alive, before this enclosure door had shut her in for all eternity.

He said, "I'm Jervais Le Strand, Earl of Conniebrook. I've come to collect the Lady Norah of Ramsay, my betrothed, whom you are harboring."

The turn sister, her voice now startled, directed him to a small receiving room to his left. The grille in the door closed, but for another moment Jervais stood with his head on one side, staring in a considering way at that door.

The receiving room was furnished with a bench, a table, and a bronze crucifixion plaque. There was no fire. The whole place was as chill as a tomb. One wall of the room was grille. Seeing it, Jervais realized the uselessness of his attempt to make an impression by way of dress. Looking at that grille, he was the one who was stunned.

The morning after her uncelebrated birthday, Norah prayed feverently, *Lord, I can't stay here. What shall I do?* Since yesterday's vision of climbing the nunnery's walls, she'd begun to feel pulled, drawn—in no way she could explain or even understand—to act out what she'd seen herself doing.

After matins and lauds, fifteen minutes were allowed for breakfast. Then the nuns did odd chores until terce. Norah worked in the kitchen where, wrapped in a huge apron, she stood on a box to reach the sink with its wooden washbowl while another nun dried their simple dishes and put them away. Following terce, they began their real day's work.

Even nuns must make their living. In Coxgrave, to earn their bread, they sewed. Norah had discovered a talent for needlework here. She'd been advanced from hemming to embroidering the altar cloths the priory produced, white on white. She spent her work hours before a broidery-frame, deftly poking, finding, and returning her quick needle in its endless journeys.

The labor was done in silence. The profound quiet of the enclosure made her restless. Except at mealtimes, when one nun read aloud to the others, they never spoke. Special dispensation was granted by the mother prioress if it would help a nun spiritually; otherwise, they were to keep their minds on God.

Norah's mind was on her vision: She'd scrambled up onto something in order to reach the top of the wall. What had she stood on? What would be tall enough?

The turn sister wobbled into the workroom. Sister Gabriel was over eighty, and had the frailty of the old and the near-blind. Nonetheless, she was obviously agitated, obviously laden with news. She tugged on Mother Fae's sleeve and signalled toward the passageway outside the room. Her demeanor spoke of urgency. The prioress stabbed her needle into her work and rose. As the two left the workroom, Norah's heart began to beat harder. She couldn't think why.

Mother Fae went to the receiving room with great reluctance. She'd heard the Earl of Conniebrook's name spoken when Sister Norah was brought to the priory, but under the influence of the dowry promised if they would take the girl in and make a nun of her, it had seemed the name of a man far away and not to be worried about, and since then she'd never thought about this earl to whom the girl had once been betrothed. (It was difficult to remain vividly alive to a world one scarcely beheld.)

In the receiving room, she unlocked and opened a pair of creaking, ceiling-high shutters. These folded back to reveal a low partitioning wall fitted with a formidable double grille. These grilles consisted of a wooden screen of thick, dusty slats on the nun's side, and on the visitor's side an iron grid fitted with wicked-looking spikes. Between the two was a musty curtain of heavy black material. These barriers served to keep the nuns from their parents, their brothers and sisters, their former friends.

Mother Fae could make out nothing of the visitor on the other side. "Lord Conniebrook?" she said, her voice steady and cold, despite its being used so little.

"Who is there?" a masculine voice came back quickly, a deep voice, imperious, autocratic.

"I am Mother Fae."

"Enchanted to meet you," the earl said. She heard the dry irony in his tone. "I've come to collect my betrothed, the Lady Norah of Ramsay."

"There is a postulant here of that name." The earl made a sound halfway between fury and triumph, and she continued quickly, "Tomorrow, when she takes her vows, she'll be given the name Sister Katherine."

"What the devil is this game? Lady Norah was betrothed to me twelve years ago."

"God has broken your betrothal, as is his right."

"God had nothing to do with this! She made the mistake of thinking she could rebuff and insult me—and now you're doing the same. I warn you, by all that's holy, I don't deal kindly with troth-breakers." It was clear by his voice that he was in danger of losing control. Then, suddenly the murder in him was dismissed by a humorless laugh. "She's nothing but a skittish girl. She doesn't have the slightest idea what she's doing, let alone what's good for her. But she's heir to a fief, and she has obligations."

Mother Fae was surprised. Evidently he had been told that the girl had come here of her own accord. The prioress saw no reason to enlighten him.

She had nothing by which to judge the man but his voice. It was one that carried without obvious effort. It had the full thunder of someone who was accustomed to making himself heard—a voice that sounded as if it were giving orders even when it wasn't. Her mind formed a dim picture of him: a tall, powerfully built man with a straight back and a strong physical presence. Exactly the sort of man who was the antithesis of a woman with a vocation for God. The only thing you could do with such a person was stand up to him, because the only thing he would respect was strength.

"She will never wed you, my lord. God brought her here." She believed that was true, if not in the way he thought. "Her fief is meant to be her dowry to His church. Tomorrow she will become Sister Katherine, and Ramsay will become the property of Coxgrave. Please accept this and go in peace."

There was a pause, a long, dragging moment. It dawned on her that he might not have known the fief was promised to the nunnery. When he spoke, his voice penetrated the grille harshly: "She hasn't taken vows yet."

"She will on the morrow." Mother Fae felt querulous; she wasn't used to being argued with. "Please, Lord Conniebrook, in the interest of peace, go away."

His patience suddenly broke altogether: *"No!* God strike me—*no!* I will *not* go away!" His voice came closer to the grille. Mother Fae swayed back as she heard him grip the iron with his hands. The entire grille shuddered as he heaved at it. Then he pushed his fingers through, to feel the wood behind the curtaining. Mother Fae gasped. Her hand went to her mouth. She could only picture him as someone huge and menacing.

She heard him turn and stride from the receiving room. Briefly, he tried the enclosure door. It rattled in its frame as he pulled against it. The door was stout, and not only locked, but barred top and bottom. Yet he shook it so terribly that it seemed to loosen from its very hinges.

Then the noise stopped, his footsteps echoed in the foyer. The outer door was wrenched open and slammed shut.

The aura of unrelieved femininity and quiet settled back on the convent like ancient dust.

Mother Fae left the receiving room feeling quite wrung out. *Sister Norah!* she thought vengefully, *so thin, so unwholesomely tender—like the flesh under a scab!* The escort that had brought her had warned she could be trouble—the devil's spawn, they'd called her.

Rain continued to drip from the roof of the priory

with bleak insistence. The bell rang for sext, and every nun stopped what she was doing and started for the chapel. Among them, Norah prayed fervently, clutching her plain wooden rosary as a life line—though she had grave doubts it would save her.

Twenty minutes later, everyone shuffled to the refectory for dinner. They took their noon meal without speech, though at a wooden lectern a reader went over the rules for the month and then read from the Book of Daniel. Each nun was given a bowl of thin soup, a scrap of cold fish, and a plate of cabbage.

After dinner there was the washing up, then more needlework. The bell pealed seven times for vespers at four-thirty. Supper afterwards was soup and a hunk of coarse bread. They ate in silence again, this time with only the cooling slurp of mouths against spoons.

The bell rang softly one last time, calling them to compline. The chapel was dark. The single light on the altar shed shifting shadows through the grille.

As the others rose stiffly to shuffle toward their cells, Mother Fae grasped Norah's shoulder. She nodded Norah toward her office.

In the prioress's cell a single candle burned. She sat, and Norah knelt beside her. She was always nervous around this woman whose manner seemed so cold and unsympathetic. A prioress was powerful within her realm. For even the slightest things, the nuns must ask a "permission" from her. And often she refused.

Mother Fae felt nervous herself tonight. Even ringed by walls, she was afraid. Lord Conniebrook's sudden arrival, and the thunderous impression he'd made on her, had shaken her confidence to its roots.

His voice had seemed so purely masculine, so peremptory, so full of sulphurous rumblings. And the way he had tested the grille! What if he were to—

Nonsense! This is a monastery. He wouldn't dare violate it.

She said to the bowed head of the girl at her knee, "You are yet contaminated by the world, Sister. You lack faith."

Norah felt the woman's dark, close-set eyes, sharp and accusing. "I—" she stuttered, "I don't believe I belong here."

Mother Fae's expression was not kind. "I don't suppose you do, someone like you, so infested with sin. We are willing to help you cast out your demons. I am truly convinced that by taking holy vows you will purify your soul. Tomorrow you will join us or—" she looked away with indifference, "or you will suffer God's punishment. There are other ways to discourage demons, you know. You must choose, Sister."

Norah answered in bright, defiant haste, "I choose to be free!"

Mother Fae's scowl was fearfully reproving. "Free? To go where? To do what? You have no place, no one. Your own father doesn't want you. He's broken your betrothal to the earl of Conniebrook. You have no friend in all of England who would take you in, no one who would feed you and clothe you—except us." She shifted in her chair. "I suggest you pray tonight. Perhaps that will help you decide."

The interview was over. Norah made her silent way through the dark, cold passageways. She felt crushed, both by the facts Mother Fae had so mercilessly pointed out to her, and by this stone building which surrounded her body and seemed to imprison her soul. Her daydream of escape seemed utterly foolish. Mother Fae was right; even if she could find a way out, where would she go?

Her cell was so small she could see every corner in a quick look through the wooden door. And it was bare, except for the narrow cot and a stand holding a wooden wash bowl. By the glow of a rushlight, she poured water into the bowl, removed her headgear, and bent to rinse her face.

She caught sight of her reflection in the water. Her hair was her only asset. It was thick and long and black as midnight. They would cut it off tomorrow. She frowned at the thinness of her face. She was not pretty. If Lord Conniebrook had even seen her, he no doubt would have thought her a liability to her dowry.

Her father, Roger of Ramsay, had certainly thought her a liability. His last words to her had been, "Satan's spawn!"

Had his penance been effective? Had he recovered from his illness? She realized with a slight sense of guilt that she didn't care. She could think of him dead without tears. He had never been a loving man. His wife had died in childbirth, and he'd left Norah's upbringing to chance.

Chance, as it was, had exposed her to a great assortment of ideas and made her mind hospitable to novelty. Though she had the occasional tutor, her real school had been observance, for Roger's indifference had left her free to come and go as she pleased, to run wild, in fact, as long as she stayed within the confines of Ramsay. Consequently she'd seen the poverty of the cripple, and the puffed pride of the

46

bailiff, and the laughter of the harvesters on the day the corn was cut. She knew what it was to wander through fields alone, daydreaming, her soul loose and floating.

She washed her face and shed her robe, then stood in the full shame and disgrace of her nudity. As the burning rush threw its softly guttering glow, she looked down at herself. Like her face, her legs were thin and attenuated. Her body was still a child's. She believed she would never look better than she did now; probably she would get worse.

Her father had been handsome in his prime, despite his remoteness. Before his illness, he'd been tall and distinguished, with a lined and deeply tanned face and brilliant, unfaded blue eyes. She sometimes wished she'd inherited more of his looks. (Was that vanity? Conceit? Pride? Mother Fae would say, "Yes! Tamp it down!")

Naked, she pinched out the rushlight. The straw mattress of her cot was only slightly thicker than the coarse, heavy sheet and blanket that covered her. The tomblike blackness and the quiet of the priory were immeasurable. Listening, she caught tiny muted sounds that were a part of it: the dripping rain on the roof, the snores and snuffles of the older nuns, and, yes, a few sobs. Sweet-faced Sister Suzanna's mother was dying of a deadly sore on her shin, and Mother Fae wouldn't allow her to go to her. (Though they weren't allowed to speak, whispers were sometimes exchanged between the nuns, in the linen closet, or on the cellar stairs.)

Enclosure. The word rang heavy with denial. Norah heard Mother Fae's stern, uncompromising tone: *You must choose.* She felt a sick fear that what the prioress spoke of as God's punishment was in truth Mother Fae's punishment. Norah would take her vows or she would be beaten. Or starved. Or . . . who knew what else they might do to her for the good of her soul?

But how could she disclaim the world? She felt no vocation for this life. She was an outsider here where everyone went about with their eyes turned inward, searching for that deep, inner place where God and the soul met. She had looked and looked for that place and couldn't say she'd ever even glimpsed it, not once. What she found when she looked inward was the girlish dream that yet persisted within her, despite all that had happened to negate it. Sometimes she was seized with such a seemingly unfulfillable yearning—and it was not for the Almighty.

Her stomach growled. She opened her hand against it. When that didn't help, she rolled onto her stomach and pillowed her cheek on her bony arms. The position placed a certain comforting pressure on her small breasts, a comfort she knew was not innocent. Mother Fae said it was a sin to feel any pleasure in the body.

What would it be like to have a man press himself against her, to clasp and twine with him? She would never know. She would never marry now, never have children. She'd dreamed of having children, the earl's children, for so long . . . but if she stayed here Mother Fae would beat or starve her into submission. It was only a matter of time.

She felt a sting of tears. Suddenly she wanted to go home. She wadded her fists against her eyes, rolled onto her back and adjusted her fusty bedclothes. She had no home. She could never return to Ramsay, never.

Everyone at Castle Ramsay woke at sunrise. On Norah's last day there, a subdued bustle had started in the kitchen as the watchman pulled the banner from its nook and planted it in the socket atop the tower. When he blew his horn, that was the signal: day had come, the ninth of November, 1154.

Roger and Norah slept in the bower, Roger alone in his carved marriage bed and Norah in a smaller inner chamber. She was his only surviving child. She'd been a deliciously pretty and engaging infant, impish by nature, and brimming with laughter and smiles, though he'd hardly noticed. Now she was a gangly and unattractive fifteen-year-old.

As soon as the horn sounded, she sat up, feeling broad awake and full of the dream she'd had during the night. In it, the bell of the church in the village of Toomesby had fallen from its tower.

After a moment, she tumbled out of bed and dressed. She wanted to be outside, filling her lungs with cool fresh air. The autumn morning awaited her.

She heard no sound from her father's chamber, not even from the priest who had all but taken up residence there. Once, when she was younger, she'd heard Roger shout at a cleric, "God will never see Roger of Ramsay a good man—I've suffered too much harrassment at His hand!" But then, several weeks ago he'd fallen into a fever and hence had been ill with the ague. When she'd suggested that a physician be brought for him, her notion was scorned. The castle priest, Father Hughues, was in charge now, and he believed that ailments were evidence of the wrath of God, with which no man should interfere. Roger, in his weakened state, had been convinced of this. On his sickbed, glimpsing the possibility of death—and the certainty of his damnation—he'd turned desperately to the deity he'd once shunned, seeking comfort and assurance.

He kept Father Hughues by him day and night. Norah disliked the man, who always looked at her as if he wanted to step on her, and so she visited her father even less often than she would have ordinarily. For a week the priest had been urging some act of penance and mortification. She'd heard him admonish Roger, "You have led an iniquitous life; now you must do something extraordinary for the salvation of your soul." It had made Norah shiver to hear that.

She seldom stayed within the castle unless the weather was really nasty. Today, the sun hadn't been up an hour before she was trotting her piebald pony toward Toomesby. There was little to entertain a young girl at Ramsay, and if the old bell in the nearby village was going to fall, she wanted to see it happen.

The turfy path wound through thickets of bramble and bracken. Though the day was sunny, under the trees she felt the creeping chill of winter. Riding out of the woods, she came to a dreaded obstacle. She had to pass through the tall, autumn-dry grass of Toomesby's graveyard. She put her head down, not wanting to look at the little stone hut among the markers.

Many years ago a pock-marked peasant woman,

Helen Oaks, had murdered her husband. That he'd beaten her almost every day of their married life was not considered, for it was a man's right, his duty, to discipline his wife, and Helen was meant for the gallows. But Roger, with unusual cruelty, proposed she be imprisoned within a small house beside her husband's grave. The village priest, Father Geoffrey, applauded this judgment, pointing out that the woman could thus do penance to the end of her days. A stone hut was accordingly erected, and the unhappy woman conducted thither. She was put inside. The only opening was then closed off, except for a thin chink to admit air, light, and a small dole of bread and water from her relations.

She'd been vegetating inside her living tomb for nine years now, existing in filth and darkness, and prattling most insanely. Her fate had caused Norah many a nightmare, and hence she avoided even looking at the hut as she passed it.

She left the graveyard and joined the cart road that led into the village with relief. The local wain-maker was plowing one of his long strips of land which had lain fallow all summer. He wore heavy leathern boots, loose woolen trousers (which once had been blue), and a shirt of dirt-colored cloth fastened by a leathern belt. Like most peasants, he possessed no other raiment than what he was standing in. His heavy, wheeled plow cut and rolled a continuous slab of dark soil to the side, forming a ridge and furrow. He looked her way, but didn't wave. She might have been a complete stranger to him instead of his lord's daughter whom he had known all her life.

She rode on, passing another surly fellow from the village. He also merely watched her ride by, with no gesture of recognition. She was used to encountering this kind of ostracism from people, and it never failed to hurt. It was a mark of her youth and her unfailing optimism that she continued to ride out at all.

Toomesby was a compact village of a dozen two-room cottages. Their roofs were thatched with rye straw and had been patched and patched again. Each house sat on a croft divided into cattleyards and fruit orchards and vegetable gardens. All were gathered about a green where chickens clucked and scratched. The old church, also extensively repaired, had an ancient bell whose toll had always brought a feeling of melancholy to Norah.

She dismounted on the green, and tried to seem casual as she let her pony drink from the trough there. She turned, oh so nonchalantly, as if it meant nothing, toward the church.

Unknown to her, however, her presence was marked. It was whispered in the village that she was a sorceress, and none took her visits lightly. People who had mouths to feed and backs to clothe over-looked no danger in their environment. Hence, as Norah looked at the church, all who watched her looked in the same direction.

For a long moment the air was uncannily still, then, all in an instant, the church bell's ancient and frayed rope snapped—just as it had in Norah's dream. The bell bonged terribly as it fell to the ground.

Chapter 4

Norah jerked with surprise. Her pony tugged against the reins in her hand. The falling of the bell hadn't been so much entertaining as it was sad. She bit her lip as she stared at it. She wished now that she hadn't come. Why had she? Why did she sometimes know when things were going to happen? She lacked the words to explain what her ability was.

The village priest, Father Geoffrey, had come out of his hut to look at the damage. Eventually he turned from the bell and spied Norah. He started toward her, walking swiftly with the shepherd's crook he affected. The villagers had come out of their houses and fell in behind him—there was Bert Forest who loved horses so much, and litte Paley Marshall dressed in garments of the shoddiest sort, and Lewis Delangre, crippled after serving as a foot soldier in the wars. They stopped at some distance from Norah, their faces pallid with fright and outrage. Father Geoffrey alone ventured nearer. Fury gripped his features. He raised a pointing finger and hissed, "Demon!"

Norah's hands made such tight fists that her fingernails cut into her palms. Her eyes went from one face to another. Fear tingled in her arms and neck and drew all the strength from her legs. She felt she could not budge.

The priest took a step toward her. She saw his twisted mouth and bloodshot eyes, and suddenly power surged through her. She leapt onto her pony and rode at a hard gallop for the forest.

She headed for a place she considered her own, a glade where she'd built herself a rough three-sided shelter of sticks. She'd spent many an hour here. It was one place where she didn't feel outcast. As a child, she'd simply accepted the impossible things that happened to her, but she'd gradually learned that others were not so tolerant.

She leapt off her pony and went directly inside the shelter. On a splintery shelf sat her most precious possession, a sea shell. It had never been disturbed, and she wrongfully believed that that was because no one knew where it was.

She took the shell in her hands and put it to her ear. What she heard soothed her. She wondered at the sea within, at that smothered whisper which slept in the shell.

She'd always known she would be married on her sixteenth natal day. For as long as her memory stretched back she'd been betrothed to Jervais Le Strand, Earl of Conniebrook. In that future marriage she placed all her hopes for love and joy.

She'd never seen or met the man who was going to be her husband, but she'd imagined him. She didn't require that he be handsome, only that he have a good face, a strong, open face. And that he be kind.

She'd imagined their first meeting a thousand times: Their eyes would meet; understanding would flash between them. He would say something wonderful, something like, "To me, you are unique in all the world." And she would feel as if the sun had come to shine on her life.

Exciting dreams.

She'd considered Conniebrook, as well, and imagined the castle as a fairy-towered place of stopped time. She'd heard that it stood overlooking the sea. She couldn't really imagine what the sea looked like, but she knew how it would sound.

Years ago, when the old earl of Conniebrook had come to Ramsay to arrange the marriage between his son and Norah, he had given her this shell. She didn't remember the moment well, but she recalled the old earl as being vaguely gentle. Far from the sea, she had listened again and again to the roaring of the breakers that he'd told her were captured within the big, pink-throated shell.

She shivered slightly. It was alarming to contemplate giving up all that had been home to her during her lifetime, yet when she recalled the scene she'd just flown from, her heart clenched. She was seized by a powerful longing for her birthday to arrive. She could hardly bear this anticipation anymore. She believed she stood on the brink of a wonderful and unknown future, and that was what kept her from despair.

She'd been at her special place for perhaps an hour when two men-at-arms rode into the glade. One was Raymond De Vor, Roger's castellan. He was not a vassal but a mere mercenary who protected Castle Ramsay for pay. He had a two inch scar on his left jaw. There was no smile on his mouth or in his eyes. His hand was on his sword. His voice bit through the silence: "You're to come back to the castle with us."

Norah looked at the other man. He went white and looked away. Sir Guibert Monad was one of the Roger's household knights, a young unmarried man who also served for a wage.

She said to the castellan, "How did you know where to find me?"

"Did you think this place was unknown—just because it's rigorously avoided? The folk know that it's here that you consort with your spirits and demons." He said to Sir Guibert, "Destroy everything."

The knight dismounted. Norah turned, intent on protecting her shell, but that was the first thing the knight smashed. She watched helplessly as he pulled her flimsy shelter down. When he was finished, Ramond De Vor said to Norah, "Get on your pony."

There was no sense arguing.

Back at Castle Ramsay, she strove to keep up with the men's long strides as she was escorted up the stairs to the bower. There was tension throughout the castle. Her father's steward, a small man as spare as a whip, met her near the top. He pressed himself back against the wall as if she were a passing leper. She didn't pause, for the castellan was behind her, and his size and his hostility made her feel as if she were being followed by some large predator.

Her father's chamber was overheated, despite the

mildness of the day. A fire blazed in the elaborate fireplace.

Roger was propped into a sitting position in his richly curtained bed. Norah was shocked by his flush and the feverish brilliance of his eyes, by his emaciated frame. Death had truly laid a finger on him. His eyes shifted away from the priests, Father Hughues and Father Geoffrey, who were both talking to him urgently; he looked at her. His face seemed charged with blood. She saw in a moment that there was a madness in him, a reckless abandon; he was not the same man he had been.

After an instant's pause, in which he said nothing, the priests began talking again. Norah was left to meekly listen.

The village priest said, "She possesses the evil eye. This time it was fixed on a bell; next time she may fix it on a sheep—and I shudder to think how dangerous she could be to men."

Father Hughues held up a hand. His fine, silver-gilt hair was cut into tonsured cap, and his neat robe put the village cleric's shabby robe to shame. "May I remind you, my lord, of the incident of the boar?"

The castellan, standing near Norah, crossed himself in brisk gestures. Her nape bristled. She wanted to shrink so that she couldn't be seen.

She'd once, when she was very small, wandered outside the castle walls. She'd gotten lost in the woods and fallen asleep in what seemed to her a perfect nest between two roots of a gnarled tree. When her absence was finally noted at the castle, men came in search of her. They found her sleeping in the nest—with the boar to whom it belonged calmly rooting nearby. Norah woke, and being a child, smiled to see so many people gathered around her. She couldn't understand why they were all frowning and shouting. Only later did she learn that a boar was a most ferocious animal, the most difficult of all to kill.

Hers was full grown; it weighed perhaps two hundred pounds. When the men-at-arms appeared, it placed itself between them and little Norah, in what seemed a clearly possessive stance. It killed two dogs in "protecting" her, and then charged right up a spear. Though its heart was stabbed, it severely gored a knight with its knifelike tusks before it died. Ever after that incident Norah had been shunned by the men of the castle.

Father Geoffrey was pounding his shepherd's crook against the wooden floor, saying, "Incarcerate her as you did Helen Oaks. She should never see the sun again!"

Norah's mind flashed on the hut in the graveyard; the vision struck her like a hard glint of light, and she flinched. "Father!" she said, moving forward. "I haven't done anything wrong. Don't let them poison your mind against me!"

Father Hughues had moved into a beam of weak November light filtering through the western window, and the pale cap of his tonsured hair shone like a silver halo. "Woe unto them that call evil good and good evil." He turned to Roger. "One of baron's duties is to render justice, which is the reason God gives him power over others. My lord, may I suggest a better solution. Send the girl away, far from Ramsay, far from anyone whom her incantations or charms might harm." His voice grew more intense. "Here is your act of contrition, my lord baron! Here is the way for you to cleanse your soul."

Roger hardly paused. Laboriously he answered, "Since she is clearly the embodiment of my sins, through her will I do my penance. It shall be as you advise: she will be sent away, she shall be committed to God in a nunnery."

That was inconceivable. It took several seconds for it to sift through to Norah's mind and make sense. Then the inconceivable became fact. The skin of her arms drew up into goosebumps. "What about . . . what about the earl of Conniebrook . . . my marriage?"

The question provoked Roger's high anger. He strained up off his pillows. "Marriage? You, who are Satan's spawn? Ensnared by the Devil's wiles?" He fell back, momentarily breathless. His next words were calmer, and reflected his new-found piety. "Alas, you show too much love for this world, daughter. Go into a nunnery. Embrace this opportunity to avoid further decay and corruption of your soul. Do what you can to avoid the jaws of hell."

He looked at his castellan. "Raymond De Vor, deliver her thither, to a place far from Ramsay. And for my own sins, offer as her dowry . . . offer Ramsay. Yea, 'tis only just," he finished in a whisper.

The castellan moved behind her. She turned. There was nothing tender or affectionate in his expression. She whirled. "Father!" But Roger of Ramsay lay with his eyes closed, his breathing shallow.

The castellan clasped her arm and pulled her from

the chamber. "A nunnery's a good place for you," he muttered as he pulled her down the stairs.

"No!" She was making a useless struggle, striving futilely against him. "No, I won't go!"

"You'll go." His grip became painful. They stood in the castle courtyard now. He gave her a look of warning.

Other knights gathered, their eyes unpitying. In the face of such masculine solidarity, she stopped shivering and stood as still as stone, horribly caught.

They left Ramsay that very day. Raymond De Vor's scarred face was rigid all during the trip south. He and young Guibert Monad kept a steady pace of twenty leagues a day. Father Hughues had told them of a nunnery noted for its abstemiousness and abnegation. They looked infinitely relieved when they came out of the woods one purplish evening and rode up to Coxgrave Priory.

Norah would never forget the sound of the tumblers of the lock turning as the enclosure door was opened. Slowly it swung in. It was very dark beyond. Standing there were two gaunt figures robed in brown.

The castellan repeated what he'd been told to say: Take this demon-child and the fief of Ramsay is yours.

The nuns listened and nodded. Finally one of them put her hand out. Norah wanted to fall onto her knees and beg the men to allow her to stay with them, so frightening was the prospect ahead of her. She remained erect, however. Her emotions had tired during the long journey, as muscles tire, and she was less capable of responding. She was drawn over the

60

threshold. The door was shut and locked behind her. New fears breathed on her. Beneath her clothing, her budding breasts drew up into points.

During her first weeks in the priory, Mother Fae drilled her to join her hands in a special way, to walk on the balls of her sandaled feet, to observe the rule of silence. Norah soon learned that her obedience must be literally blind. The prioress wasn't just instructing her in what to do, but in the exact, precise way she must do it. If she were taught to scrub a stone corridor in a certain way, misery betide her if she attempted the least improvement.

She found it hardest, among all the restrictions of her suddenly narrowed life, to "martyr her senses." When at work in the priory garden, she was not to smell the fragrant earth. When she ate or drank, she was to think of something unsavory, to mortify her taste. When she could do nothing else to punish herself for being alive, she was to put her body to some inconvenience, such as keeping one foot lifted.

Through all this, she desperately missed the freedom she'd once had to roam the forests of Ramsay. She missed the birds and the trees, the sun and the wind. She dreamed about days sweet with hay and ripeness. And at odd moments, when she considered the loss of the future which she had dreamed of and imagined and pinned all her hopes on, she felt an edge of indescribable pain.

In her fitful, remembering sleep, Norah saw an old crone in a stone hut amidst a grave yard. She drew nearer. The woman was sitting, mumbling into her lap. She held a spool of embroidery thread. She looked up . . . and beneath the pock-marks the face was Norah's own.

She sat up, wide awake, gripping her blanket to her breasts, rigid in her cramped bed. The room she was in was a stone room, its hard floor was unrelieved by even a rush mat. The cold of the nunnery pierced clear through her. Her empty stomach knocked with apprehension.

Dear God in heaven, don't let them bury me alive!

Early on the morrow, Norah roused from her troubled night. She stretched her legs beneath the coarse blanket, and rubbed her face. As usual, she was hungerstricken. Memories flickered: roast beef washed down with rich red wine, mutton pies steaming with gravy and mushrooms. . . .

She rose to the cold of her bleak cell. As she put on her heavy brown robe, she tried to still the furious emotion that filled her, the clamor which told her, *Escape, escape while you can! Run!*

During the first silent interval in the choir, she knelt as if she were a meek postulant ready to sacrifice herself to a life of calling down God's help for the world. As she saw to her chores—tidied her bed, emptied her chamberpot—she looked for a way to get to the kitchen, where a door opened onto the garden.

The nuns breakfasted on hot, honey-sweetened water and a single small loaf of coarse, crusty bread each. Having eaten, she thought, *Now.* But instead of being allowed to go with those who were headed for the kitchen to wash up, an older sister, Diane, led her away in a different direction. She followed, hardly knowing where she was going, for her mind was so strangely dizzy. In her cell, she let the older nun cut her hair. Working in silence, Sister Diane cut and cut, until Norah's mane hung no longer than her earlobes. She might have wept at this loss of her only fair feature if that image of the garden wall had not remained so urgent in her mind.

One thing did penetrate the pressing need in her mind: she kept thinking she heard the sounds of a forester at work beyond the priory enclosure.

"I've seen this mood before," Sir Gian muttered. "If anyone dared to argue with him just now, he'd strike the man dead."

Charles thought he would. They were speaking of Lord Conniebrook, whose men-at-arms, in full armor, were hacking at a tree they'd just felled. Breathing harsh and heavy, they were chopping the branches off, leaving a long log. There was not so much as a small ruffle of laughter among them. Now and then the earl's voice issued an order, whipcrack sharp. And once his head flew up at a man's suggestion, which he answered with cutting sharpness, "Who is master here, you or me?" The man turned as pale as a birch.

They were in the woods near the priory. The rain had stopped in the night, but the day was grey and damp, with clouds unfurled to the verge of the world. Charles's cloak was wet from brushing against the low growth under the trees all about. He felt shivery, and his muscles were knotted at the thought of what they were about to do. His lord's chestnut war horse snorted behind him, as if it too were nervous. He looked at Sir Gian, standing four-square beside him. The knight only shrugged and smiled hard.

Most of the nuns were in the chapel. Norah was in her cell with Sister Diane. She had been made to shed her brown habit and don a ceremonial one of white Cistercian wool, soft as spidersilk. The white veil fit much better without her hair forming lumps beneath. The time had come, with no chance yet for her to make a quiet escape. Her heart knocked in desperation. Sister Diane seemed to accept her trembling as natural, considering the enormity of the vows she was about to take.

Dressed in bridal white, she and the sister left her cell. Norah searched for a moment alone, a moment to break out. She had to escape! But the sister had her arm firmly in hand, no doubt believing Norah needed the support.

In the chapel, the sister gave Norah a last, skin-deep smile, then took her own place with the other kneeling nuns. Norah was left standing alone between them and Mother Fae. She knelt. A moment passed in which she struggled. She could not make herself voice the question expected of her: May I be taken into this community?

At last Mother Fae opened her mouth to say something. Her mouth stayed open, yet no words came out, for at that moment men descended upon the priory like a rush of rocks. There came the sound of a great spill of horsemen, shouts, and finally a *boom* that echoed through the thick-walled, silent passages. A confusion, like a fluttering of leaves, passed through the nuns. The *boom* came again, wood booming against wood. Relief, a feeling of deliverance, came as a bright, cold tingling in Norah's veins. She stood.

Boom!

The other nuns stirred on their knees; many stood. All were looking behind them through the chapel door to the passageway from whence the sound came. Mother Fae muttered, "It's him, he's using a battering ram." She hurried though the antechoir.

Boom! (The sound was rhythmical, accompanied by male grunts.)

The enclosure door was already beginning to give way. Norah had no idea what this intrusion meant. All she knew was that she'd been given a reprieve. And a distraction. This was her chance.

The nuns broke their silence and began to squeal.

Boom! (Norah felt the shiver of it in the air.)

"Sisters, pray!" someone called above the din. Some of them followed the directive and sank back to their knees. Others, however, did not. In the midst of their squealings, Norah edged toward the passageway. She came up against Mother Fae.

Boom! (The center section of the enclosure door was shattering.)

The prioress's face had turned a volcanic red. "This is your fault! You are Satan's child indeed!"

Norah gave her a look of surprise. She had nothing to do with this attack. But the expression on the prioress's face was familiar to her—a look of revulsion.

Boom!

Norah turned from the sight of the door at the end of the passage, which the ram was breaking through with a splintering crash even now. She pushed though the nuns blocking her way to the back of the priory. One or two of them, their faces the no-color of stone, fumbled for her, but she slipped away from them and picked up her white skirts and ran. She flew through the refectory. In the kitchen, the fire on the hearth was reduced to red-hot ashes which blew up in gusty embers with the draft now finding its way into this room from the broken enclosure door.

Out in the garden, the high stone walls showed naught but sky. She dashed to the nearest, paused, then saw a deep wooden bucket used to haul water to the summer crops. She up-ended it and used it for a step. Her fingers just reached the top of the wall. She couldn't get enough purchase to raise herself up. Frustration made her feel weak. She pressed her forehead into the wall and tried to get hold of herself. Out of the corner of her eye she spied a wooden barrow. Quickly she trundled it to the wall, placed the upended bucket inside it, and stepped onto it again.

The barrow wobbled, its legs sank into the damp soil; yet Norah was now above the wall to the height of her shoulders. Full of violent energy, every muscle fully alive, she threw her arms over and scrabbled up.

The wall was thick enough to sit on. Beneath her was a drop. The ground was some five feet lower than the garden's level and sloped away from the convent. The clamor behind her rose. Nuns were screaming in terror. Men's shouts echoed through the shocked rooms of silence. Norah only briefly wondered what this *mêlée* meant. Then she jumped.

She staggered and stumbled when her feet struck the ground, then found her balance and remained upright. She heard shouts in the garden now. She crouched and moved into the rambling growth of rhododendrons that grew in wild profusion outside the wall.

Her hiding place was not secure. The eaves of the green forest were near, though separated from her by an open strip. She stared across at the green—and the green stared back. It was her only hope. Shaking off her hesitation, she left her cover and ran.

Behind her she heard, "Here's one gone over the wall! She's headed for the woods!"

Those words struck a deep, primal response of fear in her. Her senses were flooded with fear. She knew not what the attackers wanted; she knew only that she'd nearly been prematurely buried and that now she was free—and that she must remain free!

Chapter 5

Norah plunged into the moist green woods. Leafy limbs lashed at her. The smell of fresh cedar surrounded her. She ran until she was exhausted, then walked until she could run some more. Stopped by a stream, she fell to her knees and splashed cold water onto her face. Fatigue struck in her breast like a blacksmith's hammer. She simply had to rest, just for a moment. A nearby clump of bushes offered a temporary hiding place. She crawled in among them and sat with her arms around her knees.

Fear made her senses harrowingly sharp. She saw how she'd muddied her ceremonial habit. Just as well. The stark white was too easy to see; her old brown habit would have blended with these surroundings better.

Who were those men? A gang of outlaws? But there was nothing worth stealing at Coxgrave. Had they attacked merely to ravish the nuns?

The forest seemed to encompass her. She had to formulate some plan. She would run until she stumbled upon a peasant's dwelling, where she could no doubt trade the fine wool of this habit for clothes less clumsy, and then—she wasn't sure what would come next, but down among the tendrils of her thoughts was a notion of making her way north to Conniebrook. Perhaps the earl would yet want her. After all, she still had her dowry; the nuns hadn't won that prize.

But that was of secondary importance for the time being. The thing now was to get up and put more distance between herself and the nunnery. Whoever those men were, they had noted her escape. When they finished with whatever was their purpose at Coxgrave, they might come after her.

She rose, crossed the stream by way of some wobbly stones, and picked up a jogging pace. Soon she was breathing hard again. Her legs burned with exhaustion. She fell twice, but struggled up and continued on. Her breath hissed—and that was why she didn't hear the horses until it was too late.

When she did look over her shoulder, past her white veil, it was to see a man-at-arms mounted on a war horse plowing through the underbrush and thistles at great speed. The aventail of his hauberk was fastened to his helmet, and it partially covered his face against the lower branches of the trees. His sword was not in his hand, but he was leaning forward on the horse's neck, riding as hard as the animal could carry him, charging after her as if he meant to run her down. The rhythm of his horse's hoofs seemed suddenly as loud as thunder.

Behind him came more riders flattened to run through the thorny bushes and clumps of rock, their destriers leaning on their bits, stretching for more speed. Norah was stunned. With an anguished cry, she ran faster than ever. She could see nothing ahead of her; low branches masked her path until abruptly the growth opened into a clearing.

The pounding beasts came on with no shout from the men. She glanced back; the leader was rushing down on her. His horse's eyes seemed blood red; the bit pried its jaws apart and its tongue lolled. Its great forehoofs tore up chunks of turf and flung them aside as it hurtled its full weight forward. She dodged. The horse reeled after her; she felt its hot breath on her face. She veered again, and the horse swerved to meet her, and then she stumbled and sprawled on her stomach.

In another instant they were all around her. The earth trembled with their hoofs. She lay with her cheek pressed to the forest floor, with her eyes shut, waiting to feel the first hoof on her back, on her head.

"Is she hurt?" one of them shouted.

For another second she didn't move. Then she looked up to see the riders working hard to steady their mounts. She pushed herself up onto her feet, breathing laboriously, noisily. The men closed their horses about her as though she were dangerous. She turned in a drunken circle, her hands raised to ward them off. She was dizzy; all her blood was drained from her head. One man's horse reared up and spun on its hocks. She staggered back from it, lost her balance, and fell onto one hip.

As she forced herself up yet again, the first of them, who had his horse under control, said grudgingly, "Are you hurt?"

She found it difficult to find her voice. "No," she said. She had leaf mold in her mouth, and raised her fingers to take it off her tongue.

He watched her, his gloved fist resting on his thigh. She felt his enmity coil about her. She sensed that he was struggling to restrain some primal warrior instinct. He said, "After the chase you led us through those trees, you *should* be hurt."

He dismounted. He was very tall, both head and neck taller than her, and very broad of shoulder. A tall, lithe, fighting man. Her eyes tried to pry between his aventail and his nosepiece to find what kind of expression was on his face. All she could see, however, were his eyes. Lustrous, pale silver eyes. There was an icy command behind them which warned her.

"Who are you?" she said, trying desperately to sound calm.

There was no answer from him, just the quiet, brutal fact that he was there. And that was only the beginning. He motioned with his gloved hand to one of the men who was still mounted. "Charles!" The owner of that name dismounted. His youth and lack of armor clearly made him a squire. The tall man said, "Bind her." At the same time he drew nearer, so that his height was almost as menacing as his tone. Norah felt very certain that she should not try to move.

From among his equippage the youth pulled out a length of hide rope. He pulled off his gloves with his teeth as he stepped toward her. Panicked, she whipped her hands behind her back. Her eyes darted between the squire and his master, who said nothing.

71

"My lady, if you will give me your hands," the squire said in a firm tone.

"Please—no!" In her ragged voice was a beseeching note. "I don't understand—what do you want? Who are you?"

The squire looked at the tall man. Norah turned her pleading face to him as well. At last he said, "You know who I am."

"I don't, truly!"

"Come, don't take me for a fool. You didn't think I could stop you from taking vows, but when you saw I could, you went over the wall. You're very determined not to honor your father's contract, but honor it you will."

She stood staring at him, trying to comprehend. The truth dawned on her, but it was too unbelievable. She said tentatively, "Lord Conniebrook?"

His head leaned to one side, signifying scorn and impatience with what he evidently believed was playacting on her part. His eyes shot back to his squire. "Bind her."

The youth reached for her arm. She didn't struggle. He was not more than three years older than her and was not as tall as his lord, yet he was taller than she was. And stronger. Standing rigid, she suffered his big bony fingers to wind the leather around her left wrist first. He tied it very tight. And then around her right wrist. As this was taking place, Norah lifted her eyes to find perhaps eighteen men staring out at her from behind the nosepieces of their helms. Large men, with expressions that did not indicate any particular benevolence toward her. In fact, they seemed men who might do anything, any irrational thing. Her eyes flicked without stopping from face to face, until she met those silver eyes again.

He was staring down at her awfully. Every pore of him breathed hazard. "You have led me a merry chase," he said softly, then turned for his horse and remounted.

She tried to think what that might mean. What had he been told? That she'd come voluntarily to the priory—to avoid marriage to him? It was absurd—yet possible. Looking at him, she could imagine that if her father had died, or was too ill to speak, the steward and the castellan and the priests of Ramsay would have wanted to escape this silver-eyed warrior's wrath. She tried to picture the scene: His arrival to claim his bride only to find her gone. And her dowry with her. If he'd exhibited even half the cold fury he was exhibiting now, she could well imagine the cowardly men of Ramsay giving him any lie that might absolve them.

She felt close to tears, close to the humiliating prospect of weeping before these men who were looking down on her. She fought hard for control.

The earl maneuvered his war horse behind her. To the squire he said, "Lift her up here."

The youth stepped even closer, and she tried to prepare herself, but there was no time before she felt the shock of those bony hands grasping her waist. She shuddered. He gave her a heave—and for an instant she felt amazingly weightless.

The earl's horse shied a little as he hooked her with his arm and dragged her over the beast's sweating withers. He settled her on the hard leather roll of his saddle, without care to her comfort, as though she were no more than a piece of dead wood. Every instinct told her to draw away, but she couldn't; she was forced to lean against him as closely as a head fits a pillow. She said, striving to be calm and reasonable, "I could ride better pillion—and with my hands free."

"My lady," he said, not even looking at her, his tone not quite matching hers in reason, "may I suggest silence?"

She fell even closer against his solid, chain-mailed body as he spurred the horse and it leapt into a gallop. His arm tightened around her, holding her hard against him, so tightly that his fingers hurt her. She felt his strength—and his desire to vent his anger on her. He was certainly not her ideal of a courtly knight. All her daydreams of their first meeting—and this was the reality.

She built up her courage, and ventured, "Where are we going?"

No answer.

"I insist on being told."

His reply, made in the rudest possible tone, was, "You're in no position to insist on anything."

Hence she entered the nightmare of being helpless in the hands of a man who seemed determined to make her suffer.

The remaining hour of that day was both interminably long and much too short. Norah, in dire discomfort wedged between the earl's mailed chest and his hard arms and poised on the forward edge of his saddle, felt a tension new and terrible. He

74

never slowed his tall chestnut horse. He refused to speak to her, or look at her, or in any other way acknowledge her as more than a captured animal. When it began to rain again, it seemed part and parcel of her day's luck.

She tried to calculate: She must reason with him. Not right now, but when he was calmer.

But what if he didn't believe her?

Given time, she felt sure she could convince him and gain his trust.

While she puzzled, however, her discomfort wore at her will. The horse moved on, hoof after hoof. She rested a little against the earl. She would have liked to put her head on his shoulder and close her eyes and feel safe in his embrace, feel rescued—but she couldn't. She felt, instead, afraid. And so she rode unblinking and exhausted, so that her head wobbled on her neck with the horse's movements.

Water began to drip from every leaf of every tree. At last she spied a lodge spouting smoke. The forest opened as they moved closer. The meadow around the lodge was hazy with lowered smoke and dim with twilight and rain. They stopped before the building as the last of the ashen light faded from the sky. From a nearby shed a mule brayed. The knights dismounted. One of them, a hearty-looking fellow who had removed his helmet, appeared beside the earl's war horse. "My lady."

Norah straightened up like a soldier. The earl released his hold on her as the knight reached up; his big hands spanned her waist and he lifted her down. She thought there was something of compassion on his face, but it was masked by wariness.

Her betrothed dismounted behind her, and at the same moment the door of the lodge banged open. A single figure appeared, craning his neck to see, muttering, "He has her?"

He was answered with a grim, "Yes."

Norah's whole body screwed tight with tension. When the earl took her arm, she was startled, and she winced away. His grip tightened and, with long, straight-ahead strides, he pushed her toward the door.

A lodge such as this was usually the property of the king, a place where he and his fellow huntsmen might ride out through the hemming forests where stag abounded. There was light within, and the delicious scent of burning wood. The hall was marvelously warm. Two fires burned. Meat was roasting on a spit in one of them. Norah was assailed by the smell of the food. Her stomach groaned with hunger. Squires, seeing their lords returned, immediately began to lay out trenchers of bread and wooden wine cups. One tall blond went around with a burning twig lighting candles.

The earl shoved Norah toward the fire opposite the one where the cooking was being done. She found herself shut in by big rugged men. The heat was a welcome luxury, however. She hadn't stood next to a warming fire for months.

The squire, Charles, muttered, "My lord," encouraging the earl to take off his hauberk and helmet. Norah saw that her future husband was built on the heroic scale. He was an inch or two over six feet, long-legged, lean-waisted, and broad-shouldered. He sat, and Charles dutifully removed his lord's high boots and put fur-lined shoes on his feet. On the hearth was a warming basin of water. The earl pulled off his tunic, and the squire held the basin for him to wash his face and hands. He dried himself and sat again, in his white shirt.

Through all of this, Norah was left to stand where she was, damp and miserable in her soiled white nun's habit. She felt homely and gauche, but stood as stiffly as a soldier on parade, determined not to seem weak. The earl never looked at her—but she looked her fill at him. In the moving firelight, his features revealed the strength in him. He had a finely chiseled, straight nose, a square, thrusting jaw, and a wide mouth. And of course those piercing silver eyes. They were beautiful, but there was hardness in them, a quality that said they had looked upon terrible things and would not flinch to look upon them again.

When they at last flicked toward her, she looked away. She dared not meet anyone else's gaze either, so she studied inanimate things with pretended interest: the table and benches of blackened oak near the fire, the candle standard that stood at the end of the table furthest from the hearthlight, three painted shields that hung on the wall. The lodge was rough, intended for men. The rain suddenly increased; it thundered on the roof overhead and roared off the eaves.

Anon, all the knights sat down to eat by the light of the fire and the six or so candles. Charles indicated that Norah should sit on the wooden bench at his lord's right hand. The hearty knight who had helped her down from the horse—Sir Gian, she'd heard him called—sat opposite her. No one spoke. It was raining on the roof, raining hard.

The earl drank his first cup of wine in two swallows. Charles placed a slab of hot meat on the trencher before him. The earl drew his dagger from his belt and began to cut bites from it. Norah was served by Charles as well, while Sir Gian had his own squire, and there were two others who moved around the table, at the edge of the light, serving the other knights. All the men began to eat without ceremony. Without speech. The rain came down even harder.

After a moment, the earl noticed that Norah was not eating. Without looking directly at her, he gestured and Charles came to cut her meat for her. When she continued to sit without moving, the squire bent over her shoulder and murmured with a hint of scorn, "Is the meat not to your liking, my lady?"

In the thundering silence, this quiet question rang loudly. Since everyone was bound to hear her answer anyway, she saw no reason not to make it in a normal tone. She said, "I will not eat with my hands bound."

All eyes at the table swiveled to their lord. He nodded to Charles, and in the next instant the squire's knife was bared for her; all she needed to do was lift her hands, and he would cut her bindings.

The earl chewed a mouthful, swallowed, and reached for his refilled wine cup, totally disinterested.

She lifted her wrists, and Charles's blade did its work.

The earl did not pause in his eating. She didn't look at him. She was sure that she would see in his expression nothing but contempt. It was hard for her to think he could have any weaknesses, as lesser mortals did.

Down the table, the silent, weatherbeaten knights were intent upon their trenchers. Norah felt agonizingly alone in their midst. She picked up a piece of meat and put in in her mouth. It was lamb that had been boiled in mint. Often she had wakened in the nunnery with her mouth making chewing movements from dreams about such food, but now her appetite had been driven away. She chewed and chewed, but had no saliva to swallow. She reached for the ivywood cup the squire had placed before her, and she washed the lump of meat down with the yellow wine.

The rain paused then began again. The meal remained a silent ordeal. Following the lamb came cold chicken and crusty loaves of bread. There was stewed fruit and a jug of cream. Norah had not seen so much food since she'd been banished from Ramsay, yet what little she could eat of it became an indigestible wad in her stomach.

"My lady," said Charles behind her shoulder, "will you take a cake?" He held a plate of brittle simnel cakes spread with red jam. She hated this boy's tone, so grating and pompous. Here was a youth infatuated with his own importance. He would be a bully if he thought he might get away with it, and clearly he thought he could get away with it with her.

"No, thank you." Her face felt as stiff as untanned leather. The strain was overwhelming her.

The earl muttered, "You eat like a sparrow. No

wonder you're so sk- . . . so thin."

She looked at him quickly, but already he was turning away and rising from the table. He seemed impossibly haughty. He was treating her as though she were scarcely worth breaking his stride for, as though she were a dog to be tossed a piece of gristle and then kicked away lest she ask for something more. She wanted desperately to answer him back, if only to make some point of human contact with him. But she was too tongue-tied, in this strange place, with so many strange men about her.

He muttered, "Gian, light my lady upstairs."

The knight, who had risen and turned for the fire with his lord, now hesitated, then turned back, picked up the candle from the table and stood over her. "Lady Norah?"

The men were as silent as ever. She rose stiffly, as if carved of wood, and followed him. After a few steps, however, she realized with the clarity of something seen by lightning the meaning of this evening-long silence among the men. Upstairs . . . a bedchamber. Her mind was swept clean of every thought as seldom before in her life. She hesitated, stopped, stood on the very edge of bolting. Sir Gian looked down at her. He put a hand under her below. She recovered and went on, letting herself be led.

The knight was good-looking in a rough-hewn way, with thick brown hair and thicker eyebrows. He went before her on the stairs, which were narrow and dark. Feeling more hopeless and more helpless with each step, she said, "Will he . . . does he mean to . . . please, I will wed him willingly, he needn't. . . ."

The knight seemed embarrassed. He opened his mouth to speak, closed it again, and rubbed his hand over his chin. He said finally, "I'm sure he won't harm you, my lady. Sometimes he looks to have a bullbear riding his back, but if you, er, behave. . . ."

She felt a rise of hysteria. It took all her control to keep it from showing. Her face felt hot. Tears pooled behind her eyes. She looked piercingly at this knight, this Sir Gian; she looked at his hearty features and his evasive eyes.

He had brought her to the door, which he now threw open. He offered her the candle. "I'm sorry you have no waiting woman to help you. Is there aught I can get you? Anything at all?" His voice trailed off. His hand went to his chin once more.

She squinted into the shadowed room and at the same time broke into a chill. He reached for her hand and pressed the candle into it, then gently urged her over the threshold. He pulled the door shut behind her. When she heard the lock turn, she whirled. Her candle went out. She stood staring in the direction of the door, listening to Sir Gian's quick, guilty footsteps clattering down the wooden stairs. She turned away, willing her eyes to adjust to the absolute darkness.

She'd been born in the midst of war and reared among men, and certain stories which a mother might have kept from her ears were common to her. Tales of captured men stretched upon racks, or chained by their arms from the beams of dungeons so that they were unable to sit or lie down and sleep, until they simply starved to death; rumors of prisoners dragged to the top of tower walls and cast into the moat below; tales of unprotected women beaten and ravished, of well-born ladies made mock of with violence, even of girl-children forced into debaucheries.

And stories of brides captured and forced into marriage.

Men, it seemed, took delight in torture and rape.

An hour later, Jervais, nightlight in hand, climbed the stairs. His impression of the girl was of a clean, erect little creature, pale-faced and travel-weary, and he had to vigorously remind himself that she was devious, that she'd led him in a chase far from Conniebrook, far from Ramsay, and had even forced him to break into a holy nunnery—while she tried to slip out the back door! His temper flared. She deserved no quarter from him. He would force her into marriage, and ever thereafter make her properly respectful of him.

Yet he had to admire her courage. At supper she'd said, "I won't eat with my hands bound." Not *can't*, mind you, but *won't*.

A voice, like a finger tugging at his sleeve, said, *She's a mere girl, Le Strand. Painfully thin, plain, and totally sexless.*

What matter's that? he argued, all icy calm and reason. She was his marriage prize and must be gathered in.

She's a child.

Every girl-child must be made a woman sooner or later.

And if caresses fail, will you use blows to subdue her?

"I might!" he muttered aloud.

In this mood of ugly determination, he stepped up the last stairs to the chamber door.

The room was pitch dark. His candle threw confusing shadows away from him in all directions. He couldn't locate her at first, and he thought maybe she'd chosen to be wise and had gone to bed to await him. But the bed was empty.

Maybe she'd squeezed through the narrow window and jumped, probably breaking her neck in the process. He'd find her lying in a heap on the ground outside—

No, he heard her voice now. She was kneeling by a stool with her back to him, a little nun praying swiftly, desperately, in a quaking whisper.

He closed the door. Her voice stopped. For an interminable moment she didn't move. And neither did he. Then he went to place the nightlight in the sconce over the bed. When he looked again, she was standing. Her face was white, her breathing labored. A little nun, like a little white moth flitted out of the dark. She looked no more than twelve years old. He'd expected youth, but not a terrified infant. This was his challenge? This girl? He clenched his hand into a fist behind his back. And he let a bitter laugh burst from his throat.

When he was still four feet from her, she reached for the stool and, holding it like a shield, came at him. His body reacted as it was trained to do: he stepped aside and used her own momentum to push her past him. His strength was greater than he realized, however, and she lost her balance with his shove, and stumbled. The stool, which she was holding before her, hit the wall, and her right cheek hit the stool, hard enough that he heard the *thunk* of the bone. She made a short, wordless sound as her head bounced back, then she crumpled to her knees. He crossed to her, bent, and grabbed her arm roughly. He'd had enough of this nonsense.

Her eyes were open, but not focused. For the moment they seemed made of cloudy glass. The little fool had dazed herself. He gathered her up, lifted her—and was shaken by how light she was. He heaved her onto the bed. She didn't struggle; she was too close to unconsciousness to defend herself. "Mercy," she whispered.

He still had his hands around her torso and could feel her heart dashing against his thumbs. Her body was tiny; it shook with an invisible tremor. What had she thought, that she could fight him?

Her cheek, where she'd banged it, was already beginning to bruise. Tears were draining from the sides of her eyes. A sob broke from her throat. She rolled weakly onto her side and curled into a ball.

And then she started to weep.

Chapter 6

The girl wept as Jervais had never seen a woman weep before, softly, hopelessly, as if he'd done something to her from which she could never recover. He found himself patting her shoulder, and his voice came deep from his throat, "There now."

She tensed and went silent. He felt like an idiot. He backed off from the bed and crossed to the door, opened it and called down the stairs, "Charles! Bring a bowl of cold water and a cloth!"

Charles soon appeared at the top of the stairs, steadying a basin and with a cloth thrown over his wrist. Jervais's expression gave away nothing as he took the items and turned away, telling Charles to shut the door.

He crossed to the foot of the bed and stood there, feeling foolish. The girl was huddled, clutching her cheek; her mouth trembled. Tears stood in her eyes, making them look huge and dark. He came around, put the bowl on the floor, and sat beside her. She cringed away, but not too far. Not a word or gesture of resistance remained—but her fright filled his nostrils. He pulled her hand from her face. "Let me see." The cheek was swelling and bruising fast. He wrung the cloth in the water, then laid it on her face. The garnet on his middle finger glowed like blood in the light of the night candle.

She eyed him owlishly. Only a little of her face was left bare by the compress and her white wimple. He suddenly wondered what color her hair was. Her brows were—he squinted through the shadows—dark. Lord she was skinny! Fragile-boned and thin-skinned and starved-looking. The flesh on the back of her hands was so pale it seemed almost transparent. "Our Lady!" he cursed softly.

After all his so-called gallant deeds—his attacks of towns and captures of castles, his hard-won battles and skirmishes, he was reduced to this, to knocking a terrified girl about. The last of his anger drained away. He hadn't meant to hurt her. Or at least hadn't realized what it would feel like to hurt her. It felt bad.

He lifted the compress. Self-disgust filled him. That blue-ish redness would be purple by morning. She might even have a black eye. He wrung out the cloth and replaced it.

Meanwhile she said nothing, simply submitted to his ministrations. As he held the compress in place, he looked away from her. Outside, the rain was rustling again. He would give just about anything to be out there in it just now, out of this room, out in the sweet open air among the resin-scented pines.

He cleared his throat and said, "We'll be married on the morrow." He looked back at her, daring her to disagree.

"Yes, my lord." Her voice didn't quiver, but he could see her lips trembling slightly.

"You don't mean to cause me any more trouble?"

"No."

He wiped at his mouth with the back of his hand, relieved that she realized her position. "Good. Would you like to undress, to get into bed—to rest, I mean." His eyes slid back and met hers and the look of terror in them. "God's bones!" He felt a rush of frustration. He stood and tossed the compress into the basin, splashing water on the floor. "Sleep in your clothes like a peasant if you want!"

He was filled with an uncertainty, a sense that he had somehow lost control of this situation. It disturbed him, because it so seldom happened. Except with Eleanor. He felt his temper rising. He had a terrible temper, as his men-at-arms could testify, and it had clenched itself against this girl, collected to itself a dozen small resentments.

He pulled the top fur of the bedcovers over her, bundled her into it roughly, and went to the other side of the bed. He pulled off his shoes and shirt and lay down under the second covering, with his back to her.

He told himself that within a few weeks theirs would be an alliance like all feudal alliances, a purely rational matter. A lady went with her fiefs, and if she were stubborn, or impertinent, or even too drenched in cloistral disciplines, well, a man didn't fail to plow a fallow field simply because it threw a few stones and roots up in his way. Women were known to be perverse. They went against all reason. She might be skinny, but all her limbs seemed well set. She was unmaimed; nothing was amiss with her as far as he could see. Except that she was naught but skin and bones, she was fit and properly fashioned to bear children—and by the saints, that's what she would do.

Closing his eyes, he felt her move. She was crying again, silently, her rake-thin little body shaking with sobs. He rolled over, threw his cover off to his waist. "Does your cheek hurt?" No answer. He moved closer, put his arm over her blanket, trying clumsily to soothe her. "Sleep," he advised. "No one is going to . . ." He stopped and started again with something else. "You shouldn't have tried to break our troth."

"I didn't."

He clucked his tongue in impatience. Was she going to prove a liar on top of everything else?

She turned suddenly, right into his naked chest. Her hands against his bare skin came as a shock. "I didn't!" she insisted. "You must believe me. They sent me away, my father and the priests. I wanted to marry you. . . ."

Her voice faded a little, with an almost convincing virginal shyness.

"Father was dying," she said less urgently, "and the castle priest told him he must atone for all his sins. He was a great sinner. And he decided I should be his penance, that he should give me to God, me and Ramsay. So they sent me away to be a nun."

He considered this. At Ramsay he'd come up against a certain Father Hughues. And a castellan, Raymond De Vor, who was a mercenary and everyone knew what kind of men that sort was. They had certainly seemed shifty enough. Still, he couldn't help but feel there was more to this.

She's telling the truth, Le Strand. You're a dour bastard, too grim by half.

"Why did you go over the wall when I came for you then?"

"I didn't know it was you. It was my last chance. They were going to make me take the vows or . . . or Mother Fae was going to beat me."

"She didn't tell you I visited there yesterday and demanded she give you to me?"

"No." She sat up. "So it was for me that you broke down the door? To rescue me?" She smiled as if he'd done something terribly brave and gallant. She even blushed a little. She said, her eyes downcast, "I was going to try to get to Conniebrook somehow. I always knew you would be kind."

Guilt stabbed him. His entire picture of her was reshaping itself. She was like a puppy suddenly, almost too eager to love and be loved. He said gruffly, "I will be, uh, kind—from now on."

She put her hand to her face, felt the bruise. "I'm sorry I'm not pretty."

Oh lord!

Her hand moved to her veil. "I had nice hair, but they cut it off this morning." Tears filled her eyes. She quickly covered her face with both hands. A sob shook her.

He sat up with her and took her into his arms. "There," he said awkwardly, "there. It'll grow back."

He pulled her down among the pillows and held her. All his anger was turned from her and focused elsewhere. From his brief search through the nunnery he'd gained impressions of cold stone, dreary cells, and endlessly bleak lives. Even the chapel was gloomy and without comfort. It was more like a dungeon than a place of God. And after meeting that old crow of a prioress face to face, he didn't find it hard to picture her giving this child's thin back a dozen stripes—or as many more as necessary to get her submission.

She didn't cry long. She stopped, sniffed, and asked, "Is my father dead?"

He sighed, unwilling to be the cause of another burst of weeping. "He died in November, probably right after you went away."

She didn't cry again, however, merely let out a deep, audible breath. Was it grief, or weariness, or just relief? Probably all three.

After a while, she murmured, somewhat drowsily, "Your father gave me a shell when he came to Ramsay to arrange our marriage. I listened to the sea in it almost every day. Is the sea very beautiful, my lord?"

"Yes."

She said, nearly asleep, "I've longed to see it. And Conniebrook . . . I've longed. . . ." She lay very still in his arms, sleep having come to her abruptly, as to an overexcited puppy.

He considered: In view of her apparent meekness, he could take her back to Conniebrook for a real wedding, but he'd already sent Gian out with two men to bring back the good Brother Ignatius. "There must be a wedding tomorrow," he'd said to Gian privately. "Oh, nothing to make a noise about. A few signs of the cross waved over us. Arrange it." He'd believed (was it just an hour ago?) that he could make himself force her, and that once the deed was done, and she was made to realize it would be done again and again until she conceived, she would gladly agree to a wedding for her honor's sake.

She sighed in her sleep. Her small fingers curled

against his naked chest.

Probably it was just as well for them to be wed as soon as possible. She could be even cleverer than he thought, and all this seeming shyness and puppy-like eagerness to please could be a ruse. It all seemed too easy suddenly. Experience had made him a pessimist. The traumatic course of his life to date had precluded smiling optimism.

On the morrow, before the earl left the chamber he told Norah to take off her nun's habit and leave it outside the door. She lay late in the big bed, naked, while she waited for his squire to clean the garment. The earl had told her Sir Gian had gone in search of a certain monk who would marry them. She wasn't sorry for her solitude, though it was a cold, dark, wet February day, and the chamber was not heated. She was used to the unheated rooms. And she was too shy of the knights downstairs to want to go down among them. Especially since they must think the earl had dishonored her last night.

She was glad when Charles finally returned her robe and veil, however, for she dreaded the thought of the earl coming in and seeing her hair. She must look like a pageboy. As soon as she could, she clasped the nunnish coif tight around her head again; the linen wimple and white veil were safely back in place as well when the earl came for her.

He told her on the stairs, "I've told my men-at-arms that we were lied to about you and that you aren't to blame for causing us this goose chase."

She gave him a nervous smile of gratitude.

Though she kept her head down to hide the bruise

on her face, the monk, a Benedictine outrider, two hundred pounds of man all in one package, insisted on lifting her chin with his pudgy hand. He complained, "Not only dressed in a holy habit but she's clearly been beaten. I can't marry a woman against her will, my lord."

The earl's eyes appraised him with something like disgust. "You *will* marry us." He casually took hold of Norah's shoulders; it was a gesture of possessiveness which she found thrilling. "Or I swear to God and all His saints—"

"Brother," Norah broke in quickly, "I *was* in a nunnery, but never was a nun. And this mark on my face is my own doing."

The monk shook his tonsured head in disbelief. "This makes sorry hearing. Did he threaten you to make you say that, child?" He looked back at the earl. "I should think you'd be ashamed."

Norah started to object again, but the earl silenced her with a squeeze of her shoulders. "I haven't laid a hand on her. Nor will I. But you, Brother, are a different matter."

The monk said, "I fear you reap beyond your mark, my lord."

At a gesture from the earl, Sir Gian slowly drew his sword. The monk straightened up instantly. He made no further protest, except to murmur in a voice that was now a little frayed, "I hope you've asked for God's guidance."

The earl took Norah's arm and she knelt with him. His knights and their squires assembled behind them, in a rustle of straw and rushes. The monk began to intone muddy Latin over their bowed heads. Norah studied the hem of his fine robe and the toes of his soft boots. He was like no monk she'd ever known, and as unlike the sisters of the priory as any creature could be.

She kept her face hidden from sight as much as possible within the sides of her veil. She had no mirror, but she knew the bruise had disfigured her.

The rain began again. It streamed against the lodge's outer walls, joining with the drone of the monk's voice. At certain moments in the ceremony Norah crossed herself, as did everyone else, right arms moving in unison. She promised "to honor and to wife" the man at her side. Her voice sounded firm and distinct, not at all nervous.

The monk asked the earl, in formal French, "Hast thou the will to take this woman as thy wife?"

"Yes."

"Will ye love her and hold to her and to no other, to thy life's end?"

"Yes."

"Then take her hand and say after me: I, Jervais, take thee, Norah, as my wedded wife, forsaking every other, in sickness and health, riches and poverty, well and woe, till death us do part."

When he had made the vow, the earl kept her hand and placed the gold band from his little finger on her middle finger. The monk blessed this ring-giving by laying his hands over their joined hands and intoning: "It is fitting for a man to be a woman's lord and master, yet let the yoke which Norah of Ramsay will bear be the yoke of love and peace." His several chins shook so when he spoke that Norah was tempted to giggle, and pressed her lips together to keep it in. She felt the earl squeeze her hand, and when she peeked at him, she saw that his eyes were alight with suppressed humor. She secretly, shyly returned the pressure of his hand.

He turned her face toward his. She felt something unfamiliar, a strange excitement. The expression in his pale eyes was immeasurably somber now as his glance centered on the bruise on her cheekbone. What was he thinking?

He leaned nearer. She quickly closed her eyes. She knew what was coming, but didn't know how to make her mouth ready for it. She'd never been kissed, not by anyone. Her heart fluttered up in an instant of panic. She felt his lips against her mouth—and it was all over, a kiss so quick and light she'd hardly felt it. Yet she was transfixed. She opened her eyes and gazed up at him an instant too long after his hands had let her go. Realizing how foolish she must look, she hid her face once more. She ran her tongue over her lips whilst, in doomlike tones, the monk pronounced them man and wife.

As they stood, a cheer went up among the men. One of the squires began to sing and play his harp. The earl went to the table where chilled wine was already poured. "Holy God," he said to Sir Gian, with a little smile. He snatched up a cup and gulped down its contents. His knights gathered to slap him on the back and offer congratulations. Norah stayed where he'd left her. She felt so strange, so light-headed, that it occurred to her she might faint. It seemed to take a moment for him to realize she hadn't moved. He came back to her with an extra cup of wine. "Come, it's done, drink up."

She clasped her hands about the cup and said in a voice for his ears alone, "By God's Passion, I swear I will do my best to be a good wife to you." The chilled wine slid down her throat like an icicle.

The thin edge of humor he'd shown grew broader. He even put an arm about her and lifted his cup and actually laughed. "A toast to my bride!"

As the men drank to her, she clenched her teeth. She found it hard not to break into open tears. She had no armor, no defense against the hot emotions she suddenly felt. She didn't even care that Charles didn't join in the toast. He'd had a slight pout to his lower lip all day, and now he pulled a face and stared stubbornly into his cup as if he'd just found a bug swimming there. Norah couldn't think of any reason for this continued negative reaction to her, and frankly she didn't care. She felt safe now, encased in a relationship that was invincible.

"To my Lord Conniebrook!" the monk cried, forgetting his earlier reluctance. The drinking went on. Norah felt the weight of the earl's hand on her waist, and of all the eyes on them, and she couldn't stop herself from edging away a little. He let her go and raked his fingers back through his hair and let out another laugh, this one tinged with uncertainty.

She sat at meat with him—and blushed when the knights nearest her plied her with the choicest tidbits. She'd never been treated with such amazing friendliness. Plump Sir Corbett, to her right, said to the earl, "You see, my lord, she sees no sin in eating heartily when she gets the chance. 'Twas only the cloister made her appetite so skimpy. I didn't see much food in the larder there."

The earl smiled. "You checked their larder, Corbett?"

"Well," he said uncomfortably, "you told us to search every nook."

"The cloister hasn't slowed this one's appetite," another knight said, gesturing toward Brother Ignatius. "The nuns of Coxgrave may be kept from the sins of gluttony, but the Benedictines haven't yet curbed their good brother's propensity."

The monk was picking clean the carcass of a once-juicy bird. He said pompously, "There is a time for pheasant and a time for piety," which made everyone so merry there had to be another round of wine.

At last, when the heavy, rainy darkness had lowered, Norah asked to be excused. She caught the earl casting a look around the table and felt beholden to him, for it warned one and all to make none of the usual ribald remarks that sent brides to their nuptial beds. So effective was it that, as she rose, the men rose politely with her.

"Goodnight, my lady," said Sir Gian. The others echoed him.

"Goodnight," she murmured, and quickly took her leave.

She was no more than half way up the stairs, however, when she heard someone begin to tease the earl about the charm of young virgins. A toast was proposed: "To Lord Conniebrook's first heir—may his seed be well and truly planted this night!"

Norah had vague ideas about what must precede her giving birth to an heir, and what she knew at the moment seemed terrifying.

No, to be truthful, she was as pleasantly thrilled as she was nervous. The earl would be kind; she trusted him completely. In fact, her spirit seemed permeated by a sense of flashing exhilaration. She almost floated up the stairs.

In the chamber, she undressed, except for her coif,

and blew out her candle. She lay waiting with her eyes wide open to the dark, holding the bedclothes tight beneath her chin, marking each minute that came and went.

It was not much later when the earl came in. He had his own candle, and in its light his silvern eyes pierced her like two stars. The moment was come, and Norah felt a chill in her heart.

He said nothing, only began to undress himself. She watched him intently in the dim and wavering light, his face, his body, his manner of movement. He was older than she was, and the winds of time had written on his face, but he was handsome and handsomely proportioned.

When down to his hose, he looked at her—and she swiftly looked away. There was a suggestion of wry humor in his voice as he said, "Are you going to wear that helmet all night?"

Her hand went to the coif. "My hair . . . I look like a boy."

"I'll make you a bargain. I'll blow out the light to strip off my hose if at the same time you'll take that thing off your head."

It was done. In the pitch darkness, he joined her in the bed. She felt a moment of sheer terror. But he lay without touching her. She was encouraged to make the speech she'd planned out. "I don't know what I am supposed to do, my lord," she said, her tongue faltering on every word. "I hope you will be patient with me."

Jervais wanted to groan. He wasn't sure he could even manage to perform with her. She was so young, so sexless. Maybe if he thought of Eleanor. (It wouldn't be the first time he'd taken a woman while fantasizing about his beloved.)

He leaned up over her. At the same moment the night sky opened; the noise of the rain was clamorous on the roof. The racket seemed to bring all her fear swiftly to the surface. She said quickly, "I'm frightened!"

"No need to be; I'm your husband now."

He leaned to kiss her. He was intentionally gentle and coaxing. His tongue slid over the planes of her lips, then slipped between them to play over her teeth. By applying more pressure, he persuaded her to relax her jaw. When she did, his tongue dipped into her mouth. She made a small sound of surprise, pushed at him, and turned her face away.

For an instant he was quiet. *Slow. Allow her a moment. Allow yourself a moment. Don't defeat your purpose by hurrying. She doesn't know how to make love any more than a child.*

He said, "I understand that you know nothing. The only thing I ask of you is to let me do as I will." His voice had a rare gentleness to it, which surprised even him. "There's no need to be afraid."

"Will it hurt?" she whispered.

He was caught by the question, and searched for an assuring answer. "It sometimes hurts the first time, just a little, but after the pain there is pleasure." His hand drifted over her shoulder, his fingers stroked the never-touched skin of her upper chest. "Give yourself to me now; don't be frightened. I swear you will have naught to fear ever in my bed."

Still, she made a sound when his chest lowered over her breasts. She flinched away. Had there been light in the room, her eyes no doubt would have met his pleadingly. "Soft, soft," he whispered.

Norah felt his arms about her. He was showing great and unexpected tenderness, yet she couldn't keep from panting at the strength of those arms, the feel of his shoulders, his chest. They enclosed her.

"Shhh, now." He gathered her whole body into his larger one. She'd been cold, even under the bed-clothes, but he was very warm. Hot. Suddenly she sobbed. The armor she'd gathered about herself, the thin shell of self-mastery, broke up and disintegrated.

"Shhh, now. Are you so terrified?"

She nodded her head.

Jervais let out a laugh, in spite of himself. "You're just a baby, aren't you? A fresh young girl with tender skin, a little postulant wife." He let her lay in his embrace for a while, holding her with no more purpose than to let her get used to the feel of him; then he found her mouth once more and kissed her deeply. Gradually he took her up into a more demanding embrace. Her mouth shuddered under his. She moaned. He pulled his head away again. "Am I hurting your cheek?"

"No," she answered slowly, as if surprised, as if she'd all but forgotten about her bruise. He felt a flash of triumph.

Armed terror was not Jervais Le Strand's only tactic. He had obtained many a victory with caresses. But though he hadn't led a monk's life—why should he?—he wasn't used to initiating young nuns into the mysteries of marriage. Hence he'd been more than a little unsure of himself. But not any longer. She was a girl, but she had a woman's instincts, instincts he knew well how to manipulate.

99

Chapter 7

Jervais resumed the kiss. His hand began to move on Norah's back. She imagined that hand, which had placed his gold ring on her finger. It was a long hand, with square-tipped fingers. It smoothed up and down, and then slid around her waist, and then worked its way toward her breasts. It was so large, and her breasts so small, his palm was able to cover the whole of one of them.

She melted. She grew dreamy and drugged with his kisses, so much so that when he lifted his mouth, hers followed, seeking more. She pressed her lips to his hair as his mouth nuzzled her throat.

He began to pull at her nipples, as if to elongate them, harden them. How knowing he seemed, how skilled! And how wonderful it felt, how unexpected, how unimagined! Excitement surged through her even as she wondered if such pleasure could be entirely sinless.

His roving hand left her breast and stroked down her hip and thigh, then slid lightly to her belly. Gritting her teeth, she told herself to stay calm—

simpler said than done. She shuddered, but he kept her held in his powerful embrace.

His mouth drifted up over her chin, and she found herself opening her lips to the approach of his completely fascinating kiss. She thought he smiled as he whispered, "I think you'll learn to like this." Then his mouth took hers. His tongue darted to part her lips and go into her. Again his kiss overwhelmed her. He gathered her even closer to his hard body. His strength was unnerving.

Now his manhood pressed against her thighs, hard as a rock; his left hand spread open over her bottom and pulled her into him. How unbearably sweet the tight hold of that hand!

Cradling her thus, he rolled her onto her back and wedged his knee between hers. She yielded—until his fingers found her. She gasped.

His answer was to kiss her again, defeating the brace of her hands on his chest meant to push him away. There was nothing she could do but lay there under him and fall obediently under the spell of his mouth once more. And meanwhile, she forgot to preserve her most intimate secret. His careful fingers began to open her, petal by petal. She felt a curious tug-of-war in her senses as he explored her. She whimpered under the relentless domination of his kiss, under the sensation of his touch which flowed through her like honey. Her knees separated and lifted of their own accord.

He kept on, kissing her, pressing his rough chest against her sensitive breasts, touching her, until she felt a gathering in her pelvis, like a hand very slowly gathering into a fist. Then there came a priceless moment when she felt everything, everything: her delicate breasts against his hard chest, his muscled shoulders under her palms, his remorseless touch between her thighs, and within her pelvis that gathering, that tightening—and then a clenching of pure sensation.

She pulled away from his mouth—she couldn't remain absolutely silent and still—"Sweet God!" Strange cries sounded in her throat, delights unimagined sang through the core of her. She heard them; she recognized them. She knew she was meant for this, that this was right, that her calling was to marry, to join with a man and bring new life into the world. She had not found God's presence in the nunnery, but she'd received his message at last. *This* was what she was meant for, with this man.

No sooner had it started than he moved over her. His first nudge terrified her, but then he pushed into her. She cried out—a sound like nothing she'd ever heard from herself before. There was a pang. "Have mercy!" she cried. He went still. The pain passed, as he'd promised. Then, enfolded in this wedlock (appropriate word that!) she told herself to relax, to trust him.

He proceeded without haste. His fingers threaded through her short hair, his hands held her face, and his mouth touched hers. He withdrew from her and pushed in again. She jerked toward panic only to have that feeling smothered in something more pleasurable.

The next time she found herself lifting to accept him, and was rewarded by his deeply fulfilling presence within her. She felt joined with him, felt a self-dissolving closeness to him. She hoped it wasn't wrong. She didn't think it was, because it felt nothing but right. He withdrew and slid in again. She imagined his male part . . . elegant. Into her again, again. The torrent of feeling threatened to overwhelm her. Each thrust left a long, incandescent trail of pleasure that slowly melted away, like the ribbons of fire left by a falling star. Behind her eyelids a door opened into a chamber flowering and falling with flame, until her mind went white. . . .

It was a moment before she realized she was lying sated and limp and wrung out beneath him. He still occupied her, as hard and fast as ever whilst he held himself on his arms above her. She had walked unharmed through that chamber of fire. She'd plunged into the flames and was scorched to the heart, but now she was returned, unharmed yet forever changed.

He bent his head to take a kiss from her unresisting lips. "All right?" he said in a quiet murmur.

"Yes," she sighed, then added, "—just . . . I feel so sleepy." A most curious languor seemed to have come over her. He was still occupying her deeply, and one of his hands was pressing and pulling her nipples again, yet she felt only a pleasurable relaxation and acceptance now.

He chuckled. "Don't go to sleep yet. You may not realize, but I haven't finished with you." He moved in her again. The pleasure of it was enough to make her want to purr. It was not the fierce pleasure she'd felt before, yet it was good, full of little tremors of passion. He could go on forever, and she would not mind.

He didn't go on forever. In fact, he was already tunneling his hands beneath her and pulling her up into his body and thrusting hard-hard-hard in a last trio of pleasure-edged pangs. Thoughts slipped away, were dismissed in the surge of lust that enveloped him. He cried out as the sensation deepened and took him.

Yet part of his mind felt her lock her arms around his neck and felt her lips moving at his throat and heard her whisper, "My lord, oh! *Je t'aime!*" It was a breath, nothing more, as if she weren't capable of more.

In the profound peace that followed, he lifted himself off her, brushing her sore cheek with his lips as he fell onto his side. It was all over; the universe was restored to its silence. He felt grateful.

Norah lay next to him with her hands resting at her sides, still rapt, her flesh still sensitive. A delicious heaviness held her. It seemed she was in a state of grace. She considered what had happened. It was as though two bowls of water had poured together, then divided again, each drop returning to its original bowl. How was that possible?

Jervais felt a curious embarrassment. He realized that this consummation had meant something entirely different to her than it had to him. *"Je t'aime,"* she'd whispered: I love you. He couldn't offer that back to her, yet felt a desire to offer her something, some recompense. He said, "On the morrow we start for Conniebrook."

She was tranquil and did not comment.

He rolled up onto his elbow. "My chamber—*our* chamber overlooks the sea. I've often thought the sound of it, muffled by my bed curtains, was like the sound in a shell."

She reached up and cupped his cheek. "My lord?"

"I think you can call me Jervais when we're alone

104

like this," he said dryly.

"Jervais," her fingers curled so that she stroked his cheek with the tender backs of them, "will I have a baby now?"

Impulsively, he slipped his hand over her flat stomach. "It's possible."

"I want lots of babies. Boys and girls. Five or six of each, and all with silver eyes. All strong and good and dear, like their father."

He felt a lump, like a rock, in his throat. "Go to sleep, my lady."

"Norah."

"Norah." He smiled. "Go to sleep. The morrow will be long."

Jervais was still not sure what color his bride's eyes were. He was ashamed of that fact as she came to stand next to him in the hall where he and his men-at-arms were breaking their fast with bread and ale. She gave him a smile that seemed to say, "You look so noble and big in your mail." Gian saw that adoring smile and gave him a broad grin and a wink.

Charles saw her adoration as well, but seemed unhappy about it. Jervais wondered if he should take the stripling aside and find out what was troubling him. And nail his ear with the fact that his respect must now be stretched to include his lord's lady.

Gian, in a mischievous mood, said, "Did you sleep well, Lady Norah?"

The girl's face flared bright red. "Yes, thank you," she murmured.

Jervais found he was irritated. Why couldn't she just lift her head and speak up? He downed his ale in one gulp. It wasn't her fault, he knew. She was just what she appeared to be, a soft-spoken, timid, woman-child brought blinking from the cloister only yesterday.

He was going to have to get her some new clothes somewhere. It was either that or go on feeling like a nun-defiler as long as her face, her eyes, even her shorn hair were hidden beneath that veil.

He saw that Gian was on the verge of saying something more to tease her; to stop him Jervais said, "The rain's let up. We'd best be off." He added, "We won't be returning through Benley."

He wouldn't care to be in the same castle with this girl and Eleanor. Nor would he care to have to explain to the king why he'd used Rusmorgan without permission. And especially he wouldn't care to explain how he'd got the girl out of the priory.

The sky was a leaden gleam when they closed up the lodge. The panniers of the sumpter mules were packed with the party's tents and traveling gear. Jervais lifted the girl up onto a saddle horse, an ambling hackney that wasn't too good but was the only extra horse they had mild-natured enough for her to handle. In arranging herself, she inadvertently displayed a too-thin leg. He pulled the skirt of her habit down to cover it.

"Thank you," she said, that adoring look still on her face.

Why must she be so grateful for every crumb? he thought, irritated again.

The monk sat on a beleaguered mule. Jervais handed the man a purse of coins. "That should buy you some good wine and well-salted pork."

"Am I to have no escort back to Benley? There are

106

outlaws in these woods."

"If you didn't look so criminally and damnably rich, you wouldn't have to worry about outlaws," Jervais answered heartlessly, swinging onto his bay hackney.

The girl looked back at the hunting lodge as they passed into the forest. What was she thinking? Was she going to make a shrine of the place in her memory?

Riding through the endless forest, the thing that played over and over in his mind was their lovemaking. It hadn't gone at all as he'd imagined. He would never have guessed the girl's potential for passionate response.

Without thinking, he found himself riding nearer to her. She turned her head a little in his direction. She was all cheekbones beneath the shadow of her veil. And he felt a totally unexpected throb of affection in his chest.

As the day passed, he found himself daydreaming about making love to her again tonight. He looked forward to teaching her, arousing her, even pleasing her. He savored his memories of her innocence, her tears, her quaking breath—and the tenderness and deftness they'd called up out of him. It embarrassed him, yet it seemed to be a fact that he was physically pleased by this nursling woman.

How could that be? He tried to turn the matter over in his head—and soon found himself immersed again in a daydream of pressing his cheek to the tiny points of her breasts.

The day continued to hesitate on the edge of light. All through it Jervais had hard work reigning in errant thoughts of running his hands over those tiny

107

breasts. He could almost feel her trembling slightly beneath him. Poor child, she needn't fear him. He hoped she would never hear anything of the reputation he had with women. She would be shocked. Poor little simpleton.

Je t'aime, she'd said; and he grimaced, feeling terrified suddenly. He was no one for a young girl to love.

In the dark afternoon, Norah straightened in her saddle and looked about intently. She hadn't heard a voice or seen anything untoward, nor did she have any reason to feel the least fear, yet an odd alertness was on her. Someone, or something, was in the woods. She was on the verge of saying so to Jervais, when it occurred to her that she must not. Since they hadn't denounced her to him at Ramsay, she had a real chance to begin a new life with him. He must never know of her strangeness. If there were danger in the forest, well, the caravan was under good watch and guard. She must tamp down these feelings, and the urgings of her visions and dreams. And she must stay away from wild boars.

The afternoon became windy. The road they were following was naught but a ditched and muddied track. A flooding river crossed their way. The willows and cattails that grew thick along the sides were all but drowned. The party had a struggle in fording it. Beyond the lift of the bank, Jervais called a stop for the night. The men neck-roped the horses and mules together on a flat place, and they prepared to set up Jervais's tent of scarlet taffeta. Three other tents for his knights would be arranged around it.

All this was easier said than done. The men shouted and strained to put up the big shelter against the wind—and cursed when it blew down just as they were about to stake it. A lock of Jervais's hair lashed his cheek as his knights stood looking disconsolate, their shoulders drooped. Gian kicked at the tent on the ground and muttered, "You whoreson Judas." Corbett said without emotion, "May God damn this piece of scarlet horse manure." Charles, however, was looking at Norah with cool aversion.

Jervais glanced her way and saw why. She had her hand over her mouth and was trying not to laugh at this scene of sorry knighthood. Jervais forgot his squire's ill temper and suddenly felt unaccountably merry, enough so that he joined the next attempt to get the tent up.

At last they all three were raised. He and Norah took their supper in two canvas chairs within the scarlet shelter. Their folding table was lit by a waxen taper whose flame wavered with the flapping of the walls. The set-up was not luxurious, but it was adequate. There was always some worry about outlaws while traveling like this, and Jervais had ordered that nothing should be left out in the open for easy theft. Hence, all around them stood packed baggage.

He made an attempt at conversation: "Ah! yellow wine, my favorite, and this is better than usual, don't you think?"

"It's very good," she answered.

An uncomfortable silence ensued, and then she made a try herself: "Does Sir Gian live at Conniebrook?"

"He breeds war horses at Lesterhouse, north of there. He owes me another month of service—but perchance I'll let him go home early." He felt magnanimous. His journey had been successful; he had his bride—and her dowry, and though she was no beauty, she was meek and inoffensive. And surprisingly responsive in bed. He felt a sweet frustration in his loins, an eagerness for the meal to be over.

Charles brought the last course in through the flap, a tray of honeyed fruit. Jervais bit into a wedge of apple; the sweet taste filled his mouth with juice. When the squire went out again, Jervais gestured toward the bed casually. "I suppose you're tired." He didn't wait for her to answer, but rose, saying, "I'll dispense with Charles again tonight." He began to remove his own tunic. He turned to her, "Can I help you? When we get to Conniebrook, you must have a waiting-woman."

"My lord," she said shyly, "I know the weather is foul, but will you go out while I undress?"

He frowned, and it was on the tip of his tongue to say, "You're not in a nunnery anymore." But he decided that her modesty was worth preserving.

Outside, the knights had built a fire with dry wood cut from the heart of a dead tree. Jervais stood around it with them and listened as the musical squire played his harp and sang of a knight of the road. Was it only Jervais's imagination that his men-at-arms swiveled their observant eyes from him to one another with knowing looks? He didn't care. He was too bemused by his strange impatience to be with the girl again, to hold her and taste her and touch her.

The sight of Charles reminded him of the talk he needed to have with the boy. He might as well use this time to get that chore over and done with. He motioned Charles aside. "What is this dislike you've taken to Lady Norah?"

"My lord," he said stiffly, "I don't know what you mean. Surely I've done all I should in serving her."

"But those faces you pull—you could kill a girl so slight with those looks."

"It was not my intention to offend you, my lord."

"It's not me I'm talking about."

Charles's mouth worked, as if he were chewing his cheeks, gathering moisture. At last he blurted, "She bears no resemblance to the queen!"

"God above! Why should she?"

"But she is besotted with you!"

"She is my wife. There is naught wrong, I trust, with a wife caring for her husband."

"But she can never be to you—even *hope* to be . . ." His words were mangled, but what he wanted to say was clear: *Who does she think she is?*

Jervais hardly knew what to say. Men were looking over from the fire. "I see this conversation must be postponed until we can go deeper into the matter." He leaned back from Charles's bent blond head. "That's all. You're dismissed."

The boy's direct eyes measured him before they turned away.

When Jervais went back inside, he was troubled. The girl loved him. But he loved Eleanor. Yet there she was, waiting for him in his low traveling bed, against a nest of cushions. He refused to feel guilty.

111

He hadn't lied to her; he hadn't claimed to love her. What he did feel, this odd affection, was honest. So why should he feel guilty?

She'd blown out the candle, but the fire outside snapped and flared, and its light leapt up the scarlet walls. In its red glow, she made the classic feminine gesture of lifting her arms to her hair. He disrobed and joined her. He took her into his arms, and, homely as she was, young as she was—too young to know anything worth knowing—her gentle yielding brought out that unfamiliar tenderness in him once more.

In the flickering shadows, he satisfied himself that her cropped hair was dark. He brushed it back from her face. Very thick it seemed, and sleek as satin. She'd said it was her best asset. How long would it take to grow back?

He kissed her, and to his surprise, she met his tongue with the hot tip of her own. A kitten's tongue, he thought.

She lifted her hands, hesitated, then finally touched his forehead. He didn't move. Encouraged, she brought her fingers slowly over his face, the way a blind girl would. Her discovering touch slid down his neck, over his shoulders. Her shadowed smile was gentle and dreamy. Stimulated unbearably by those hot, timid fingertips, he became extremely conscious of the rhythm of his blood in his veins.

He buried his face in her throat and inhaled her scent. She might look like a nun by day, a sexless child, but she didn't smell sexless. He'd never been aroused by the mere scent of a woman before, but now his heart skipped.

The men retired to their tents. The three knights

doing watch shared a bit of low laughter as they left the fire to take up their positions. Jervais hardly heard them; his ears were schooled to quieter sounds.

In dreams thereafter he would relive that night: the sound of the tent walls flapping, the flaring of the firelight that filled the interior with a moving scarlet glow. He took his time with her, determined to know her better—and so got to know her ear, which was small and shapely, and the arch of her foot, and the curve of her lips and brows. His hands contemplated her barely-rounded little breasts; his lips kissed their delicate buds. She let him ease her legs apart. She didn't make a sound, but she trembled violently as she waited for his touch.

At first she was troubled by his caresses, but then he knew the exact moment her distress was replaced by passion: her fingers that had been spread out flat on his chest now slid up to his shoulders and held onto him. Her right hand went around his neck, and she pulled herself up, offering her mouth.

As he kissed her, he felt her body soften and then abruptly clench. He was surprised and delighted by this honeyed response, and waited in patience till her pleasure completed itself before he took her.

He went into her with restraint, though by now his body was thumping and thrumming. His patience was rewarded by the tender clasp of her. Ah, the sweet warmth.

They came together silently, tangled, and then locked with intense feeling. As his body convulsed in long spasms, he heard her whisper again, *"Je t'aime!"* And when he heard his own moan, it was filled with such solace that it surprised him.

He fell onto his back beside her. She rolled and

hesitantly, timidly, stroked his chest. He captured her hand and brought her sharp little knuckles to his lips.

He could have done much worse in marriage. Roger of Ramsay's daughter could as easily have been stout and big of bone. At least this shy, small, plain creature wasn't gross or vulgar. And it seemed that all she needed was a little affection to win her loyalty.

His attraction to her was odd, but pleasant. Getting her with child wasn't going to be nearly the chore he'd dreaded, for what she lacked in woman-flesh she made up for in sweetness.

And her dowry was never far from his mind: the quarries and knights' fees and the fief of Ramsay. They were all his now.

Her impertinent fingers had been busy, and the blatant curiosity of her touch had inevitably aroused him again. He turned to her. "You've done it now."

"What?" She was startled; yet even so her arms opened—no, her whole being opened to him. And for a moment—for a moment—a transcendent feeling flooded him, like a hand laid on his head.

"What have I done?" she asked.

He laughed. It was low, easy, not mocking. "You'll learn," he said. And his heart leapt in anticipation.

Norah woke an hour before dawn. Suddenly she was sure the encampment was not alone in the forest. She'd been sleeping with her back to Jervais, and now turned toward him in fear; but before she could voice her alarm, a shout—"Outlaws!"—came from one of the guards. Jervais woke. In a trice, Charles was in the scarlet tent with a light, helping his lord dress; then they were going out, Jervais in swift, powerful strides despite his unshaven, disheveled condition, Charles hurrying behind him.

Norah heard her husband speaking outside:

"What did they steal?"

"Naught, my lord, we scared them off. They were cutting at the horse ropes."

Jervais issued several orders, his voice vibrating with anger. In another moment Norah heard horses gallop from the dark camp. She sat up in bed, holding a purple quilt to her breasts. Her short hair touseled around her face, leaving her naked back unprotected from the chill. She was just wondering if she'd been left all alone when a voice called, "My lady? It's Charles." His tone showed all his lack of regard for her. "My lord said to tell you he's left eight of us to protect you and that you shouldn't worry."

"Thank you, Charles."

The commotion had left her with an impotent sense of disaster. She knew she would never get back to sleep, and so she dressed and went out. The fire had been built back up over its bed of glowing coals. Most of the men had returned to their tents, except for those on guard. The shadowy figure of Charles offered to heat her a bowl of wine. She accepted.

She knew very well he didn't like her, but she was a little frightened by the idea of robbers coming so close to the camp, and so she said, "Would you mind if I sit with you for a while? I could bring out the canvas chairs."

"I'll get one for you," he said, scorning her lack of authority.

He handed her the bowl of hot wine, grudgingly, his eyes squinting from the smoke of the fire. He moved to stand across the flames from where she sat, with his arms folded tightly, his mouth pressed shut, staring straight into the fire with an expression of withheld antipathy. She sipped the wine silently, troubled by his attitude—but really her mind was too full of thoughts of this sudden, new, fabulous love she felt to be very disturbed by anything else. Her joy, she thought, would wring her to the bone, would pierce her to the heart. She studied the gold band on her finger.

We have slept together.

And it wasn't frightening, as she'd always secretly worried; it was just utterly right, magical.

Jervais wore another ring, one with a red stone that burned like a flame. She glanced up at Charles and plucked up the courage to ask, "What is that stone in my lord's ring?"

He said, smiling softly, "A garnet."

Seeing that smile, she felt with a *frisson* of intuition: all was not well here. "It's very pretty," she ventured, like a child anxious to look under a scab.

"It was given to him by, er, a highborn person."

Norah felt another pang of unease. "Someone close to him?" she prodded gently, fearful of touching a nerve, yet unable to resist.

"Very close, and very distant."

She said nothing for a long while, then said, "A woman?"

Chapter 8

Charles didn't answer—and didn't deny—that Jervais had received the garnet ring from a woman. Norah sickened all over in a plunge of fear. Her heart, her very soul dropped through one lovely dream-layer after another. Yet her voice showed none of this. "Does he love this woman?"

Charles gave her a vicious, sidelong look. "No less than he loves himself."

Her heart and soul finally hit bottom, where they lay among certain shattered memories—of herself naked, her limbs twined in abandon about him; of her long cry of delight during that moment which she hadn't dreamed existed before; of her whispers, *"Je t'aime!"* Beneath her coarse woolen habit, her skin, every inch, felt rimmed with frost.

"Why—" she took a casual-seeming sip of her wine to soothe the dryness in her throat, to soothe her secret panic, "why did he not wed her?"

"Because she was already wed when he met her, and is wed again now."

117

A wind blew through the forest, strewing the rosy clinker of the fire. "He loves her though she's another man's wife?" How could she sound so idle when she felt broken into a thousand shards?

Charles answered impatiently, "He can't help himself. She is to his heart what sunrise is to the birds; it sings for her."

Norah almost gasped at the pain. For a moment she was unable to believe her reaction, its inner intensity, its outer calm. She sipped from her bowl again. The wine could have been corrupt, and she wouldn't have noticed. "Does he see her often?"

"Hardly ever. She has her duties and he has his."

She was tempted to do something half-witted, like cry out to God, like shout in a fury of refusal and shock, *I don't believe one word! You're making this up!* Somehow she managed not to. Anyway, her reason told her it was true. Charles was in a position to know all the details of his master's affairs. The truth was, Jervais simply wasn't the bridegroom of her dreams. She'd thought he was. She'd been a fool. Her voice came again in that same I'm-asking-out-of-mere-curiosity way, "What of her husband? Does my lord have no conscience about plowing over another man's landmark?" Raised among men, the crudity came to her lips naturally.

"Lady, he has never defiled his love's honor! Fie! He would never allow her to lower herself to the level of priests' lemans and the lost women who parade outside town walls. You don't understand at all. You can't possibly understand the kind of lady who would draw his love. She is of noble birth, fair and good and chaste and—and *beautiful!* So beautiful

118

she has a sort of glow, a kind of sheen. It reminds me of light on gold." He sighed. "In her service, the earl's heart has dwelt well nigh eight years, however far apart they may be."

Long before he finished this tirade, his words had set up a jangle of sound in her head. She was striving to digest it all. "But he married me." Her voice was all right; it seemed casual and steady. "Won't she be unhappy about that?"

Charles gave her a cold look. "She understands how badly he needs building stone from Ramsay's quarries for his work on his castle, and that he has a need to provide Conniebrook with an heir."

Her dowry, of course. She'd all but forgotten it, and since Jervais had never brought the subject up, she'd even fooled herself that he'd come to Coxgrave simply to rescue her. Now she nodded. "I see." Her voice had no strength left; it came out as if she were standing in a gale that hollowed the words out of her mouth. The hour's long gradual swell of feeling had left her heart tripping along much too fast and the blood thundering in her ears.

She was nothing to him. She was only a girl, just like a hundred other girls, except that she was dowered with Ramsay. Of course he didn't love her, a man like him, with his looks, his charm, his undoubted abilities. He had no feeling for her except as something useful for his fief, for the gleaming ramparts of Castle Conniebrook which overlooked the wrinkled sea.

Somehow she finished her wine, then rose. She said, just before the lump in her throat hardened to a rock, "I think I'll try to sleep again." Across the leaping flames her gaze met Charles's. For an instant her eyes rested on his, undissembling, withholding nothing. He was the first to look away, his mouth thinning with impatience at her pain.

She made it to the tent without breaking down. Nor did she break down inside. She thought of tears, but she had passed beyond weeping. She felt as if something within her had torn. Her sorrow was so powerful it precluded anything so small as tears.

He set out to fascinate me, like some brilliantly plummaged, flashing bird. And he succeeded. Oh yes, he is a resolute and audacious man. When he wants something he gets it, and to get Ramsay, he bewitched me. And I was eager to be charmed. I was like a young cat rubbing against his ankles, back curved, tail raised, legs stiff—my hinder-parts turned enticingly toward him!

Without undressing, she lay down on the cushioned bed, lay down as a shell on a curved ribbon of luminous surf, empty of everything but whispers of the sea.

The darkness was never-ending. The only sound she heard was an occasional frost-crisped leaf giving way from its tree and dropping. She longed for the light.

It came at last. She watched the tent walls lighten, saw the first low shafts of sunshine hit them. A few winter birds called and answered. The night was thankfully over. She lay unrested, more strangely tired than ever before. Sitting up seemed to take the most enormous effort; the simple act of standing took thought and concentration. She straightened the bed, moving with care, making no sound, listening to the calls of the birds.

Her tiredness came from the need to suppress what she wanted to do. She wanted to tear things apart, to run and run until she fell down unable to breathe, to bite her lips until they were raw. *Tonight*, she promised herself. But it was so long until nightfall! Meanwhile, she must avoid Jervais, because the extraordinary thing she'd learned must surely show on her face, and if he tried to give her any of his false care, she would surey break into shrieks of fury and pain.

Yet at the same time her longing for him was so acute she was terrified she might weaken and throw herself at his feet and beg him for his love. She mustn't do that. She had to keep her pride. It was all she had left. She thought of this woman he loved, a woman who was so beautiful he couldn't help but love her. If it was beauty such as that which called forth his love, then Norah had no weapon. She was plain—ugly. All she had was her pride.

Bishop Bartolo d'Orenish thought of himself as a precise man; Henry Plantagenet thought him fussy and effeminate. The bishop was thin and dark-complected, with a clean-shaven, lunar face. His hair was cut even with his ears, the top tonsured. His eyes had a concentrated stare that was completely without wit. He dressed gorgeously—no rough woolen monk's robes for him. Today he was wearing a blue satin surcoat. Henry could never look at him without thinking of the act which d'Orenish's kind coyly referred to as "Greek love."

While the man stood talking in his strident voice, Henry moved restlessly about the chamber. D'Orenish had brought a complaint for which he was determined to have justice. He was going on and on about Jervais Le Strand, the earl of Conniebrook.

Yes, yes, Henry thought impatiently as the man's high-pitched voice ran on, *by the cross, I already see the point you mean to make fifteen minutes from now!*

He stopped listening. He strolled to the tall slit of a window and squinted out at the cloudless, blindingly bright, wind-swept sky. As he waited for d'Orenish to make an end, he thought of the brilliant plans for Conniebrook that Le Strand had left for Henry's approval. And he thought of Eleanor's "secret" visit to the earl's bedchamber.

He was called Henry II, or Henry fitz Empress (he was the son of Empress Matilda), or Henry of Anjou (where he'd been born). He was bigger than the average man, broader in the shoulder, more muscled, ruddier of complexion, though not exceptionally tall. He was a good warrior, being more comfortable in the saddle than out of it. He was prompt to anger—but his most noted characteristic was his restless energy, which bordered on the frenetic. Hence he was used to being one step ahead of most people, as he was ahead of d'Orenish now. Even so, he had little time to spare from the management of his vast empire, which stretched from Scotland to the Pyrenees.

He'd been bred a king. His education, both in books and experience, had brought him to a precocious maturity. He appeared, at age twenty-three, striking, if not quite handsome. For handsomeness he substituted, when it was needed, resplendence.

He was just about to turn to d'Orenish and shout, *What in thunder do you want to say?* when the bishop's whining voice said, "—hence, considering all of this, my lord, I must insist you bring the man in."

Henry lifted one eyebrow, as if inquisitively. "Insist? Now, if this were a cleric we were talking about, I could see where your authority could insist; however, since Lord Conniebrook is not a cleric . . ."

D'Orenish blinked. "Lord Conniebrook at this moment stands in dire danger of burning in hell forever."

"Hold, sir!" Henry said like a shot. He didn't mean for the man to go so far as to make his ultimate threat. *Damned boy-lover!* "The fact is, I have already sent eight fighting men out in search of Lord Conniebrook."

D'Orenish's face went blank. And then he smiled. He had a fine bland smile, so cool, so superior, so proper to a papal flea.

"I'll talk to Le Strand—"

"He will do penance!"

"He will do the wise thing, I'm sure," Henry promised with a polished tongue. "My lord bishop, the moment is for healing injuries, not inflicting them. England is still deeply scarred by the wars. In all the kingdom there is enough disorder to occupy every one of us for years. Now, Jervais Le Strand may be a rascal, but at least he's a noble rascal, the very model of a courteous, brave knight. A better comrade-in-arms would be hard to find. I pray you, out of courtesy to me, have patience. Let me talk to him.''

Privately, Henry's opinion was that Le Strand's stout-hearted way of handling this broken betrothal positively stirred the blood. Not many men would have plotted so brigand-wise. Henry couldn't fail to mark that it would have been his own way.

And then there were the plans for Conniebrook. They were brilliant, and would serve the nation well.

The nation. Henry had fought hard to make that concept a reality in England. He moved to look up at a map on the wall. Pride like a shrill of horns moved in him. To ensure his struggle was worthwhile, he had an urgent need of men of high endowment and character to whom he could delegate works of the first importance. The north was his weakness, and Conniebrook was in the north. Le Strand had the drive to make Conniebrook an impregnable fortress, but he needed stone, which was why Henry was prepared to overlook a small matter like coercing the little Ramsay into marriage. In actually ramming a priory door, the earl might have carried things a bit far. Surely he could have been more deft?

The bishop, satisfied, bowed himself out, all his blue satin crackling softly. Henry went to the fireplace where a blaze roared. He considered the report he'd got after his return from Rusmorgan.

What had they done, Le Strand and Eleanor, alone in the earl's bedchamber? Talked? An innocent lovers' tryst? Henry could almost see the amusement in Eleanor's face at his flash of jealousy, and silently he cursed her. 'Twas exactly how she meant him to feel. 'Twas exactly why she chose to take with her that night from among all her society of beautiful and ornate women the very lady-in-waiting who was in Henry's debt.

Still, it couldn't have been more than a completely innocent half-hour. Eleanor might still be exceptionally beautiful and incredibly elegant, but just now she was too big with child for any sexual treason. She would never have risked meeting Le Strand if there had been any possibility of it being thought that she'd actually let him enjoy her intimate favors.

What a subtle mind the woman had! She wanted Henry to delve into all the rumors about her, rumors dating back to the last Crusade, to Antioch, all that ill-natured tittle-tattle which included (though by no means ended with) certain long and animated conversations between the young earl of Conniebrook and the unhappy queen of France in the gardens and terraces of the prince's palace.

What was her purpose? To gain some kind of bargaining power? Or was this jealousy her sole aim, to keep him off-guard, to keep him intrigued?

Le Strand, of course, was simply her means. Henry had learned the first rules of statecraft at his mother's knee—the "hungry falcon" politics by which Matilda Empress had imposed her will in Normandy. Hence, he recognized the technique when it was practiced by Eleanor. Poor Le Strand. "Dangle the prize before them," the astute empress had taught her son, "but be sure to withdraw it before they taste it. That keeps them eager and devoted." The prize Eleanor had dangled before Le Strand was herself, fresh and bright and cool. But Henry wanted the earl, with all of his good fame and gravity and experience—and his strategic castle—devoted to *him*, not to his cunning wife.

The men-at-arms he'd sent out this morning had been carefully instructed in how to treat Le Strand once they found him. The earl needed a reminder of the fact that he was subject to the royal will. And it wouldn't hurt to pacify d'Orenish. Henry could never control England for long without the support of the church.

All in all, this entire incident, which seemed such a tangle, was in truth a golden opportunity for him to press certain facts home to his turbulent vassal—and perchance to his intriguing wife as well.

The fire made blistering, crackling, fumbling sounds. Henry rubbed his hands together contentedly.

Jervais and his men-at-arms returned in the late morning. They had not run down the outlaws, but they seemed confident the villains had been frightened off. The day's travel was taken up. The wind had shredded the clouds and harried them eastward. Norah kept her eyes on the rough track. Jervais didn't seem to notice any change in her. Slowly, slowly, the hours passed, until at last the sky went blood red with the sunset. The day died down, then ceased.

That night, she was ineffably relieved when Jervais only bade her goodnight and fell asleep. As soon as the rest of the camp was abed, she rose cautiously. The interior of the tent was brightened only by the light of a sliver of moon. While lying awake, her eyes had adapted to the dark, and since she'd laid out her clothes in a convenient manner as she'd taken them off, she was able to dress without a sound.

She stood over Jervais. Something even now held her bewitched. Throughout the day she'd suffered moments when she wanted to be the author of his ruin, but now . . . now she couldn't seem to get up a single evil emotion. He was still the only person in all of England with whom she wanted to spend her life. She believed that in some way he must have cared for her; in his arms she'd felt more wanted, more prized, more accepted than ever before. The first time he'd taken her, in that moment of her deepest passion, it seemed her heart had opened up and taken him in forever. That moment she had added him to herself. And so, standing there, she hesitated. *"Je t'aime,"* she breathed. Then, bracing her shoulders, and her soul, she turned away from him.

It was an easy matter to creep under the side of the tent, but not so easy to by-pass the three sentinels posted around the camp. She had to crouch for an endless hour, praying desperately that Jervais wouldn't notice her absence, until at last the changing of the watch created a few brief moments of inattention among the sleepy guards. A brief moment was all she needed; quickly she was in the woods.

She was alone. The relief! It was darker under the trees; she could hardly see. The air was peculiarly still. A quiet, dark, cold night. She heard no footstep, no voice. She walked cautiously until she was well away from the camp.

Where was she going? She had a vague idea of finding people who would befriend her. Or she would live in the forest and make her own way, be her own mistress. Of course, she'd never been absolutely alone in the forest before. At Ramsay, she'd wandered the woods, but always within range of the castle. And she'd never been out in the heart of the night like this, alone.

She was uneasy, but not afraid—until she stopped abruptly. She'd seen no movement, heard no sound other than her own footsteps and raspy breathing and the thudding of her own heart; only her sensitive instincts had told her that she had company. She stopped, turned, looked back the way she'd come. No one was there, only shadows. Yet she felt sure that if she'd looked only a second sooner she would have seen something. Someone.

The intense quiet was broken by the sound of a twig snapping. Her first thought was that the camp had become aware of her absence. But the sound wasn't repeated. Perchance it was only a deer. She started on again. But now came the sound of a branch whisking against cloth. She stopped again.

Jervais had believed the outlaws were frightened off, but the threat of them came abruptly down on her, a heavy weight.

It's only a deer.

She knew she was trying to slay a dragon with a wish. She stood a long while without moving. The whole forest was unnaturally still, naught stirred in the tall trees, not even a rustle of wind. But when she moved again, the ominous sounds resumed immediately: a rustle, a soft footfall. She shuddered. When she thought she heard a breath—too close!—she began to run.

Which way was the camp? She didn't know anymore, her sense of direction was all turned around. Treacherous shadows grew everywhere. She stumbled several times. She saw a movement from the corner of her eye, thirty feet to her left, a fleet shape cloaked by night. It slipped out of sight again. Then it seemed the forest was full of a host of phantoms, repeatedly startling her and keeping pace with her. The eerie, palpitant light contributed a dreamlike quality to the chase.

Too soon she saw that they were not phantoms after all: a man was to her right; another to her left.

She came to the river which she had crossed yesterday with the earl's party, and now she saw that they were driving her, as dogs drive a sheep. They and the river forced her to turn south.

She thought she might outwit them by crossing the water. The current was swift, almost black, disclosed only by an occasional dark gleam and a chuckle. She no more than stepped in and the churning water roiled cold about her calves. Another step and it reached her thighs. It had considerable force; it pushed and pulled relentlessly, as if it were alive and had a mean desire to topple her. She clamored back onto the bank and ran south along it again.

The mysterious figures flanking her drew closer.

Finally, exhausted, she tripped on a surface root and fell to her knees. As she scrambled up, the sounds closed in around her. On her right the river glimmered darkly. By the faint moonlight she made out a flicker of movement between the trees to her left, and before her, and behind. Shapes emerged. Men. Of course, men! What else could they be but men? And not the earl's men. Her hands clamped over her mouth. Oh how foolish she'd been, when she should have been so careful.

There were four of them. She was nearly encircled. She had nothing with which to defend herself but her fingernails. Panic rose, though she wanted to stay calm, to do the right thing, the wise thing, the safe thing. Never had she felt so very young, so very vulnerable.

She was brought down. The first outlaw leapt on her. She fell and was pinned by his great weight, and the other three swarmed in, touching her, plucking and tugging at her clothes. She cried out—but it was not much of a cry because she was breathless. She kicked and flailed with her hands, desperate to strike them. The one atop her paused suddenly, then straddled her and sat up. He said in the common tongue, "She's a nun."

He was pushed aside. A bigger fellow yanked her to her feet. She could make out little of him—a broad bearded face, dark eyes that glistened like a hunting wolf's. She struck at him with her fingers hooked. He captured her hands easily. Another one caught her arms from behind. "Hold her!" the bearded man said. He ripped her veil and wimple off. She heard the fabric tearing—and felt his coarse fingers gouging her throat in the process.

Caught by the one behind her, with both her arms wrenched back, she couldn't escape. Her scream was cut off when the bearded one raised his fist at her.

"Don't do that!" At the same time the man holding her changed his grip, now squeezing her wrists together in one large paw while his strong free hand came over her mouth and yanked her head back against his chest.

The one standing aside said again, "She's a nun." His words were almost lost in the mutter and rush of the river.

The man before her lowered his fist and grinned. "Yeah, a juicy little virgin." He started to feel her roughly all over. Details imprinted themselves on her mind: his tunic was of falding, the roughest cloth; his legs were bare below the knees.

A fourth one, shorter than the others, had been dancing from foot to foot, loosing frantic bursts of words: "Hit her! . . . Juicy! . . . Now! . . . Now!" Finally he shoved the bearded one aside impatiently and took to feeling her himself.

"Hey!" said the bearded one, jostling with this impatient fellow. Four hands fondled her, tried to strip her, pulled at her, found the hem of her robe and lifted it, scratched her thighs. The fourth outlaw, still standing to one side, said, "You can't do that to a nun." The others seemed not to hear.

The nauseating stench of their sweat gagged Norah. She made strangled noises behind the hand over her mouth, and tried to bend at the waist, to step back. From behind her, the man's voice grumbled, "Fine as her little fanny feels shoving into me groin, if ye two're going to fight over her, I'm going to have the first dip me-self!" When they didn't stop haggling, he swore under his breath. "Irvin, step back! Ye know Judd got to her first."

The impatient Irvin stood aside with a curse. "Hurry up then!" Now only the bearded one, Judd, was before Norah, showing her a foul smile. He fumbled with his dirty tunic, and kicked her sandaled feet apart with his heavy boots. She would have fallen if the one behind her hadn't held her up. "Grab her ankles," he told Judd.

Norah knew then that she was going to die. She would be pinned and defenseless, and she would die before they were through with her—but suddenly Judd fell to one side. The outlaw who was reluctant to defile a nun loomed before her, a club of dead wood in his hands. Shock and disorientation doused Norah like water. Nonetheless, she got her feet beneath her again; her robe fell back over her legs. The man behind her tightened his painful holds on her and grumbled, "I told ye, no fighting, joltheads! Dicky, ye'll get your turn—"

But Dicky dropped his club and reached for Norah. He yanked her right out of the man's grip. He turned with her, and flung her away, saying, "She's a nun!" Norah fell onto her backside with a yelp. She rose to her knees immediately, feeling dazed, thinking she must scramble away—but now the impatient Irvin caught her arm.

Then, with a look of frozen surprise, he too fell aside. Norah's mind seemed to be twisted out of true—until she realized Irvin had been hit in the side of the head by Dicky.

The one who had held her, the leader, rushed forward, using shameful profanity, and Norah saw his fist rise and fall. Dicky took the blow to his head and fell almost on top of Norah. "Run, Sister!" came

132

his quiet voice as he struggled to lift himself off her legs. In the faint light she saw a dark wetness that could only be blood streaming down his cheek. But he stood as if unaware of being hurt. *"Run!"* he said again.

Life was the strongest reflex in her, and so she painfully detached herself from the ground. She staggered until her legs recovered from her shock, and finally she broke into a run. She looked back over her shoulder to see that Dicky had a knife out now. He was surrounded on three sides by the other outlaws, one of whom had picked up the club of wood. The bearded one jabbed in at him. Dick caught the man's arm and plunged his knife into his stomach, all the way to the hilt, then as quickly yanked it out again. The outlaw went to his knees.

"He got me! Irvin!"

"Well, we'll get him then," said Irvin.

"Yeah," said the leader, swinging the club.

Norah slowed, stopped. They would kill him. And then they would come after her again. A cold instinct for survival set her pace as she ran on, leaving the man to die for her. Frightened, confused, lonely unto sickness, she fled deeper into the forest, into the night.

Chapter 9

For the tenth time (or was it the twentieth?) Norah fell. And got to her knees. And rose unsteadily to her feet. Eventually she slowed from a jerky run to a walk, and then she simply stopped. She had to; she couldn't go any farther. She leaned against the thick trunk of a pine whose branches began just above her head. This alcove of the woods was like a dark chamber. The walls were tree trunks; the roof was black foliage. The one star that winked down seemed to magnify the silence. She would sit here and rest a while. She wouldn't sleep, though. Her eyes fell shut, but she tried to keep her slipping mind alert. . . .

One big hand supported her breast so that her tiny nipple could be captured by his lips and exposed to the ravishing and random attack of his flicking tongue. This was the wonderful, wild thing she had wanted all her life. Wave after wave of sensation struck her and filled her with an almost unbearable sensitivity. Jervais, Jervais, Jervais . . .

Norah came awake to find herself rolled in a tight and miserable ball, straining for . . . what? Her lips had fallen apart with her dream, and the heat between her legs mourned for—

She came to her feet with a start. The sky had lightened. She'd never meant to sleep. And never meant to dream of him.

She found herself near the edge of a grassy clearing. The frost and the faint light made it a tiny field of silver. Just then the sun came up and, as urgent as a lancer, hurled its golden spears over the whitened grass. Norah felt as cold as marble. To escape the shade, she stepped out onto the meadow. The sunlight felt warm on her skin but failed to relieve her chills. She had only one means of getting warm, and that was to start moving again.

She looked around, hoping for inspiration, for a twinge of fore-knowledge to tell her which direction to choose, but her "talent" was not that convenient. She started out at random, searching for a deer trail, a path, any traveled course that might provide passage through this deep-shadowed, moist forest.

Miles away, heading in the opposite direction, a dozen horsemen traveled through the forest in the grey half-light before dawn. Occasionally there was a sharp sudden sound, which always turned out to be some animal startled by their approach. Jervais was in the lead. He kept his hackney to a slow pace as he leaned from side to side searching for a sign of Norah's passage. All too soon he found it: her veil and wimple on the forest floor. He slid off his mount and picked them up. They'd been stepped on, ground

135

into the soil. There were other stains. He realized he was deliberately not letting his eyes focus on these, and he made himself look, made himself take in what they were. Smears of blood. He felt something like panic grip him.

Why had she left the tent?

The place about him had clearly been the site of a struggle. Gian found a rough club of wood that showed more blood. And Charles found the prints of dragging footsteps. The knights remounted to follow these further into the damp, green depths.

The injured person was not hard to find. He was a bearded, rank-smelling outlaw clad only in an unadorned grey wool tunic and heavy black boots. His tunic was soaked with blood from a deep knife wound in his belly. He said, as Jervais squatted by him, "Left me to die, God curse 'em. They ain't worth cat's piss."

"Do they have the girl?" Jervais asked.

"What girl?" His eyes were glassy and strange.

Jervais shoved the veil in his face. "This girl!"

The outlaw was breathing in wheezes, clearly in mortal pain, yet somehow he managed a grin that showed teeth abraded down to stumps in his gums. "Ah, that girl, the nun."

Jervais grabbed the neck of his filthy tunic and lifted him several inches off the ground. "Where is she!"

The man drew his breaths in gasps, like a dumb beast who couldn't speak, his eyes getting wider and wider and more desperate. "Mercy!"

"You'll get no mercy from me."

The man's eyes hardened. "Dead!" he said. "Little

thing she was—screamed and cried a lot till we punched her quiet. We had our fun of her—and when she weren't fun no more we tossed her in the river. Last I seen, she was floatin' face down towards the sea."

Jervais felt his face go blank with horror. He'd thought that along the way of fighting holy wars and civil wars he'd become indifferent to death. He'd been sure that death had no ability to shock him anymore.

He'd been wrong.

He stood slowly. Gian, his features grim and set, whispered to him, "Let me hang him. It's the only way these brutes learn anything."

The bizarre humor of that almost made Jervais laugh. But he only shook his head. He looked down at the man, whose eyes were glazed over. "No, leave him. He'll die in God's own time, which if there's any justice, won't be for several days hence."

He strode into the forest. He was going to hit someone if he didn't get off by himself. He had to be alone, just for a minute.

Safe from curious gazes, he closed his eyes and tried to imagine the scene the outlaw had described. He couldn't—or rather, he couldn't bear to. His mind recoiled from it.

Time passed. Still he lingered amidst the pines, struggling to bring before his mind some feeling of grief. Sadness, regret, and anger touched him, but only lightly and briefly. This inability to feel strongly was, queerly, the one thing that provoked strong feelings. He was frightened by it, this emotional disconnection, this unwanted and apparently irreversible petrifying of his heart.

Eventually Gian brought his horse. Not looking at him, Jervais said, "I didn't know what color her eyes were."

Gian handed him his reins. Tears shimmered in the knight's eyes, though Jervais knew he was not going to let them fall. Still, Gian took a deep breath, and another, and the tears glistened brightly. *"Courage!"* he said at last, giving it the French pronunciation. Jervais gave him a bitter twist of a smile.

He discovered that the rest of his knights were mounted and waiting for him. There was no talk among them, only the creak of saddle leather, and now and again a smothered oath. He still had Norah's veil, and knew he must keep it, yet he couldn't bear the sight of it. He handed it to Charles, saying, "Keep that for me." Charles's face bore a peculiarly stricken expression. Looking at what Jervais had given him, his mouth worked awfully. Jervais thought he wanted to say something, but then he stuffed the veil into his tunic and put his head down. He looked boyish and vulnerable. Jervais thought that perhaps he was feeling guilty about his treatment of the girl.

They rode from the dying outlaw without a backward look.

Norah's keen instincts told her she was being followed. She plodded on through the woods, exhausted, every step she took jarring a whimper of misery out of her. Toward noon a black pig crossed before her, and she came to a stock-still halt in the icy winter air. It was a small but plump pig, moving leisurely across the ground with its head down. Then, at a sound, it lifted its slit eyes and trotted away.

Norah, not knowing why, followed at a safe distance. She stopped on the brink of a lightly wooded vale. A thin column of blue smoke rose from a mean hut. Outside it, chickens were everywhere. They objected as they were scattered to make a path for a woman. Though Norah believed she was safely hidden behind a bush, the woman's eyes found her.

"Hello, there! No need to hide. Come on out where I can have a look at ye."

She sensed something mysterious, something weighted with silence, with things felt and not expressed; a cobweb of the inexplicable dwelled here. *Something like me.* She cautiously revealed herself.

The woman recognized her garb. "Ye're running from the cruel nuns. Ah, I know, they're bitches them. Always a-starvin' and a-scourgin' theirselves." She spat, as if to clear the words from her mouth. "The father or step-brother who locks up a girl amongst 'em ought to spend just one week eatin' their cabbage. He wouldn't come out lookin' so well-fed and content, either, would he? I don't blame the girl who makes a run for it. I admire them who're bound to be free."

Norah didn't answer. The chickens went on clucking indignantly at the woman's feet.

"What's your name, Sister?"

"Katharine," she said, a little amazed at herself. "That is, I would have been called Sister Katharine if

I'd taken the vows."

The woman shook her head. "Nay, ye were never bred for the cloister, Katie. Truth is, I been expectin' ye. The air—" she gestured sweepingly, as if she meant the air, literally, "has been thick with rumor about ye."

Norah stepped toward her. She felt oddly drawn to this weird crone whose face was broad, with high cheekbones and a wide mouth. She was old; time had left purple reminders on her nose and chin. But it was her eyes that compelled Norah. They were jet-black, set wide apart; they shone and were unblinking.

"Who are you?"

As the hag stepped forward, her breasts rolled under her loose dress. "Why, I'm Sidella," she said, smiling to show nine black teeth. That unwinking stare held Norah. "Ye seem a bit addled. Ye've never met anyone like me before?" Her eyes narrowed with amusement. "Are ye sure, 'Sister Katharine?'"

Norah felt an almost savage longing, such as she'd never felt before. She wanted to run forward to this woman, and had to hold herself back. Her spirit was straining like a hound at its leash.

"Come inside, Kate. Let me make ye something hot to fill your poor empty belly."

Norah blinked stupidly and took another step toward her. This was dreamlike. Yet more pungent and clumsy than a dream ever was. She took another step. Then stopped. The woman's eyes had veered away from her. Norah turned and saw a man behind her. She jerked. Dangling from his left hand, a knife blade glistened in the light. His breath was hoarse and hammering; his face was bloody and his stance was strangely stooped. His broad shoulders bowed under his head like a yoke. His left arm hung as if the bones had been pulled out of it. He swayed, and Norah saw that his left leg was as limp as his arm.

Unafraid, she went to him. "Dick?" she said. "Oh, Dick, what did they do to you?"

He stared back through wall-eyes, and slurred, "Sister Katharine."

Jervais was not really surprised to find the king's men-at-arms waiting for him back at his camp that evening. A certain Sir Crespo and a Sir Ruben officially arrested him. After spending the day following the river, looking for Norah's body, he hardly listened to their charges. And he didn't object when his ankles were chained together beneath the belly of his horse and his hands were bound. Gian and Charles and some of his knights were on the edge of revolt at this shameful treatment, and would have drawn their swords had he given them a nod. But he didn't. He let himself be led out docilely, saying only, "Gian, keep searching for her."

The furrowed fields around Benley lay awash in winter sunshine. The trees waited to be roused like restless sleepers. The day was golden, drowsy, dreaming of spring. Soon the pilgrims would be set loose, and the roads would throng with their multitudes; for now, however, everything was still, hazed, silent.

The day was far spent, and it was about the hour of

vespers when Jervais rode beneath the king's banners billowing heavily in the light breeze from the castle ramparts. The cobbled inner courtyard was a-clatter with horses' hoofs. Jervais's ankles were unchained, and a groom stood waiting to take his horse when he got off. Other grooms were loosening the girths of the king's men's horses. The bitter scent of horse sweat lay in the air; Jervais's throat itched from it. Sir Crespo and Sir Rubin helped him dismount, for his hands were still bound. Between them, he climbed the steps to the great hall.

Two sentries in blue tunics and scarlet hose stood before the door. One stepped back to open it. Jervais entered before his escorts. Sir Crespo, on his left, was tall and lean, with grizzled hair and a steep upper lip. On his right, Sir Ruben had a crisp, clipped way of speaking and a strong Angevin accent.

The hall was not large, but at present it was full. Several barons stood rubbing up against one another, flanked by their squires, all in their court finery. The Angevins among them stood out as the most colorful, in their French particolored coats. Jervais shouldered his way through them. Sir Crespo's grizzled, close-cropped head remained at his side. Jervais gritted his teeth. It had been Crespo who had shackled his ankles beneath his horse's belly.

The gathering made way; an aisle formed between him and his objective: the heavy chair on the dais at the head of the hall.

The throne was empty. Jervais stopped at a discreet distance from it. A sudden horn blew two notes, loud enough to hurt his ears, and a herald bawled, "Make way! Make way for Henry fitz-Empress, Duke of

Normandy, Duke of Aquitaine, Count of Anjou, and Lord King of England!"

The mob quieted completely and pressed itself tighter together, opening a corridor from the side of the hall. Henry made his appearance looking young and casual. In his hand he held a book with a jeweled cover, as if he'd just paused from an hour of reading. He crossed the head of the room, stepped onto the dais, and sat in his throne. Without apparent effort, he made everyone else in the room seem drab. He leaned on one arm, the picture of an idle, unconcerned man. Jervais was accordingly all the more alert.

"Lord Conniebrook."

Jervais worked his way free of the audience and bowed.

Henry pretended shock at seeing his earl bound as he was. "Crespo, unbind my earl of Conniebrook." His voice had the sharp crack of authority.

Jervais wasn't fooled. The manner of his arrest had been ordered by Henry. Crespo would never have risked humiliating him like that otherwise. While the knight was freeing his hands, he noticed a man who had come in at Henry's heels, a thin, dark-complected bishop, whose hair was tonsured in the way of a monk. Ostentatious in blue-and-silver satin and silver fox fur, the bishop cleared his voice but did not speak. No one spoke. Jervais rubbed his wrists.

Henry's pale eyes shone. "I've been studying," he said quietly, glancing down at the jeweled book in his lap, "and I wonder, just out of curiosity, my lord, what your opinion is—what do you believe constitutes a man's service to his king and his country?"

Jervais was Henry's senior by four years, but he was not his senior when it came to learning. Though intelligent and well-schooled, he did not have the born scholar's fire for the acquisition of pure knowledge. "I would say his loyalty," he began hesitantly, "his skill as a man-at-arms, and his desire to see both king and country prosper."

"And what about his obedience to the law?" Henry came back, his eyes slanting and sly.

Jervais remained silent.

"Come, my lord, surely you have an answer. 'Tis a simple question."

"Laws are important, but on occasion a man must disregard them—in order to better serve his country. And his king."

Henry remained as he was for an instant, and then—"You are *wrong*, my lord! *You are wrong!*" Abruptly his famous temper began to leak from all his pores. He put both his hands to his hair as if he meant to pull it out. He leaned forward and shouted, "In a man's obedience to the law *is* his service! And you, Lord Conniebrook, are not beyond that law! You are subject to the judgment and condemnation of your king!"

The silence in the hall was absolute. A moment passed. Jervais stood at military attention, his jaw tight, his eyes pointed at a tapestry just above Henry's head.

At last Henry lounged back in his chair. The high color had faded from his face. "Le Strand, you have done much mischief in these parts." The bishop nearby stirred, his mouth pursed. Henry amended hastily, "Far worse than mischief, yes, you have

144

committed grave crimes." He gestured with one finger, and the bishop produced a document from which he began to read. He had a compressed, mincing voice. He charged Jervais with ravaging a holy Catholic nunnery, with abducting a nun, and with forcing her into marriage.

Jervais gave himself a little shake. This was important. He must stir up enough feeling to defend himself. "She was no nun," he said. "She was the Lady Norah of Ramsay, my betrothed. And she left the nunnery willingly and married me willingly."

The bishop stepped forward. He seemed to think he was a true hawk of Rome, for he warned, "Bethink thee of thy soul, Lord Conniebrook."

"Silence," Henry said to the whispering audience. To the bishop, "My lord, I myself have sent to the prioress of Coxgrave, who told my man that the girl was as yet a mere postulant. In any case, she was betrothed to Lord Conniebrook for twelve years. I rather think he had a right to expect her to fulfill her obligation."

"She was in a priory, dressed in a holy habit! This man broke down the enclosure door and chased through the entire cloister trying to find her." He turned to Jervais. "Where is she? Let's hear her speak for herself."

Henry held up a hand. "My lord Conniebrook, did you take the little nightingale from the priory?"

Jervais felt tired. He wanted this to be over. He hardly cared what end it came to, just so long as it was over. He dredged up the will to shake his head. "She was climbing the wall to get out just as we were breaking in. We found her in the woods. I'd expected that I would have to be stern with her; I'd been told she'd fled the priory to evade me. But I discovered that she'd been put there against her will. Her father went mad during his last days, and at his priest's urging, he decided to give both her and Ramsay to the church as penance for his own soul. As I said, she was making an escape as we broke in, not knowing it was me coming for her."

Henry stirred. "How very romantic you make it sound. And you were wed?"

"The lady became my good wife four days ago. The marriage was consummated," he added. A spark of memory flared in his mind. He braced himself against even that slight tremor or vestige of feeling.

"Yes, well, where is she then, my lord?"

His answer came out in a hard, clipped tone: "She was captured by outlaws who, when they finished with her . . ." He swallowed. His throat felt as if it had been scraped by knives. "We found one of them yesterday who told us she'd been thrown into the river. I left my knights to continue the search for her body."

Loud murmurs filled the hall.

"Indeed," Henry said softly. "I'm sorry to hear that. Please accept my condolences, my lord. Your grief must be great."

Jervais felt the smooth cliches wash past him as water washes past a stone in a current.

At this point Sir Crespo took it upon himself to say, "We found no sign of the lady, Sire, except for a nun's veil in a squire's possession. It looked as if he'd been searching for her when we got to him."

Jervais was surprised to hear the man speak up for

him, and then and there forgave him for the chains and the humiliation.

The bishop said, "My condolences as well, Lord Conniebrook, but still there is the matter of breaking into a holy sanctuary."

"I broke in, yes," he said in a monotone, "but only to claim my rightful marriage prize. They wouldn't turn her over to me, so I took the most efficient course of action."

"Efficient, but dishonorable," Henry said. "To war on women reflects badly on a man-at-arms, especially women that live in poverty and chastity." Henry shook his head. "This is a far from chivalrous piece of business."

Jervais knew that Henry didn't care a fig for chivalry. Eleanor was the person behind the fashion of chivalry.

"Le Strand, you have reached your position at this royal court through valor, but lately you seem to have forgotten the cardinal virtues, especially temperance and prudence. Our enemies learned to fear you dreadfully for your unrelenting perserverance, but that was during wartime. We are not fighting anymore, my lord. We are supposed to be at peace. You have broken that peace and mocked the law."

He put his chin in his hand and looked as if his heart were in pain. "Dear Le Strand, zeal is invaluable when it is right, but when wrong . . ." He seemed to consider. "I should punish you severely, but in the light of your bereavement—"

"Does he look bereaved?" the bishop broke in, waving his effeminate, ring-adorned hands. "Does he look in the least bit sorry the lady is dead? Had he left her where she was, had he not pillaged a cloister—"

"Your precious nuns were starving the girl," Jervais said acidly, "and they would have beaten her next, to make her take their vows. They wanted Ramsay as much as I did, and were as ruthless as me in trying to get it."

"You are unrepentant!" The bishop turned to Henry. "He has broken more than English law here. He has flaunted the church that bred and nursled him. And unless he confesses his crimes with all meekness and humility and agrees to a suitable penance, he will be brought before a church court." The man turned ominously toward Jervais. "And the verdict I will seek will be excommunication."

Chapter 10

On the ramparts of Castle Benley, the torches of the
night watch fluttered like flags on the wind. Within,
lying helpless in his enclosed featherbed, the king of
England dreamed he was surrounded by a swarm of
furious bishops and abbots, by armored knights with
unsheathed blades, and by peasants wielding scythes.
Henry jerked all over; his eyes opened. He crossed
himself uneasily and sat up. The hanging nightlamp
inside his bed fluttered with his movement. He sat
silent for a moment, still stunned and terrified by his
dream of mutiny by the three orders of society. The
nightmare had brought on one of those peculiar,
lightning-struck moments when a man sees himself
with a stark clarity. And what Henry Plantagenet
saw was the frailty of his power, that a king remained
a king only as long as his liegemen chose to obey
him.

He was doing his best, but it was no easy work to
reconstruct a shattered realm. Among his first
priorities was enforcement of the law—a difficult

149

task when people had grown so used to ignoring it.

He thrust his bare legs out through the bed hangings and called to the page who slept on his floor, "Get me a robe!"

The boy appeared, looking as if he'd been kicked awake, his face white. He was no more than nine or ten years old. Henry said again, less sharply, "Get me a robe, lad."

Fifteen minutes later, wrapped in a deep-blue brocaded dressing gown, he grasped the iron ring of Jervais Le Strand's chamber door and shoved it open. Le Strand sat up with a start, with much the same expression as the pageboy had shown. Henry dismissed the boy, who had lit his way through the castle. Le Strand would have risen, but Henry gestured him to stay where he was. The door closed and they were left alone. He sat on the end of the earl's bed.

A night candle burned in the wall sconce near Le Strand's head. Otherwise the room was draped in shadow. Le Strand had lifted himself up, one arm making a column of support between him and the bed. His bedcovers had fallen away to his waist. Henry felt an altogether unfamiliar twinge of envy. The man was well-shaped, and handsome, too, which was just the final touch to make him appealing to a woman like Eleanor.

In contrast, Henry knew he was a little too thick-necked, that his eyes were too prominent and his cheekbones were set too high. And his lips—there was no doubt about it—they were coarse. He tended to talk too much and be too outspoken, and Eleanor couldn't possibly be blind to any of these faults.

Stop thinking like a foolish schoolboy!

He tapped his fingers on his brocade-covered knee. "You've put your head into a hellish noose, Le Strand." He gave a harsh laugh. "It behooves a man to do a little wickedness once in a while, for the good of his soul, but you seem to have a talent for it, my lord. And now this bishop—damned insufferable eunuch." He made a scornful smile for Le Strand's benefit. The earl didn't smile back.

Henry shook his head, picked at the gold stitches sewn into the silk of his dressing gown. He felt at a disadvantage here. He felt young and gauche. Had Eleanor ever pretended, behind her closed eyes, that it was her handsome Jervais who was making her moan so pleasurably. He felt a scalding rush of humiliation, a feeling he didn't like at all.

"D'Orenish needs to be appeased. I've given it some thought, and I believe a just settlement can be made. If you promise to go on a pilgrimage, besides making the usual penance-of-the-purse, the man should be satisfied."

Le Strand seemed peculiarly torpid. Was he still combating the shock of being awakened so abruptly, and by—of all people—his king? Was he trying to pick up the shards of Henry's words and fashion them into some intelligible pattern? "A pilgrimage?" he said at last.

"That's right." Henry gathered his authority about him. "I believe the discipline will be valuable for you, even though it's a distasteful concession, I know."

"But what about Conniebrook? I've just got started there—and Ramsay? I can't possibly leave them just now."

Henry's nostrils flared. His occasional rages gave

warrant to the legend of a demon ancestress. He felt one of them coming on him now. "You durst argue with me, my lord? I'm trying my best to save your miserable skin—and you can't leave your fiefs for a few months? *God's Rood!*" He stood slowly, his fists clenched. His heart was a hot thumping hammer at his throat. He swore, kicked over a chair. "No, you ... who are you to ... *are you defying me?* Do you think me your servant?" Finally he lowered his face close to the earl's. "I am your king."

He stood straight, his fists still clenched. Looking at his handsome liegeman, he was suddenly conscious that his veins must be swollen in his bullish neck, that his prominent eyes must be bloodshot with fury. He raked his fingers through his thick hair, then wrapped his dressing gown closer about him. "Mark you, my lord," he said in a stiff voice, "You can leave *everything* you treasure—forever! Just let this nose-picking, boy-loving bishop bring you up before a church court, and *see* what you can leave!" He marched to the door. "Let you find yourself excommunicated, turned away by office of book, bell, and candle from all the sacraments on which your soul depends, and then we'll see what you can and cannot possibly leave behind!"

He left, slamming the door resoundingly.

Jervais heard his voice in the corridor shouting fiercely: "God *damn* him!" Jervais swallowed. He'd made a mistake. There were things that were unimaginable, and saying no to Henry Plantagenet was one of them.

Excommunicate? This was all so absurd, so humiliating, and so *treacherous* when his numbed emotions gave him no clue as to how he should react from one moment to the next.

Excommunicate? He couldn't think about that seriously.

He lay back on his pillows. If he took time off to make this pilgrimage, he would lose his architect. With Henry encouraging castle-building all over England, Master Thomas Dhaene was in demand. He wouldn't sit on his hands for a spring and a summer, not when he had others willing to pay for his advice. Conniebrook needed the man, it needed revisions, and that was all that Jervais could take seriously right now.

The drowsy sentry clattered to attention when Henry arrived back at his chamber door. "Sire, you have a guest—the queen is within."

"This time of night?" His eyes narrowed. She couldn't have found out so quickly that he and Le Strand had quarreled. His lips compressed. He gestured for his page to remain outside and entered the chamber alone.

The room seemed empty. He crossed to the bed with barely a whisper of his billowing robe, and pulled opened the hangings. "I see you've made yourself at home, my lady." It gave him satisfaction to see her blush and smile uncertainly. She was holding the bedclothes to her plump, bare breasts. Her long blond hair, the soft yellow of morning sunlight, lay on the pillows in disarray. She was Eve, the first betrayer, the first seductress. Henry could never look at her without the awareness that he was a man, full of blood and a beating heart. And yet he was never comfortable with the conflicting emotions she stirred in him. He hesitated, then threw off his robe and sank into the featherbed beside her.

Beneath the covers, he took her into his arms. Her body was a silken, rounded thing in these final days of her pregnancy. His flesh leapt into sensuous life as the softness of her pressed against him. Then her belly moved against his, and he pulled back, startled. She laughed. So did he. Then he held her again, crushing her naked bottom in his fingers, as he tasted her lips for the first time in weeks.

He broke off with a groan, determined not to be ruled by this woman. "You have chosen your time to visit me well, my lady, for I am in need of enlightenment this night."

"Enlightenment?" she said in her sweet, cool voice. "How so, my lord?"

He smiled into her eyes, into that jeweled territory of iris. "Push back the shadows for me, if you will, on the subject of Jervais Le Strand, the earl of Conniebrook."

Her expression changed. "What will you do about him?"

"Hah!" At least she wasn't going to dissemble, for which he was grateful. "First, you will answer me a question: They say women like him well, despite the fact that he is indifferent to all but one of them. What sets him apart from, what makes him more attractive than the rest of us mere men?"

"He . . ."

(Was she truly on the brink of revealing her feelings, or was this part of her cunning? Oh, why couldn't women ever be the purely passive objects of which the poets sang?)

"He was a friend to me once," she said. "And

154

behind his performance of the hardened man-at-arms there is a particularly tender heart."

Henry got up on his elbow and gazed down at her, trying to reconcile this perception of Le Strand against the earl's ruthless pursuit of what he deemed to be his duty.

"You would be unwise to kill his loyalty, husband."

He sighed and rubbed his hand over her small shoulder. Her skin was petal soft. "My goal, 'wife,' is surrender and capture, not bloodshed. Marry, I'm willing to do what I can for him, but that worm d'Orenish is hungry for public penance. I've advised Le Strand what might be done, but . . . he has fire, this earl, but he only burns his own fingers with it! I'm trying to help him, but he's stubborn. Perchance you would do better to visit his bed than mine. By the saints, it's his will that needs seducing."

She blinked up at him slowly, no doubt fully aware that her long golden hair made a delectable frame for her beautiful features. "I don't think he would welcome me in his bed just now; I am waxed so unshapely. Nor would the feel of your babe kicking against his belly please him as it does you."

He gave her a look of smoldering mistrust and pulled her close against him again, feeling the babe's movement intimately. "Too bad for him."

"Let me talk to him—on the morrow, when his mind has steadied."

"Alone in his chamber?"

He thought she smiled, but her face was hidden beneath his chin, and he couldn't be sure. "The orchard will do well enough."

"Ah, yes, the orchard, with a platter of figs and

raisins and a jug of muscatel to remind him of the gardens of Antioch."

"Are you jealous, my lord?"

He didn't answer. He felt all his anger rising up again.

"I think it's another son," she whispered provocatively.

He took a handful of her radiant hair and pulled her head back so that he could study her face by the nightlamp's glow. A sudden hunger threw shivers of anticipation through him. The birth, then six weeks in childbed . . . such a long while for a man to wait. Thank the saints the court attracted perfect swarms of brazen females of the accomodating kind.

He said, "My grandfather always claimed a king couldn't have enough children—as long as they were bastards. It's legitimate ones he should be sparing of. Too many official sons can cause friction."

She laughed off his venom. "Then it shall be a girl. Shall we name her Matilda, for your mother?"

He wasn't mollified. "If you can get Le Strand to kiss the bishop's ring, you can name her what you will."

The night opened onto another clear day. Jervais was reminded of his basic dislike for being at Henry's court. Bad enough was the racket and the disorganization, the fawning flatterers and the wicked backbiters—and the court prostitutes—but to any man with a delicate tongue, the meals were the worst torture. It was with the taste of half-baked bread and sour wine in his mouth that he was escorted to the small castle orchard. He heard a hunting horn sound

156

far off to the north. Men were out with their mastiffs and packs of deerhounds. Was Henry with them?

He was left at the gate of the walled orchard. He walked alone through the quince and pear trees that were protected and warm in the morning sun, their unleafed branches flung motionless against the fragile blue sky. Squinting, he discovered Eleanor.

"My lady," he said, bowing over her hand. She was seated on a cushioned stool beneath a tree of quincebuds. Her silk dress was the color of new leaves. A gold circlet lay on her brow and around her hair, and a gold filigree bracelet clasped her wrist. The borders of her sleeves were embroidered with an elegant pattern. Her hands played idly with the tassel of a small scroll in her lap. She didn't rise, and there was no seat for Jervais, so he had to remain standing like a peasant in the presence of his chatelaine.

She seemed cool. She smiled cooly. Her voice, though sweet, was cool and taunting. "My lord earl, it seems you stand in a poor way just now. What folly. To actually raid the priory. I wonder at you, Jervais. And now Bishop d'Orenish will have his revenge. Perhaps it is only just."

"Perhaps," he said, answering her coolness with a stilted chill of his own.

Her face sharpened, as if with a new perception of him. Belatedly, she seemed to remember that he was now a widower. "I was saddened to learn of your bride's death, my darling. It must be hard for you— and now this trouble with the bishop."

His bride's death. Somewhere just beyond his reach there was an emotion. Even as he noted it, it receded. And then it was gone. What kind of man was he? He should at least be sorry, if not devastated.

"It's a great tragedy," Eleanor was saying, "but life must move on. And it's your life that seems very insecure at this moment."

"D'Orenish!" he said. His hands clasped behind his back worked against each other. "And Henry—he thinks I should go on a pilgrimage, you know."

She raised her brows, those features which seemed too exquisite to be natural. "You think that's asking too much?"

"For breaking down a single door? Yes."

"Jervais, you were too long at war. Doors are not, in the natural order of things, meant to be broken down. Be wise and save yourself."

He turned away from her. "You think I should do it?"

"Henry is your king and you defy him to the danger of everything you hold dear. He has pledged himself to establish a firm peace in the kingdom, and he shall require it to be kept."

"But he knows the work I've started at Conniebrook is important. D'Orenish . . . the man is as stupid as stone."

"You underrate him. Bishop Bartolo d'Orenish is dangerous. Yes, he is stupid, but he also sets a very high value upon himself. That combination makes for the most dangerous of men. If you will not humble yourself to him, you will find yourself before a church court. The trial would be over in no time— and you will be condemned."

He stood with his back to her. Her warnings beat at his mind like a bird trying to get in a shuttered window. "I'm not in the mood to play these court games."

"Jervais!"

There was an edge of fear in her tone. He turned to see that she seemed genuinely vehement.

"You have always been a rational man. I hope you will listen to rational advice now, especially from one who loves you and has your welfare at heart."

He tilted his head to one side. "If I give in to this witling it's as if I'm admitting to a dishonor."

"I know it is difficult for you, and yes, d'Orenish is a witling—but you must learn to bear yourself as a wise man among wise men and as a fool among fools."

He gave her no answer.

Suddenly her composure broke. "*You* are the fool! For your pride you'll find yourself thrust out of the church itself!" There was a pause as she considered him. She proceeded to unroll the scroll in her lap. It was the rhetoric of the judgment of excommunication. She began to read aloud of it. Its tones were not gentle:

"May he be seized with jaundice and smitten with blindness; and may he bring his present life to a miserable ending by a most wretched death and undergo everlasting damnation with the devil, where, bound with red hot chains, may he groan forever and ever, and may the worm that never dies feed on his flesh and the fire that cannot be quenched be his food and his sustenance eternally."

By the time she came to the finish, his shoulders had drooped. The message was clear for anyone who had ears to hear. He had no choice. He'd known as much all along. Why had he fought it?

She said, "My darling, I speak sharply because I fear sharp things for you."

He gave in abruptly. "All right. I'll drink d'Orenish's poison."

Her smile was sad. But as he looked down at her, he felt an uneasiness. In times past he would have had the impulse to reach down and touch her gentle, sparkling face, to run a finger down the pale satin of her throat, to ask, *Do you love me?* He had no such impulse now. "Forgive me for being so mule-headed," he said. "My heart is in such a tumult, I'm afraid I'm being rude to everyone."

"I understand."

He doubted that. "What do you think?" he tried to jest. "Do I have the face of a holy ascetic?"

She smiled softly. "You're not emaciated or wild-eyed enough."

He forced a laugh. "Give me the summer. I'm sure I'll be a perfect horror after walking the roads with the vulgar herd. Where should I go? What will please this buffoon of a bishop?"

"Compostella."

He nodded. One shrine was as good as another. Then he remembered: "Your father is buried there."

"He died in the shrine and was buried before the main altar in the Church of Saint James. Will you visit his grave in my behalf?"

"Of course." Once this would have made him almost eager to make the journey; to do any small favor for her would have made six months of wearisome travel a small sacrifice indeed.

She stood, with some difficulty, due to the ripeness of her body. "I will not see you again before you leave. On the morrow you will break your fast with

160

the bishop and Henry, and you will tell them your decision. I suggest you be ready to leave immediately afterward. It will spare you the irritation of meeting people in the castle once the news is noised abroad." Her hand reached up to touch his cheek. Her look held him. "I shall miss you."

His gaze traveled over her brilliant eyes, so full of assurance, her sweet mouth, her neck whiter than snow on a branch. Who could say when he would ever have her all to his pleasure like this again? Why didn't he kiss her? Where was his fleshly desire? Though he *knew* what he felt for her, though he remembered it, he did not feel it now. The love, the passion, the melancholy longing, all seemed to have faded. Studying her perfect face, he was aware of those previous feelings, yet they were like a chamber in him that had been closed off.

He said, "How farsoever away I am from you, your light will shine in my heart." It was the first time he had ever mouthed empty words to her.

The pilgrim roads of Europe were crowded each spring and summer with wayfarers bound for the various shrines in which were housed the lock of hair of a martyr, or the piece of a garment or some other keepsake of a saint. By going to see these, the faithful hoped to gain remission of their sins and cures for their ills. At the least, the journey made an adventure for folk who knew naught but toil all their lives. Three destinations were thought to bestow special blessing: Jerusalem, where it was possible to visit the True Cross and the sites of Christ's Passion; Rome, with its relic-filled churches built to serve the Papal

Court; and Compostella in the northwest of Spain.

Compostella, or *Santiago* in the Spanish language, claimed possession of the tomb of Saint James the Apostle. It drew pilgrims from as far afield as Scotland and Greece.

Traveling alone, as was his preference, Jervais rode south from Benley and crossed the English Channel in a small boat crowded with passengers. Most of these suffered fearful seasickness and filled the vessel with a sickening stench before the coast of France was gained.

There Jervais purchased a horse and rode to Paris. From the city on the Seine it would take another month or so to reach Compostella. As he traveled, he displayed his holy endeavor, for it was not considered fitting to travel in great state on such an errand. Accordingly, he was dressed in a long coarse tunic, like monk's habit, with a cross sewn onto it. He let his hair grow long, and his beard became full.

Only persons of rank and some wealth rode on horseback, as he did. Most people walked, carrying wooden staffs cut and blessed in their homelands. Jervais avoided contact with everyone, but especially with these commoners.

He needed no guide or map, for the way was marked clearly enough by the crowds that traveled it. For accomodations, there were hospices, which were resting places maintained by the donations of pilgrims and local benefactors.

One night, while sleeping in such a hospice, he was awakened from an uneasy dream by the late arrival of a sobbing, stumbling woman and a strangely silent girl. He rolled deeper into his cloak and turned his back on the commotion, hoping his

162

sleep wouldn't be disturbed for too long. He wasn't curious. By now he'd heard every complaint of the road—confidence tricksters, stolen purses, unscrupulous vendors who sold the unwary stale bread and rotten meat and "miraculous" mirrors, cutthroats, even wolves. Most of the time nothing affected him anymore. Day by day, hour by hour, he felt less emotion.

In the morning, the sight of the two women wrenched him, however. The one who had been crying was older. She sat against the hospice wall with her feet bandaged. By her side was the poor mute girl. Both of them were bruised, and their clothing was torn.

One of the monks who staffed the hospice, a tall, stooped man, was offering the pilgrims a dole of bread and meat and a draught of rough red wine to set them on their way. Jervais had the story of the two women from him:

"Bandits kept them for two days." He nodded at Jervais solemnly, leaving the obvious unvoiced. "Then they burned the mother's feet and cut her daughter's tongue out."

Jervais studied the woman's face, so lined and drained of color by her ordeal. The eyes of the girl were small and showed no feeling at all. She sat erect and still-faced. For an instant Jervais felt a terrible pity, he was gripped by it, dazed, frozen—

No.

It vanished, as suddenly as it had appeared. Yet he wanted very much not to look at her again, he wanted to get away from her. He could not make himself face this girl who had been raped and tortured by outlaws. Sweat trickled down his temples. He said to the monk, "Give them my horse."

The man blinked.

Jervais gave him a frosty sort of a smile. Then he started out immediately. He wanted no scene of gratitude.

The girl's face followed him all that day. And that night a monk had to lance his blisters, for he was not used to walking.

Dick's head was tilted in a permanently quizzical attitude. He held up his trapping gear with his good left hand. His speech came out slowly, as if he had to concentrate very hard on what he wanted to say: "I . . . I'm going t' get us a . . . a rabbit today, S-sister Katharine."

"That would be wonderful, Dick."

Norah watched him disappear into the summer woods. His step was unmistakable, a pitiful step-drag, step-drag. It was a daily reminder of her silent unspeakable memories of that night in the forest. Despite his seeming loss of wit, he was still able to keep their dinner pot filled, however.

She gave vent to a sudden sigh. She had a roof over her head, and friends, but she hadn't forgotten anything. Not her girlhood dreams, nor the rejection she had suffered; not her time in Coxgrave Priory, nor her escape. And not Jervais, not for a minute, nor his perfidy. His face was sharp in her memory. She grieved for him, and for the love for him that she'd dreamed up in her lonely youth and had actually lived for two days, before it was taken away from her by the hateful truth of reality. Recently, though, she'd been filled with a struggling radiancy of better things.

She and Dick lived with Sidella. She'd gotten used to that odd old woman who prepared the table with four knives, even though there were only three of them to sit down. The fourth place was for the fairies, that they might bring good luck to those who lived in the hut. Norah loved even the taint of madness that sometimes clung to Sidella. The old crone contended that she'd once flown out the window of her village church while being questioned about her witchcraft. "I told them, 'Ye're goin' to judge me—three men I wouldn't trust with a pear lest ye'd eat it soon as my back was turned?' And they said, 'They that come of the devil should go to the devil.' So I up and went. Oh, I'm Christian by name, but devilish in deed," she cackled.

Norah had never seen her actually do homage to Satan, however. And the only witchcraft she'd ever seen Sidella do was some trick or other, or perhaps a mildly heretical ceremony in the gathering of her medicinal herbs, when she would chant, "Holy Goddess Earth, Nature's parent, who dost generate all things, Thou guardian of the land and the sea . . ."

The old woman was known thereabouts. Now and then someone made a journey into the forest to visit her vale. One day a girl with a rival for her man had come, scattering the chickens about the hut before her, setting them to clucking. Sidella advised her to gather up her rival's "tracks" by cutting up the turf upon which she'd trodden. The girl was to put this soil in a cloth over a fire. "Yer rival will shrivel up and die."

The girl looked horrified. After she'd gone, Norah asked, "Will it work?"

The crone grinned; her eyes crinkled. "Oh, it will work."

"Will she do it?"

"Nay, her rival's her own sister. She wanted the man, but not at such a cost. 'Tis sometimes necessary to show people what's most important to them."

Norah had no reason to doubt that the woman was able to change people by sorcery and enchantments. She'd come to believe that Sidella could charm a bird from the sky or a snake from under a stone. In the atmosphere of her vale, Norah's own eerie peculiarity took on a feel of normalcy.

It was the month of May now. Where Norah stood watching Dick disappear into the forest a hundred small birds sang, making a gurgling sound, above which a single lark's call rose repeatedly. She was in the lowest part of the vale, and could hear water moving, deeper than the birdsong, and from everywhere came the smell of warm, wet ground. It was time to approach Sidella on her own behalf, to make her own request of the witch.

Chapter 11

"Ye thought I didn't know?" Sidella said, in answer to Norah's blunt telling of her condition. They sat in a place where the mystic play of the forest's shadows undulated and twisted as if they had life.

"I must decide what to do."

Sidella shrugged. "Ye either want the babe or ye don't."

"Of course I want him!" She knew the child would be a boy.

For a moment there was only the passionless chant of the insects, continual, insistent. "Then ye either go back to yer earl, or ye rear it as best ye can on yer own—if he lives that is. Peasant life is chancy for an infant. There's the sicknesses, and the starvation—"

"He's not going to die. He's going to be the next earl of Conniebrook, and heir to Ramsay."

Sidella allowed herself a flickering smile. "Then ye've decided to go back to yer man."

"Perchance."

"Perchance! Give me naught of yer perchances!"

"All right, I'm going back to him—but not just yet. And not as I am."

The witch frowned. "Ye'd better not wait too long. I got a pain in my side that's goin' to take me before the next winter's out. I'm not complainin', I'm on to fifty, a ripe old age. But I'll not see another spring, and by next summer a dent in the ground will mark my grave. Once I'm gone, the outlaws and ruffians will move into this vale—and yer Dick won't be able to save ye from them again."

Norah felt a start of alarm. "Sidella, you must teach me what you know!"

"Nay. Ye'll not be a witch! Nobody loves a witch—and it's love ye want, I know."

"Then teach me just one spell." Norah paused, working up the courage to say it. "A spell of beauty."

"Beauty!" Sidella gave a shout of laughter, showing her nine blackened teeth.

Norah did not join in her amusement. "My husband loves a beautiful woman. I must get his attention before I can hope to win his love."

"I'll reveal to ye this much, a love potion without medicines, without any witch's magic: if ye want to be loved, ye give love."

"Sidella, I am determined to be the mistress of my own fate. If you won't help me, I'll experiment on my own. I've watched you, and I have some idea how to accomplish—"

"Nay! Ye'll end with donkey ears and club feet. Beauty!" she muttered. "Mistress of yer own fate!"

Norah continued to look at her evenly. Her old face

considered, and gradually relented. "All right," she said cautiously. "If ye're willing to take the risk."

"Risk?"

"Haven't ye learned yet that every spell has its dark side? For every gain of brightness in the day there's an equal deepening of the darkness of night. The world demands its balance. Oh, there's always risk, Katie, there's always danger."

"Don't talk in riddles. What danger could there be in a spell of beauty?"

"I'm telling ye that if ye want beauty, ye must deal with its opposite."

"Ugliness? I'm already dealing with that."

"Ye're not ugly."

"To a man who loves beauty, I might as well be ugly. Sidella, I trust you. I must be beautiful."

"Aye, well, 'tis not a matter of trust but of power." She thought. "Ye have some power of yer own. If we worked together—"

"Yes!"

The old woman's face took on a look of evil glee. She began to cackle, "Aye! By the time we're finished with ye, the poor dolt'll have a time passin' ye by without wantin' to bed ye! If it's beauty ye want it's beauty ye'll have—why, the stars'll faint from the sky to see ye, Katie!"

When at last Jervais reached Compostella, although he was worn out by so many weeks of travel, he went immediately to the shrine. At first he could only blink and let his eyes grow used to the semi-darkness within. As his sight adjusted, however, he saw that the building surged with hungry, filthy, sick humanity. So eager were the pilgrims to touch the precious relics that they risked injury in the crush. Jervais shouldered his way to the forefront and went to his knees before the gold-fitted altar.

He tried to pray. It was impossible. The saint's martyrdom was celebrated in a cacophony of musical instruments, shrieks and sighs of religious ecstasy, and prayers in polyglot tongues. After a mere three *Paternosters*, he gave up. Pulling his cloak tightly around him, he escaped the tumult.

The heartless noon sun of Spain smote him as he emerged from the candlelit shrine. He strode down to the beach where legend claimed the body of Saint John had arrived in a miraculous stone coffin in the ninth century. A west wind was winnowing the breakers. The boundary of the sea was crossed by his gaze, and he envisioned Conniebrook. Norah had wanted to look upon the sea from Conniebrook's towers. Norah, his bride of three days, for whom he'd felt a foolish affection. He had a vague memory of a small, sharply boned face. His hands vaguely recalled the feel of her delicately sloping shoulders. She'd been so young, and so very unwise.

He stood as still as a pillar, looking out to the ocean, seeing naught that was before his eyes.

He'd spoken to Gian before leaving Benley on this journey, and learned that they hadn't found Norah's body. He couldn't even give her proper burial.

Why had she dressed herself and left the tent that night? Was it possible her puppy-like devotion was all a ruse? Had she been trying to escape him? He couldn't believe that. More likely, he'd said or done

170

something that had hurt her. What careless words would have prompted her to run so foolishly? He would never know.

He stooped to pick up a shell from the beach. It was too broken for the sea to whisper in it. Poor little Norah, poor little simpleton.

On the morrow he would visit the chapel where the former Duke of Acquitaine was buried, for Eleanor's sake. Then he would start for home. He'd accomplished all he could with this pilgrimage. He felt let down, for he realized now that he'd secretly hoped to feel something, *anything*, upon visiting the shrine. That wasn't to be.

He would go home, and gradually this numbness would wear away. He would feel again. He would feel remorse for his bride's premature death, and he would again feel his love for Eleanor—and therein would be his real penance.

Where the moonlight poured, it lay like frost. Norah proceeded on a path entirely her own through the dark. It ended at a large flat stone overhanging a stream. She stood listening. When she was sure she was alone, she lifted her robe over her head.

Her old nun's habit hardly hung so loose on her as it once had. In fact, she had to struggle with it to free herself of it. Then she stood on the rock naked of everything but her wedding ring. A night wind blew softly; she took pleasure in its gentle touch. She stood feeling it and listening to the leaves of the dark forest. A tiny bird appeared on a willow twig and sang a song like thin ice falling from high branches. She

171

also heard an almost inaudible, indecisive, little voice asking, *What are you doing, Norah?*

Ignoring it, she sat on the edge of the stone and lowered herself into the moonlit black water. Her eyes narrowed in sudden, all but unwilling pleasure. The water covered her thickened waist as she sat down on the pebbly bottom. She leaned forward and used her hands to douse her face, again and again. The golden band on her finger gleamed. She had never taken it off, not since Jervais had given it to her. But one day she would have to. She ducked her head back to soak her hair.

At last she stretched out. She felt very peaceful. The August moonlight was so bright it seemed to warm her. Her mind was blank, and she had a sense of clear limpid translucent Being.

Her trance was disturbed by the still-startling movement of the babe in her body. She lifted her hand to her rounded belly. He was stirring, her son. After a while, her fingers drifted to her breasts. There was no lingering immaturity there. She was buxom and womanly now. Her wet hair hung to the middle of her back, thick and sleek and dark.

She smiled drowsily, remembering that younger Norah who had thought she was as full-grown as she was going to get, that strained and hungry girl whom the nun's had tried to mold into their own image. They wouldn't know her now. No one who had known her would recognize her in "Kate's" form.

She heard the sudden muffled sound of a voice: "Aye, ye're beautiful. More beautiful every day."

She sat up. Bound in the deep and potent spell of the pool, she had lost awareness of her whereabouts.

She hoisted herself up and, damp as she was, pulled the confining nun's robe over her body. As she twitched and yanked the once-white wool over her belly, Sidella came out of the forest. It was the first time she had intruded upon Norah here since they had together said the necessary words and cast the necessary ashes into the water. Norah now bathed here every night that the moon struck the water.

A rooster followed Sidella out of the greenery. It seemed wherever the old woman went she was followed by some animal or other. Norah recalled the boar who had tried to protect her when she was a child. She knew why now. She knew what she was.

Under Sidella's rapt looks, she was never free of the feeling that she was doing something irresponsible. "Ah, yes, the spell's takin', girl." Sidella puckered her lips. "I've watched ye bloom and grow radiant. Ye're like this." She held out her hand, palm up; she closed her fist, and when she opened it again, a butterfly flew forth.

Norah laughed softly.

"Ye laugh, but do ye see how the pretty thing flutters this way and that? He's out of his element in the dark, night-blind, lost."

Norah sobered.

The old woman seated herself and crossed her large, able arms. The rooster stood back, pretending indifference. With her head cocked over to one side like his, Sidella said, "Ye've even grown taller. I swear ye've stretched up a full foot."

"Not that much, but I am taller."

"When are ye goin' to send word to him?"

"After the babe is born."

173

From the thick branches overhead, unseen birds sent forth bursts of untimely song. Sidella shifted into a position where the pain in her side was less. Norah sat near her in quiet fellowship. The moonlight was gentle, and the birds sang songs of desire.

Sidella said suddenly, "I'm afraid for ye."

"I made my choice."

"Aye, ye were a little late comin' to it, but we all learn cunning, and even how to be cruel, in this world."

Norah quickly faced her. "Sidella, this is not an evil spell, is it?"

"To love is good, it bein' no simple thing." The old woman paused. "Ah, Katie, we're sinners all and there's the truth. What we want we tell ourselves is right and good." She nodded, her mouth pulled tight. Deep lines had gathered between her brows. "But for one person to love another is perchance the dearest task, the test and proof, the pain for which all other pain is but making ready. It must be good."

Her face was wearing an expression Norah had not seen before, and yet she understood it. There was hardly an expression of loneliness that she didn't understand.

Sidella lumbered to a stand, with creakings in all her bones. "No sense in having second thoughts. There's no going back now. Ye are as ye are. I wish there was some way to get ye out of it—to break the spell just in case. But even if we could, I'm not sure what ye'd be."

"What do you mean?"

Sidella shook her head. "'Twas all a chancy thing,

as I told ye from the first. Were the spell to break, 'tis possible ye'd be . . . something God never meant to be created."

Norah shivered. "But there is no way of breaking it." It was a statement—and a question.

"None that I know of—though I don't know it all. Perchance . . ."

"What?"

"If he were to learn who ye really are."

"Would that break the spell?"

Sidella shrugged. "'Twas a powerful charm we made. I'm more afraid ye'll wish ye never wetted yerself in that pool than that the spell'll be broke on ye."

Norah couldn't imagine wanting to ever break it, even if it were only to revert to that thin body and those childish breasts. Beauty was her most urgent quest, the grail of all her happiness. With beauty the rest would follow naturally.

Sidella sighed. "I hope it works out for ye." Her voice was full of sleep. She was ready for her pallet. "But be careful. There's no guarantee that what's good can't cause evil. Even love. A love that's too fiery and strong will burn all to ashes in the end."

When she and the rooster were gone and Norah was alone again, she listened to the stream flowing quietly by, slipping darkly beneath the overhanging branches, rippling with reflected light. So much more lay under the surface.

What she had done, and meant to do, was terrifying—but so was the lonely and forlorn life she otherwise saw continuing to the end of her days. Whereas, if she could make Jervais love her . . . For a long while she sat dreaming, her eyes focused on the glimmer of the pool. At last she removed her robe and slid down into the mysterious water once more, determined to emerge invulnerable, so that she would never be spurned again. The black pool accepted her; she felt herself slipping into the power of the magic. The feeling was intense, deep and sweet. Sweet, very sweet. She felt herself slipping away, exquisitely away.

Part II: 1156

Amor vincit omnia: Love conquers all.

Chapter 12

Jervais stood on the wall walk of Castle Connie-brook watching the April sky melt softly from the blue color of the sea to a pink haze. As usual when he was quiet and alone, all the little gnats began to settle, all the regrets and sorrows. He sipped the rich, red Aquitaine wine in his cup and felt it lull his pain. Sometimes his soul seemed to ache. He didn't fully comprehend the nature of this pain, except that it was part of the intolerable loneliness he felt.

Winter had broken a week ago with the cracking of the frozen Barset River. In the sweet mistiness of one perfect spring morning, the black boiling current had carried the softened masses of ice out to sea. The sky had been lapis since then, or white with star-blaze. Scholars with their astrolabes were prophesy-ing marvelous things.

The construction of Castle Conniebrook was going forward again after the long year's pause. In whatever direction Jervais turned, there was evidence of the small horde of stonemasons which his new architect had brought with him. Currently, the builder was marshalling this army to the construction of housing for themselves. Thanks to Jervais's brief marriage, they could begin to build the outer walls of the castle next, for they would have an unlimited supply of stone.

Jervais didn't have the enthusiasm for the work that he'd once felt. He had loved Conniebrook, yet he could not find that devotion in himself now. He remembered a good deal of happiness related to it, and to his parents, but he couldn't feel that happiness anymore. Laughter had graced his life here, but now that laughter was faded until the recollection of it was too faint to even bring a smile of remembrance.

These days his smiles were all false anyway, with no humor behind them. All laughter and joy had somehow seeped out of his life. They seemed ancient memories.

He'd taken a baron's widow, a woman with thirsty eyes, for his leman during the yule month last winter. She was fair and comely, yet there was no feeling between them beyond bodily sensation, no tenderness or concern. They had thrust hard and fast at one another, pushed and pulled and flexed and twisted against each other, striving for the maximum excitation. Neither had cared for or about the other, only about themselves, their own gratification. It had been mere pleasure of the senses.

He'd considered asking this woman to marry him. In the back of his mind was always the thought that he must marry again eventually, to beget sons if for no other reason, for an earl must have an heir. But without the emotion factor, every act was hollow. It seemed at times as if his whole being was exerted toward the acquirement of nothing.

Christmas came and went, to the brawling accompaniment of mumming and revelry. The last time he'd taken his widow to bed, on Twelfth Night, he'd had a vision of the whole effort of his body straining to raise a stone, to roll it up a slope; he'd seen his mouth screwed up, his cheek tight against the stone, his shoulder bracing the mass, his legs wedging it.

The next day he'd sent the widow and her thirsty eyes away. His solitude since then had intensified and deepened. He'd once believed that there was no fear that could not be surmounted by mockery. Now he knew better.

Eleanor, I love you, but I need someone who can share my days and nights.

Not long after he'd last seen Eleanor, in the orchard of Castle Benley, she'd taken to her bed and provided Henry with a second son, Geoffrey. Jervais imagined her now in another garden somewhere else, surrounded by minstrels and ladies-in-waiting and courtiers, all dancing and playing the harp and reciting poetry and songs of love.

He heard light footsteps and turned, wondering if it would be Charles. A page emerged from the tower. He gave Jervais a deep, almost ceremonial bow. "A . . . message, my lord."

The boy waited while Jervais put his wine cup on the stone rampart and took the disreputable looking hide-purse. It was frankly dirty, showing signs of much handling. His eyes narrowed. "Who brought this?"

The pageboy flinched. Jervais knew he had become broody and difficult since his return from Compostella. He'd been given to unpredictable bouts of black rage. Sometimes the coldness of his own voice surprised him. He believed that was why Charles was so quiet now, and why the youth avoided him as much as he could.

"A beggar," the pageboy answered. "He was mute. The guard gave him a few coins and sent him on his way."

Jervais opened the purse. Inside was a ring and a letter, which was indecipherable in the dim light. "Bring me a candle." The boy left, and within five minutes was back with a light.

The ring was the one Jervais had given to Norah for a wedding token. A shudder went through him. As he read the letter, he started to shake with reaction. When he finished, he glanced at the darkening sky. He said to the boy, "Tell my squire that first thing in the morning we will strike southward. Have him send someone to Lesterhouse to tell Sir Gian to meet us at the Barset River at dawn."

To hear him giving orders, no one would know that his mind was torn asunder by a dozen clashing considerations. The boy left him standing deep in thought. The letter dangled from his hand. A son. Norah had lived to bear a son—*his* son, the letter said, though that remained to be seen. She'd died after the child's birth, according to the writer, someone named Kate.

It could be a hoax to extract money from him. Or a trap of some sort. It could even be a scheme to place an illegitimate child in his house as heir to Ramsay and Conniebrook. It could be anything. Or nothing. In the grip of this deep and fearful loneliness, he tended to believe it was nothing. But he had to know, of course. He felt *compelled* to know.

Norah had lived?

How?

Where?

A voice speaking low in some barred-up, secret place within him cried, *Please God, let this be no hoax. Let it be my child. Let me have a reason to care again.*

In her sleep, Norah saw a castle on a promontory, standing blue-silver under the moon. A soft wind blew. There was someone leaving the gate. His face was hooded. He commenced to walk with slow, rhythmic steps. Shadows shrouded him. There was eerie deliberation in his tread. She knew he was coming for her for, like a waking voice, she heard her name called.

She lifted her head off her pallet and opened her eyes. She was in the hut in the vale. The shutter was closed, and only a thin ray of moonlight fell on the floor beside her. She lowered her head. She recalled the moonlight of her dream, and that call: *Norah!*

He was coming. But he mustn't ever know her— that *she* was Norah—or the spell might be broken. She felt a pang of dark unease. Sidella had warned that if the spell ever broke she might become "something God never meant to be."

Across the room, Dick snored softly on his own pallet. Nearer, Norah's babe breathed evenly in his cradle. Sidella was dead. Norah missed her. Could she go through with this alone? She must, for her son's sake if not her own.

Bright, hot sunlight blenched the sky; the newly green grass of fallow fields stretched out on either side of Jervais. Flies buzzed about his horse's neck and ears; he kept a leafy branch in his hand to brush them away. His nose caught a hint of honeysuckle, and he sniffed. In the field beside him bright orange butterflies lifted out of the grass and circled, higher than his horse, making the air vivid with their bright wings. A shepherd with unruly copper-red hair raised his eyes and shaded his face from the sun as Jervais passed.

He was traveling alone again—without the provision of a tent, a chair, a real bed, nothing except for what was packed in the panniers of the sumpter mule on the lead-rope behind him. Gian, Charles, and his armored men had left him yesterday to travel to London and there await him at Henry's Easter court. In his liking for privacy, Jervais had often dispensed with what Gian considered the barest decorum of a retinue, and lately the tendency was more marked. Yet if there was naught to this letter, he wanted to find out on his own.

He swiped the branch at a fly. Memories chafed his mind. The things he'd been remembering lately! His father lifting him high onto his first pony. His mother brushing back his hair and calling him "my chattering little daw," both of them kissing his forehead the day he left their care to begin his education as a page. Daydreams, scraps of time.

He'd dreamt of Norah, too, often and often lately, that frightened, desperate, barely nubile girl he'd

184

taken to his bed nigh a year and three months ago. Once he dreamed they were together in a bed of wildflowers, almost stifled by warmth and sweetness.

Empty dreams.

He closed his eyes against the glare of the sun, just for a moment. . . .

When he shook himself out of his drowse, his horse was taking him past a wild plum tree like a silvery cloud moored beside the road. He was weary, and his teeth were on edge for food. He would give anything for a bowl of cool white wine. But he'd come past the place of cleared fields and any possibility of a tavern. He was back in the forest once more, a forest full deep and most strangely wild. He was markedly aware that there was neither castle nor village nor even an abbey nearby. The branches over his head were densely interlaced, allowing only thin gilt threads of the late sun through. The air was heavy with the scent of pine.

Ahead an almost imperceptible footpath led off the road at an angle. Beside it sat a peasant, an extremely hideous fellow sitting against a stump and holding a great club. Jervais reined his horse. Behind him, the sumpter came to a halt and waited, standing under its panniers. He saw that the peasant's huge brows overhung a pair of wall-eyes. The man had a white and tangled beard, and his body seemed somehow awry as he stood now by leaning on his club and heaving himself up. He was wearing a strange garment of wolf hides. He lifted his free hand as though to shield himself from some powerful light while he looked at Jervais.

Jervais's hand was on his sword; he was ready to defend himself. But the old fellow looked at him without a word, like a dull-witted animal, until Jervais began to think he probably couldn't speak. He struggled to remember the words in English to say, "Are you friend or enemy?"

"I am a man," came the slow answer.

"What kind of man?"

The peasant shrugged, slowly. "Just as you see."

"What do you do?"

"I live." He shuffled on his feet; his left leg seemed twisted. "What do you seek, my lord?"

Jervais stared into the leafy woods beyond the man's head, then with a shrug of his shoulders said, "A babe, a woman named Kate."

"Who are you?"

"Jervais Le Strand, the earl of Conniebrook."

The peasant seemed to take that in. He had a quality of immobility so total that Jervais could have believed he'd been here for hundreds of years, waiting just for him. Finally he said in his halting way, "You want to rest. I . . . can show you a place where you won't be bothered."

Jervais wasn't sure this wasn't an outlaw posing as a witling in order to lure travelers off the road. And more fancifully, he thought for a moment that the old man might be of the fairy folk, trying to trick him to an enchanted world. Still, he needed a place to rest. The stretching sun was turning the sky above the trees to flame. It was time to find a copse and make an end to the day's journey. He raised his arm and wiped his sweated face on his sleeve. "All right," he said without gratitude, "lead on."

The peasant started into the forest, and now Jervais saw how crippled he was. His gait was a slow step-drag, step-drag. Jervais reined back his mount, reassured that he had little to fear from this old cripple.

The peasant led him to a clearing deep in the woods. "This is called Satan's Arrows," he said in his halting way.

"Why?" Jervais asked, dismounting.

The peasant shrugged. "You'll be safe here."

Holding his horse's reins, Jervais turned to look about. He inhaled the fragrance of the trees and the grass, and caught sight of a bird dyed golden by the last of the sun. When he turned back, the peasant had disappeared into the dense growth. He decided to scout around.

He soon discovered that the ground had been leveled and cleared sometime in the ancient past, whether by the hands of men or by some magic he couldn't say. The original boundaries, though overgrown, made very nearly an exact circle. The heavy growth on its edges concealed three ancient, undressed, vine-draped stones. They were not quite evenly spaced. Each was about four feet wide and twenty feet tall. He couldn't imagine where they had been quarried or how they'd been brought here, but obviously this had once been a sacred site, erected by some demon-adoring cult in a dark time long passed.

Though Jervais was more curious than frightened, he thought that probably this was still considered a powerful place to the primitive folk of the neighborhood. He imagined it would be as safe a place for him to rest as any, for the sort of ignorant, superstitious men who made up bands of outlaws no doubt avoided such spots.

He cleaned his horse with wisps of grass, and tethered it and the mule to a tree. Ignoring the fact that the silence and the emptiness made the back of his neck prickle, he pulled off his tunic and settled down against a tree in his shirt-sleeves. He considered the name of the place, Satan's Arrows, as he ate the remainder of the bread and cheese he'd bought that morning from a villein living in a wretched roadside hut.

With his belly full, he grew drowsy again. He sat listening to the day dying and the night being born. A great peace overcame him. He felt himself dissolving into the imponderable forces of nature, felt himself a part of the docile rhythms and the perfect chords of time. It was a feeling that surpassed waking reason, that went to the core of his despair and found it baseless. He as rightfully belonged to this harmony as did the forest and the field and the day and the night. Never had he felt such an appreciation of the sheer wonder of simply being alive. His eyes fell closed.

Sometime later, he wasn't sure how long, he heard a noise, like a peeper's silver croak. He willed his eyes open, but they would not obey. Nonetheless, they saw:

It was full dark, with only a sickle moon above the trees. Through a muslin mist, he saw a woman standing above him. As he got to his knees, she stepped back, quickly, and stood barely balanced, her whole body poised to flee. She fixed him with an intense gaze, with luminous jewel eyes. He lunged to his feet, and now she did turn and flee. He gave chase and caught her. She seemed frighteningly pale and cold.

"Norah? *Norah!*" He shouted the word at her as though she were deaf. She struggled and they fell . . . and he seemed to fall back into his sleep. His head fell, and his sight of the moon blackened.

Jervais lay in the profoundest silence, in that suspension between sleep and wakefulness. The word "Norah" again raced up from the fathoms of his dreams and broke the surface of his mind, softly, as softly as the dawn light now met his slowly opening eyes.

The moon was settled and the sun risen, large and graceful. He sat up, trying to shake off the soft, grey, smothering dust of his strange sleep. The dew had settled on him and chilled his skin. He marveled a little that he'd fallen asleep so directly, and slept so soundly that he hadn't even put his tunic back on or rolled up in his cloak.

A cricket creaked nearby. The birds were murmurous, not quite awake in the trees yet. He wasn't in the place where he'd half-expected to find himself—where in his dream he'd fallen in the struggle with the woman, with that apparition he'd taken to be Norah. Instead, he was by the tree where he'd dozed following his meal. And Norah wasn't there. She'd never been there. She'd been a dream.

However, there was a woman sitting hear him. His heart clanged when he finally spied her. For a moment he couldn't make her out clearly. She was all filmy edges. Then her face burned through. He just managed not to gape—he could feel his jaw dropping, and he jerked it closed again just in time. Her face seemed too flawless to be human. Her lips shimmered ever so delicately; her eyes were the color of green pools reflecting a blue sky; her expression

189

was innocent and full of some doubtful curiosity. And yet she was human, and poor and common at that. At her hand lay a black pig, which she petted idly, as if it were a companion dog. Otherwise, she was motionless, waiting for him to make the first move, which he did:

He stood.

So did she.

And so did the pig, which began to move about, nosing the ground for acorns. It was so fat it could barely walk.

Jervais stood there stunned, with nothing in his mind but the alchemy of this woman who was the most beautiful woman he'd ever seen. Like the experience of a many-colored dawn, or golden trees reaching for the sky, she lifted him out of himself, shortened his breath, set his heart to hammering, and started a grind of desire in his loins. He struggled to concentrate, to get his senses back. Meanwhile, like a bird, she seemed lightly perched, ready to fly. As she stood facing him, her shimmering lips parted a little, her green-blue-water eyes were wide and wondering. *Don't fly off,* he almost said.

She was tall for a woman, though not terribly tall compared to him. Her hair, which was dark and exceedingly long, fell freely over her shoulders and past her waist. It was sable in the dawn light. In contrast, her skin seemed as white as morning milk. She was dressed in a shapeless, loose-fitting gown of rough cloth, of an unknown color, which fell to her bare ankles and feet. It revealed her collarbones and clung to her breasts. Despite her commonness, despite the pitiful way she was clothed, she was astoundingly beautiful. And he wanted her.

"My lord," she said softly in the common tongue, "hence lies no travelled way. Tell me what you seek and perchance you'll find it."

Jervais had things to tell her all right, things they hadn't made words for yet. "Who are you?" he said, unable to take his eyes off her. His gaze was focused now on her mouth. It was a small mouth, slightly pouted, luscious; he could almost feel its fullness.

She seemed to hesitate, as if reluctant to reveal herself. She crossed her arms, each hand curved around its opposite elbow. At last she said, "You can call me Kate."

Her voice had a natural musical quality, the music of leaves and wind. It was the perfect voice for her, so perfect that it was a moment before he realized what she'd said with it. His heart pounded in his chest once more. "You're Kate?"

Something suddenly frightened the birds. In a cloud they rose, piping, from the trees into the pale air. Their calls grew dim.

He said, "You knew my wife, the Lady Norah?" Without realizing, he twisted the gold band on his little finger.

Norah's name seemed to go through the woman like a chill. She shuddered, something in her seemed to teeter, but then she steadied.

"Yes," she answered, smiling prettily now, "and I have your son."

Jervais drew himself up, found his tunic and pulled it over his head. He located his sword and drew the broad belt about his waist. The woman was silent through all this. She stood with her head tilted, giving away nothing. She was clearly in no awe of him, and he was disgruntled to have to dance to the tune of a peasant—even this peculiarly exciting, darkly attractive peasant. If she did indeed have Norah's babe, however, it was worth it.

She said, "I notice you don't ask how I came to know your lady, what trials she endured, or how she finally died. I'm not surprised. She told me that you cared naught for her."

"Keep your improper words in your mouth, woman, or I shall have to beat respect into you."

"Oh-ho." She was suddenly full of mordant humor, her eyes half-closed with it. "Yes, my lord, by all means, my lord. Would you like me just to hie myself off? No? Are you sure, my lord? I wouldn't want to offend you with my lowly presence, you who are so well regarded by virtue of your fame and your wealth."

It was intolerable to be insulted this way, yet she was as sinuous as a circling, glittering fish. And so shatteringly beautiful! While his desire came in flashes, while he stammered to find a retort to put her in her place, she gave him another careless laugh. He felt the carnivore in him bare its teeth. If she only knew how he wanted to devour her. He stepped toward her.

"Careful, my lord," she warned in a wool-soft voice. "You need me if you want to see your son."

The growing light glimmered on her. With each passing breath he saw her features more distinctly. Her face, with its creamy skin and deep-set, green-blue eyes, was remarkable, as was the red of her mouth and her dark, shapely brows. There was something truly strange about her—and yet she was maddeningly beautiful. Who on earth could she be?

He forced himself to ask, "Are you a fairy?"

Her face lit up with delight; she laughed again. "Perchance."

That left him without words for a minute. However, when he asked, "How did she die?" the woman's face sobered.

"She was about six hours in travail, and though it was sharp, the saints were good to her in blessing her with the strength to go through it and endure it, and they gave her, in their own good time, the sweet babe."

"You helped her?"

"I did, and I have nursed the child these five months."

Jervais was not disturbed by this news. He knew that noble wives did not always nurse their infants themselves. They paid a low-born woman, usually one whose own babe had died, to be a wet nurse, or *damosel*.

"By the next morning," Kate continued (all the good humor was drained out of her face now), "your lady was gone."

"How could that be?"

"She was unhappy when she first came upon my vale, stumbling out of the woods in terror and misery. She never recovered her spirit. I believe she willed herself to live just long enough to give birth to her son."

Jervais said softly, "'Twas a miracle she lived that long. She ran from my camp soon after our marriage—I don't know why."

Kate cocked her head to one side. "Really? Not even any suspicions?"

He didn't answer that. He said, "She was beset by outlaws on the forest. The one we found told us they'd—" he halted, looking for a word that wouldn't hurt his tongue, "that they had ravished her, and bludgeoned her, and thrown her in a river. My men searched, but—now I know why her body couldn't be found."

He knew he was revealing too much of himself, and she was regarding him with intense interest, as if surprised by what she saw. And as if out of pity, she said, "She was never ravished. The outlaw you found lied. Be at ease, my lord. She was neither ravished nor murdered."

He wanted to believe this, and in a corner of his heart he did believe it, and it seemed the world was brighter than it had been before; and yet at the same time he recognized the convenience of her saying it, for if Norah had been raped, there would be every chance that the child this woman claimed was his was in truth some outlaw's byblow—if it were Norah's at all.

He couldn't allow himself another pang of sentiment. Regaining his distance, he said, "I'd like to see this babe."

"You will see him—and you will know him when you do, but first, my lord, I will tell you my price."

Chapter 13

"Your price?" Jervais said, scornfully.

Norah hadn't thought it would be like this. She'd feared being near him again, but in a corner of her mind she'd felt she would surely be in control of herself, after all that had happened to her, after so much time. She hadn't wanted to be so drawn to him again. She thought he looked a little older, but he was even more ruthlessly handsome than she remembered. And he still possessed that piercing, brilliant gaze which could fix her so effortlessly.

Oh, this was going to be so much harder than she'd imagined. For one thing, the lies. She'd always taken comfort in telling the truth and had found it difficult to make herself tell a lie. How very hard it was going to be to *live* a lie.

"Yes, my price," she answered him. "There is naught for naught in this world."

"Tell me then, what is your price, Mistress Kate?"

"Take my hand."

He hesitated, bending on her a look that seemed

both questioning and ominous.

"Do you want your son?" she prompted.

Abruptly he offered his hand, palm up. She placed hers in it. (She tried to stand rigid, tried to defeat the involuntary trembling that started in her at his touch.) "Now promise me that you will grant me one wish, my lord, whatever I ask of you, as long as it lies in your might. And for this pledge I shall provide that for which you have come."

He reacted as if she'd struck him with a knotted whip. "God's rood! You could ask for anything, woman! My property—my life even! Do you take me for a fool?" He seemed to grow larger in his anger.

He would have withdrawn his hand, but she clasped it with both hers. "Promise!" she urged him. "Or I'll never show you your son! I'll rear him as my own—if he lives beyond the diseases of poverty, that is."

At last, with disbelief and contempt he said, "Very well, I will grant you one wish, whatever you ask of me—*as long at it lies in my might.*"

She didn't trust him. She suddenly remembered everything—how he'd used her to gain Ramsay, how shabbily he'd tricked her into loving him. She looked down at his large hand captured beween hers. "That ring," she said impetuously, "that garnet—give me that, my lord, in token of your word."

He stared down his nose at her; the corners of his mouth were turned down sharply; his chin stood out like a rock in a river. "I am a man of honor, and I have given my pledge."

"You seem to think much of your honor. Or is it that you hate to part with the ring?" she said with a desperate recklessness. "I wonder if you think more

196

of keeping it than of gaining your son?"

For a long moment their eyes dueled. Then, with a suddenness that made her heart bound, he pulled his hand away and tugged at the ring. He wrenched it off his middle finger and held it. She reached for it—but for an instant he did not relinquish it. They held it between them in their fingertips.

A most quiet and terrifying manner wrapped him like a cloak. He said, cruel and resolved, "If you value your life, this ring will be returned to me."

This flick of his temper sent a shiver through her. She brushed a wisp of hair from her cheek and looked down at the red stone in her palm. It made her feel tired, heavy. She looked away, at his horse calmly grazing. "I will return it to you," she said dully, "when you fulfill your pledge."

"See that you do. And now, what have I given this foolish pledge for?"

She ignored the ruthless overtone in his voice, and gestured for him to follow her. The sun was a warm liquid pouring through the sieving trees as he led his horse and sumpter mule behind her (and as Sidella's pig followed this cavalcade) to the vale, to the low daub and timber hut with its single narrow window. Approaching it through the steam that was now rising from the dew, she realized that once she took him inside there could be no turning back.

The hut seemed more wretched now as she saw it through his eyes. A small outer room was for storage and contained several setting chickens and Dick's squirrel-hoard of tools, together with certain other debris of the mean life they led here. The floor was earth.

The second room was hardly larger. It was cool

and dark and smelled sweetly of herbs and flowers. To her and Dick it had been a modest, homely, serviceable room. The floor was covered with dried rushes, and curling smoke rose from the open fire that smoldered in a clay-lined hole. In the far wall the open window shutter let in the light.

Not looking at Jervais, but feeling his presence behind her, Norah crossed to the rough cradle. Her hands were shaking. She waited until he came to stand beside her. She said, impulsively touching the babe's spider-silk hair, "Your son, my lord, born five months ago."

For a long instant Jervais merely stood staring down at the sleeping babe. She could almost hear him thinking: *There is no proof here.*

It was not until the child woke that the hidden trait that father and son shared was revealed: the child blinked and squinted and then stared steadily up at his father. And silver eyes met silver eyes. Norah heard Jervais's breath catch. He reached out his big hand and laid his fingertips on the child's round cheek. He boldly smoothed the babe's head. He even bent and pressed his lips to the spider-silk hair. There was a father's pride in that kiss, and Norah felt the most secret, glorious relief. But then, glancing up at him, she saw the flash of paternal possessiveness in his eyes as well, and she resented it.

"His name is Roger," she said harshly. "Norah said it must be so. Her father's name was part of her patrimony—she explained that to me, and that the boy will inherit Ramsay as well as Conniebrook. I promised her that her child would have his rightful place, and I will keep that promise."

Jervais pulled his eyes from his son and stared at

her. Somehow he seemed blind to her. He was clearly far away in his thoughts.

"You need me," she emphasized. "I've been his—" She stopped, realizing belatedly that she had lapsed into French. The mistake was too late to correct now. The only thing to do was brazen out. "I've been his *damosel* since Norah died."

"You have it all figured out, don't you?"

She stiffened. The moment had arrived when her plan would either fail or succeed. He stood so tall that the low thatch of the roof ruffled the top of his head. One look at his face was enough to bring on a sense of doom. Roger started to rub his eyes with his small fists. His face puckered to cry. She quickly lifted him. "There, there, my dearling. Yes, yes, in a moment, my love."

She couldn't stop the babe from nuzzling at her breasts. From her ankles a heat rose and branched to all the limbs of her body. Yet what embarrassed her seemed to bring home the truth to Jervais. While her face burned, his voice seemed constricted and harsh: "I suppose I have no alternative just now. I certainly can't nourish the child myself. I'm going to London from here, however, and things may change there, so don't get above yourself with me, woman." His expression was full of cold distaste. "This is my child and I will decide who will rear him. If you will not bear yourself mannerly towards me, God is my witness, you will be replaced."

Fear crackled within her. He was after all a remorseless man. If he wanted to be rid of her, he would be rid of her, one way or another, despite the sanctity of his given word. If she wanted to stay near Roger, she must not push Jervais too far. She must prove herself useful to him. And she must appear submissive.

She had only two weapons. She used them now, both at once: she tipped her head seductively and met his silver gaze, saying, "Don't forget the pledge you made to me, my lord."

Their first day of travel together was as blue and warm as summer. Jervais made a nest for the child in one of the mule's panniers, while he and Norah took turns walking and riding his hackney. (The two times he helped her onto the horse, she noticed that for a long while after he kept his pale eyes fixed like a statue's before him.)

He was nervous about outlaws, and suspicious to discover Dick following along behind them when they left the deeper forest for the sunshiny woods of the road. Norah said in a pinched voice, "Dick goes where I go. I take care of him, and he takes care of me. Never fear, my lord. He won't murder you in your sleep. He'll keep us informed of outlaws while he provides us with small game for food."

"As long as he can keep up. I won't be delayed by him."

"I've explained to him that we're going to London. If we get separated, he'll find the way."

Jervais said wryly, "At least the pig isn't coming too."

In the slanting, sinking sunlight at the end of the day, they made something of a camp in the middle of a meadow. Norah roasted two rabbits Dick brought in at dusk. The old man took his portion off into the woods. He seemed afraid of Jervais. When he was gone, Jervais said, "How did he get to be so ugly?"

Norah gave him a side-long look. "I think he was born with the wall-eyes, and probably he was a bit simple all along. But then he had his head nearly clubbed off by some churl." Her voice was low and roughened. "He's not been the same since."

Eager to change the subject, she asked what Henry Plantagenet was like. Jervais answered tersely, "With the king, there is school every day, and constant conversation, and the discussion of 'questions.' He likes to surround himself with able men—to hone his mind on them."

"I think I would enjoy meeting him, but I fear I would be unwelcome. Sometimes I wish I were a man."

He gave her the ghost of a smile. "No one treats men so prettily as they do women."

"I haven't noticed men treating women so prettily." The look she gave him was narrow-eyed.

She was ignored. He watched her eat with a steady, unsmiling look. She saw a change in his eyes. He seemed full of a strange and edgy hunger. Yes, he seemed hungry, *starving*, but not for food. She understood this hunger, though she was uneasy with its apparent intensity. It seemed to grow so hot that she had an impression of whiffs of it drifting from him like steam off boiling water.

Disquieted, she ate faster and faster, until her cheeks bulged. When he couldn't stand it anymore, he said, "Your manners would bear improving, mistress."

"My manners are mine," she said, with her cheeks stuffed with meat. "I am quite—" she packed more food into her mouth between words, "—content

201

with them."

He seemed to lose his appetite, both for her and for the rabbit, and ended his meal with a wrinkled apple he'd had among his packs. When she was finished eating, she strode, still barefooted, across a carpet of mint to the stream that watered the meadow and there washed her hands. As she came back she plucked some mint leaves and crushed them in her hands and rubbed their perfume on her wrists.

She stooped and gathered Roger, gazing down at him with adoration.

She was clearly besotted by the infant, which made Jervais feel slightly ashamed. Even though the child was his, and she was only its *damosel,* he was as yet incapable of such transparent devotion.

The child evidently needed changing. He watched her take care of it. And then she nursed him, sitting on a low log with her back to Jervais. He was in something of a turmoil over her. He was impressed with her concern for the infant, yet disgusted by her peasant way of eating, and yet again, overwhelmingly attracted to her beauty. Such a tangle of attitudes!

He said, "You're not completely ignorant. You speak French. And though you eat like a sow at a trough, you keep yourself clean. Where were you reared?"

Her answer didn't come immediately. He guessed beforehand that it was not going to be entirely truthful. He doubted that anything she said was the complete truth.

"I lived in a castle—worked for a castellan, actually. I did embroidery for his wife."

"And was it his child you had?"

Her back stiffened. Her hair hung down in a black shadow about her shoulders, like a veil.

"You've had a child else you wouldn't be able to do what you're doing now." All the time he was trying not to think that her breasts were naked to the infant. He tried to ignore that his blood was buzzing like a wasps' nest.

"It might have been his," she said sharply.

Once the babe was asleep on the deep bed of leaves she'd made for him, she stood and stretched her back with enormous satisfaction. Seeing Jervais was watching her, she stopped. Trumpets of desire sounded in him. They rose in pitch, sharp and brilliant and chilling. Her mouth was indescribably luscious in the firelight.

Accursed female! She *was* a fairy! Or a witch!

She lay down beside the child. She'd brought a wolfskin to use for a covering. Her last words were a mumbled, "God rest you, my lord."

Jervais rolled himself into his own bedding and retired to another mattress of leaves. He didn't sleep immediately, however. He was awake to watch the moonlight turn the meadowgrass white. When he did fall off, he had an eerie dream wherein he saw himself caressing her. It was her naked shoulders he touched, and his lips moved over her pretty throat, and then over the curve of her breasts. He came awake in the deep of the night, sweating and miserable.

On the morrow, they left the road at midday to rest. The peasant, Dick, was nowhere to be seen. Kate said she wasn't worried about him.

Jervais led the way into a grassy, park-like section

of woods, seeking a place where they could pause for their noon meal. The babe was packed into the makeshift nest on the mule, and both Kate and Jervais were walking. By the way she stepped, he could tell she liked the feel of the new tender grass under her bare feet. She lifted her chin and breathed deeply, gazing at the soft blue, feather-stroked sky above the wide-growing trees; hence, when a vine caught her foot, she tripped and sprawled in the grass and buttercups.

She rolled onto her back, laughing at herself. Jervais stopped. The sound of her laughter seemed to startle the clear air. He stared at her, down among the butter-colored flowers, smiling. He felt his manhood swell.

"Let's stop here," she said. "I'm too comfortable to get up."

He tied the horse. Roger was asleep, so Jervais left him where he was. Kate's hands were moving over the grass, petting it as she might pet a cat. Without thinking, he sank to the ground and knelt over her.

For a long time he had denied himself certain pleasures. That denial had caused a tremendous pressure within him, pressure that he desperately wanted to relieve. And here was a peasant woman, a woman without a man, a woman with whom he was free to indulge his suppressed urges.

No, he mustn't. He tried to think.

But the only thing he could think about was the lower half of his anatomy, and how the woman looked and smelled, what her body must feel like.

Her hands had stopped moving. She was so beautiful his heart almost quit beating to look at her. Her glossy hair, black as a raven's wing, fell back from her exquisite oval face. Her large eyes shone like burnished green-blue water stones. They were huge and long-lashed and held an innocent aura that proclaimed she was a virgin. But she couldn't be. She'd borne a child.

He bent nearer, placing his hands on either side of her. Her look became startled, as if she'd suddenly seen smoke pouring from his nostrils. She tried to sit up. But it was too late. As her head raised, he kissed her and bore her down again.

Her mouth opened to him. It was like losing consciousness, like candles going out about him, like walls vanishing.

Oh, this was fine—all his principles flooding away in the breaking of this dam! All his scruples lost in this longing for her moist mouth.

Yes, it was fine! He felt raw, ravenous. A bitterness welled up in him, poisoning him, poisoning the beauty of this enticing place. He opened his clothes, and yanked her skirt above her waist, and stretched her out on the ground beneath him and went into her with a fast hard motion. His body blazed. He plunged into her again, brutally, as heartlessly as an animal. It felt as if some grim devil, some bullying, brutal devil was forcing him to it. He was driving into her, right into the core of her. Sensation positively raged through him, and he stoked it, stoked it.

His hands found her perfect breasts and closed on their full roundness. His mouth found the pale skin of her long neck. He lost all sense of when and where, existing only to stir up the fire in his loins, to stoke it relentlessly. He was pinning her down; he must be bruising her. He didn't care. He wanted to let go, to cast off the restraints on his emotions, to go wild, to surrender, surrender, and please God, let the void be filled.

His mouth found hers again, he moaned into it— then his breath stopped. He went rigid. The climax erupted in waves, one following another, forceful spasms around which his whole body contracted, an apogee he felt in every fiber of his being.

When it was finished, for a moment he was without enough strength to rise. It took effort to disengage himself from her and sit upright on his knees again.

I've had her, he thought. Now he would be free of that terrible lust he'd felt since he'd first set eyes on her.

And for the moment it was true. He felt no desire at all for her. Without looking at her, he got up, refastening his clothes as he did. He heard her rising from her bed of buttercups behind him. He felt no desire, nothing but a sense of disgust.

But then he thought he heard her sob. He turned. His eyes fell to the broken flowers and broken grass where he had taken her. His gaze lifted to see her making her way to a little seeping stream. Her head was down in her hand, her shoulders were hunched, and yes, she was crying, stumbling and crying.

His fury flashed; he felt it heat his face and twist his mouth. He strode rapidly after her, caught her shoulder and spun her around. She cringed and covered her head with one arm and her breasts with the other, and she made a sound, a mewl of deepest anguish. He experienced a quiet shock to hear that.

Yet when he spoke, his defensive anger was excessive. "Stop that! Why are you crying?"

The arm over her head lowered slowly to the other, so that both were crossed over her breasts, but she would not look at him. Her sulky-sweet mouth was bruised, and her eyes were swimming.

"The way you were lying there—you as much as shouted you wanted it." He caught her by her upper arms, wrapped his fingers around them and brought her up against him. His frustration was exceeded only by his outrage. "You *did* want it! I take no one who is not willing. So what are you crying about now? Say something!"

With her eyes downcast, she said, "You hurt me."

All his rage and frustration dissolved. A groan issued from him. Without thinking, he gathered her to him. He kissed the top of her head. She stood stiffly in his embrace, jerking a little in her attempt to keep from sobbing. He took hold of her hair and pulled her head back in order to look at her face. Her eyes were closed, her cheeks wet; her full lips were trembling. He realized for the first time how young she was—no more than seventeen or eighteen. And he *had* hurt her. He felt an empty, achy feeling in the pit of his stomach.

He'd taken his yuletide leman that way, savagely, but then she'd been older, and she'd had any number of men, and she'd invited his roughness. She'd seemed to prefer mock-rape to tenderness. This fairy-woman had wanted him to take her—but in all fairness he'd used her willingness as an excuse to make her a threshing floor for all of his emotions. Here was something that was going to be hard to set aright.

He let go of her hair and put his arms around her again. His lips brushed her forehead. A whisper rose from deep in his chest: "I'm sorry. Is there anything . . . will you be all right?"

"Please, just let me go."

"Go where?" He sensed that, as tight as he was holding her, she was tenuously tethered and ready to break loose.

"I just need to be alone for a while."

He knew she did. She needed to accept what he'd done to her, to understand it—to try to find some solace for it. "You won't go far? And you'll come back?" He gave her a little shake. "You'll come back?"

She nodded in absolute obedience, though he could tell she was forcing herself to remain calm, restraining herself from any resistance. "Please, let me go, please."

He did, though he felt such a resurgent wave of desire for her that he could barely stand it. He knew then that the urge was going to stir again—and he was not at all sure he could successfully supress it.

No, I won't do that again, I can't, not again.

Yet could mere will restrain such a ferocity of desire?

That night, as the blaze Jervais had kindled of vine branches and dry sticks sank into glowing coals with a smoky column spiraling up from it, Norah lay down with Roger under a quilt of misery. She listened to the sound of the small, fast-running stream nearby. Why had she tempted Jervais? Why had she been surprised at his cruel kisses, his brutal ravishment?

She'd done it because she'd hardly known the

208

strength of her spell; she knew it better now and knew it was of incalculable and mysterious power.

She was eager for the relief of sleep, though she hadn't come near it when she felt his presence an hour later. She turned her head to see his face above hers. His silvery eyes were slitted. For a thundering moment she thought he was going to fall on her right there with Roger beside her. But he said, "Come to me." His voice was peculiar, thick and slightly blurred. Taking her wrist, he tried to pull her up.

She resisted. "No, I don't want to."

"I won't hurt you."

She continued to resist, and finally he scooped her into his arms and stood with her. In that one act, she was made to realize his build and bearing, his competence in war and strategy, and her comparable vulnerability. "Please don't."

But then she remembered that this was exactly what she'd wanted. This was all part of her plan, that he should want her, that she should demand his entire attention long enough that she could make him love her. Hence she stopped trying to escape him and let him carry her to his bed of leaves.

The impression of his strength was both frightening and wonderful. A woman needed a strong man in a world where disputes were settled and needs were met strictly by the application of muscle. Yet she'd already felt this strength turned against her, and she was wary.

She let him undress her, between kisses, and lay her down on his bedrobes. He came to her naked this time. He lay half over her, his arms around her, enfolding her so closely she could feel the vital drumbeat of his heart. Her face was nestled into his warm shoulder; his fingers were twisted and tangled in her hair. She could smell him. Jervais. Her husband. Her love. Desire radiated from him. He kissed her mouth. They kissed like lovers who had been parted for years. He touched her breasts, the nubbins of her hard nipples, with exquisite tenderness. And all the while the look on his face and in his molten silver eyes said that he was doing something that he couldn't help but do.

She was unwilling to stop him, but dear God, this was as terrible as anything she could ever have imagined. The spell was too strong, too strong; he was all but maddened by it. She had no idea what he might do to her. She closed her eyes. She didn't want to look at his grim face. She felt his near smarting touch, and his arms enclosing her, she felt his chest against her breasts and his mouth tearing at hers now. A sound of fear came up in her throat.

Immediately he checked his passion. He pulled his mouth away and fell onto his back beside her. He lay as though if he so much as touched her he might do her harm. "You aren't a mere woman," he muttered fiercely. "You must be a demon."

"I'm not!" She hated that word above all others. And she'd never wanted to hear it from his lips.

"Then what are you?" He leaned up over her. "What manner of woman are you?"

Chapter 14

Norah and Jervais lay apart for several heartbeats. Norah felt their separation like a rent in her flesh. Her breasts ached. A sensual suffering came over her. At last she could bear it no more. She leaned up on one elbow; her eyes probed his face, looking for anger, and her hand tentatively reached for his chest. She said, "I'm yours." He didn't move, but she felt him flinch as her fingers toyed with the light hair of his chest, slid to his belly, and then to his manhood. She touched him only with the tips of her fingers, yet even that seemed too much. He groaned. She lifted her hand away immediately. "Does that hurt?"

He was panting slightly, and now huffed in ruthless humor, "No."

She touched him again, curious—and a little wonderstruck. His eyes were open, watching her. He said, "You don't have any notion what you're doing, do you?"

She bit her lower lip. "I'm afraid not."

He seized her hand, stopping her untutored caress.

"How many men have had you, besides your castellan?"

She was shocked—and could not think what would be the best answer. Two? Twenty? She said, "No more than your fair and courteous ladies who keep friends, two and three together with their wedded lords."

He seemed to study her. "None, is my guess," he said. "Just one old man who probably treated you well enough, until you had the bad grace to conceive his child, then he threw you out. Or his wife did. Am I right?"

She said nothing. He was concocting her story for her. She let him.

He rolled, taking her half under him again. He leaned down and peered into her eyes. She automatically put her hands against his chest to protect herself. He said fiercely, "I have to have you. I won't hurt you this time, but I have to have you." His determination was so strong it cut deep lines into his face. "Pretend I am someone you have loved. Suppose he is me. I won't abuse you," he whispered. He touched her shoulder, then let his hand smooth down her arm in a caress.

She didn't answer, only moved against him, wanting him closer, welcoming the strong arm he put beneath her to arch her back and lift her breasts against his chest.

"I need you," he murmured on. "I need to possess you, to possess you completely—but I promise to make you feel all that I feel."

His face seemed suddenly so unguarded that she raised her arms around his shoulders and held him hard against her. That was when his hand parted her

212

thighs. Oh, the icy-hot pleasure! The rush of sensation! It swallowed her completely. She sank into its bottomless, limpid well.

"Ah, you like it, you want me to take you, you want me."

At last his weight came down full length on her, crushing her. His eyes were gleaming like flickers of silvery fire. She gave a long gasp—and then her body opened, welcomed him. Her thudding heart seemed to swell until her lungs had no room to expand. Her apex was more satisfying than anything she'd experienced before.

From his guttural moan, she knew when it was all but over for him. In the deep peace of passion spent, they lay quiet, entwined. He fell to his back beside her again, and she told herself to expect no more, that he was finished with her for the time being. Yet she felt in that moment she could have begged for any crumb of affection.

Hence, when she felt his hand, so heavy, so strong, roll her so that she faced away from him but with her back curved into his chest, she gratefully thrust her heated face into the crook of his shoulder which he offered for her pillow. It seemed all of him curled around her, even his fingers that were so sure and warm. He even lifted her touseled hair and kissed her neck tenderly. He made her feel precious beyond value, as if she were so exquisite he had no words to adequately describe her.

He whispered drowsily, "I wonder if you'll have faded away when I wake in the morning."

A bird sang; its voice punctured the silence of the

grey dawn. Jervais opened his eyes. The woman was not faded away. "Good morrow," she said. He sat up, giving her a polite nod that he hoped would plainly discourage any further conversation. He'd held her through most of the night, but now he was cautious again. Why did she affect him so strongly? Why was he so utterly enslaved by this passion for her? Some wizardry was afoot.

"When will we get to London?" she asked.

He wished she wouldn't talk. Her voice was an irritation. Her voice was . . . in fact, it was thrilling—silver-toned, reaching deep into him, stabbing him not like a blade but like music. He wanted her to stop speaking to him because her voice enticed him so; it made him want to shed his responsibilities and concerns and all his defenses.

She sat up beside him, sleepy looking, her hair all touseled. She seemed steeped in a serene contentment. She took no care of the blanket, letting it fall to her waist, and he clearly saw her wonderfully full breasts. The nubbins of her nipples were puckered, like lips asking to be kissed. He felt a tightness in his loins, a thickening in his throat. Though he hadn't intended to, he turned and bore her back down into their leafy mattress. He felt utterly abandoned and beyond himself.

For an instant her entire face blossomed with surprise and delight, then a guarded expression settled over her like a visor.

"Don't be afraid of me." His voice sounded peculiar, thick and slightly blurred. He stroked one of her soft shoulders. "I didn't hurt you last night, did I?"

She relaxed a little then, and even smiled. "Last

night was wonderful."

Her breasts were squashed against his chest. The pressure in his loins was greater. His throat was tighter, too. As he gazed into her wildly green-blue, unwavering eyes, he said, "Let me make this morning wonderful, too."

Her smile became a tease. "And noon? Can you make noon wonderful, my lord?"

He slipped a hand between them and caressed one of her rosebuds with the ball of his thumb. "Yes . . . I don't know . . . noon is a long way off." There was such passion in him he could hardly take part in her banter.

Now that all signs of nervousness was gone from her face, he crushed her in his arms and bent his head to devour her mouth. She responded with equal fervor.

Though she was naturally responsive, she was clearly not a woman who knew exactly what she was doing, hence he reminded himself to be gentle, to proceed slowly, to train her appetites even as he appeased his own. He seemed to have some mastery over himself now. He was pleased with his self-control, and realized it came from knowing she was his, his completely, that she belonged to him. Knowing that, it was possible to be considerate.

Soon enough, however, all his good sense was thrown aside. He had her naked in his arms again, and he thrust into the luscious wetness of her with all the power of his long, hard body. In an instant sensation ravished him. She threshed about under him, and when he heard her orgasmic cry, he was galvanized to know he had done that for her.

When he lay still, his ecstasy over, he felt a newly

kindled awareness of the potentials of his own body.

She said something, softly, a murmur.

"What?" he asked, still full of his knowledge of her, of his possession of her.

"Nothing."

He let it go. Lying alongside her, pressed against her, he felt comfortable. Content. He had felt something of this before with women who had let him love them, but never as strongly. He kissed her lightly; she traced his lips with a loving tongue-tip; he inhaled the perfume of languor and summer that was her scent. He loved the feel of her against him; he couldn't hold her close enough. She made him feel . . . happy.

When they rose at last to dress, he watched her secretly. She looked and felt frighteningly essential to him. Just looking at her made him want to take her into his arms again. A vision flashed through his mind: returning to Conniebrook without her, leaving her in London for another man to claim. Something in him made a broken little protest. There was a moment . . . and then it ended, and the balance beam that had for a breath tilted in doubt came down. His decision was made: he would take her to Conniebrook. He *must* take her to Conniebrook with him.

She took up the babe, and did not turn from Jervais this time when she suckled his son, or in fact do anything to shield herself from his scorching gaze. He watched spellbound as the soft light played over her cheeks and the mounds of her breasts. The child's tiny hand caressed the breast he was suckling; the rosebud of the other stood firmly. The sight made Jervais want to strip himself, to take her to the ground yet again. That was when he did what he didn't know he could do: he turned away. He felt like a man who had just pulled back at the brink, yet he hardly felt in full control again until she'd closed her bodice sometime later.

All that day, as they traveled through the rolling, forested land, he was obsessed by his desire; he thought of little else. He felt an unusual tenderness for her, and insisted that she ride most of the day while he walked along beside her. He felt protective of her. And he felt happy beyond belief. Was this . . . could this be . . . ?

No, it couldn't. He loved Eleanor, and this woman was, after all, only a peasant.

But, his mind argued, just because a man is perishing for the love of a woman he can never possess, his natural instincts don't disappear. He can (the idea came slowly to him, soft-footed as a lion despite its mighty weight) care for someone else, if in a far different way.

And in a single instant it was as if the door of a dark and confining chamber had been thrown open onto a brilliant panorama that had been there all the while, a view laden with the most extraordinary possibilities:

This woman was young, and from his experience with Norah, he knew that young girls were apt to become infatuated very easily. He could care for her and make her care for him in return. He could keep her in his own bedchamber. By day he would dress her in gowns the color of ripe apricots, and by night he would move over her in his great bed. She would be like a mother to Roger. Like a wife to him. They would be like a family. He'd never wanted to marry again anyway, and he needn't now that he had a legitimate heir. Instead, he could have this woman, who owned such an odd, terrible beauty, who pleased him so, who seemed so right for him, so necessary.

Yes, he must have her at Conniebrook with him. She was too necessary to him to even think of giving her up now. Too beautiful. They would spend many of their hours with their children. (She would have children of her own, inevitably, given his desire for her, half-brothers for Roger, and little sisters.) Theirs would be a simple life; their conversation would be basic and uncomplicated, and though she was lowborn, he would be comforted by her.

Looking about him, his passion remade the world. Everything seemed alive and significant. Each bird on the boughs sang now to his heart. The clouds had faces, the trees, the swaying grass, and the flowers seemed aware. Behold the fine madman! He traveled through a palace of sweet sights, feeling twice the man he was, feeling the blood of the violet and the clover course through his veins.

The day progressed. And Kate remained on his mind.

And this happiness remained in his heart.

Happiness! Yes! He recognized it from his memories of his days before Antioch. It was like being a boy again, before his heart had been maimed.

When the sun set and the sky was radiant with purple light, they stopped for the evening. As he helped her off the horse, she said, with a shyness that made the words all the more seductive, "Can we make love again, my lord?"

To his amazement, he grinned. "I expect your friend Dick will be coming in soon with something for us to eat." Nonetheless, he discovered his hands were holding her. He made himself release her, made himself focus on something other than the siren song of her. There would be time, after they'd eaten, after the babe was put to bed. Then there would be time.

The roads around London were no better than elsewhere in the country—a danger right up to the city's gate. Before entering, Norah looked back. Dick was nowhere to be seen. To Jervais she said, "He probably won't come inside."

"He'll be all right."

She agreed, reluctantly.

Once inside the gates, they reached a marketplace just as a hangman was finishing one of his fateful ceremonies. The event had drawn a crowd. Any public execution served as both a grim caution and a stirring amusement. Norah had never seen one before, however, and she felt shocked to see the man swinging from the gallows. She also felt bruised by the din and the press of the traffic.

London was a strange and noisy and crowded place, with huddled buildings that didn't seem welcoming to an outsider. Once, when her nose had drawn her attention to a spice shop, she found herself shoved aside into the crowd. A fishmonger shouted in her ear; then two glaze-eyed youths, who had evidently gulped down a gallon and a gill each for their breakfasts, got her between them and slid their hands over her and winked at her. While the one behind her softly hummed a bawdy drinking song in her ear, the one before her said, "Come with us." She broke away, and half-ran, half-shoved her way back to where she'd last seen Jervais.

His cloak was a splash of rich red color disappearing from sight among the butchers, tanners, shoemakers, drapers, and purse makers. He didn't realize she wasn't right behind him anymore. Indeed, since they had spied the city in the distance, he'd seemed to change; there was an urgency about him, a sense of hurry. Something at the end of these cold, damp, malodorous streets seemed to be drawing him.

As he continued on, she caught only tantalizing glimpses of him while she fought her way around a fat housewife bargaining with an apple for a skein of wool, past a gaunt beggar, and through several dirty children who were making a game of leaping over a pile of dung in the doorway of a small cookshop.

Her heart was throbbing like a drum when she finally caught hold of the sumpter mule's tail. With relief she saw that Roger slept on in his pannier. Jervais had never noticed her disappearance. He was shouting in his deep voice, "Clear the way there! Clear the way, you damned, lowborn dogs!" No one paid the least attention to him. His voice was drowned by the grumble and grind of the wheels of a heavy oxcart and the clip-clop of the oxen's hoofs. She saw his nose wrinkle at the stench of unwashed flesh and watched him try to escape brushing against the more unsavory of the beggars.

Finally they were safely through the jostling markets, across the Thames, and installed in Castle Bermondsey. The Plantagenets had been obliged to take shelter here because the palace of Westminster had been so despoiled by Stephen's followers that it could not be inhabited. Norah was left in a chamber with Roger while Jervais went . . . she knew not where. And something of his demeanor had forbidden her from asking. He'd seemed more arrogant suddenly, more the earl of Conniebrook. He'd pulled her into an alarming embrace and kissed her, but when he had stopped, when he'd stepped back, he'd left her. He hadn't said anything; he'd simply left.

Had he gone to inform his knights of his arrival? To see the king? She didn't understand that turning from her, that warding off, that refusal. After the closeness she'd felt during their journey, it confused her.

Unless the woman he loved, that great and noble beauty, was here with the court. Then the reason for his mood became clearer.

While she waited, sitting alone, she observed London's wooden houses standing wall-to-wall along twisted alleys from her chamber's unshuttered window. Across the river from the royal residence the streets ended in docks and wharves. Cookshops and wine shops lined the Strand. Stray scents of fish, wool, and beer drifted over, and the calls of boatmen and eel-wives made a distant babble. Smacks and wherries were gathered about the stairs beneath the ancient bridge. Along the wharves ships from Flanders, Nantes, and La Rochelle, even from Syria, lay with their oars banked. Directly opposite Norah's window stood the Tower, its mortar drenched with blood according to legend and its dungeons already rich with the dark harvest of history. Sprawling westward, beyond the walls of the old city, newer suburbs were growing helter-skelter, set amidst orchards and stockaded gardens.

Once her eyes had grown used to these sights, her mind turned back to Jervais. He'd been given the chamber next door. Would he summon her to his bed tonight?

Where was he now? The question was an itch in her brain.

Long shadows stretched across the cobblestones of the castle court below. Pigeons landed to strut majestically, as if they were royal themselves. A noble couple crossed on their way to some entertainment. Norah thought the woman was overdressed and too made-up, and the man looked like a show-off. As they hurried across the courtyard, the pigeons fluttered thickly.

Roger stirred in his cradle. The sound was enough to make her breasts tingle, for it was time to suckle him. She rose and crossed the rough, unpainted wood floor. He lifted his arms for her to pick him up. She held him so that she could see his face. The light from the window etched his little mouth.

"My son, everything is going to be fine," she said with intensity, with utter certainty. "Already your father loves me a little. Time is all I need. Just a bit more time."

The infant responded by smiling at her as if she'd told him a heartwarming secret.

Her room was simply furnished with a small bed and a carved oak dresser. After feeding Roger, and playing with him on the bed, she put him back in his cradle. A knock came at the door. She opened it to find Charles of Silda, Jervais's squire—her old enemy.

But this was not the too-tall, overly-eager boy she'd been defeated by a year and more ago. At this first sight of him, she felt a rush of galling resentment, yet even that couldn't prevent her from thinking how magnificently he'd grown.

He was even taller than before, but now his muscles had developed as well, so that his height was filled in. He was suddenly a man, a powerful twenty-year-old dressed in court finery—blood-red garments lined with bluish-grey taffeta.

"Mistress Kate?" he asked belatedly, for he was clearly as nonplussed by her appearance as she was by his. "My Lord Conniebrook asks if there is aught you need."

Norah repressed her disappointment that Jervais had not come himself. "I could use a fire," she said, "and a candle—it grows dark in here. And food, I suppose. And perhaps you could show me to the nearest garderobe."

When she was back in her chamber, she hesitated, then asked, "Where is the earl?"

Charles frowned, clearly wondering what business she thought it was of hers where the earl was. Yet he answered courteously—much more courteously than the old Charles would have. "He is with Sir Gian of Lesterhouse. They are discussing his appointment with the king on the morrow. I'll send a pageboy to light your chamber and bring you some supper."

"Thank you."

He was looking past her. He said, "Could I, er, may I see my lord's son?"

At the cradleside, he seemed awkward. Finally, lowering his voice to an oddly funereal hush, he said, "You knew Lady Norah?"

She gave him a sidelong glance. "I knew her."

"Did she ever mention me?"

Instinct made her wary. "She hardly mentioned anyone except Lord Conniebrook. Did she have reason to recall you?"

He stood straight. "I'm glad her son lived. I've said prayers for her soul's safe journey. I pray she didn't suffer overmuch."

"She suffered." Something about his expression made her take pity on him. "But she was happy in the end."

"How could she be happy?"

"She saw her son, saw his silvern eyes, and she was happy. She loved the earl, you know."

He nodded. "Yes, I know. I'm grateful to you for helping her. If there is aught I can ever do for you . . ." He left it at that, and quickly exited the chamber.

On the morrow, Norah was brought a breakfast of bread that had been hastily made without yeast. Her wine was sour and reeked of pitch from the cask. She ate the meal alone, as she had eaten her supper last night. Though she'd lain awake until her candle-end had guttered out, Jervais had neither visited her nor sent for her. The first she heard of him was when Charles came to her door again.

The squire still gave no sign of recognizing her. She'd expected to resent him, to hate him even, for the pain he'd caused her. But she found she couldn't remain armed and armored with that old ill-feeling, for he was changed, in ways she couldn't quite understand (because he was in all ways remote now). And, after all, he was not to blame for the fact that his leigelord loved a beautiful woman and not the scrawny stranger he'd made his wife in order to gain her dowry.

MORE PASSION AND ADVENTURE AWAIT... YOUR TRIP TO A BIG ADVENTUROUS WORLD BEGINS WHEN YOU ACCEPT YOUR FIRST 4 NOVELS ABSOLUTELY *FREE*
(AN $18.00 VALUE)

Accept your Free gift and start to experience more of the passion and adventure you like in a historical romance novel. Each Zebra novel is filled with proud men, spirited women and tempestuous love that you'll remember long after you turn the last page

Zebra Historical Romances are the finest novels of their kind. They are written by authors who really know how to weave tales of romance and adventure in the historical settings you love. You'll feel like you've actually gone back in time with the thrilling stories that each Zebra novel offers.

GET YOUR FREE GIFT WITH THE START OF YOUR HOME SUBSCRIPTION

Our readers tell us that these books sell out very fast in book stores and often they miss the newest titles. So Zebra has made arrangements for you to receive the four newest novels published each month.

You'll be guaranteed that you'll never miss a title, and home delivery is so convenient. And to show you just how easy it is to get Zebra Historical Romances, we'll send you your first 4 books absolutely FREE! Our gift to you just for trying our home subscription service.

BIG SAVINGS AND FREE HOME DELIVERY

Each month, you'll receive the four newest titles as soon as they are published. You'll probably receive them even before the bookstores do. What's more, you may preview these exciting novels free for 10 days. If you like them as much as we think you will, just pay the low preferred subscriber's price of just $3.75 each. *You'll save $3.00 each month off the publisher's price.* AND, your savings are even greater because there are never any shipping, handling or other hidden charges—FREE Home Delivery. Of course you can return any shipment within 10 days for full credit, no questions asked. There is no minimum number of books you must buy.

Charles said, "My lord asks that you ready yourself and the babe for an audience with the king within the hour."

That hour was an eternity. When finally it was passed, and she met Jervais outside her chamber, his only words to her were: "Listen to me. You are to do nothing but stand in the back of the hall until you are called to show the child to Henry."

Frightened, she stammered, "What if someone questions me or tries to put me out or—"

"Charles will be with you. He will say that you're under my protection."

She drew back, feeling the oddest pulse, the strangest vulnerability. Not a loving glance, not a sympathetic touch, not a quick kiss had passed between them, yet with a few careless words, an indifferent reference to his "protection," he could make her feel like this.

What did *he* feel? Ever since they'd entered London he'd seemed to put a shield of iron will between them. She should have expected it was not going to be as easy as it had seemed when they were alone on their journey. Now she remembered that he'd warned her that once they reached London things might change. She was suddenly afraid that he intended to dismiss her and find another *damosel* for Roger.

She suffered under the weight of her nervousness as, carrying Roger, she followed him and Sir Gian across the castle's inner ward. She couldn't drive away a ghostly intuition that something awful was about to happen. She looked up at the thick, crenelated, stone walls surrounding her—and then made herself look higher, at the clear sky. Hidden in her hand was her only guarantee that Jervais could not separate her from Roger. She clutched the garnet ring secretly and thought, *Dear God, let him honor his pledge to me!*

The largest building within the fortress housed the great hall. The doors were guarded by men-at-arms wearing helmets and swords. Within the doors, the hall was much longer than it was wide. The walls were plastered and painted and covered with tapestries. Except for benches along the gallery, there was no furniture. A fire in an open hearth scented the damp air with smoke. A young man sat in the only chair at the far end. Could he be—yes! that young, square-built man with russet hair had to be Henry Plantagenet!

Barons and knights and court attendants, many with their ladies, stood about. They looked at her briefly, but no one questioned her. To them she was only a servant, of no more import than a leaf in a breeze.

Feeling glaringly shabby, she shifted Roger in her arms and stood where Charles indicated, near the rear of the hall. Though born a baron's daughter and a lady by rights, she felt foreign to this place. She looked furtively about her. The garments of the court women were sewn from the finest cloth. Several had trains, so that when they walked they dragged their skirts after them in the rushes. Many had their hair covered in a way she hadn't seen before: their heads and throats and shoulders were draped with fine linen swaths, one corner falling over their left arms. They were held by chaplets of wrought gold.

Costly furs lined and bordered the men's cloaks. Some of these men were not so much graced as they were loaded down with gold and jewels.

Norah dragged her eyes from all this pomp to see that Jervais, with Sir Gian behind him, had made his way to the forefront and was bowing to the king. His plain and elegant clothing contrasted with the bright fabrics of the other ladies and gentlemen, yet he seemed confident.

Henry wore a coat of white sewn with gold and silver threads. He looked to Norah like a temperate young man whose smile came from prudent habit, a man who harbored his passions until he decided to launch them. With a raised finger, he commanded silence of the assembled crowd. Into this he spoke with a surprisingly authoritative voice, "Lord Conniebrook. Sir Gian tells me you have learned that your lady did not die last spring after all?"

Before Jervais could answer, a door opened near the front of the hall. Norah couldn't see over the craned heads, but she heard a cool feminine voice: "My lords—why, here is Lord Conniebrook! How wonderful to see you again, sir."

A murmur started up. Through the shifting crowd, Norah caught a glimpse of a tall woman of thirty or more, immensely graceful. She could be none other than the queen, Eleanor.

Chapter 15

Eleanor wore a samite dress woven with more gold than silk. Her sleeves were so long they touched the rushes. Over all was a white samite mantle. Jervais went down on one knee to kiss her hand ceremoniously. She gave him a smile—a peculiarly conspiratorial smile it seemed to Norah who had found a place where she could see from the back of the great hall. Eleanor bowed her head to him slightly, while keeping her back straighter than a Spaniard's.

She turned to Henry. "Why wasn't I told of Lord Conniebrook's presence? You know that he's an old and dear friend of mine." Shimmers of light and shadow appeared and disappeared in the long folds of her dress. She was holding a book. Norah knew that she had a reputation for reading and for her patronage of peaceful, leisured activities. "But I'm interrupting, aren't I?" she said. "Forgive me." While speaking she'd gestured to a page who quickly brought a chair and placed it beside Henry's throne. A cushion of Bagdad brocade was placed upon it.

Norah was enraptured by Eleanor's beauty, though she was a little shocked as well—at the queen's lavish dress and her free-and-easy manner. Still, Norah couldn't help but gape at her long neck, her fine bones, her white tapered fingers. At first glance she looked frail, but it was clear that this was deceptive. Something about her posture suggested a soundness hardly less than that of a great tree of the forest.

She sat regally, careful that her sleeves lay well. Her face was painted with a fixed and intensely dulcet smile for her husband. "Please continue, my lord."

"Thank you," Henry said irritably, shifting his great shoulders and full chest back to Jervais. "You were saying, Lord Conniebrook?"

Jervais seemed to have to think—where had he left off? "I was saying that though I believed my bride was dead . . ."

For the next quarter of an hour he exhumed the past and went into a grim inventory of the bones, ending with the tale of receiving the letter, with Norah's wedding ring, and his journey to find his son.

"I have the babe with me." He gestured for Norah to come forward. When she hesitated (so many eyes had turned to stare at her!) Charles's hand at her back gave her a push-off. Charles, she discovered, was not going to move forward with her. She must go alone. Her bare feet made no noise as the barons and ladies opened a narrow aisle for her, each one peering with curiosity at the bundle in her arms. Low, uneasy discussion ran through the crowd. She clutched Roger—and he seemed to give her the courage she needed to walk boldly through all that silk and purple and rouge.

She curtsied before the king, who crooked his finger. She took the babe nearer, right up to the throne and, with her pulse pounding, she uncovered Roger's face.

Henry seemed more interested in her than in Roger, who was sleeping. She recognized the veiled desire in his eyes. Ignoring it, she patted Roger's little face tenderly. His tiny lips pursed and worked and his little face wrinkled. "Come, my sweet," she whispered, "meet your king."

Henry seemed calm and untroubled over the whole affair. He chuckled to the crowd, "Marry, 'tis *someone's* babe all right." Uneasy laughter swept the hall. Norah glanced back to see Sir Gian fingering his chin thoughtfully. Usually good-natured to a fault, he looked worried now. Henry said to Jervais, "You must have better testimony than this, my lord."

The child's eyes fluttered. "Come, sweeting, awake," Norah cooed more urgently. Any moment now Henry was going to wave her away, and Roger with her.

"Bring the child here," Eleanor commanded. Reluctantly, Norah straightened and threw back her long hair, which had flowed around her in bending near Henry. The queen took the babe from her, and suddenly Roger's translucent eyelids lifted. Child and queen eyed one another. A stillness fell over Eleanor. Her polite smile froze. "My lord . . . sire . . . look. These are Jerv—Lord Conniebrook's eyes."

Henry leaned to look at the child again. Then he looked at Jervais. And then at Eleanor.

The queen had lifted her eyes from Roger. Her smile was intimate, loving. "My Lord Conniebrook, you have a beautiful son, as handsome as his father."

Jervais's face colored in a way Norah had never seen. "Thank you, my lady." Beyond that he seemed wordless, past discourse. His and Eleanor's eyes held.

And suddenly Norah understood.

For a moment she stared, disbelieving, taking it in. She felt tears of hurt coming, and fought to keep them back. Then she felt a jealous fury—and she let it rise. The noises of the hall unified into a distant hum in her ears. Dimly she heard Jervais saying, "I'm convinced the babe is mine, and I will rear him as mine and the Lady Norah's, as heir to Conniebrook and Ramsay—if I may, sire."

Eleanor was cooing at Roger, bearing him in her lap with as much possessiveness as if she had mothered him herself. "Life is so quaint!" she interrupted. "Think of it—this poor babe, born in the wild where he was deprived of his mother and cared for by naught but a peasant, will be the heir to an earldom! It's so romantic!"

Norah watched her sidelong. Here was an adversary about whom she had no ambiguous feelings.

Eleanor lifted her head and blinked her clever youthful eyes at Jervais and said with a smile, "My lord, you must have the boy baptized right away."

"Indeed," Henry said; he added with special heartiness, "And that this good beginning of your dynasty should come to full honor, we must find you another wife, Le Strand, someone to mother this little one and give you others like him. As a matter of fact, I have a lady in mind, the fairest creature of sixteen years, widowed, yet already the mother of twin daughters—I hear they are lovely—"

Norah heard no more. The thought of Jervais married to another made her pulse thud suddenly. She froze. She felt a chill run the length of her arms, the length of her entire body. How could she stop this? She had to do something. There had to be a way. She had to think straight. The air became heavy; there was a strange pressure, something she'd never felt before. Hardly realizing what she was doing, she stepped toward Henry, saying in clear Norman French, "I call for justice, my sovereign king! Before this court is dismissed, give me my right!"

Henry looked startled. His mouth twisted, but before he could speak, she went on:

"'Twas I who saw that a letter was sent to Lord Conniebrook. 'Twas I who suckled his babe after Lady Norah's death. 'Twas I who delivered Roger to his father. In return, Lord Conniebrook made a pledge to me that the first thing I should ask of him he would do."

She turned to Jervais. She'd intended only to ask him to assure her the position of Roger's *damosel* and nurse, in case he tried to dismiss her. But now, in the space of minutes, she'd learned that he was in love with the queen, and that there was every possibility he might marry again—bigamously—something she had naively never considered.

As shocked as she was, her mind of its own volition plotted ahead. She found herself saying, "Before God, and the king who is the source of all justice in England, and in the hearing of these knights and their ladies, I pray you, my Lord Conniebrook, to take me for your wife."

She imagined she could hear a collective gasp, but in fact the silence was complete and deadly. The leaden bread of her breakfast stirred in her stomach.

Jervais reacted like a cheerful man who had set out to enjoy himself for the day, and who now found himself stabbed without warning. His lips parted; his jaw seemed to lose all tension.

Norah waited with pent breath. Her back tingled. She felt as though she were naked before Eleanor and Henry and the entire court. Jervais's eyes were unblinking, as colorless as splinters of glass. Should he deny her, she knew that she would be separated from Roger forever. She both loved Jervais and dreaded him in that instant. Her heart hardly dared to beat. The moment stretched, and in the end, she knew she couldn't trust him not to renounce the oath he had sworn to her. For all she knew, promises were to him merely knots to be severed by his sword.

Roger was whimpering. Without thinking, she turned and took him from Eleanor's arms. The queen, stunned, let her. Shifting her son into the crook of her right arm, unconsciously feeling this flesh as familiar as her own, she held out her left for Eleanor and Henry both to see. The garnet ring sparkled in her palm. "He gave me this, sire," her eyes did not look at Eleanor, though she heard the queen gasp. "He gave it to me as a token of his most solemn word."

Henry's eyes narrowed and he held out his hand. He wanted the ring. Gladly Norah dropped it into his palm.

Jervais's voice came out roughened. "I did make

the woman a promise, I won't deny that." His eyes regained their focus and now pierced Norah. "But for God's love, woman, make a reasonable request! Money—fie! I expected you to ask for money! But if it's marriage you want, I will be heartily glad to find you someone of your own class. Forsooth, you can have a croft, cattle—" His stare shifted and converged with Henry's. Norah looked as well, and saw the king's face.

Henry's fist was closed about the garnet ring. So. He understood as clearly as she did what that ring meant, what lay between his regal wife and his vassal. Norah could hardly guess what bitter pride she'd unleashed—and she hardly cared. A demon of obstinacy had driven her to an edge from which even now she would not back away. Crystalized in her mind was the thought: *He is* my *husband and this is* my *son and no woman will claim either of them but* me.

Clutching the babe, her next words came out softly. "I will not take any bribe. I have made my request: I will be your true wife."

"My true wife?" Jervais's voice was killing. He smiled without a touch of humor. "Rather my true damnation. God's curse on you that I should ever be so foully dishonored as to share my name with a peasant slut."

Pain flashed through her. She set it aside, to be felt and felt again, but later. She said, "I had no need to give you this child. I love him as my own and could have kept him as such. I gave him to you out of love for him, that he might come into his own. I have lain with you—again out of love—for which you repay

234

me with cruelty." Her voice nearly broke. She steeled herself. "Now it is for you to behave honorably. You joined hands with me and gave me your solemn word—and your token on it. 'Tis for you to deal honorably with me, my lord, or may God's curse be on *you*."

Jervais took a step toward her. "You—"

"Enough!" Henry broke in. His fist remained clenched around the ring. "I have heard enough." He stared at Jervais for a long moment, then his eyes shifted to Eleanor. And at last they rested on Norah. "Guard! Take this woman back to her chamber."

He dismissed the court just as she was escorted through the doors of the hall into the courtyard. The man-at-arms gave her no time to tarry—and no time for Jervais to catch up with her. He remained outside her door once she was back in her chamber. She'd no more than stirred the fire back to life and sat on her bed when the door opened. She started up, with Roger still in her arms, then curtsied deeply, for her visitor was none other than the queen.

Eleanor waved back the tiring woman who had accompanied her. The woman stepped out and closed the door quietly. Eleanor didn't come far into the room. She was still wearing her rich, golden samite gown, but she'd knotted the extremely long sleeves to prevent them from trailing the floor.

She stood majestically erect and simply stared at Norah. At last she spoke: "You must listen to me, girl. Give up this insane fantasy. I'll see that you're given a generous purse of, say, eight marks—do you know how much that is?—and safe-passage out of London. You'll need safe passage if you expect to survive the earl's rage. If you won't go, I warn you, I'll feel no sympathy when your grasping heart reaps its inevitable reward.''

Norah felt herself trembling, yet she answered, ''I cannot do as you say.''

Eleanor's face was like a carving of marble, beautiful and hard and cold. ''You don't know what you're doing, you pitiful child. So the earl took you to his bed in the woods. Did you think because he used your warm young body when he had no other to use that he loved you? You're nothing, a peasant, slender of learning and slow of wit. The earl of Conniebrook is deserving to court any woman in the land. Any lady would be honored to catch his attention. And it will be a *lady* he will take for a wife, not a beggar-woman. The classes are clearly ordained by Heaven, and to rebel against your status is to question the judgment of Providence—a damnable sacrilege if ever there was one.''

''I will make him as good a wife as any lady would.''

''*Tsk*. Excellent wine may become vinegar, but never contrariwise.''

Norah studied the woman. Eleanor was tall and handsome. Her eyes were large and lustrous. Upon first seeing her in the hall this morning, Norah had thought they were her best feature. Then Eleanor had smiled, and after that Norah hadn't been sure. She was commanding, as well, this queen, a woman born to rule. And she was also extraordinarily sensual. The knowledge fell on Norah that Eleanor cleverly used each of her assets to enhance the power of the others. Did Jervais realize this—that she used her sensuality as much as her mind to rule those about her? Probably he didn't. Men did not easily see evil in those they revered. Norah feared that all of her magical art wasn't able to produce the superior, nor even the equal, of this marvel of sensual manipulation.

In the face of her silence, Eleanor tried another tact. "You have made Lord Conniebrook a figure of fun, you know. Already there are broad songs being composed for singing in the streets about him. A marriage such as you suggest would destroy his reputation and humiliate him. And infuriate him. When he left the hall, everyone could see the fury rampaging in him."

Still Norah didn't answer.

Eleanor went on thoughtfully, "Your beauty is remarkable for a peasant. But Jervais Le Strand is a particularly fastidious man. To my knowledge, he has never taken a lowborn woman to his bed before."

"He took me."

"You seduced him. I wonder how."

Norah said, very gently, "However I may have done it, most beautiful queen, he did take me, and most lovingly, I assure you."

Eleanor's only sign of reaction was a slight widening of her eyes. "Are you a sorceress? Have you cast a spell on him?" She seemed to read her answer in Norah's silence, and she turned away abruptly, as if in fear. With one hand on the doorlatch, she said, "Should you change your mind before this time on the morrow, send word to me. After that, I shall be deaf to all your pleas."

Norah spent the day peering at London from her

237

chamber window, feeling as imprisoned as she had in the cloister. When the sun set, she turned away from the gloaming light reflected on the pearl-colored river. The big-jawed guard let a pageboy deliver a supper tray to her. She struggled to eat, for Roger's sake. The main dish was slices of pig's liver, wrapped with fat and baked, or rather, burned brown. The tastiest thing on her plate was the dry, crisp biscuit, which she softened in the strong ale provided.

A few minutes after the pageboy took the tray away, her door opened again, with no forewarning knock, and briefly she saw a male figure outlined by the torch roaring in its sconce outside her chamber. The door closed, and she was alone with her visitor. In the smoky, ruddy light of the chamber's fire, she swept into a deep bow. "Sire."

Henry came toward her, and walked around her slowly, ending his inspection by lifting her chin with his blunt fingers. His gaze was intent. His question was a surprise: "Where does a forest-girl learn Norman French?"

She lowered her eyes from his piercing look. She scraped her memory for what she had told Jervais. "I was reared in a castle. I learned French there."

"Which castle?"

She resisted the urge to let her eyes fly about the chamber. "Well, it was a manor, actually, a place called, er, Cranelock." Innumerable manors dotted the untamed forests, most of them self-sufficient, and the smaller among them virtually anonymous.

"Hmm." His hand dropped from her chin. "I know many a servant woman who can't speak proper English, let alone the French of her masters. You must be very clever. Very clever indeed. So, you were reared in a manorhouse and then left it to live in the forest. Tell me, what did you learn *there?*"

"What do you mean?"

The fire glinted on his eyes and lips. "How did you live?"

"With an old woman, and a man, lame and bent. We all looked after one another, in a fashion."

"In what fashion?"

"I don't understand. What it is you want to know?"

"Who was this woman you lived with?"

"Her name was Sidella. She was good to me."

"How good?" His eyes narrowed where he stood with his face in the dull gold from the fire.

She stole a look at him. She had the sharpest impression that by some unnatural clarity of sight he could see right through her lies, that he knew everything. "Is that guard at my door—am I a prisoner?"

He raised his brows. "No—except that you can't leave—but no, the guard is there to protect you from Le Strand. You haven't done yourself much good with him, young woman. He's furious." He added, "And the queen is convinced that you're a sorceress, full of evil spells."

She lifted her head proudly. His eyes narrowed, as if he were looking into some dark interior. "Have you used sorcery?"

"I also refused the purse she offered me, and the safe passage out of London."

He grinned abruptly. "So, the golden key to open this door is not money then. Nay, of course not, after all the trouble you've gone to." He rubbed his hands

239

together. "Oh, this is perfectly delicious."

Through the heavy wooden door came a voice from the passageway beyond. Norah turned in a panic. It was Jervais's, that cutting, precisely articulated voice, that confident tone which carried so easily: "I *will* see her!" it said.

Of the guard's reply, Norah heard only, "The king is with her. . . ." She heard no more, except the door of his chamber next to hers boom shut. She heard naught of what was taking place in there, for the stone walls were too thick.

Henry was watching her with a raised eyebrow. He gave her a little cat-like smile, *shared* it with her, as if they were partners in some way. He even laughed. Then, without mentioning what they had both overheard, he crossed to look at the babe in his cradle. "Le Strand's firstborn is of surpassing promise, comely beyond most children's wont."

Norah volunteered, "He was a Sunday's child."

"He'll be taken from you briefly come morning. Eleanor is set upon him being splattered with lustral water as soon as possible."

"Taken!"

Henry clasped his fingers behind him and looked back at her over his shoulder. "I'll see that he's returned to you, set your mind at rest." For a time he studied her. At last he said, "Did you plan to ask him for marriage all along?"

"I wanted Roger to have his rightful place, but I knew I couldn't bear to be separated from him. I meant only to make the earl pledge to keep me as Roger's *damosel*."

"But then Eleanor made you realize that you must

240

have more than that."

Her temper blazed in sudden ire. "And so did you, when you spoke of my lord marrying again." Another marriage! That hair shirt of bristles pricked her deeply. She would do everything within her power to prevent it. "He cannot marry anyone but me."

"Why not?"

"Because . . . because I love him."

"Well, 'tis clear you *want* him—for revenge or love, I'm not sure. Nor do I think you are." He paused. "My conscience bids me to call your attention to the anathema that would greet such a mating as you suggest, the prejudice against you it would cause, the price it would cost you both—should it ever take place, that is. Are you certain you don't want to back down? You may come to consider all this too heavy a burden. If money will not persuade you, perchance the promise of a home would." His look became sly. "I could arrange for you to retire to a nunnery."

The very word caused her to shudder. Images flashed: the suffocatingly small, tomb-like cells of Coxgrave, the dark, dank, enclosing walls. "Nay! I will not be buried again whilst I am still alive!"

She recalled too late that it was her king at whom she was shouting. She lowered her head, letting her hair fall forward, yet continued to peek at him. "Forgive me."

Was that glint in his eyes from the firelight, or was it amusement? Had he noticed that she'd used the word "again" in her outburst? He seemed delighted to the very marrow. Did he know who she was? If so, why didn't he simply say so? She'd been at court for hardly more than a full twenty-four hours, and already she hated these noxious games and vanities.

He was studying her. "Le Strand is a powerful man, a strong man, practiced and renowned in arms and surely fearsome in chastising those who cross him personally. Should I grant him this love of yours—and your body with it—I hardly know whether you would suffer more from shame or from pain. Aren't you afraid?"

She brushed back the veil of her hair and answered honestly. "Yes."

He shook his head. "I cannot sufficiently marvel when you of the frail sex dare to advance into such presumptuous things." He stepped closer to her. He reached out a hand and stroked her cheek. Though he still seemed to find the situation amusing, he was not quite as lighthearted as he had been. "'Twill be an interesting thing to see who wins this war—as well as what the victor exacts of the vanquished. I wish you luck, my lady—er, Mistress 'Kate,' is it?"

"Yes, Kate."

He smiled. His parting advice at the door was: "Whatever happens, you should prepare for a sorrow as infinite as the love you are proceeding with."

Those words stayed in the chamber long after he took his leave. In them, Norah felt the essence of prophecy. She went to the window again, and looked out upon the unquiet water of the river, which shone with the sky's last light. Suddenly the world under her feet was no more real than a dream. Instead of the Thames, she saw an entirely different scene: there was wind, and the sound of the sea, such as she'd heard as a child in her shell. The setting was obscure, as if a mist curled around him. Jervais was walking through that mist away from her. Seeing him brought her an immense feeling of sorrow and regret, a sorrow as infinite as her love.

Norah woke suddenly. Jervais was bending over her. He had one hand on each side of her, and his weight on her blankets effectively pinned her. He said nothing. He simply looked at her with an icy calm that felt worse to her than if he had surrendered to his obvious temper.

"How did you get in here?" she asked calmly.

"The guard had to visit the garderobe sooner or later," he said in a soft, paper-dry voice. His control was more chilling than anger itself. His grey eyes were cold, remote, unexcusing.

She knew that any self-defensive move would doom her. She said, "I've missed you."

That affected him. In an instant he was livid and straining, the cords were standing out on his neck. "I could strangle you for what you've done."

She wisely remained silent. The castle had that hushed quality the world possessed only between midnight and sunrise. All was silent. Still. The darkness was loud with his breathing, loud with her heart. At last she dared to lift her hand to his face. Her touch crackled in his eyes; he jerked away as if she'd burned him.

"My lord," she said, struggling to sit up. But he was already leaving. "Jervais," she whispered to the closing door, *"je t'aime."*

Chapter 16

Following the debacle before the court, as a special biting mark of Henry's disfavor, Jervais was made to wait six days before he received any word from the royal quarters again. Meanwhile, Roger was baptized—blessedly without Kate's attendance. The christening was a formal acknowledgement of the babe's legitimacy, and it settled his claim as Jervais and Norah's heir. At the font, he'd had three godparents, two of his own sex, and Eleanor. Regardless of the honor, Jervais knew that her insistence on becoming his son's godmother couldn't help but worsen his own position with Henry.

The fair weather turned sour during this time. Clouds hung over London in gloomy, black masses echoing Jervais's mood, for he was the embodiment of pent fury day after day. None of the court's buffoons or fiddlers or timbrel-players could distract him. Occasionally he would say aloud: "I could kill that woman!" If he could only get to her again—or so he told himself—he would leave no marks, but in five minutes she would recant this lunacy.

At last Henry sent one of his Angevin knights, a tall man with mournful eyes to summon Jervais. Gian and Charles were with him in his chamber, sprawled in chairs, leaning on their elbows, their tunics off and their shirts open. They'd all three been drinking for hours.

When the Angevin arrived, Jervais tried to pull himself together. He yanked off his soiled shirt, and Charles held a bronze water vessel for him to wash his face and hands, then helped him into a clean shirt and laced up its front. Jervais wished desperately for an hour to clear his wits, but one did not keep Henry waiting at any time. Charles pulled a clean tunic bordered with precious ermine over his head.

A few minutes later he was striding with the tall Angevin across the inner ward. Their boots rang on the stones. They skirted two pageboys at their basic practice, fencing with toy swords and shields. The raw and icy wind cleared his mind somewhat. Swift, sharp wings overhead caught Jervais's attention. His eyes followed their flight up the tower he had just left, and he saw Kate at her window looking down at him.

He stopped to stare; it was the first time he'd seen her since that night when he'd all but fled her chamber in order to resist the siren call of her. Her long black hair was caught back from her face and . . . she was beautiful. The bone structure of her cheeks and brow was as resolute and sure as the vaulted ceiling of a great cathedral. He felt a clenching of desire in his groin. But something unspoken, mysterious, something he couldn't even name, told him that she was different, that she was no perfectly ordinary miracle. Could she really be a sorceress? He almost wanted to believe it, because if he didn't then, by the saints, he was just another fool among men.

She stood in the full light, such as it was on this gloomy day, and she faced him with a gaze that was unblinking. Her expression was determined, yet he imagined he saw a trace of panic. She was the first to draw back, out of sight from his stare, and immediately he was filled once more with impotent rage.

He found Henry faultlessly dressed as always, pacing an inner chamber as he dictated letters to a clerk, a tubby little man with a long nose and a constant look of affliction. Henry looked over the clerk's tonsured head to greet Jervais. "You're pale, Le Strand."

The clerk's pen scraped on over the parchment. Jervais said, "I have not been out much, Sire." Henry turned, and Jervais watched his profile. He needed to know how close he might be to the limits of the king's good will. Very close, he decided. He could almost see the anger stirring in the man, like a large snake shifting its coils.

Henry pinched the Norman arch of his nose and said in a soft, absolutely flat voice, "It appears that you are consistently most imprudent, Le Strand—if a king may comment upon his vassal's behavior." He looked at the ceiling. "I must stop being amazed by you. I must just accept the fact that naught you could do would amaze me anymore. Your affairs are never dull at least. But this time," his eyes swung back, "this time you've brought me something really hugely interesting."

There was a pause in which each man took the measure of the other. Jervais saw in Henry a serpent's readiness to strike, and he knew the blow would be irresistible.

Henry said, finally, "I've given my best thought to it, and I have come to the conclusion that you will do as the wench asks."

Jervais couldn't repress a jerk. He waited for the clamor in his head to recede. On some lower level he was aware of the clerk's large-eyed stare, but it was Henry who demanded his concentration. As the shock faded, it was replaced by anger again. "I came hither to your court for one cause alone—to establish the legitimacy of my son. For none other will I answer."

These words, uttered in blatant defiance, made Henry's face go as white as wax. Nothing was changed in his voice, however, which was as cold and inert as venom as he said, "You will do as I say, my Lord Conniebrook."

Time seemed to slow. The clerk shifted uncomfortably on his stool. It was on the tip of Jervais's tongue to shout, *Never!* but a whisper of reason reminded him of the last time he'd raised his voice to this man. It had nearly cost him the excommunication of his soul.

The chamber was heavy with frustrated silence, that deadlocked quiet which follows the wordless rejection of a spoken demand. Then Henry suddenly roared, *"Do you hear me? You will do as I say or you will disobey me on pain of curse and exile!"*

"Exile! On what grounds?" Jervais shot back.

Henry's eyes blazed. He tossed something down on the clerk's table. Disdain glinted along the edge of his tone as he said, carefully, each word quivering, "You ask me on what grounds, my lord?"

On the clerk's parchment lay Jervais's garnet ring, Eleanor's gift, the token of her love, which he had so foolishly entrusted to that forest-witch. He stared down at it while his mind's eye made a turning and glanced backward over his life. Was this fall inevitable—was the weakness in him, or in his stars? He contemplated all the unrelated actions which had become this fate, and he saw that it was created by him, fragment by fragment, all fused together now in this sharp-cut moment of amazing regret.

The clerk sat absolutely still, his eyes on the ring, while Henry turned away, a flicker of distaste in his gesture. He said, "If you can give your word to a peasant girl and then duck the consequences like a coward, why should I believe that your word is worth any more to me? I begin to think the name Le Strand is all vainglory and empty honor."

What answer could Jervais make? He could not proclaim that he had never had a disloyal thought, not when he loved Eleanor, not when he knew that if given the opportunity he most certainly would commit the most intimate act of perfidy imaginable.

Henry added, "You are as aware as I am of the downfalls that have overtaken men through women since the beginning of time. You are as aware that the wise man fears all of that other sex."

He added more softly, "I wonder why you would ever make such a vow to a woman, in particular one you claim to scorn so."

Jervais realized he was meant to answer. He struggled to start his tongue into motion. "I did what it seemed I had to do at the time, to get my son."

"Still, to promise so wildly—is it possible your wits were seduced by the woman's remarkable beauty?"

Jervais suffered flashes of memory: his ridiculous frenzy of possession among the buttercups; and later, laying her down naked on his bed of leaves as he more gently caressed her elegant legs, her breasts, finding out how far she could be aroused; and still later, when he imagined her at Conniebrook, in his chamber as his leman, his companion, his comfort. Well, he would have her there now. But not as he had fantasized. There could never be anything but bitterness between them now. The knowledge made him feel unfulfilled, as if a great prize had been offered to him and then snatched away just as he'd touched it.

He said weakly, "She is clever."

"Is she? Or is there more to this than you're willing to admit?"

Jervais shrugged bravely. "I believe she has practiced some sorcery on me."

"Ah, so she only bleared your eye with some spell or an incantation." Henry let out a great noisy sigh, as if he were weary of this whole conversation.

Jervais said quickly, "Sire, I cannot take this woman for my wife. One does not select soft wood to fashion a chatelaine; one chooses the hardest of oak. Can you see this *Kate* taking charge of a castle the size of Conniebrook? She knows nothing—she's not even a lady."

Henry remained unsympathetic. "Le Strand, you

are unsubtle—a fearsome warrior, yes, but in your private life you make mistakes. I want to know that I can count on you, but in just over one year you have plundered a nunnery and disturbed the *religeous* living within—"

"That debt was properly paid."

"Yes, but what about the girl you rapt away, a lady of good repute, whom you married and then lost in the woods?" He managed to make it sound like an incredible act of carelessness. "She was defiled and beaten—and where was her husband? She was strong enough, *clever* enough, to survive and give birth to your son—and where were you, Le Strand? Have you paid that debt? And now, *now*, you have pledged your most solemn word of honor to a mere peasant." He shook his head. "By this time you should be learning better." His tone hardened. "'Tis *time* to learn better, my lord. Wed the woman. She seems teachable; *make* her into a lady. She has common sense and sharp instincts; the rest can be cultured into her.

"Or lock her in a tower with the shutters bolted to the mullions and there make her into a courtesan to please you and breed your dynasty. Bed her well. Spear the dragon of evil in her. Do a good day's toil every night and sire yourself a fine brace of sons on her."

He threw up his hands even as his voice grew in energy. "Frankly, I care not what you do with her once you get her to Conniebrook—as long as you aren't brought before me again tainted with tittle-tattle and rumors!"

The clerk sat biting his thumbnail, gazing down at

the ring on his parchment as though something dreadful was about to sprout from it. Jervais slowly reached for it. He said stiffly, "This sentence you hand down to me is insupportable. I can't turn dross into silver, nor dregs into wine. The woman is a common harlot."

Henry moved to the fireplace. Jervais had the impression that the room tilted with Henry's weight. His young face was white again. He said, his voice gone deadly soft, "According to what I have seen, she is not at all common. According to what I have seen, she has more honor in her than you, my lord. According to what I have seen, she is worthy of naught less than my whole-hearted regard and admiration. By Saint Christopher, you shall take her to the altar. You have no choice. I have made my decision."

This was said inexorably. Jervais took a step back under the jolt. He recalled having ordered a deceitful baker carted through the streets of Conniebrook last autumn with a telltale "short" loaf slung around the man's neck. Retribution by public humiliation.

"And keep in mind," Henry was saying, moving back toward the afflicted-looking clerk, "that once wed I will not countenance the dissolution of your marriage for any reason, so don't think to force the girl into a nunnery and then ask the pope for a divorce. I will not tolerate it. Do I make myself plain?"

Jervais's face was stiff with humiliated pride and fury. It was hard to make his lips form an answer. "Very plain," his voice broke from him gruffly, "as plain as oven-baked bread."

"Good! Now that is all I have to say to you. Good morrow, my lord."

Jervais stood outside the door for a moment. The garnet ring, back on his middle finger, seemed heavy.

Henry's vengeance was just. Jervais was repaid for his treason with treason. It was a perfect triumph of royal justice, a perfect balance between fault and retribution. Jervais shuddered with a sudden chill. He'd heard it told that a serpent's venom was frigid; now he knew it to be true.

The gloomy day's light eventually leaked away, and the purple glow of dusk at the windows did not adequately light Jervais's chamber, yet when supper time was come and a page with a scrubbed appearance brought him food, he wouldn't let the boy light the candles. He didn't want this cramped stone chamber to be lit; he didn't want to see it, didn't want to be here; he wanted to be at Conniebrook; he wanted to look at the sea again. There the cows would be in milk and the peasants' wives bustling about to make butter and cheeses and collecting the payment of eggs due their earl at Eastertide. Spring planting would be finished by Holy Week. And work on the new castle walls would be in full swing.

As the twilight faded toward night, the shadows in the corners of his chamber intensified. When full night came, he at last allowed Charles to light the place and freshen the fire. No sooner was that done, than he received two messages. He read the first, and said to Charles, "The king is in no mood to wait for the marriage." The second note was a summons from Eleanor.

Charles accompanied him. They found her in her bower, where candles bloomed everywhere. Near the flickering light of a huge hearthfire Eleanor's beauty blazed. Her clothing was all silk and damask and fur, and jewels of worth. She gestured, a smile pinned to her lips, and Charles and the courtiers surrounding her moved away, leaving Jervais alone with her in the midst of them. Her voice spoke blandly, "So, you are going to wed her, that poor, dirty, clod-pated peasant."

"I have no choice. And there is to be no delay. The king is very eager for it to take place at once. I just received word he prefers tomorrow afternoon."

"That soon?" Her face was remarkable; no emotion but bland pleasure showed, for the sake of those who were watching them. "Beware of this woman, Jervais. Tread soft. I believe she might be a sorceress of some sort."

He laughed hollowly. "I'd already concluded that."

"You must stand firm against her bewitchment."

He could not explain his sense of helplessness. "I've tried. It avails me naught. She is so . . . beautiful, so irresistible!"

He saw at once that was the wrong thing to say. Eleanor's face suddenly pinched, as if she were about to explode in fury. "You gave her your ring. Tell me, the love which I cherished, was it a lie all this while? Because if it was, I damn you for worse than any Saracen."

Like a coward, he looked away. He felt ashamed that he'd debased an object that meant so much to both of them—another shame to pile upon the several he already owned. "I did what I had to do to get my son. Lady of heaven, but the woman is uncanny! She somehow knew the ring held importance for me—and knew just how to use it to vanquish me."

Eleanor gestured for a page with a tray and busied herself in pouring them some white wine from a half-full ewer. The page faded back. She and Jervais sat in uneasy silence. She swirled the wine in her cup, sipped it, her lashes lowered. Her face was more in shadow than in light. He searched for some crumb of reassurance—but this was Eleanor! his beautiful Eleanor! and he could not serve her crumbs. He cleared his throat. Finally, with genuine deep remorse, he said the only thing he could say: "I have on many occasions showed lack of judgment, but this was the worst. I'm sorry, my darling, so very sorry."

She nodded, as if with sympathy, then said slowly, with mixed humor and resignation, "We are creatures of obligation, you and I. We go from this to that and try, always try, to perform our duties creditably. We try to be kind and fair to all." She sighed and sat up straighter. "The splendid thing about life, my lord, is that though it is cruel, it is also filled with wonder and amazement. Perhaps things will work out better than we can now foresee."

He took a mouthful of wine, composing himself. "'Tis hard to imagine." What he foresaw was his humiliation being bruited about, carrying his shame to the edges of the kingdom.

Her eyes met his. "You know I have loved you, Jervais."

Suddenly he was angry. How could he know any such thing? He felt a shocking sting of tears. He needed her companionship, her presence in his life—right now he needed her hand in his, but even that he could not have. To fill his empty heart, he'd been tempted to turn to a handsome peasant. He suddenly saw all his tribulations as Eleanor's fault, because she made him love her. He felt a great wave of self-pity.

The log on the grate burst with a shower of sparks. As if that were a signal, she rose. "You must go." Her smile seemed sad, yet there was the faintest movement of her curving brows. "Henry will know of this meeting within the hour."

He hadn't missed that movement of her brows. So she meant for Henry to know. In a flash of insight he saw that his loyalty was being deliberately stretched between them. They each wanted complete claim over him, this king of his country and this queen of his heart. They each had a hold on him, and were both pulling. If they were lucky—if he was lucky—he would not tear down the middle.

He rose with her, clearing his throat as he did. He was all right; he was not going to weep; the self-pitying tears had receded. He said, "What if he does? What more can he do to me?" He felt reckless with the judgment already hanging above him.

She tilted her head to one side. "Much. He's a man who always knows his advantage."

Despite the fire, Jervais felt chilled again.

Back in his chamber, as Charles helped him undress for bed he said, "My lord . . ."

Preoccupied, it was a moment before Jervais answered. "Yes, what is it?"

255

"This woman who is to be your lady—Mistress Kate—she seems to genuinely care for your son. She seems very gentle spirited with him."

"She *seems* many things."

Charles was silent for a moment, then proceeded. "You told Sir Gian that you found her pleasant enough company on the road, and that you'd even decided to take her to Conniebrook as your leman."

The reminder set Jervais's nerves on edge. He felt his instincts awaken. He eyed Charles narrowly. "What are you getting at?"

The youth shrugged. He'd learned to hide his emotions some time ago. His noncommittal features could seem carved of alabaster for all the expression they showed. Still, Jervais sensed that the thoughts behind them raced like riptides. Charles said, "I only mean that perchance you should marry her with an open mind. And an open heart. Since you must marry her anyway. There is always time later to revile her, if reviling is what she deserves. Meanwhile, for all her vulgarity, she is a truly beautiful woman."

The sense of betrayal that Jervais felt shocked him. He looked at Charles coldly. "Has she bewitched my own squire, as well then?"

"No, my lord," the youth mumbled.

The rounded apse of the castle's small church blazed with tapers; its vaults were clouded with incense. Jervais stood before the altar, his back to Norah as she entered on Sir Gian's arm. With furtive, uneasy eyes, she gathered an impression of saints' images and carvings, of rich paintings. As Gian led

256

her forward, her heart pounded up. She felt the anticipation in the chapel, the unnatural quiet.

Gian halted at Jervais's side. Jervais held his arm out, and she settled her fingers lightly on his wrist. She saw then that he was wearing the garnet ring from Eleanor again. It took all her will to smile at him.

He ignored her. He looked over her head and muttered to his friend, "God but this is tedious."

Gian said nothing, only backed away. In the candlelit darkness of the place, a priest in gorgeous panoply appeared and began to mumble, coiling the solemn oaths and promises about them, binding them together. The priest's vestments, of the finest sendal set with gold and pearls, flashed in the candleflicker.

Norah felt behind her the curiosity of the courtiers who had come to witness this unusual marriage, and she was grateful for the king's gift of clothing. He'd sent it with a message: "In as much as from the beginning of time a wedding has seemed first and foremost a matter of clothes, please accept this." He'd signed it simply, "H." She was inexperienced in luxury and felt quite opulent in the bright green gown, which was the first silk dress she'd ever owned. It had a silver girdle, and silver embroidery, like cobwebs glistening with silvern mist-drops, on the bodice and skirt. In her hair she wore a garland of flowers, and on her feet were felt shoes.

She covertly looked at her bridegroom. Apparently pride had compelled him to clothe himself grandly for this ceremony, however unlikely his bride. He stood beside her in a tunic of red-and-gold brocade, beautiful—but his expression struck her more forcefully. He looked grey and seemed seized with some pain. Frightened, she jerked her eyes forward again.

What was she doing? She wasn't the kind of person to deceive and connive, the kind to cause pain to someone she loved.

Yet here she stood, and her actions said that she *was* that kind of person.

Jervais's resentment must at least equal his pain, she thought. He must hate her now; he would do everything he could to hurt her. Dazed with dread, she told herself she must not expect much from their life together at first. She must somehow shield herself against the blade of his resentment. Then, later, when the edges of that sharp sword had dulled, she could make him love her.

What if you can't?

She must!

But what if you can't?

The sharp, heavy scent of incense filled the air. The voice of the priest sounded as if it came from a great ways off. She tried to concentrate. He made the sign of the cross, blessing them, and everyone present dutifully mumbled and crossed themselves. Someone behind Norah had a wet, thin cough. Jervais's body was stiff beside her.

Stop this now, Norah. It's a lie. You're a lie. And no good ever came of a lie.

Another voice in her shouted, *It's too late! The spell is in place. The die is cast. There's no going back. If he ever learns who I really am, the spell could be broken—and I could become a monster, a being neither beautiful nor merely plain, but something else, something unnatural.*

Her knees began to quiver with tension. She became conscious of her breath; it seemed she couldn't get enough air, it was all incense, she breathed faster, then faster. Just when she was afraid she was going to swoon, everyone knelt.

Throughout the chapel, voices lifted. She spoke the prayers along with the others, the words rising up from memory and long usage. Her tension didn't leave her, however. As she waited for the next thing to happen, everyone stood. She hurried to do the same, feeling a heartbeat behind and a need to hurry to catch up. She stood so quickly her head swam.

More prayers, underlined by that anonymous, wet, thin cough. She gripped her hands together. Jervais gave her a sidelong glance. Her eyes met his. She felt him staring at her as though he'd never seen her before.

Or as though he had. He seemed on the verge of shouting, *Wait! stop! by Christ, I know this woman!*

Her vision dimmed. The altar began to fade into one long blur. Panic stifled her. Her legs gave way. Jervais reached out, clasped her arm—but too late, she was on her way down. He went down with her, controlling her drop so that though her knees hit the stone floor hard enough to make her teeth click, he kept her upright. She wavered, and felt his arm go around her waist.

Belatedly she realized that no one had noticed that she'd nearly fainted because the time to kneel and pray had come again. Her head cleared; she sent up a swift and heartfelt thank-you.

At last the mass ended with the chant of the

"Agnus Dei." Jervais advanced to the altar and received the kiss of peace. He turned back and embraced his wife, to hand down the kiss to her. As his head lowered, she saw that the aura of power and menace he'd evinced during his brief night visit to her had not left him. His face was sullen but determined. She'd expected nothing more than a respectful kiss, and made a sound of surprise when he opened her lips and thrust his tongue deep inside her mouth. For the instant that it lasted, she glimpsed glory and fire and mighty wind and the savage music of the spheres.

His act left everyone murmuring restlessly. The ceremony was finished. He took her arm and turned her from the altar. He kept a tight grip on her, no doubt fearing that she might falter again and disgrace him. A ray of brilliant light cut into the church's shadow through the open doors. She heard a hum of voices beyond, but the light fell like a bright veil, hiding whatever lay behind it.

They stepped into it, and walked out the doors and down the stone steps into a sunny, gusty afternoon. The air smelled clean and blessedly free of cloying incense. Norah blinked at the dazzling brilliance.

A clutch of humbler folk, scullions and knaves and castle workers, people who gave thanks for a solid meal and a bed of rushes, had gathered in the courtyard. Two kitchen maids, their cheeks like red apples, gave a cheer for "Lady Kate," probably seeing in her a heroine, one of their own risen to unheard-of heights. Other voices joined in, crying, "That's the way! Good fer ye, m'lady!" Their shouts broke taut and vibrant over the voice of the wind. Norah's glance swept their attentive faces, and the blood at once came back into her cheeks—a blush of shame for this new facet of her deception.

A bitter, humorless smile tightened Jervais's mouth. He let go of her arm and stepped a little away from her. Their shadows separated on the cobblestones and lay aslant with the angle of the sun, as parallel as two arrows. He'd probably seldom ever talked to a peasant, beyond handing down judgments and giving orders and asking directions, and now he was bound to what he believed was one. For the first time she felt his humiliation. The tally of her sins was rising by the minute.

The witnesses were crowding out of the chapel to watch the end of the drama. As they came down the chapel steps they separated around the bridal couple, the way flowing water parts around a stone. Norah and Jervais were surrounded, yet they occupied a space that no one else dared to enter. The onlookers found places at a safe distance and lingered about, as if waiting for something more to happen. Someone to Jervais's left coughed wetly and thinly. Norah took in a woman with an angular frame and red-gold hair that looked heavy and lumpy beneath her coif. She was no one Norah knew. Only someone who had come to watch the entertainment. After all, an earl didn't wed a low-born "slut" every day.

The crowd remained oddly quiet. The king, ceremonially wearing his crown and an elegant gold chain about his neck, came out from the church now, with his square soldier's hands clasped before him. All bowed in acknowledgement of him. Several of his Angevins hemmed him, but he broke away and came forward to kiss Norah's hand and raise her up from her curtsey. He turned to Jervais and said quietly, "You've arranged no feast?"

Jervais's voice trembled with charged emotion. "I saw no reason to celebrate this madness."

Henry's jaw tightened. He had to look up to meet Jervais's eyes, but he did so without blinking. With his feet set apart, and his thumbs hooked into his belt, he exuded menace. "Are you saying you think me mad, my lord?"

"Of course not."

"If you persist in this discourtesy to me—or if I hear of you ever once misusing your wife . . ."

Jervais said tightly, "You won't," although Norah sensed that at that moment he hated her and wanted to punish her more than anything else in the world.

Henry gazed back at her. She pretended to busy herself with controlling her long hair and the skirt of her emerald and silver dress, both of which were rippling and fluttering in the wind. He said to Jervais, as if she couldn't hear, "She's really quite a beauty, Le Strand. Or is that only her sorcery?"

Every muscle of Norah's body clenched. Did Jervais know that her beauty was naught but a spell then? His face was tight, giving away nothing. When she looked at Henry, however, to her astonishment his face was lit with amusement. He took a step back, turned, and let his Angevins encompass him again. Norah heard only one more comment from him as he departed. "It's a brave mouse who undertakes to bell the cat." Jervais heard it too. Norah saw him flush.

Now came the priest, bearing himself with self-important magnificence, smoothing his robes like a plump peacock grooming its plummage. He was moving toward them, obviously intent upon congratulating them. But evidently Jervais could bear no more. He stretched his neck, found Gian, and signalled to him. The knight threaded his way through the crowd. Jervais said to him, "Take her to her chamber—carefully—she nearly swooned in the church, and I can't have Henry saying I haven't looked to her welfare."

Gian nodded.

Then, without speaking to Norah, Jervais left.

Chapter 17

In the normal course of events, a great feast culminated the marriage of a nobleman. In the evening, after hours of revelry, the ladies put the bride to bed. The groom got under the covers with her, and a priest blessed their chamber to dispell any curse that might compromise their fertility.

But this was a *mésalliance*, a marriage between an earl and a peasant, a thing begun under the worst auspices, and though all the court was immensely curious, no one wished to actually be a part of it. Not even the groom. Hence, not only was there no feast and no bedding ritual, there was not even any husband. Jervais had disappeared out the castle gates on his chestnut stallion, and that was the last Norah had seen of him. She was escorted from the church by Sir Gian, who kept his head screwed down as if out of the wind, hence managing to do this duty silently.

Henry had ordered Jervais's and Norah's things to be moved. Their bridal chamber was much larger than the one in which she'd been kept before. It overlooked a small orchard planted within the broad sweep of the castle's outer curtain wall. The branches of the budding trees moved in the wind. Seated in the window, Norah waited as the cast-up light from the departing sun burned like a bonfire on the horizon. Waited as the evening star shone out, an unblinking diamond. Waited as the sky turned white with stars. As a monstrous red moon rose and drowned out the stars. As fireflies began to spark among the orchard branches.

Finally, tired of simply waiting, she stood and arched her weary back. Her breasts were full. Evidently Henry had thought to relieve her of the care of her child during her first wedded hours, but now she needed her baby. She pulled the iron latch and opened the door to find Sir Gian standing guard over her. He straightened, his hands on his sword belt.

"Could I have Roger brought to me?"

He nodded and pulled the door closed again.

Later, with Roger in her arms, her breasts bared so that he might drink his fill, she felt only a little less lonely, for he gazed up at her solemnly with Jervais's silver eyes. When his eyelids drooped and his lips went slack, she eased her bodice closed. His little mouth yawned.

She troubled Sir Gian once more to have the child's cradle brought. He saw to this, again without speaking to her. The relationship between this knight and his lord might be an easy one, but it was clear that she was going to be barred from it. Gian's great, gruff, cordial ways, his large grins, his large gestures, his large, hearty affections were not going

265

to be for "Kate." No doubt all of Jervais's men had thus armed themselves against her with concerted disapproval.

Roger sighed in his sleep as she settled him down. Shortly thereafter a page with a freckled face brought her some supper.

For all its pomp, the royal court had an exceedingly poor kitchen. The food was plenteous yet consisted of the coarsest roasts of lamb and joints of bad venison and tainted gamebirds. Under the best circumstances, any wine had a short life and became undrinkable within a few months. But here Norah had been served with wine so muddy that she had to close her eyes and clench her teeth to filter it rather than drink it. Out of her memories of Ramsay, even the roughest bastard wine allotted to the servants was never as awful as this. The royal ale was equally horrid to the taste and revolting to the sight. And as for the bread . . .

After the page took the remains of her meal away, she removed her felt wedding shoes and lay down on the bed. She listened to the muffled sounds of pages carrying dishes and candles and messages about the castle, to the whisper of the night-softened, southerly wind at the window, and sometime she fell asleep.

Jervais came in very late. She woke with a start upon hearing the clatter of the doorlatch. He came in still dressed in his red-and-gold finery. Smiling to hide her embarrassment (she hadn't planned on being caught asleep), she leaned up on her elbow. He didn't meet her smile. In fact, he took pains not to even look at her. He went to a small table where a ewer of the king's terrible wine stood and poured himself a draught into a shallow, maple-wood bowl. Using both hands, he drank what looked like half of it in a single mouthful. Wry-mouthed and shuddering, he crossed the room to set the bowl down on the mantle. He began to undress himself before the embering fire.

When he was naked, he drank the rest of his disgusting wine, quite casually, his muscles stretching and relaxing. In the silence, Norah's gaze strayed over the contours of his form, from his straight shoulders and deep chest to his strong arms, from the whirl of crisp hair beneath his waist downward to the place were his manhood nestled in its lush curls. It was resting quietly now, yet she had seen it aroused and knew it could be amazing in its power to take, to plunder, to incite her woman's body to flames.

Still casual, he walked to the bed. He pulled back the covers on his side, got in, and lay with his broad back to her.

Norah, leaning up on her elbow atop the blankets, felt completely at a loss. She was nervous, and shy of being alone with him, and more than a little frightened. He was, after all, a huge warrior. And he had reason to want to punish her. She studied a faint, jagged scar on his right shoulder. What had made that, what violence had he been about? She really knew very little about him. She should be wary.

Then she asked herself, where could he have been all this time? With carousers, with wine-soakers? With another woman—the queen? And she thought with savage purpose, *He is mine, twice married to me, and before this night is through, he will know it!*

She made a little gesture with her hand, allowed

herself a small laugh, and asked: "Good sir, does every nobleman treat his bride as you are doing?"

After a moment he muttered. "Does every peasant woman go begging for a husband who doesn't want her?"

"No, indeed, usually it is men who take women who don't want them."

He didn't answer.

She said, "You wanted me badly enough when our beds were made of leaves. What makes you so fastidious now?"

"Fastidious?" That word roused him. He lifted enough to punch his pillow into a better shape for his head. "Aye, by Peter, I *am* fastidious! If you knew the honor it is to bear a good name—and the shame it is to see it sullied—"

"Sullied!" Her eyes narrowed. "You feel sullied? But you have no right, not when you took—" She stopped in time. She'd almost said, "—when you took my love and used it, while your own heart was pledged to another!"

She gave him a sidelong look and said instead, "Not when you took me like a beast and used me as if I were less than human. What makes you any nobler than me? How we live, my lord, measures our nature."

When she got no answer, she leaned to breathe in his ear, and she used a wheedling voice, purposely trying to goad him. "Turn to me, sweetheart. Why do you not turn?"

He stiffened but didn't move.

"For God's love," she went on, "tell me what it is, and I shall amend it, dearling."

He turned toward her at last. He was so close she saw the shadow of the beard that darkened his chin. He seemed huge suddenly, and completely masculine. She felt her courage, such as it was, abruptly ebb away.

"It will not be amended," he said quietly, dangerously, "not ever. You are loathsome to me, do you understand?"

She briefly hated him for all his meanness and cruelty, and she vowed to make him pay for it. She rose and lit a candle in the fire and brought it back to the bedside. She placed it in a sconce and stood next to him in its light. Her hands went to her face, her hair. "Am I ugly, my lord? Is that the cause of your loathing?"

Those steady silvern eyes didn't leave her. Looking at her in cold accusation, he said, "You are ugly inside, ugly and stupid—and no wonder, being only one level above a serf, some blinkard's byblow, no doubt. You could be a harlot for aught I know. Who can say how many men have had you? It sickens me to think of the brutes who may have rutted between your legs."

She hid her pain with a smile (though it was hard, it was hard). "I have been poor, but never cheap, my lord. I assure you, none but so-called gentlemen have ever taken their pleasure of me." Her eyes dropped. She picked a bit of fluff from her sleeve. "Still, I understand your disappointment." She nodded sagely. "As a widower, you naturally hoped to seek a second marriage more in keeping with your dignity and interests." She made her voice a gliding feline whisper, "Yet I wonder if you can't find some consolation in having me for your wife instead?"

She began to remove her dress, teasing him as she did with sly glimpses of this or that part of herself. It was the most brazen thing she'd ever done, and she felt almost sick with anguish, yet she wanted to open his eyes to her wholly, so that he would be forced to take her measure from head to foot. And this was only a prelude to her full intention.

She saw his face darken and his mouth tense. When she was naked, she strode around the bed and got into it beside him. She drew the covers no higher than her hipbones. The candlelight fell over her softly. His eyes had followed her movements; she'd managed to concentrate his senses, no question about that.

Her courage was as brittle as an eggshell, but he had found her desirable before, and she was confident that nothing had changed. She was too modest to look down at herself and so stared up at him—and fought an impulse to run. She scarcely knew what he would do next, though she could think of a dozen possibilities.

She let one of her hands lay open, palm up, beside her head, in a desperate effort to seem at ease. She surprised herself by saying in a heavy, languid voice, "Before God and men, I am your wife now. You pledged me one request, which has been fulfilled. I swear this oath by salt and bread to you, that I will do naught to purposely cause you unhappiness. From now on I shall dwell in your will and do whatever you decide. As Ruth said, 'Intreat me not to leave thee, or to return from following after thee: for whither thou goest, I will go, and where thou lodgest, I will lodge. Thy people shall be my people, and thy god my god. Where thou diest, will I die, and there will I be buried.'"

She saw a vein pulse in his temple as he leaned up beside her. With seeming great reluctance, his hand lifted, and moved to touch her bare breasts. Her senses almost leapt with delight. Her nipples rose. She lay complaisant, not once trying to stop him or to in any way break into the rapt attention he had focused on her. As if unaware that he was conceding, he began to kiss her, her mouth, her neck, her shoulders. He pushed the covers down further, to see her belly and stroke it lightly. When he tasted the flesh of her breasts, her hands went about his head, pulling him closer. He immediately tore his mouth away.

His look was blurred with desire, yet confused—and angry. "Every time I get near you, I feel like a man biting into a poisoned apple. The more I taste of you, the more I want to taste, to savor, to swallow—it's despicable!"

"Ah," she said heartlessly, "the temptations of the flesh." She had no sympathy; he was far too puffed with pride.

"You know the arts of enchantment, don't you?" he persisted. "You've used them on me, haven't you?"

She ran her fingertips into his close-cropped hair, feeling its soft texture. She felt wanton. "Perchance."

He drew back, but she twined her arms around his neck and lured him closer. Encouraged by the heat, by the unbanked embers of his eyes, she said, "I am your mate, your perfect partner, and you are mine. You must feel this now, as I do."

271

"No." The strength of her arms was nothing compared to his, and he could have flung himself away. Instead, he let himself be drawn down. "No," he groaned.

"Yes," a whisper, "yes." Her lips were parted and ready for him; all of her was simply waiting for him. His kiss was like red wine and honey, and the taste of his tongue burnt her mouth with sweetness. Her fingers clasped his neck, and he was feasting on her, his tongue inside her. Her skin all over was alive. He kissed her throat and shoulders. Her hair had fallen down and was partially covering her breasts. As his hands brushed it away, her head moved from side to side on the pillow. The touch of his fingertips was too light, too delicate. She made some faint protest, unable to control it. He answered by tugging her face around and kissing her once more, his tongue going into her mouth.

She sensed that he was seething with excitement, as she was, yet he was torturing her with this leisurely lovemaking. There was nothing she could do about it. He was in control, by the sheer authority of his size and strength. She could make him want her, but there was no sorcery, no spell or incantation, no magic, black or white, that could give her power over the pace of his lovemaking. He would, in his own tempo, take her to that world he created, that region of great wonders and strange storms and lights unbearably strong, where the mysteries of time and space became briefly known to her and where marvels were wrought.

He lifted his head and looked at her. The light in his eyes had kindled until they seemed like sparks of lightning. She closed her eyes, unable to look. She felt his tormenting lips on her cheek, his teasing fingers stroking her neck. She whispered, "Don't do this to me."

"Why not?" He gave her a soft, silky kiss.

"I can't bear it."

"Yes, you can. If I can, you can."

"Please, I want you."

"How so?"

"Inside me."

He parted her legs with his knees and got over her. "Like this?" He went up into her.

"Yes!" Her entire body moved in an undulation to receive him. Her arms went around him. There came that exquisite sensation of penetration, of being distended, that gorgeous violation.

But then he just lay over her, wracking her with pent desire. He said, calmly, cooly, "Your face is so seemingly fragile, your lips so deeply rose red. But you aren't fragile, are you? There are threads of steel in your fiber. When I get you to myself at Conniebrook . . . what do you think I'm going to do to you? Guess."

She was making soft, wrought, helpless noises and moving beneath him, but the feelings she invoked were too gentle, too faint. He was in her to the hilt, and lying heavily on her pelvis, keeping her legs spread wide. He held her so that her naked belly and breasts were fastened against him. She could only rock back and forth. A low buzzing pleasure ran through all her limbs at that overpowering sensation of being filled, but it was not enough.

He moved, suddenly, and there was that rich,

exquisite friction—yes, there!

He stopped again. Holding himself on his elbows, he used his fingers to stretch her nipples. She wanted to weep. "Please . . . don't."

"Don't?" His fingers left her breasts. He lifted his hips and slipped out of her with a kind of searing sensation. She felt his hot weight moving away.

"No!" She tried to hold him.

He kept himself poised above her. His fingers burrowed into her hair and pulled her head back, forcing her to lift her chin. He licked his lips, looking at her mouth, but he said, "Your eyes are all bright with tears. So you see how it feels?"

She couldn't bear it anymore. She had to escape him. She tried to rise up, to get away from him. He scooped her into his arms and lifted her higher on the nest of pillows, and thrust into her instantly, impaling her again, slamming into her. Through slitted eyes, through the wash of sensation, she saw the deceptive look of tragedy and pain on his face.

She was under the full weight of his body. He grabbed at her mouth with his, and kissed her, making her face be still under his. This, while he moved like a battering ram within her. The power of him stroked her with a sureness that bespoke his necessity to ease his own tension. She could feel a slow exhilaration building. And when he exploded within her, she exploded as well.

Who had won the battle? She didn't know. In its aftermath, he folded her against him, and she gave up all thought to her inescapable drowsiness. She fell asleep to the feel of him caressing her breasts and her damp sex very gently.

All through the night their bodies slept and woke and moved as one. He woke her with whisperings: "You're so wet and hot, it astonishes me. Your hair is so silken." She felt the loving touch of his sensitive fingers on her tiny swollen bud until she dissolved into long rhythmic shudders again. And once more she dozed off into the sweetest sleep.

His lips woke her sometime later, touching her again, his hands having crept slowly back to her parted thighs to repeat his attentions, and his mouth feeding on her neck. There was nothing hurried or strained about him when he moved over her and took her. He squashed her breasts under his weight when he penetrated her. She cried out and clung to his splendid shoulders. It was intolerably beautiful, intolerably sensual, and so slow that eventually she gave him her moans and quivers, her spasms of ecstacy a third time. Hearing her, feeling her surrender, he scattered his seed within her fields with broad sweeps of his body.

Sleep came to her again.

Before even the first cock crowed and spread its feathers and fluttered its wings, Jervais rose. In something of a fury, he roused Gian and Charles and called them into his bedchamber. It gave him satisfaction to humiliate Kate by bringing his vassals in while she still huddled in the uncurtained bed, to treat her like a common harlot. He wanted, in whatever way he could, to deny the power of her enchantment over him. Her nose was just visible above the edge of the drawn-up bedclothes, and the tips of her

275

fingers where she held the sheet in mock modesty—as if he didn't know just how brazen she really was. Gian stood pretending he didn't see her while Charles helped Jervais dress. Jervais bristled with orders for their departure from London. Then, without a word to his bride, he left the chamber.

He shouldered himself back inside the door again just two hours later, and found her dressed in one of two gowns he'd had Charles buy for her. (Charles had chosen with the woman's eyes in mind, he noted; one of the gowns was blue and this one that she had on was salt-green.)

Her bodice was open. She'd just been feeding the infant who now lay beside her on the bed in a slant of fragile sunlight from the window. The child seemed entranced with his own tiny fingers and feet, and Kate was smiling down at him. For an instant Jervais stood lost in wonder, not of his son, not of the woman's loving smile, but of the exposed, ovoid, feminine, white flesh of her breasts. Enhanced by the light, the sloping skin was poreless and creamy. In an instant, his blood was up and he was filled with a desire to go to her, touch her, place her under him and run his hands over all her curved surfaces.

He saw then that he was doomed to a repetition of these sudden, furtive snatches of sight, moments when her gown would slip, when her knees would part beneath her skirts, when her sleeve would fall back from her wrist as she raised her hand to smooth her hair from her forehead.

Only very slowly did her smile fade. Only very slowly did she think to close her bodice. Slowly and seductively. By what magic was she granted such a quality of seduction? How did she manage to capture all the fleeting beauty of the world in her small person?

His mind had clogged, but finally he found his thoughts again—and his voice, and he said, "Have the babe ready to leave within the hour."

She slowly rose off the bed. Her milky throat lifted like a pillar from the white frame of her collar bones. Jervais stammered, "I'll . . . I'll send Charles to help you." He suddenly wanted some piece of furniture to hold on to, something to stop him from crossing to her and lowering his lips to that throat, from pushing her back and crushing her onto the bed.

Her long, delicate-fingered hands at last finished their work over her breasts. "I'm ready now, if you like."

He nodded, struggling to the surface of this seemingly bottomless well of dark desire. He watched her gather his son into her arms, then he escorted her down into the castle courtyard where all was last-minute bustle. With his scabbard tapping lightly against the tanned yellow of his halfboot, he led her past the cart with food supplies and tents enough to shelter them as they traveled, past several horses belonging to his retainers. He pulled her out of the way of some knobs of horse manure clustered with oats which she would have stepped in because she was gawking about like the naive peasant that she was. Meanwhile his men, some of them striplings, some in their prime (and some of them abashed and some of them insolent) looked her over.

He led her to the litter he'd purchased just an hour ago. From its box, long shafts attached to the saddles of four horses, two before and two behind. With its embroidered canopy, it would be far more comfortable for his son than a pannier, or even solid-wheeled cart.

Though it would be several minutes and perhaps as much as a half hour before the caravan set off, he said, "Get in and draw the curtains. And keep them drawn."

He didn't want her to be seen. Even after last night, even after he'd taken such warmth and comfort as her honeyed flesh could offer, and filled his hands and filled his mouth and filled his eyes with her, he was ashamed of her.

She met his look—and gave him back one that was full of remembering silence. He could see no shift in them, no expression, and yet he sensed hurt. All she said was, "Will you hold Roger while I get in?"

She casually held the child out to him. He took the baby gingerly. It was the first time he'd held his son, and he contemplated the feel of the little wrapped package with alarm. The child was sleeping at the moment, but what if he should waken and begin to cry? Meanwhile, Kate was struggling to get into the litter, and he had to shift the baby to one arm and half-support her with his other arm around her waist. What if he should drop Roger? Or squeeze him too hard? Kate sat down, and as casual as before, held out her arms to take the child back. Jervais watched her settle him in a nest of cushions without the slightest sign of awkwardness. She met his eyes again, then solemnly bowed her head on the flower-stem of her neck and closed the curtains.

When they moved out, it was with proper military

caution. First came two spearmen on their common nags. Were they to meet trouble upon their way, these two would dismount and fight. Behind them rode a clump of men-at-arms, Jervais among them. Then came the litter containing Kate and Roger. Behind them, the sumpter mules and tent cart were led by two grooms. At the very back of the column rode a rear guard of more knights.

London was as crowded and noisy and dark as ever. The caravan forced its way past men with baskets full of cabbages, oranges, and used clothing. A merchant's wife returning from mass got out of their way, as did a laundress and a stone-carrier who were out about their morning's work. A baker's wife with cheese pies called out her goods at them from a stall. A carter bearing fish up from the coast in a lumbering wain pungent with the smell of seaweed called out curses at them when he was forced to turn into an alley to let them pass.

They were held up themselves by a drover with a herd of cows trotting uncertainly before him, claiming the whole width of the city gates for several minutes. While they waited, several of Jervais's men broke into calls at a saucy milkmaid with two brimming buckets hung from a wooden yoke about her neck.

Outside the city lay the light and openness of the fields. Now the country sounds once more took over—the complaints of the shorn sheep on the slopes, the rising wind that stirred the tops of the trees, a dog barking, a great black corbie-crow rising from a stile with a hoarse *caw*. Peasants were out on their strips of land with seed baskets slung around their necks. As the men scattered the seed, their wives threw stones at the crows and doves.

Soon after they left London, Jervais saw an old man at the side of the road. He knew him immediately: Dick Jackson, Kate's ugly peasant friend. Had he been standing here every morning, watching for them? Or had he somehow known that this was the morning they would be leaving Bermondsey Castle? Jervais rode right past him, but Kate, who had opened the curtains of her litter just enough to peek out, of course spied the old man. "Stop! Stop, I say!" she called to the pageboy leading the litter's horses. She was already half out of the box and would have tried to jump to the ground while it was still moving if Jervais hadn't wheeled his mount and shouted, "Halt!" to the boy.

He rode to the side of the litter and bent from his saddle to speak to her quietly but harshly. "I intend to travel as swiftly as I can. An old man afoot will never be able to keep up with us."

"Then let him ride," she said, jumping out of the litter without help, disgracefully exposing her legs to the knees. "You have spare horses."

Her tone fanned his already strong indignation. "Those are *destriers*. They'd never let that old cripple get within ten feet of them. Now get back inside that chair. You're making an unpardonable exhibition of yourself."

"My lord," she said, the words tumbling out quickly, "recall that I told you how Dick came to be as he is—that someone tried to take his head off with a club? And perchance you recall a night when your Lady Norah ran from your camp and was beset by outlaws in the woods? 'Twas Dick who saved her from all they intended.'' She paused to catch her breath—and to let her words settle in. "Aye, you owe poor Dick for this son you have. He pulled your lady from the hands of those filthy devils and told her to run whilst he stayed to keep them from following after her.''

Jervais didn't know whether to believe her or not. The peasant had limped forward along the line meanwhile, and now stood looking at Kate with a foolish grin of greeting on his face. She smiled in return, and even reached up impulsively to hug him.

Jervais dismounted and pulled her away. To the peasant he said in halting English, "Did you know my Lady Norah?''

The man looked at Kate. Jervais put his hand on her shoulder, forbidding her to prompt the man. He said, "Did you help a nun in the woods?''

It seemed to take forever before Dick gathered his words. The focus of his wall-eyes was uncertain, but it seemed he was looking more at Kate than at Jervais. "Aye,'' he said at last.

"Well—what did you do, man?''

"She were in the woods. 'Twas . . . night. They were hurting her." He frowned. "I can't remember. Irwin . . . I hit Irwin. I told her, 'Run! Run,' I said. Then somebody hit me." He rubbed his left hand over his face. "I can't remember.''

Jervais watched him with a still heart. Kate stepped forward and patted the old man's arm. "It's all right, Dick, it's all right. You don't have to remember any more.'' Her voice had that deeply feminine sound that almost pained Jervais. She looked at him. The leaves of a nearby tree whispered and shifted. He inhaled deeply, then turned with the knowledge that he was compelled once again to accept her humbling terms. "Somebody give this man a mule to ride!"

He handed her back into the litter. He would have turned away without speaking, but she stopped him with a touch on his hand: "My lord, thank you." Her color was high; she wore, somehow, that extra flush that glowing fruits sometimes wear. He pulled away as if her fingertips were burning brands. Indeed, they sent a fire racing through him.

Though he tried not to look her way, he was aware of her all that day. And because of her, he couldn't seem to keep his temper. The slightest thing vexed him almost beyond bearing. He alternately throttled his rage and let himself explode with it.

They traveled through fallow and tended fields and, here and there, areas still seared and blackened from battles once waged. The villages which they passed through had grown according to the lie of the land and the need to preserve the fertilest soil: in one the squat cottages would face inwards around a green, while in the next one they would straggle along the road. Before each cottage grew a few onions, peas, or beans.

The fair afternoon, full of long vistas with the smell of grass and the murmur of fat and fuzzy bees, gave way to a rough camp and darkness. Jervais didn't make love to Kate in the tent they shared that night, ringed round by knights and squires. By that seemingly simple (but really nigh impossible) act of self-discipline he regained some control over his anger. The next day it was checked enough for him to keep it from leaking out over just anyone.

Meanwhile, they joined an old Roman road, one of the old thoroughfares of conquest, and proceeded north on it. Made of stone, with fur-leaved weeds sprouting in its cracks, it ran directly up the countryside. They met other travelers on it, groups of half a dozen or more. Jervais noted that Kate opened the curtains of her litter just enough that she could observe every passing peddler and dancing bear and wandering monk, every troubadour in bright, ragged clothes, every beggar and wealthy burgher.

That second night he again slept with his back turned to her, albeit he was aware of her every movement, aware of her naked beauty behind him, calling to him. He couldn't hold out against her much longer. He yearned to reach Conniebrook, somehow sure that there he would find some method of self-defense.

Chapter 18

The journey seemed endless. Norah got tired of the movement, of the tension in the tent at night, of the early reveille. But at last she got her first glimpse of Conniebrook and the sea. Just before sunset on the last day of their journey, the caravan climbed a narrow road that leaned uphill. At the crest, there in the distance stood Conniebrook Castle, poised high on a rocky plateau overlooking the moving sea, its fortress towers hung with scarlet pennants of welcome.

Seeing what she could through the narrow opening in the litter's curtains, it was all just as she'd imagined it. Or almost. Something forewarned her and, unexpectedly, she felt afrighted. Perhaps it was the very size of the place, the massive fortifications and the stark towers.

As they started down into Jervais's broad and fruitful domain, Norah caught glimpses through gaps in the trees of a town at the castle's gate. A wooden palisade surrounded it. Smoke rose straight from the evening fires in the small houses crowded together along the narrow streets.

Suddenly they came out of the shadowed woods and under the sky. A sharp bend of the glassy Barset River lay before them, flowing deep and narrow between its high banks. They crossed it where a toll bridge spanned it. They followed the river's course for a while, until it broadened into wide water meadows filled with cattle. Now the road split away and turned directly towards the castle.

They came through fields that had lain open all day to the sun, and finally entered the wooden palisade and paraded through the village. People rushed down through the huts to meet them. There was cheering for Jervais and a craning of necks, for messengers had told about the common woman who had forced their lord into marriage.

This was far from the welcome of Norah's childhood dreams—the welcome that was to be the start of a future filled with promise. Her heart broke a little.

The castle ahead was built of pale stone. The last sunlight shone on its walls and roofs. Norah could see the building Jervais was doing with the dowry of stone from his "first" wife. A great, many-towered outer wall, or curtain, was being added, amidst a confusion of mortar, rubble, and scaffolding. It would eventually surround the three landward sides of the existing castle, creating an outer ward and doubling the castle's size and defenses.

The existing stronghold appeared already impregnable. Jervais's garrison, with their lances at salute, stood along the battlement above the gate, which they'd thrown wide to welcome him and his new-found son—if not his new bride.

The cloudy sky overhead grew bright with the reflection of the pink and orange sunset, and cast a glow over all the scene. They rode up the last stretch at a smart trot and cantered through the gate, beneath the raised portcullis, into the square inner ward. Mounted knights from the castle garrison had formed a welcoming aisle beyond the gatehouse. Their horses were polished and sleek; their iron helmets and mail tunics and kite-shaped shields shone. They dipped their lances as Jervais rode past them, and the castle people cheered loudly.

Jervais reined to a halt in the center of the ward. People immediately crowded around his horse. Sir Gian dismounted and walked over to hold the chestnut's bridle to keep it from dancing in all the excitement.

Charles appeared to help Norah climb out of her litter. Dick stood nearby. She had no time for more than a glance about her. She took in that the castle enclosed an inner complex of stone buildings: a kitchen, stables, and a blacksmith's forge among other enterprises, all lined up around the courtyard's inner walls. Then Jervais caught her attention again by swinging out of his saddle into the flock of greeters.

Norah couldn't count how many attendants and servants there were to hail him. She glimpsed a chaplain in a wool cassock, pages, a falconer and a butler (servants of considerable dignity and power in any household), a kennel boy with a silent greyhound, a master cook (identifiable by his fat limbs and his apron). At the outer edges there were even several common scullions.

Jervais's eyes glittered like flint in the last breath of the sunlight, and Norah realized that, like any man, he was glad to be home. His eyes swept the march of the walls around him with satisfaction. He gave his cloak to a page, a thoughtful, sad looking child of eight or so. A great bear of a man shouldered through the pack, shouting, "Come into the hall, my lord! You must be weary."

"William!" Jervais clapped him on the shoulder. "I'll eat and drink in my office. Ale—I've had enough of the king's wine to sour my stomach for grapes for a long while." He started for the largest building, went up the steps and through a pair of bronze doors.

All eyes now turned to stare at Norah. There was some muttering. She heard an, "Oh, *mon Dieu.*" She didn't know what to do. She'd been left to trail behind Jervais like an anonymous page. As she stood in doubt, Charles appeared again, and murmured, "Will you come with me, my lady?"

She smoothed her blue linen gown and straightened her hair over her shoulders. She gathered Roger and let herself be escorted through the bronze doors. Her friend Dick followed close upon their heels.

She found herself in the castle's great hall. Old rushes were spread unevenly on its timbered floors. The windows were tall, but were shuttered against any light that might have come in. The great trussed ceiling was black from the smoke of the fireplaces. From the far end came the smells of the kitchen— delicious smells of roasting lamb and crushed mint. Norah's mouth watered. She too had had enough of the king's fare.

Charles urged her toward the group of men about the earl. One of them was very old and bent. His hands were closed and stiff, and he moved by hobbling on a stick.

Jervais turned as Charles brought Norah into their midst. He said tersely to the two most prominent men, "My son and . . . my wife." The bearish man made a faint bow which did not hide his squinting suspicion. Jervais introduced him as William Goings, "the bailiff of my lands. And this is Philip of Cotherne, my master builder. And Yves Damen is steward of the castle."

The master builder was a man with a nose like a granite wedge driven into his face. He dismissed Norah with a nod. The old man, Yves, however, scrutinized her from his bent position, pursing his mouth. "Are ye sure the babe is truly yours, my lord?"

Norah had the satisfaction of seeing Jervais's eyes turn to arctic ice. "I have said so, haven't I? He is named Roger, for his grandfather, Roger of Ramsay."

The old man was undaunted. He continued to squint from Roger's little face to Norah's, until Jervais took her arm and said to her, "You can put the boy down in my chamber."

He started her toward a door at the north end of the hall. A servant hastily threw it open. Jervais stopped. Without looking back, he said to Norah, "Tell your friend he cannot come into the tower."

Norah turned to find Dick was right behind them. She said in English, "Stay here in the hall, Dick, I'll be fine. This is our home now."

Jervais stepped through the door before her. The tower contained, altogether, three round chambers, each eighteen feet in diameter, one above the other, gained by way of a narrow, enclosed staircase that spiraled up. The treads were worn with the usage of years, and gave off a dank, musty smell. The room at ground level, which Norah hardly got more than a glimpse of, seemed to hold stores. The door of the second story's room was closed. Half way up to the third story, Jervais motioned to a small door leading to a cubby off the stairs. "The garderobe." Nothing could have been more faraway and impersonal than his bearing.

The top room, the third story of the tower, ninety feet above the courtyard, was a bedchamber. It had three windows, all with rare glass set into wooden frames in the stone openings. Norah was impressed. Glass was expensive. Of course, it was full of bubbles and bumps and so not quite transparent, yet it let in the sun and kept out the wind and gave tantalizing hints of the sea beyond.

Dusk was settling outside, and pages came after them, bringing oil lamps and candles which they arranged on corbels around the room to supplement the light from the fireplace.

A thick coat of painted plaster covered the walls, making them light and clean. The chamber lacked the warmth that a few tapestries would give, however. The bed had clearly been built especially for its tall owner. It had a dark-scarlet spread with silk coverlets and curtains, which were tied back for now. Other furnishings were sparse: a pair of stools, a chest, a small table. The floor was of wood planks.

All in all, though plain, it was a pleasant room. Norah said so to Jervais. He nodded curtly. His voice was cool: "My first project was to refurbish the existing buildings."

A pair of pages came through the open door carrying a beautifully carved cradle. Another boy, the sad-looking one who had taken Jervais's cloak earlier, came in with his arms full of infant bedding. Norah thanked them, and soon she had Roger settled. He slept, oblivious to his homecoming, to his inheritance, exhausted by the lengthy journey.

Turning to her husband, Norah said, "May I go up to the wall walk, my lord? I would so love to have a good look at the sea. I've never seen it before, and soon it will be full dark and I'll have to wait for the morrow."

He seemed surprised, then frowned as if in impatience, but gestured for a servant girl to stay with Roger.

The spiral staircase went up to the very top of the tower and opened onto a realm of light. Norah felt she was even higher than heaven, higher than the angels. She leaned over the battlement. Below her was a clear fall for nearly two hundred feet. She could see boulders and a narrow strip of beach below, where it met a churning surf. She said, "Could I walk down there on that beach?"

"It's not broad, even at low tide."

She sensed his negative mood and did not challenge it. Besides, she had the sea to delight her. It was enough for now.

It reflected the peachy-blue light of the dusk, and immensity too supreme to have been imagined. Nothing could have prepared her for this sight of wondrous, lustrous openness. Still, it had a familiar quality. She realized what it was: the sound. It was the whisper of the ocean in her seashell, amplified a dozen times over.

The wall walk was narrow, and Jervais was forced to stand near her. A glance told her that this view enthralled and excited him, as well. As if in a trance, he idly touched her hair on her back. His fingers lightly pinched a strand and fingered it. She felt a splash of icy pleasure, and dared to think, *Now comes the joy.*

She said aloud, "It's beautiful."

"I've always thought so."

But then he seemed to realize what he was doing, and he moved away from her. The moment was gone, as was all the tenderness in his manner. In full control of himself again, he said to the old man, who had followed them up in his slow, bent way, "I have things to see to, Yves. Take care of her."

The words were like a slap to Norah.

She didn't stay long on the wall walk after he left. Yves's company was too unsettling. As she gazed at the darkening sea, he shuffled back and forth, obviously impatient to rejoin his lord. He talked in a murmur, as if to himself, but really meaning for her to hear: "The earl home, so much to do, so many things to discuss with him." She gave in at last and started down the stone staircase.

She expected to be left in the bedchamber, probably to eat a solitary supper, and Yves hesitated before the door there, evidently unsure what his lord's intentions were. Finally he ushered her further down to the second story chamber. Norah guessed it must be used by Jervais for his office, and it was here

291

that he had said he would be dining.

The sad, thoughtful-looking little page stood ready to open the door for Norah. She stopped to ask, "Lad, what is your name?"

"Lloyd of Clarence, my lady," he said, shyly, tentatively.

She touched his young cheek. "Have you been in the earl's service long?"

"Yes, my lady."

"Bah!" said Yves behind her, "he's just come last month from his father's manor."

Norah gave the boy a smile. "It must seem like a long time to you, though." Despite her own battened-down misery, her heart went out to him.

Yves muttered, "You mustn't coddle him, my . . . er . . . the only thing wrong with this boy is that he was caught crying in his bed again last night and was soundly thrashed for it this morning."

The child looked mortified and miserable.

Norah asked, "Boys are beaten for being young and homesick here?"

"It's not unknown for Sir Oakley to take a boy behind the kitchen and give him fifteen strokes with a stick."

She gave the man a chill look. "Does my lord the earl approve of that?"

"Sir Oakley is in charge of the young pages." He gestured toward the chamber door. "Will you go in?"

The room beyond was smokey and warm. Its windows were the tall, vertical slits called arrow loops, which were used for defense in wartime. The furnishings were all simple and practical and masculine. A crowd filled it, with Jervais in their center, his figure overpowering even William Goings.

Several of the men gave Norah looks that clearly said they didn't feel she belonged here. For the most part they were younger than Yves and were not yet showing the same meanness around their eyes; nonetheless, she could read their suspicions and their hostilities clearly enough. Jervais gave her the merest glance. From it she knew that Yves had made a mistake. Jervais hadn't meant for her to take meat with him. But now that she was here, there wasn't any graceful way for either of them to mend the situation.

He turned his attention back to William Goings, who was saying, "We had a good harvest, even the serfs seem satisfied. In the fullness of time, methinks . . ."

Norah didn't listen. She was too distracted by all that was happening around her: A boy moved about lighting candles; another was covering the chamber's only table with a cloth; servants were coming in with covered salvers and ewers of ale.

As William talked on, and Yves joined him, Jervais went to the fire. His right hand rested easily on the mantle, above which hung a Saracen shield—a souvenir of his adventures on crusade? He continued to ignore Norah, to look into the fire, to listen to his bailiff and his steward. Beyond that first look, he didn't even acknowledge her presence. Everyone else ignored her as well. He was setting the standard for how she was to be treated. His unspoken word was: She's not important; take no note of her.

At the table, the pages uncovered the dishes.

Norah's stomach clamped to her spine with hunger. At last Jervais sat and, as if only now recalling her, gestured for her to join him. She did, uneasy amongst all these strange, disapproving men and attentive-faced boys. Yet she was starved. She picked up a strip of meat from a carved roast in front of her and started to put it into her mouth. Jervais said, in a low mutter that no one else could hear, "None of your manner-less ways now."

She arranged her features into a smile. A knave brought in a bowl that, uncovered, proved to be a fragrant venison stew. Charles ladled out sauce and meat onto her plate, but she found her appetite much faded. Another boy put an entire roast bird before Jervais. He drank his ale, sitting back so that Charles could disjoint the bird. Norah ate very carefully, hideously afraid that she would make some blunder and bring embarrassment and Jervais's disapproval down upon her.

The report of Master Philip, the castle builder, started while they ate. As the talk of things about which Norah knew nothing went on and on, she grew drowsy. She eventually put an elbow on the table and leaned forward to rest her cheek in her palm. Jervais immediately gestured to Charles. "See her upstairs."

The room went silent as she straightened and looked at him. Across the table, his eyes met hers at last. He seemed to say, *I didn't want you here, but you insisted, and now you must take what treatment you get.* She pulled herself to her feet. Some of the men looked at her scornfully; others wouldn't look at her at all.

She was glad when Charles closed the door behind them and led the way upstairs. She was more glad when he left her in the bedchamber with little Roger, who was still sleeping snug by the fire. She dismissed the servant girl, and then she was alone. Blessed solitude at last. She sank onto the side of the bed, her shoulders hunched, her mind numb. All of her was curiously empty of feeling. She'd reached the limits of her strength and her powers.

After a while, she combed her hair, and then undressed and slipped under the beautiful scarlet coverlets. Her eyes stung, but she refused to let herself weep. She turned on her side, curling her knees to her breast, and fell forlornly asleep.

At last all the ado about Jervais's homecoming was done; everyone was gone to bed, and he was left alone in his office. He leaned back, tipping his chair behind his work table. The candles had burned down to nubs, some had guttered out. The fire flickered on, however, refreshed by the sleepy page Jervais had just sent stumbling to his pallet. Along the ramparts the watch was no doubt gathered two by two, playing quietly at dice, but inside only a cat was left to keep company with the lord of the castle. It was a thin black cat who sat on the rug near the hearth washing an upthrust hind leg. Its body was as curved on itself as an elegant shell.

Jervais's work table had been cleared of the supper long ago and now was layered with documents and tally sticks. He refused to think of the summer's labor before him. He was tired, and it was too daunting to think of it anymore tonight. All he wanted was his bed.

But the woman was in his bed. Kate.

The thin cat, arrested in its toilet as abruptly as if it had heard a dog baying, gazed at Jervais, its tongue like a rose petal still projecting from its mouth. Jervais rose and went to the nearest window. He stood with his hands clasped behind his back. A late moon had risen; fog drifted at the edge of the sea below. He wondered if that had been the edge of a storm he'd spied to the south earlier today.

He needed to thoroughly inspect the castle estates as soon as possible. William said the sheep shearing had begun. Half the expected wool was already sold to a merchant from the great cloth center of Flanders; the rest would go to local markets. He also had to travel to the fiefs held of him, to Lesterhouse Manor, for instance, the fief held by Gian, and to others, especially those of Ramsay. Meanwhile, the thatch that had protected the unfinished stonework from frost damage all winter had been cleared away, and Master Philip was ready to swing fully into the year's work on the outer curtain.

He wanted her. This attempt to divert his mind was doing no good. The knowledge that she was in the chamber above, in bed, in *his* bed, stirred him unbearably. He recalled the look of her on the wall walk, when she'd leaned her arms on the rampart, her heavy dark hair shining, her lovely face alight with her first clear sight of the sea. He'd wanted to stay with her, to share that moment with her and discover the sight anew through her. It had come as a strange and powerful feeling which he'd instinctively distrusted. It had come as had that strange bouyancy, that tenderness of affection, which had carried him to London at her side. It was a feeling not to be trusted.

He'd known so many women, yet none, not even Eleanor, possessed so powerful a mystique for him as this one. In dealing with her, he needed to be constantly on guard. She was not what she seemed to be. When she handled Roger with such gentleness, she didn't seem evil—but she must be.

He turned back to the room. He stared at the Saracen shield over the mantel, trying to remind himself of Antioch, of his true and pure love for Eleanor.

It was no use. She was far away, both in distance and in position. Their love could never be consummated—and sometimes a man needed a woman's nearness, needed her attention, her body.

That was all this desire was: he simply needed a woman. And since he had a woman, why shouldn't he use her?

With sudden decision he strode to the hearth. There was a jar of spills, and he stooped to take one. He held it to the flames until it caught, then went to the door. Using the spill as a nightlight, he took the dark spiraling stairs two at a time. It was late, he was going to bed; he was master of this castle, and he was going to his chamber for his pleasure and his rest.

A drowsy Charles was waiting outside the chamber door, ready to go in with him and undress him. He nodded, and they entered together.

All through his disrobing, Jervais watched the small mound in the bed. Nothing moved. She was sound asleep, unknowing as yet of his guilty desire.

He dismissed Charles. Naked, he paused by the cradle which he himself had slept in as an infant. The firelight flickered on his son's sleeping face, showing a little pursing movement of his lips. He was dreaming, no doubt, of Kate's breasts. A like feeling moved Jervais toward the bed. He had a sudden sense of urgency. The last time he'd taken her, on their wedding night, was all too alive in his memory. Again he felt visited with that sense of an indefinable force, that pull she had on him.

He slid into the big downy bed and moved toward the warm pocket that she'd made around herself. She had her back to him. A few tresses of her long dark hair lay on the pillows; the rest was hidden beneath the covers. His hand went to her waist, went around it to cradle her soft belly. Her body was beating and warm; his own heart was beating hard. For some reason this seemed to him more like coming home than had entering the gates of Conniebrook.

"Kate," he said as quietly as his stretched nerves allowed.

She didn't wake, and suddenly he felt too fearful of his desire. He fell back onto his pillow, tried to relax, tried to give himself up to sleep.

But every part of his body felt as tightly stretched as an animal pelt nailed on a drying board. Why couldn't she be a woman of quality? At least little Norah, as skinny and uncomely as she'd been, had been a lady by birth.

But she hadn't been graceful and lovely, nor owned a body that was full and womanly under his touch.

Why even think about her? She was gone and not ever going to return.

Or could she? Somehow?

What brought that thought? How could she return—she was dead! And meanwhile, he'd been tricked into marrying this utterly common temptress, this half-faerie. His heart burned at the thought.

Yet, like it or not, she was his wife. She'd gotten everything she wanted from him—so why shouldn't he take what he wanted from her? Why shouldn't he enjoy the pleasure he had denied himself for too many nights?

He turned back to her sweet-scented warmth, stretched out behind her and took her thoughtfully and without haste into his arms. The feel of her breasts in his hands, the touch of her excitable body pressed backwards against him broke down the last of his reservations. Against the groanings of his mind, he drew back the coverlets to expose her gleaming skin. Disturbed, she moved in his arms, turned protectively onto her stomach—and presented to his sight her superb, delicious backside, so spectacularly creamy in the firelight. Spurred by the devil, he stroked those round, satin cheeks. His hand delved between her thighs. The position was unique to him, backwards and behind-wards as it was, a bit perverse—and tremendously exciting.

She was still asleep, but he didn't care. *She* didn't matter, he told himself. He only wanted to revel in the beauties of her body and become intoxicated with the pure sensation he knew it could afford him, to live for a while in that place apart it created, that world in which time was banished. The sumptuous delight in taking her had nothing to do with who or what she was.

She woke sometime, and responded to what he was doing, and though he didn't like to acknowledge it, her response increased his pleasure. A thought strayed into his head: although Henry had forced this unlooked for and miserable arrangement on him, perhaps, after all, he could enjoy it. How many men could boast of a liaison with a sorceress?

He let her turn onto her back. Her breasts were bare to him, their pink nipples excitingly puckered. Her eyes were wide; her tongue darted out to moisten her lips. She made a sight so devastating it sucked his breath away. She was perfect.

"How beautiful you are, how beautiful," he murmured as he leaned to kiss one breast and then the other, to suckle those two precious morsels at their tips. His lips eventually trailed down her stomach to a finger's breadth above the little patch of curls that safeguarded her secret place. A desire flickered uncertainly. Bold and sudden as he was in war, he was a man who had seldom indulged in sexual experimentation. His instincts were all conservative. But now, suddenly, he was filled with a mood of unusual exhilaration. She seemed so achingly rare and lovely, and so touched with the strange that, yes, he had to part her thighs and let his mouth continue its journey.

There was a tingling down his backbone, a catch in his breath—he'd never felt aught like it! a sensation like falling off a cliff!

He never hit bottom; he became lost in the taste of her, lost somewhere between immensity and infinity. At first she lay stiff, in shock, like someone who had just been caught by a terrible, cold wave. But then she began to make the small, wordless sounds he recognized, sounds which intensified his pleasure until he grew dizzy. When she called out, *"Mon Dieu!"* he heard the halting of his heart—and felt a physical weakening so unusual it made him feel slightly faint.

Yet he found the strength to rise up on his arms and storm her keep. He stretched himself over her, felt all of her exquisite nakedness against his own nakedness, and he took her. And if his mind had a shape in that moment, the shape was of an immense and endless corridor. Along it, her second cry was taken up echoed by his own: *"Deus volt! . . . Deus volt!"* God wills it! his crusader's cry of war.

Afterward, he reclined beside her, holding her as she lay passive, conquered in his arms. He fell asleep with her.

He woke about an hour later, wanting her again. The second time was always better; it took so much longer. His mercilessly self-inflicted restraint of the journey north was forgotten. If she were a sorceress, if she had placed a spell on him as he believed, then he would not fight it. He saw no reason to fight it. He was not a boy, ardent for some desperate triumph of honor. She was beautiful, she was utterly desirable, she was here for him to take, and take her he would.

Yet even in that instant of his keenest ecstasy a voice asked if he were living a dream come true or a nightmare.

Chapter 19

Jervais's expression was stark; his eyes dazzled like moonlit ice. "I've looked for you all my life." The words hung in silence betwixt them. She wouldn't have known him for the man who had destroyed her youthful hopes with his indifference, or the one who sometimes frightened her now with his terrible desires. She was filled with happiness for she knew what he was going to say next, the words she waited so long to hear from him: "Je t'aime."

Norah woke, but the happiness of her dream stayed. Had it been a foretelling dream?

She stretched langorously. She'd been miserable and exhausted last night, but all her vitality seemed returned now. Jervais's lovemaking had made her feel such wonderful things, such hope.

As her eyes gathered the shadowy details of the bed, she saw that the curtains had been untied. She was enclosed. And Jervais was gone.

She was at once completely awake. The light seeping in around the curtain edges was strong. He'd let her oversleep. Had it been consideration? Gratitude? (Not simple indifference, surely not.) She pushed back the blankets and rose.

She found a young girl with stringy, honeycolored hair waiting in the chamber for her. Startled, she snatched at the bed curtains to cover her nakedness. The girl bobbed a scant curtsy and said in an unpleasant, mincing way, "I'm Theresa. Yves, the steward, says I'm to do for you."

All was warm and orderly in the chamber—the girl's work, Norah supposed. She allowed herself to be dressed in her salt-green gown with its plain narrow girdle. She asked Theresa to part her hair in the middle and coil it at the back of her head. After all, she was the countess of Conniebrook now. Today she would begin to learn her duties here. She thought that she should look older.

She listened to the timeless boom of the breakers against the empty beach below as she fed Roger. Out the glass windows the sea was as blue as a sapphire. She would have liked to visit the top of the tower again, but she was already so late in starting the day that she decided to go directly down to the hall.

The big room was dark. She'd missed mass, and found that the first hasty partaking of the day—bread, beer, and slices of cold salt-meat—was already being cleared away. Jervais was headed toward the great bronze doors. He paused upon seeing her making her way toward him. His companions politely stepped out of hearing.

He seemed to shine out in the half light of the hall, as bright as a stained glass window with the morning sun behind it. The neckline of his grey tunic left his

303

strong throat bare to his collarbones. She stopped before him and gazed up at him, intent, waiting for some magic to happen, for him to look at her with the same love he'd spoken from in her dream.

But it had not been one of her foretelling dreams. He said, without even the prelude of a greeting, "I've instructed Yves to show you around this morning."

She hid her disappointment. And railed against it. "Thank you," she said, striving to match his coolness.

He nodded, and then just stood staring at her in a way that made a glorious inner excitement rise in her all over again. It was not a loving look so much as a look of possession; still, her heart raced to see it. She hoped she wasn't blushing.

"Good Lord!" he said finally, under his breath, and he turned on his heel. He adjusted his sword belt as he went out. He and his companions ran down the steps and out into the windy, cobbled square with a fine masculine clatter of booted feet. Before the double doors swung shut, Norah saw several horses waiting for them, sumptuously swinging their great muscled haunches.

His leave-taking left her with no doubts. He did not love her yet. Not even after last night. She held herself together by sheer will.

When she turned, her eyes found Dick sitting beside the nearest hearth. She crossed to him. "Did you sleep well, my friend?"

His wall-eyes lit up; his smile was generous and bone deep. "Sister Katharine."

"No, Dick," she said with quiet intensity. She glanced about to see if he'd been heard. No one was near. She put her hand on his shoulder. "Dick, I'm Kate now. Remember? It's very important."

"Oh, aye, that's right. I forgot."

"Try not to forget, Dick. Try very hard."

Directly after her solitary breakfast, she began her tour with Yves. She was eager to learn her way around her new home.

The existing castle was in excellent repair. Jervais had seen that everything was patched and painted and scrubbed as bright as a penny before he'd started on his vast extension. Looking up from the courtyard, she saw clouds had built up into billowing turrets and spires which gleamed in the sun like the legendary towers of Camelot. The inner ward was a scene of noise and activity. Smiths were sharpening swords and shoeing horses, bowmen were practicing from a section of the walls above, grooms were taking horses out to be exercised, or poulticing the sick ones, and carpenters were mending tables and long benches from the hall. There was an incessant pandemonium of horses, hounds, falcons, and men.

Inside the thick walls of the castle chapel, however, all was quiet. It was located in the seaward tower nearest the Barset River. This tower contained a room on the second floor that was two stories high. The apse was built into a large window recess where the stone frame was carefully fitted with pieces of stained glass retelling the epic of salvation. Backed by the morning sun, the colors melted the opposite walls to radiance and shed pools of light here and there on the floor, as red as blood, as blue as dusk. As Norah knelt to say a brief prayer, the air moved with languid, drifting dust motes, so that it seemed a world sunk to the bottom of a sun-struck ocean.

Directly across from the apse, on what would have been on the third-story level, a balcony was built out from the wall. Here the lord of the castle observed the services above the common worshippers below.

In contrast to the beauty of the chapel, the kitchen was hung with pots and buckets, and one whole wall was lined with barrels of English beer and great ale butts. Everything was busy-ness and practicality. A great copper meat pot was in action, with a boy pumping a bellows to make the fire hot so the caldron would bubble. The chief cook sat at a huge work table shredding cabbages. When Norah and Yves entered, he leapt to his feet and bowed.

A castle cook was an immensely important person. All who lived at the fortress must be fed, from the noble at his high table to the scullion who snatched and bolted her food in the kitchen. Norah said, "Master Villhard, I have recently come from King Henry's court, and I must say that the dishes I have smelled and tasted since my arrival here are in no way comparable to what I was served there." She watched his face stiffen before she went on: "Indeed, after nearly starving under the tortures of the royal cooks, I can't compliment you enough. I'm much afraid I shall grow fat on your peacocks and capons."

The man's face slowly softened; he broke into a sunrise of a smile. "My lady," he said, "you do me honor." He insisted in showing her everything within his realm, from the warren of stone-flagged larders and storerooms to the ovens for baking. He pointed out his special fireplace for cooking fresh meat, his large stone sink with water piped directly from a stone cistern; he even explained his system for organizing the storage in the scullery.

Yves wasn't pleased with her conquest of the cook. Norah was confirming what she'd suspected, that Yves was a peevish and limited man. For some reason he insisted on showing her the castle dungeon next, though it meant calling a man in to move two barrels and a bale. These covered a trap door in the floor of the ground-level storage chamber of Jervais's own tower. Yves scolded the man all the while he was moving things. He threatened to pull the fellow's teeth, to have his hands hacked off, until at last the long-unused trap door was lifted.

Dutifully, Norah glanced down into the dank, dark pit. During the anarchic reign of Stephen the dungeons of many castles had held both men and women imprisoned and tortured with pains unspeakable. Norah couldn't believe that Jervais or his father had done such things, even during those lean and hungry years, but she thought it best not to ask.

Yves explained to her in detail how the level of the outcrop upon which the castle was built was slightly lower here than elsewhere, and so the rock had been cut out a little more to make a dungeon. It could only be reached through this door. The air that came up into her face was cold and humid and had a taint of midden stench. She shuddered with a feeling of terror far greater than the moment warranted. A feeling like a premonition threatened to overpower her. It came as a sense of helplessness, and terrible cold, and terrible, terrible fear.

Yves produced a rope ladder. His dark eyes were bright. "Would you care to go down?"

"No! Thank you, I can see what it is." The thought of being locked up in such darkness, with no escape, with the weight of the whole fortress bearing down on her, made her feel weak. *Helen Oaks.* The name of the woman buried alive in Toomesby's graveyard swam to the surface of her thoughts.

Yves smiled nastily.

Uneasy visions of that vault lying below the chamber tower haunted Norah for the rest of the day. Her tour of the castle had left her listless in another way as well: she'd seen no place for herself, no position to occupy. Conniebrook had existed for many years without a chatelaine, and seemed quite capable of existing thus in the future. Jervais could make a place for her, but clearly he was not about to.

She saw him again at midday. He didn't speak to her when he came into the hall to take his meat. He seemed bent on a policy of treating her like an object of furniture—by day, at least. Listening to his talk with William Goings, she gathered that he had completed an inspection of the nearest fields of his *demesne* and had satisfied himself that the quality of the sheep wool was up to that stipulated by a contract he had with a Flemish merchant.

His talk of the outdoors and all that was happening on the land made her restless. She'd been shut up for so long, first in Bermondsey Castle, then in the litter during the journey north. Today she hadn't had even a moment to get up on the wall walk to see beyond the castle's inner ward. How many times had she dreamed of how happy she would be if she were only here. And here she was, amid days that she would remember all her life—and what she would remember was that she had been unhappy.

Reaching for a dish of eels, Jervais's glance met hers. She'd been staring at him and felt abashed to be caught at it. He stared back at her for a moment, with his jaw clenched. She pretended to bend her attention back to her meat. The food was delicious, the wine light and cool, tasting of how she imagined France, but she could eat and drink little of it.

William Goings continued his unabated discourse. At the other tables men and women were eating off their trenchers as fast as they could put food into their mouths. In the mammoth fireplaces, driftwood flashed and flickered, providing most of the light in the dim hall. There were changes needed here. For instance, plenty of sunlight was falling right outside the closed shutters of the hall windows. Yves should have them opened, at least for the spring and summer months.

A page reached to refill her wine cup. It was little Lloyd of Clarence. His face looked flushed and puffy, as if he'd been crying again. Had he been misused once more by his master, Sir Oakley?

Taking advantage of an interruption in the bailiff's discourse, when he paused to spit out a mouthful of small bones, Norah touched Jervais's sleeve. "My lord?" He turned that cold look on her again. She shuddered, but said anyway, "I would like to talk with you about the matter of servants. Yves sent me a maid, but I shall need three nurses for Roger—and," she rushed on, "I think I would like to have a page."

Without waiting for him to respond, she half-turned in her seat. "Lloyd, would you like to be my page?"

A shy smile dawned on the boy's face. "Yes, my lady."

Jervais said in a low voice, "The lad is young."

"Yes, he is. A fault he cannot mend but through time, no matter how often he is beaten for it."

"Beaten?" He looked over his shoulder. "Boy," he gestured Lloyd closer, "are you being mistreated?"

"N-no, my lord."

Jervais dismissed him, his eyes swinging back to Norah.

"What answer did you expect? The man you trust with the charge of the young pages has been thrashing that little lad for the sin of being young and homesick. Anyone with eyes can see that he's miserable. If you wish to hear the truth, and not simply what is most convenient for you to believe, perchance you should take your questions to Sir Oakley himself."

Her head rang with her own words as surely as if a cymbal had crashed and a horn soared right by her ears. Jervais's face narrowed; his eyes wore a cowl of winter. But before he could answer, an older page came to the head table with a whispered message for him. He listened, frowned, then nodded. A few moments later, a young man entered the hall and made his smiling way to the head table. He was very tall and thin, very poor looking, and yet somehow he seemed charming. He had a deep voice, cultured and pleasant. "My lord, I am Andrew Pastor, a troubadour, at your service."

"Make yourself welcome, Andrew Pastor," Jervais said, "and after you've eaten, you can entertain us."

The young man was entertaining indeed. He was about Norah's age, innocent in aspect, obviously ardent and moved by life's laments. He sang in rhyming stanzas of the great Abelard, Heloise's lover, and several other songs with exquisite lyrics. When done, he asked Jervais if he might join the household for a time.

Jervais's silver eyes traveled over him with sharp regard. Norah had been subjected to such looks and had found them unsettling. Andrew, however, simply waited. Jervais said, "Where do you hail from, troubador?"

"Originally, I was left in a bundle at a baron's door—a waif, my lord." He sounded quite untroubled about it. "Since I was twelve I have migrated from one castle to another, regaling whatever audiences will listen to me. Once I was privileged to sing for the queen. She loves literature and music."

"Yes, I know the queen." Jervais paused, then abruptly added, "I would be glad for you to join my household."

"My lord, I am overwhelmed. I assure you, you won't be sorry. I know love lyrics, war songs, witty satires," he showed a fleet grin, "and though I'm humble in origin, I have been trained from my youth in courtesy."

"Yes, well, in this castle are some who could learn from you then." His eyes flicked in Norah's direction. The troubadour also looked at her. Jervais said, "My wife."

Norah felt a flush of shame at how scornfully those words passed his lips. By night in the tower room he might insist on his husbandry, but it seemed that by day he intended to act the injured man.

Yes, I know the queen.

After that reference to the queen, she was upset and yearned to escape, but the troubadour was smiling at

311

her. He bowed. "I am honored, my lady. May I sing something just for you?"

She nodded, keeping her eyes on his hands that were long and thin, musician's hands, while they plucked the strings of his lute. The song was French. It began:

> *We'll to the woods and gather May*
> *Fresh from the footprints of the rain*
> *We'll to the woods at every vein*
> *To drink the spirit of the day.*

Norah found her arms rough with goose bumps. The verse seemed to suit her perfectly, it being an expression of her love of the freedom of the woods and the weather. How could a stranger know her so quickly and so well? When he was finished and had bowed again, she said, "That was lovely. Thank you very much."

"Nay, 'twas my pleasure, lady." He laughed. It was a mellow, easy laugh—which was either very artless or completely comprehending.

Any formality between Kate and Andrew Pastor seemed, in Jervais's opinion, to vanish quickly. The troubadour had been in residence at the castle only two days when Jervais first became disquieted by the long conversations going on between him and Kate. Andrew seemed to find her significant and richly absorbing. They often used the native dialect whose racy expressions Jervais didn't always understand, and there seemed to be a familiarity in their talk that disgruntled him.

She entertained him variously in the hall and in Jervais's bedchamber. She seemed to prefer the chamber, where it was lighter and she could work on the embroidery loom that her page had unearthed in one of the storage rooms. (Jervais had given her Lloyd of Clarence after learning that Oakley was indeed chastising the lad over-zealously.)

Since the weather was fine today, and both the chamber door and the door to Jervais's office were left open, he couldn't help but overhear scraps of her conversation with the troubadour. Their voices, if not their exact words, wound down through the still air of the spiral stone staircase. Hence, as Jervais tried to concentrate on his accounts and scratched out notes for William Goings about the work on the farms, he was always half-aware of Andrew's voice alternating with Kate's.

The companionable chatter echoing down the narrow stairs became an increasing annoyance. When the youth made some unheard comment and Kate laughed at it, the sound brought back from across the years the memory of Eleanor in Antioch, laughing lightly in the sun of the prince's gardens.

Jervais leaned back in his chair and stared at the parchment upon which he'd been writing. He put his quill in the ink bottle and twirled it. Other voices, other worlds. The ecstasies and physical yearnings of first love. He'd been tall and slender and young, and to a youthful and unhappily married Eleanor he'd seemed quite handsome. Was it possible that this was how this Andrew Pastor seemed to Kate?

His attention was sharpened. Their voices began

to hang like a dark storm brewing on the horizon of his mind.

He'd made love to her the last two nights, as was his right. And he'd found more than sexual relief, something far more than that. She'd responded, but perhaps not as whole-heartedly as she had in the past, and if he were truthful, he would admit that that bothered him. He realized now that he'd nursed the prideful notion that her passionate response meant that she must be in love with him. But what if she weren't? Strange creature that she was, she could probably separate her heart's desire from her body's as completely as any man could.

He thrust his hand into his hair. The idea that she could care for anyone else, in any way at all, rattled him. Deep inside, he knew how stupid he was being. Unless he kept her under lock and key, of course she was going to speak with other men, perhaps even befriend them, as she had befriended that peculiar peasant who followed her about like a pet dog. She might even fall in love—and what did he care?

His hand descended trembling from his head to his ribs. There was an ache there in his chest. The accounts before him seemed a tangle he would never set in order. Work of this sort always tired him far beyond any physical labor. His chair creaked as he extended his legs out under the table. Sitting like this wearied him. He hated anything that took him off a horse and made him bend himself to fit a piece of furniture—yet he'd been finding reasons to stay in the castle. These accounts, for instance, could be worked on in the evenings. Why did he find it so hard to separate himself from that woman!

314

By midday his mind was floating in fatigue. He'd had enough. And enough and more of the whispered sweet-nothings that continued upstairs with no sign of stopping. In a sudden rise of exasperation and impatience, he found he could not listen another minute. He got abruptly to his feet and forced himself out of the castle.

By evening he was better—he thought. Until he suffered the two of them together again at supper. Andrew had taken the seat to Kate's right. Jervais had set himself a policy of steadfastly refusing to talk to her any more than was absolutely necessary, and his knights were following his lead. But this troubadour had set no such restrictions upon himself. He sat next to her and their continued conversation stropped Jervais's nerves. And salted them. By the end of the meal he felt like choking her, like thrashing the boy, like jerking her away, like forsaking her forever, like giving her over to the troubadour with a quiet dusting off of his hands.

That night he made love to her for a long time.

The following day he met with his master builder in his office. It was breezy outdoors, and he had a page close the shutters on the narrow windows to keep Master Philip's drawings of two new devices, one for lifting stone and another for sawing timber, from blowing off the work table.

When the builder left, Jervais again turned to his accounts. He told himself he only had the records of the household on a parchment roll to go over, and he may as well do it now and be finished with it. However, snatches of talk and laughter soon came wending down from the chamber above. Mixed with the wind, they seemed today to have distinctly amorous overtones. Without forewarning, his imagination suddenly presented him with a vision of Kate leaning into the boy's lanky body. He dismissed it at once, yet next his ears began to imagine the sound of kisses and sighs.

He shook his head. He tried to shut it out, but—

He saw the boy crush her to him, kiss her deeply, and worse, he saw her responding.

Reason was immediately lost, drowned beneath a dashing, deafening roar of emotion. He flung down his pen and took the stairs two at a time, burning to catch them unawares, to confront them with their perfidy.

He rounded the last curve of the stone stairs and appeared abruptly in the doorway. Kate glanced up from her embroidery loom. She smiled expectantly, as though actually pleased to see him. He didn't return the smile, but just leaned his shoulder against the doorframe and surveyed them.

The scene appeared completely innocent: she was there at her loom, the boy was sitting in a window—not even near enough to touch her. Everything was sharp, stark, intense beyond enduring. Every one of Jervais's heartbeats thumped against his skull. He stared from one to the other, hating their companionship, this communion they enjoyed, in which he had no role.

He had their complete attention. Kate's smile gradually lost its spontaneity, yet it stayed there, stuck on her face. The moment strung out as fine as the thread in her tautly upheld needle.

For the first time, he looked at the troubadour's face

316

properly. It was a pleasant face, perhaps a trifle thin, the nose a trifle broad. Confronted in return by Andrew's cool and silent eyes, by his straight and unblinking gaze, an unreasoning animosity sprang up within Jervais.

He said nothing; instead, he turned to leave—without having said a word to either of them. As he took his first step toward the stairs, he felt as if he were stepping out of a pillar of fire which surely must yet be ablaze behind him. The jealousy which had for a moment cindered his mind slid away, leaving him feeling like a fool, as dumb as lumber.

He climbed up to the wall walk, where he drank the sunshine and leaned into the wind, inviting the fierceness of it, wanting it in his face, needing the last ashes of that ridiculous emotion swept out of his head.

Jealousy! How could he feel such a thing for a peasant woman, a sorceress who had wormed her way into his life?

The door behind him opened. He knew it was her without even having to turn and look, for she carried with her an aura that surrounded him with a silent, terrific jolt to his senses, a jolt that stayed. He felt as if a lightning bolt had struck and now stood shimmering directly behind him.

Her voice sliced through the eerie silence of that moment: "My lord?"

He turned, took her in, her beauty, her tresses that were black ribbons in the wind, and that look that said, *What is wrong?*—as if she really cared! He felt a rush, a current through all his body, the same as the one time he'd felt one of his teeth crack, or the time he'd suddenly, all in an instant fallen in love with Eleanor—that rush of excitement and horror that had jolted him the split second before the pain began.

And so he knew the pain was coming, and as if to get it over with, he abruptly embraced her. He gathered her into his arms and crushingly plundered her mouth.

He felt himself giving way, slipping slowly into ecstasy, bliss. Though he had her clenched against him, though her mouth was his, his body called for more. *More.*

He wrenched himself away. He held her by her arms and looked down at her and said, "You're too damned beautiful! God help me, you're too beautiful! Who . . . what . . . what in God's name *are* you?"

Chapter 20

Every night Jervais made love to Norah, every night she watched his sandy-haired head move lovingly over her breasts while he kissed them, while he kissed other parts of her until, every night, she felt the onset of that intimate dizziness, that ultimate delight. And every morning she felt less happy, less hopeful. Everytime she looked into his eyes she saw his desire for "Kate," beautiful, seductive Kate—but she did not see love.

She was in their chamber today, her only refuge in this castle full of people who mistrusted her, and Andrew had followed her here after breakfast. It had become his habit to follow her everywhere. When he sighed for the third time from where he sat in his favorite window, she said from behind her embroidery loom, "Andrew, you are so quiet."

"I'm in mourning, lady."

Her needle stopped. "Has someone died?"

"Nay." His gaze remained as cool as ever. "But I have fallen in love, and, alas, it is a hopeless love."

"No love is hopeless," she said, though the words sounded hollow.

"Mine is. The lady is married—to a wealthy and powerful man, a man who is already suspicious of me, and jealous, I think."

Norah had been alarmed, thinking he'd meant her at first, but now she was reassured. Jervais, he of the unrelenting, unscrupulous resolution, would never be jealous of her.

She went back to her embroidery. Who would have thought that her time in the nunnery would actually prove to be of use to her? But she enjoyed embroidery, as a pasttime, if nothing else. And in truth, she had nothing else to do with her time, beyond feeding Roger. His care, otherwise, was largely overseen by the three nurses Jervais had provided.

Andrew sighed again. The sound irritated her. He had been a part of the household for scarcely four days, and already he'd followed her about so much that she was weary of him. To be sure, his company was better than no company at all, but there were times when she would just like to be alone.

Hence she said, "Andrew, I feel sleepy."

He unfolded his long legs out of the window. "Are you feeling unwell?"

"Oh no," she smiled, "I'm just lazy. Since Roger is with Lloyd and his nurse, I think I want a nap. Would you mind if I excused myself?"

"Well, I could go watch the knights play at their jousting for a while."

She knew he wasn't the least bit interested in knights, or jousting, and she felt guilty for her ruse, but one can stand only so much companionship.

To ease her conscience, she did lay down for a moment after he left. Far from being tired, however, she was bursting to find some outlet for her energies. She needed to do something.

She felt like a sneak as she stepped out the chamber door. She half expected him to be lying in wait for her. She listened. No sound came from above or below. She tiptoed down the stairs. As she came around onto the landing before Jervais's office, she heard voices coming up from the hall. Yves was directing some bit of work and, as usual, was threatening to do something quite horrible to whoever it was he was bullying. This time he was going to dispose of the person's remains in a revolting manner. Norah lost heart for venturing down into his realm.

The door to Jervais's office stood ajar. She peeped in. It was empty. His morning fire had collapsed to a mound of ashes. On an impulse, she went inside.

She took in everything, foolishly enamoured by the simple clues and clutter of his private life. She touched a leatherbound book he'd left on the mantle. It was Greek, she believed, Aristotle perhaps. One of the pages was marked with a ribbon. She wished she were more literate. She could read and write French, but not without a struggle. If she could read this book, perhaps she could discuss it with Jervais, perhaps they could talk about it.

Eleanor had probably read it.

Had she been defeated from the start? Eleanor would never allow herself to be shunted aside for all but the fulfillment of her husband's physical desires. But then Eleanor was a queen; it seemed natural that her strength and guile were beyond Norah's.

She turned, just listening to the silence. From the open, narrow windows she heard the gulls and the water sloshing below on the narrow beach. She noted that Yves didn't keep even this room terribly clean. Cobwebs floated like dead skin from the ceiling.

On the work table were several parchment scrolls. These were probably the castle accounts—Master Philip's accounts telling of the stoneworkers' wages, Yves's untidy accounts of the castle, and William Goings's reports of the estates. She thought as she fingered them that those who worked with Jervais seemed to admire him.

The door behind her suddenly swung wide. She turned. "My lord!"

Jervais stopped upon seeing her in his private domain. "What are you doing in here?"

His look shocked her. "I was exploring and—" she made a helpless gesture, "I just happened in, I guess."

"You have no business in here."

"I'm sorry." She smoothed her skirts nervously. He said nothing, and she felt obliged to say more. "It's only that I feel so useless. You're always so busy— you overwork yourself, I think—and I have nothing to do beyond play with Roger and idle over my embroidery and chat with Andrew—"

"Andrew, yes. Where is he, by the way?" He came further into the room, scattering a feeling of impending disaster before him. His sleeves were rolled up, showing his powerful forearms. "Seeing you without him is like seeing you without your shadow. How can you bear it? When I asked him to

322

join the household, I didn't realize he was going to spend every waking minute with you. I must say I don't like it."

She didn't like his tone. It made some stubborn remnant of pride rise up in her. "Why not?"

"Never mind."

"But I do mind." She minded very much! "I think you're implying something. Something shameful."

He laughed harshly. "That's rich—coming from a woman as bold as a harlot."

"I'm not a harlot!"

"No," he jeered, "you're a perfect rose. A rose with a peculiarly putrid scent."

The tension was unbearable. It seemed he stood there behind a tree of thorns, a wall of thorns twined twig into twig, thorn upon thorn. Her anger melted toward frustration, toward tears. Lest she cry in front of him, lest she be reduced to a running nose and a face blotched and puffy, she said tightly, "By your leave," and stepped past him to the door.

On the stairs, she kept her back as straight as a duenna's. She climbed past the bedchamber and emerged on the tower walk. As she opened the door, all the gulls on the ramparts rose up into the bright April sunlight, wild great herring-gulls, their cries echoing the silent cries in her wild heart.

The weather was brisk. An east wind was blowing gusts of sun and shadow across the sea. Low clouds were forming and dispersing to reveal an egg-shell blue sky, blue overhead, blue in the distance. Down on the narrow beach, the tide was coming in. The line of white rollers was hazed in spume. She took all this in with the unconscious part of her mind. She was too hurt to do more than register it, for she'd allowed him to hurt her again.

He didn't matter! It didn't matter if he thought of no one but himself! How would he like to experience what she'd experienced all her life, being ignored, and ignored, and ignored? He was so smug, so self-righteous; he had such extraordinary powers of insensitivity and dim-sightedness, this earl of Conniebrook! And as for Andrew, why, that was preposterous!

Wasn't it?

She began to stroll along the wall walk, which would take her all the way around the inner ward. As she passed a pair of guards, she bade them good day and gave them a preoccupied and not very happy smile. They looked at her slantwise, then at one another, as one work horse looks at its yoke mate. She hardly noticed.

Progress was being made on the north portion of the new outer wall, which was rising up from the building site, two hundred and fifty feet long. A winch was hoisting large blocks of stone into position, and the laborers' shirts clung to their backs with sweat. She was spotted, and they passed the word from one to another that she was there, until nearly every crowbar, sledgehammer, square, measuring cord, and saw was stayed, and every mason, mortar maker, and carpenter, every plumber and common digger was looking up at her. One man shook himself like an excited dog. She didn't notice.

Near the two U-shaped gate towers, she looked down toward the village. She picked out a few shops selling produce, fish, and ale. The town was divided into lots, each holding a house, some livestock, and a garden.

She proceeded on. From the southwest tower of the castle, she could see some of the farmland. Far away, a man opened a gate and climbed a hill to where two milch cows grazed.

She moved on. Charles came out of the garrison building and crossed the courtyard below her, making for the blacksmiths' shop on some errand. He looked up, then shaded his eyes in order to see her better. A little dog came and began to run circles around his legs. He gave no attention to this little fiery particle. Norah hardly noticed either of them.

Near the chapel tower, above the small postern gate, she gazed off at the brown sheet-silk bay that the mouth of the Barset River made. On this side of the castle, the new outer curtain hadn't been started yet, though the building lines were marked out with stakes, ropes, and measuring rods. Between the river and the castle lay the exercise field, where Jervais's men-at-arms rehearsed their wars. A few of the knights were relaxing from their labors with a dip in the river.

The shadows of the day were just starting to lengthen when Andrew found her there. She was disappointed to see him coming, for she simply wanted to be alone. Why was it that the one person she wished to avoid was the only one in all the world who didn't seem to possess the will to ignore her?

"Here you are," he said. "I've written something for you, my lady."

She gave him a polite smile. "Read it, then."

He seemed suddenly shy as he unfolded a small

parchment. "'I tremble as a lyre at the touch of my mistress . . .'"

It was a love poem. Decidedly a love poem.

"'. . . you are noble and sweet, faithful and loyal . . .'"

It aroused a flurry of emotions in her. She was trying to think how to respond. At Eleanor's court, knights and ladies regularly exchanged amorous poems, but Norah was unfamiliar with such things.

"'I love chivalry, truth, and honor, but my love for you is greater than all these together . . .'"

From a corner of her eye she saw movement in the courtyard below. Jervais was rapidly climbing the staircase up the inner face of the massive wall toward them. She automatically snatched the parchment away from Andrew and hid it in her hand behind her back. At the same time she arranged her face into a bright, guilty smile.

He'd known. Even before she did, Jervais had known that this troubador fancied himself in love with her. And she'd thought him completely blind to her. Hope flared anew, only to be put away by the need to deal with the look on his face as he gained the wall walk.

He said nothing to the troubadour, only flicked his fingers in dismissal. Andrew's face glowed as red as a fire, but he bowed and disappeared. Meanwhile Jervais did not take his eyes off Norah; they fixed her harshly. His breath was coming fast—from his run up the stairs? He said, "I don't want you wandering about on your own up here again."

"I wasn't alone," she prevaricated, giving him a tight-lipped smile. "I had Andrew with me."

326

"He just joined you. Before that, I saw you myself, strolling along by the gate towers without an escort, letting every man for a mile gape at you."

She considered this. Her smile had dissolved. She said, "I didn't realize I wasn't supposed to be seen. I could wear a veil, like an Arab woman. Or I could spend the rest of my life in our chamber. You could lock me in."

"That's a possibility—unless you prefer the dungeon. That also could be arranged." His tone was blandly vicious.

"And would you visit me there every night, visit me as you do now? And leave me again before daylight so that no one might guess how well you like to lay with—"

"Come with me!" His voice cut in like a swift blade with the hard ring of steel.

He led the way back to their chamber, while she trailed obediently after him. She felt the deepest possible uneasiness, a premonition that something was about to get out of control, that she must take extreme care.

Theresa was in the chamber with the nurse who had been feeding Roger bits of soft foods. Seeing her son, Norah suddenly longed for his warm and rounded softness in her arms. Jervais looked wrathfully from one servant to the other, until the nurse put the baby down under a coverlet bordered all around with marten fur, then she and Theresa scurried out and shut the door behind them.

Jervais immediately turned on Norah. His eyes held the bright cold fire of diamonds. "You are indiscreet, woman. Your conduct is unseemly of

327

your position."

She wanted to scream, *What is my position?* Instead, she asked, "What exactly have I done?"

He took a step toward her—and was abruptly too close. "You think I'm blind? You think I can't see what every naked eye in this castle can see? Give me that note you're hiding in your hand."

Her heart stopped; she forgot to breathe. She handed the scrap of parchment over with the greatest reluctance.

He took it, read it, then read it again. From beyond the glassed windows came small noises: gulls crying in the somnolence of the aging day; the floodtide creeping up the shore. In her mind, Norah recalled the damning phrases of the poem, and when Jervais didn't look up from it, and didn't look up from it, she said, "It isn't what you think. Only this morning did I realize he had perhaps become infatuated—not with *me* so much as—"

"Not with you?" He read aloud the lyric which openly proposed, "*'Lady, touch me, body and heart, and take me for your love.'*" He crushed it in his fist. "The boy wants you! You've become his *raison d'etre*," he said scornfully. He threw the poem like a stone into the fireplace. "I should pity him. No one knows better than I what your sorceries can accomplish in an otherwise sober man. No one knows better than I how you plant seeds of bewitchment and how they grow and spread, like choking vines."

Her guilt pierced her. She'd never thought it would come to this; she'd never meant to become his tormentor. She felt the desire to console him, to place her hand on his cheek and murmur, "Jervais."

328

He went on as if he were waging war against her, ferociously, savagely. "I've been naive, for I thought you were content to seduce me only, because you wanted to be an earl's wife. I see, however, that now that you have what you want from me, you intend to try to seduce others—for the pleasure of it, I assume. You want to stretch out your wings as it were."

She would have defended herself, but when she opened her mouth he talked her down, raising his voice: "By God's precious soul, I doubt you would turn down any man who appeared vaguely presentable. You're utterly shameless. You fill me with despair and disgust. You were a whore when I first took you, and you're a whore now."

She felt the color drain from her cheeks, and felt the tears rush to her eyes. She whispered, "By what warrant do you say such things?"

"If it weren't for you, it wouldn't be necessary for me to say them. You're the one who came sneaking and pushing into my life. You wanted to be my wife; you dazzled Henry and all his court to get me for your husband. Very well! Now I am your husband—and now you must sleep in the bed you've made for yourself."

She throttled her pain enough to try to counter his anger. "Just what do you imagine I planned to do with Andrew? Lie with him—a wandering troubadour? Scheme with him, I suppose? Strangle you, strip the castle, and head for France?" she ended, her tongue tripping along, saying wild things, thoughtless, hasty things.

He leapt on her words with the speed of a cat on a bird. "No, you will not lie with him, not with him nor anyone else but *me!*"

She bit her lip, took a deep breath, and said, her voice coming out vivid and high-pitched: "And not with you either. Never again."

There was an ominous pause before he said, "You think not?" He made no effort to keep the derision from his voice as he fired his final malicious arrow: "Don't forget you are my wife—mine to do with as I like."

She stared at him. Was this the face of her love? She looked about her. It seemed all this chamber and its furnishings were alien to her. She felt contained and cold and part of naught she saw. As she looked back at him, it seemed she did not recognize this man with whom she was quarreling. She didn't know this earl of Conniebrook who stood before her as big and distant as a mountain, nor why she was here with him. She turned for the door.

He moved quickly, caught her wrist, stopped her. "You're not going anywhere."

"Let me go." Her voice was rough and low. "You hate me, you despise me, you find me loathesome—you said so on our wedding night. You've said so in your actions every day since. Well, I'll relieve you of my presence. Isn't that what you want? To be rid of me?" She hadn't exactly forgotten little Roger, but for the moment her memory was purged of emotion. She was disconnected from all the shackles, all the weights, all the commitments and duties that had held her. "Let me go." She twisted her wrist in his hand.

"You're not going anywhere. I am the absolute master of this castle—and of you. I'm not a light-tongued troubador but a plain spoken knight, and I say that a woman like you is worth only what I make you worth to me. From now on I intend to indulge myself with you—without any of the restraint or sense or temperance I've practiced before."

The realization of what he meant, that she was his chatel, that there was nothing he couldn't do to her—that he could beat her, hold her prisoner, throw her down the castle well—and that she had no one to protect her, no one to appeal to beyond him, struck her like a fork of lightning. His arms came around her, his formidable arms, and he lifted her as if she weighed less than a feather pillow. He was so startlingly quick that she found herself swept right off her feet. Her heart stuttered, then found a faster beat as he carried her struggling to the bed. He tossed her down and fell on her. She recognized the look on his face, that look of hunger which considered only itself. "No!" she cried in a thin, frantic voice, "don't!" But as her mouth opened to say this, he sealed his lips over hers. His arms held her so that she couldn't move her head, and his tongue filled her mouth. She beat at his shoulders and pulled his hair until he found her wrists and held them tightly.

Lifting his head anon, he said fiercely, "Look at me, Kate, yield to me! *Yield!* Or so help me I can't promise not to hurt you!"

She began to weep. Her long hair was pressed between her back and the bed, and it anchored her head for another deep and assaulting kiss from him. Though she shuddered and sobbed, the kiss went on. But gradually his mouth gentled. His lips became more purposeful, the kiss became a conquest. He plundered her even more deeply, yet more slowly and carefully as well. She stopped fighting him. He let go of her wrists and embraced her. "Yes, Kate, be sweet for me." His voice throbbed with quiet victory. He moved over her, sensuously, as if he couldn't get close enough to her.

Her fear faded; desire took its place in her. She felt a sensation like rising through murky waters toward light, toward music, such music as had not yet been written. She pressed her hips against him and felt his fierce passion.

"I have to have you," he murmured in her ear as his hands felt her breasts through her dress. "I have to, you know that, don't you? You do this to me. You make me feel everything at once, hatred and desire, fury and joy."

Her mouth softened and trembled, and she said, "Jervais, I never meant to make you unhappy."

His hand swooped to pull up her hems, and his sudden caress, intimate, powerfully erotic, shocked and weakened her.

He rose up onto his knees and began to undress her, not letting her rise or even sit up, but pulling things off her in haste until her body was a white field ready for him. "You're so beautiful . . . here . . . and here." He lavished her with kisses, and with compliments. "You have such lovely skin, so clear the veins show beneath it like smoke."

He pulled off his own clothes—his sword belt, his dagger, his shirt, boots, and hose—and when he abruptly took her, she cried out softly.

When he was finished, he lingered over her. He lifted her chin and bent to take another kiss from her lips. His tenderness filled her with a softening torment. She had not been satisfied by his impetuous need; she still wanted him, and dared not make the slightest movement to dislodge him.

"This is impossible, ridiculous—I can't get enough of you!" he said roughly. He was speaking of the fact that he was still swollen within her. He reached beneath her to hold her naked bottom, producing a groan from her. He moved, thrust into her with much more deliberation than before. She muffled her cry against her closed lips. He lifted himself so that he could watch her breasts quiver as he thrust into her again and again. She saw his distress behind that blank, watching expression. He was voracious, and yet, despite his threat, he seemed to be holding himself severely in check.

She ached with desire. Her heart was pounding. She wondered if he could see her excitement. Of course he could. That was why he was watching her so intently. She gave him a pleading look; she was all ardent appeal.

Then her eyes misted over, her crisis drew nigh, nigher. When it took her, he too lost control. He embraced her, crushed her vulnerable breasts to his hard chest and kissed her, her face and her hair. This went on long enough that her climax receded, and she quietly returned his kisses. The only sound, besides their breathing and kissing was the low boom of the breakers against the ramparts of rock far below.

The lord of Castle Conniebrook and his lady did not appear in the hall for their supper. While others ate, Jervais and his Kate slept, entwined and naked, the bedclothes pulled over them carelessly. It was very dark when the baby woke them. Jervais pulled on a dressing robe and poked his head out the door to order food for them, then he returned to sit cross-legged on the bed and watch Kate suckle the infant.

Their food arrived and, surprised at himself, Jervais found himself offering his wife bits of boiled chicken from his own fingers. He held her cup for her to drink. He'd only once before known such feelings—on that journey to London with her. He didn't trust them, wasn't even sure what they were. Contentment? Happiness? Hope? Whatever, in the midst of this attack of carnal fever these hours alone with her and his child were sweeter than honey, sweeter than ripe fruit.

The night nurse prepared the babe for his cradle while Kate remained inside the curtained bed. The knowledge that she was there, naked, waiting, excited Jervais, and anon, when the nurse went out, he returned to his spellbinding wife.

Her clear eyes seemed to see into his mind as transparently as if he had spoken, and when she raised her arms to welcome him, the gesture drenched him with fire. She surrendered at once and totally to his third embrace, which was the most sundering of all. He felt the basses of his body throb in witching chords.

When they fell asleep again, he was exhausted and finally sated, both physically and by an exultation of spirit that he could in no way have described to anyone.

Chapter 21

Norah awoke before dawn. For a little while she lay relaxed and smiling, remembering. She turned her head to observe with deep satisfaction the sleeping face that occupied the other pillow. Jervais had one arm tucked beneath his head, the other rested over the blankets. She touched his wrist as she would touch a chalice, just for the sheer delight of feeling the shape and curve of it with her fingertips.

Her light touch disturbed him. She drew her hand back, loathe to wake him. Her own drowsiness was gone, replaced by a glorious energy. She cautiously sat up, turned back the covers, and got out of bed.

Since she had no dressing robe of her own, she put on his. She looked briefly into her son's cradle, then went out the chamber door. She put her finger to her lips as she met the eyes of her page in his rolled-out pallet there on the landing. She gestured him back to sleep. She crept up the stairs where she knew she would find the day breaking new upon the world.

As she leaned against the battlements, she felt the

first rays of the rising sun faintly warm on her face. She brushed back her touseled hair. It was madness, but all she could feel was unbelievable happiness. Happiness foamed within her and would not settle down. *He loves me,* her heart kept singing, while her mind argued, *He's made love to you before, and each time you've felt that this time he loves you—and each morning he always seems to regret his passion.*

"But not this time," she murmured aloud; "he loves me truly now, I know it!"

The morning sea was a luminescent blue-green in the dawn, but Jervais hardly spared it a look as he stepped out onto the wall walk from the tower. Kate heard him and turned. She was radiant. Her eyes were like blue-shadowed green silk. Her hair fell over her shoulders, over her arms, and down her back. His stare drank deeply of her beauty, deeply of her poisoned draught. She gave him a winsome smile that said things to his heart, and he had to steel himself not to return it.

She was wearing naught but his chamber robe, and therein he found his first foothold back to sanity. He said, "You shouldn't be out here in that."

"I wanted to see the sunrise. And it's so early, no one else is up."

"The watch is up." His eyes skimmed away from her. He had risen and dressed as soon as he'd heard her leave the chamber. He stood now in the cool of his spent emotions, idly fingering the hilt of his sword. "I would have thought that after such an orgy of rutting even you wouldn't need to tempt a man—

not for a few hours anyway. I warn you, if necessary, if it's the only way I can get a little peace from your wantonness, I will have you under lock and key, as we spoke of yesterday."

A silence very different from any other fell betwixt them. He could almost hear his words strike her and penetrate. She seemed to die on her feet. Standing there at the ramparts with the first arrows of the rising sun catching in her hair, her smile died, as well as all her animation. Some of her beauty seemed to die, too (though not all, not all). Her eyes looked at him without life. Her expression, or lack of it, caused him an uncomfortable feeling that this time he had gone too far.

Impossible words of apology sprang to his tongue. He must not say them. She was two things: the peasant sorceress who had bewitched him and forced him into humiliation after humiliation; and this new thing that menaced him even more, against which he must take desperate action. Even now confusion was climbing in him at the sight of her, and he knew that escape was the only thing that could save him. He must find some way to protect himself from her, he must think of something, but first he simply had to get away from her.

He turned, only stopping at the door to say, "You'll notice that your troubador, young Andrew Pastor, is no longer in residence here. He was shown to the gates right after he delivered his little love poem to you yesterday."

Without a word more, he left her.

* * *

Norah arrived at the chapel just in time for morning prayers. Moving like an automaton, she climbed to the balcony and knelt beside Jervais, who did not look at her. The priest read the psalm for the day. The castle knights and servants knelt in the lower room.

Norah bowed her head. *Dear God, what have I become?*

Something evil, came her answer. *Your father was right; you are the spawn of the devil.*

She'd never meant to blight Jervais's life, but clearly that was what she was doing. And blighting her own in the process. And sooner or later she would blight Roger's. There was only one thing to do, only one way to make amends.

After morning prayers came breakfast. At the end of the hall, a hatch was opened out of the kitchen through which servants passed out the bread and ale. No one spent more than a few moments eating it; few even sat down for it. Yves was there, watching closely to make sure that no one ate better food than he deserved, for there were different kinds of bread, from fine white wheat to coarse rye, and different grades of ale, and each class of castle-dweller got only his own kind. Norah accepted her small loaf of fine wheaten bread and her horn of French wine. She somehow swallowed this down, every crumb and drop, knowing it might be some time before she ate again.

It was Lloyd, her page, who helped her escape. He brought her a set of clothes "acquired" from one of the older pages, which fit her fairly well. There was a pair of hose of the choicest red, close-gartered, and shoes, and of course a shirt and tunic. She bound her

338

hair up under a cap. Lloyd went to tell the grooms that a horse was needed to carry a message for the earl. While he was gone, Norah paused over Roger's cradle. "My son, you will never be out of my thoughts, never out of my heart."

Leaving him quickly, before her will broke, she shut the door of the chamber and started down the steps. She felt like someone torn in two.

The high-beamed great hall was not empty when she crossed it, but it was a measure of the success of her costume that she did not excite anyone's particular attention. Not even Dick seemed to note her passage.

She hoped Jervais would not be cruel to Dick. She would take him with her, but he was slow, and she needed to move swiftly just now.

She hoisted herself up onto the black mare which Lloyd held for her outside the bronze door. Next, the boy created a diversion at the gates: he pretended to run and fall full length on the cobbles and set up a wailing that distracted everyone.

On the road, Norah started out calmly. As much as she wanted to gallop away, she couldn't afford to attract any undue attention. She had no plan. She expected nothing. She knew only that she must go. As she passed the fields and climbed the road up the hill, two men on the slopes, working a yoke of oxen, turned to watch the earl's page ride by, out on some errand for the castle, no doubt.

She left the road as soon as she could, and vanished into the leafy shadows of the forest. The hours seemed both to speed by and to stand still. Noon passed. Then pinpoints of late afternoon sun flashed through the foliage. Then came the cool and scented evening; the forest faded to a frescoing of shadow upon shadow. Soon it would be night.

She was not afraid of outlaws. Jervais had been vigorous in routing them out, and she knew she could sleep in the woods without fear. She was more afraid of being chased and seized and fetched back. She was more afraid of Jervais.

From his office, Jervais could hear the water murmuring to the beach. A mist was rolling in, a dark tide of fog. There was no breeze. All was quiet and still. He sat at his work table looking at his steward who had just come in to say:

"My lord, your lady seems to be missing. That is, well, she can't be found anywhere."

Jervais looked at him blankly. "What do you mean she can't be found?" He'd been out on his horse all day, as far from the castle as he could get. He'd assumed Kate was here. He realized, too late, that he'd *counted* on her being here.

"Her maid says she hasn't seen her all day." For once there was no sign of the yeasty side of Yves's temperament; he was clearly panicked, which alerted Jervais more than anything else. "The babe began to fuss at noon," Yves went on. "He's crying hard now, as you can hear."

Jervais had heard the baby crying in earnest up in the bedchamber, but he'd tried to ignore it. Slowly the meaning of that crying became real to him: she'd abandoned Roger; she was gone.

"Kate," he said to himself. Then, *"Kate!"* He

wasted no time getting free of the furniture: he exploded into a standing position. His chair fell back with a clatter.

He stood in a silence so intense that he knew Yves—and Charles, who was there, too—were unnerved.

Had she gone after the troubador? That festered sliver of jealousy which he had not been able to pluck out suddenly erupted.

How dare she make him want her, *need* her, and then try to leave him like this! His blood was a river that was running riot. He said to Yves, "We'll have an accounting for this, you and I, but for now, find a woman from the town who can suckle the babe. Then have my horse and six men-at-arms ready to accompany me in fifteen minutes.

"Charles!" He began to strip off his coat and shirt. Charles was already holding out the quilted yellow linen jacket he wore beneath his mail. Jervais glanced at the windows. Christ, the sky was growing darker by the second!

Yves was moving slowly toward the door. Jervais shouted, "*Move*, you old nip-cheese, or I'll take a red-hot poker to your arse!"

Yves disappeared. Jervais pulled on his hauberk, and Charles tied up the sides. The weight on his shoulders always took a moment to get used to; he swung his arms while Charles got his sword.

The men were waiting for him when he strode out of the hall. Their kite-shaped shields were fastened to their saddles, and their heavy swords were braced on their thighs. They were bursting with excitement. They were wearing their Conniebrook cloaks, and one carried Jervais's scarlet standard, the bear and the lion eternally engaged in combat.

Jervais pulled on his gloves, then vaulted into the saddle of his horse. Charles handed up his helmet.

"Where are we off to, my lord?" asked one of the knights, a gapped-toothed man, brawny and big-boned.

Another knight muttered, *"Hist!* Mark his temper."

Jervais answered, "To find a page who has stolen a horse." His voice was rough and dry. He gigged his horse around and headed toward the castle gate.

Norah had been riding for an hour the next morning, through unfamiliar country, when she spotted an old Roman signal station, a ruined tower built centuries ago. It was a familiar landmark of the easternmost edge of Ramsay land. Her page's boot tapped her horse as she climbed toward it. At the top of the mound she drew in her reins. From here she could see Toomesby in the distance, and even the old cramped castle of her birth. To think that Jervais had been this near all those years—a mere two day's journey—and had never bothered to visit her. It bore thinking about.

She dismounted and stood in the thick, yellow-green grass. A light wind whispered in her ears. Her weariness and saddle-soreness and hunger weren't her only miseries. She missed Roger terribly, and not only because her breasts were uncomfortably full. She felt unsure of this impulsive flight now. She'd run from Jervais before, and what good had it done

342

her? Yet it wasn't for herself that she was doing this time. It was for—

The sound of hoofs reached her. They quickly grew louder, until they drummed—hoofbeats moving at a canter. With a spurt of panic she started for her horse and gathered its reins, but then seven men-at-arms rode out of the woods into view at the base of the mound all at once, all wearing Jervais's red. Seeing her, they milled.

Her horse reared its head, probably recognizing the scents of its stablemates. Norah knew in an instant that there was no use trying to escape. She was only a modestly skilled horsewoman. Jervais would run her into ground. She stood as still as a stone in the long grass, waiting, clearly visible to the men below.

One horse started up the slope. She closed her eyelids and saw the sun, blood red, through them. When the sound of the horse got close, and stopped, she opened her eyes.

Jervais had reined in and was staring down at her. His helmeted head was dark against the immensity of the bright sky. His face was in shadow, but his eyes were lit, silver, fiercely luminous. "Get on your horse," was all he said.

She'd never known the Jervais who led the journey back to Conniebrook that day. Damp with sweat, pale, his eyes peculiar and haunted, he was the most intimidating man she'd ever faced. They rode hard, mile after mile, until Norah thought she might fall off her mount. She tried to hold on with one hand so she could use the other arm to support her breasts, which were hot and hard and full of milk. Every bounce made them hurt, until the pain was excruciating. Her cap came off, her pins fell out, her hair tumbled in long untidy loops down her back.

The last silver-grey of the gloaming faded over the horizon, and the constellations appeared, heaving with portent. It was full dark when they rode through the wooden palisade of the town; then, at last, the entourage clattered into the inner ward of the four-square castle.

There were people here, but not one of them spoke. Norah dragged her right leg over her mare's withers and sat sideways, praying that when she slung herself down her legs would support her. Before she was ready, Jervais appeared and reached up for her. His grip on her waist was cruel, and when her feet touched the ground, he transferred that cruel grip to her arm.

She was so stiff she could hardly walk, but he had no sympathy for that. Icy and implacable, he strode long-legged into the hall, pulling her stumbling along with him. All eyes turned toward them, from the most elderly knight to the youngest cavalier. Norah had no time to feel her humiliation, for in the back of her mind sat the awful question, *What is he going to do to me now?*

Yves intercepted their progress toward the tower door. He had little Lloyd by the neck. "My lord, I found the traitor who helped her."

Jervais glowered down at the boy who was pale-faced and trembling. Norah, weary as she was, felt all her protective impulses rise. She said through stiff lips, "He is no traitor; he's just a boy."

Yves ignored her. "Does Sir Oakley have your permission to whip him? And then, my lord, I think he

344

should be sent home in disgrace."

The boy hid his face in his arms and sobbed.

Norah lunged forward, despite Jervais's grip on her, and managed to take the boy away from Yves. She felt the shivers of terror that were pouring through the lad. Her eyes darted from Jervais to Yves and back to Jervais again. She saw a vein jumping in his temple. She said, "How can you blame him for obeying me? I took advantage of his naiveté."

"He's a disgrace," Yves said; "he should be whipped."

"No," Jervais said grimly, "she's right. The fault is hers." He glowered down at the boy, however, and said, "You and I will talk. For now—" to Yves, "bring him along. Let him witness this—as a lesson."

He took Norah in hand again, and started across the sour, matted rushes toward the chamber tower. In the tail of her glance, Norah saw that Dick had risen at the far end of the hall, but then Jervais was hauling her through the tower door, and she lost sight of him.

She looked up at the dark turn of the stairs—but instead Jervais steered her into the basement storage room. Yves came with the boy behind him. Charles came in, too, and stood behind the page and the steward with a torch, which illuminated the chamber with a gaudy, flaring light. Jervais said to his squire, "Put that in the sconce and open the trap door."

Those words came to Norah with a shock far worse than if he had asked for a birch rod, which she'd fully expected.

Charles hesitated. He gave Jervais a look. Jervais

345

answered it with a thrust of his chin that said, *Do as I say!* Charles obeyed, though he moved with a suggestion of some invisible weight, as if a coat of chain mail were slowing him.

He moved a hogshead of wine, then hauled the trap door open by its iron ring. The clammy, sweating air of the dungeon came up into the chamber like the smell of something foul escaped from its grave. Lloyd stopped sniffling and wrinkled up his nose. Charles made a muttered oath of surprise. Yves, however, eagerly produced the rope ladder. Jervais's eyes met Norah's. He didn't speak, merely gestured again with his chin.

Her face felt cold and clammy; gooseflesh had risen all over her body. "My lord . . ." Her voice was nearly inaudible.

There was no relenting in his stance. His expression had none of his usual control in it. He said, "I'd just as lief see you in hell, but this will have to do for now."

She had the feeling that if she didn't climb down the ladder on her own, he might throw her down. She saw now the full fruiting of her actions. She'd played with enchantment, reached for something too rich, too fine, and now Jervais could not live without her—nor with her. There could never be any truce or peace between them.

Dick appeared outside the open door, a look of confusion and worry bunching his odd-eyed face. "Sister?"

Yves took it upon himself to call a guard: "Put this dolt out of the castle!"

Jervais was still looking at Norah with such

346

singleness of purpose that it stunned her. She took a step toward the gaping hole. Another step. She went to her knees on the rough wood floor and forced herself to reach for the rope ladder. No one helped her. If her hands slipped or her feet failed to find the rungs . . . She swung one leg down, then the other. She climbed like a marionette, all strings and joints. Tears started in her eyes. She couldn't help them; she was so afraid she hardly realized they were there.

The pit was *cold*. It was like descending into a well of cold, brackish water. Her breath came in sobs, and her pulse pounded as she placed one foot and then the other on the dungeon floor. It was solid stone. She looked around her quickly, holding herself tight. She heard a sound—the darkness was awake. Were there rats? Vermin? Snakes?

Ghosts?

The air reeked of a dozen fetid odors, some of which would not bear contemplation. And there were shadow shapes. Torture equipment? It was too dark to tell.

She looked up at the square of light a dozen feet or more above her. Her streaming eyes met Jervais's. An unnoticed sob shook her. She stood there and looked at him, stared at her husband with round wet eyes filled with terror. Long and long she looked at him, until abruptly he stepped back out of her sight. She heard his great, deep voice say, "Close it."

Charles's voice filtered down softly, "My lord, I beg you to reconsider this."

"I did not solicit your opinion," Jervais said, equally softly—but there was bloodshed in his tone.

"You will regret this, my lord."

347

"I deal with my wife as pleases me, squire. You have not a hair's width of right to interfere."

There was a pause. Then came, "But I have every right to refuse to take part."

In the end, it was Yves who hauled up the ladder. Norah heard a peculiar whimpering and realized it was her own throat making the same sound she'd heard coming from the cell that stood among the graves of Ramsay.

The trap door slammed down. The boom resounded in the vast stone pit while at the same instant she was cast into utter darkness. Immediately she was hurtled back into the helplessness of her youth—that confused girl who had been thrust into a nunnery, unloved, rejected, entombed for life for the fault of being . . . evil.

She heard Jervais's muffled voice. Something was dragged across the wooden floor over her head. He was weighting down the door with the hogshead of wine. Next she heard footsteps . . . and then perfect silence, disturbed only by a suggestion of the sound of the ocean. And now and again a rustling and scratching of something alive.

She held her eyes painfully wide open, yet could see nothing. She tried to calm her imagination. If there were rats, she could kick them—as long as she could stay on her feet. How long would that be?

(Was Helen Oaks still alive within the lichened stones of her graveyard tomb? She'd been walled in there ten years ago. Was she still talking crazily, or had she fallen silent at last?)

Norah stood, hugging herself, her arms crossed over her swollen and aching breasts, her fingers gripping her shoulders, unmoving, afraid to move.

A moment passed with no loosening of the grip of her terror.

An hour passed.

And because no mind can withstand such a squeezing clench as that for long, her thoughts gradually surrendered, gradually disappeared, gradually a dreadful trance of emptiness opened within her.

Jervais ate his supper alone in his office, dismissing Charles with a glare. And he sat alone after eating, the servants who had attended him having wisely vanished. He sat with a cup of Gascony wine, staring into the fire. He could hear the muffled sound of his son upstairs, a continuing cry that seemed weary and without hope. The infant was not taking well to the milk of the *damosel* Theresa had found. It was some woman named Wulfa. The child's little bleating, despairing cries went on and on. Jervais flattened the heel of his hand against his forehead. The child had never cried like that when Kate suckled him.

Kate, Kate, Kate—her name set up an echo in his head. *Kate. Wife. Witch.*

What was the extent of her power over him? He found her beautiful and desirable—*too* beautiful, *too* desirable, irresistibly so.

Was that all? Was that the width and breadth of her powers? And with such a puny weapon she'd pitted herself against him? Why? She'd engendered darkling desires in him, and then, foolishly, stupidly, opened her arms and let him vent them upon her.

She'd opened her arms, her body, even her heart. She'd opened herself to his ravishment—and to his scorn, his anger—and finally to his vengeance.

Why? Merely to raise herself up to be an earl's wife?

It made no sense, no more than did her attempt to run away—which brought up a whole slew of new questions, such as, why, when he knew without a doubt that she loved Roger, had she left the child behind? She'd left her great friend, that ugly peasant, as well. And where had she meant to go? Not to find Andrew Pastor; common sense told him that. Where then? Back to some hut in the woods?

But if she really was a harlot and a sorceress . . .

Was she?

If not, then who . . . what . . . ?

Still the child cried, as though purposely to disturb him and wring some reaction from him. Kate could quiet him in a moment. Her breasts must be full and over-full. What did that feel like? Was it painful? Into his mind flashed his last sight of her, her face looking up, wet with tears, her arms wrapped about herself against the cold and her terror—and against the pain in her breasts? No doubt. She and Roger needed one another. She was the only mother the babe had ever known. She probably missed him as much as he missed her.

How could she have left him?

Jervais knew how. He knew the exact moment she had decided: yesterday morning on the wall walk when she had turned to him with her beautiful hair uncombed and falling about her, with that winsome smile—which he had killed with his spite. With his fear.

His meal churned in his stomach. He had to do something about that pathetic crying, which seemed to be growing fainter, guttering out. He hadn't realized how much he depended on Kate to care for Roger. He'd taken for granted her obvious love for his son. It was clear that those women upstairs didn't have an ounce of her instinctive ways with the babe. Jervais was going to have to do something himself— order the search for another *damosel* if nothing else.

He rose heavily, tossing the dregs of his wine into the dying fire where they hissed loudly. He went to the door and started up the stairs slowly. His legs felt too heavy for the climb. Midway up, they refused to go further. He forced himself to take another step, and another, but when he tried for a third, suddenly he couldn't do it. He felt tempted beyond wisdom by the agonizing memory of that small, pinched face looking up at him, those lovely green-blue-water eyes flowing with tears. He put his hands on the wall, leaned his forehead against the cool stone. He lifted his head an inch and knocked it against the wall. And knocked it again. And at last he turned back.

He descended past his office, his legs gaining will and speed as he went. He snatched a torch from its rack along the way, and at the foot of the stairs he pushed open the door to the storage room.

When he shoved the barrel aside and pulled open the trap door, he saw her immediately. She was exactly as he'd last seen her, except that she wasn't looking up anymore. He knew intuitively that her body had not moved an inch in all this time, as he instinctively knew that her mind had fled far from this terrible thing he'd done to her.

Chapter 22

Jervais threw the rope ladder down into the dungeon. It almost hit Kate, but still she didn't move. He swung down, descending agilely, using just his arms.

The place was awful. It stank of the cesspit in which the waste from the tower garderobe was collected. It was cold and dank and fearfully full of shadows. He wanted out as soon as his feet touched the stone floor. The torch in the storeroom above did little to light the place, and left obscure wastes of shadow at the dungeon's margins. If someone were to shut the door above . . . he tried to imagine how utterly black it would be. What kind of monsters came out of blackness like that? He tried to fight off his cowardly fear, hoping it was something he could govern. It wasn't.

"Kate."

She didn't look at him. Though she stood there in her page's hose and coat, her mind seemed to have gone elsewhere.

"Kate!" He put his hand on her face. Her tears had dried; her cheeks were cold. Her big, innocent-seeming, green-blue eyes were open, but their look was unseeing, glazed over with the soap-like sheen of uncut sapphires. "God in heaven." He took her arms in his hands and gave her a little shake. "Kate!"

Her eyes focused on his now, and he felt some relief, but not much, for there was no recognition in them.

"You have to climb the ladder," he said, shaking her again. He turned her toward it and took her hands from her shoulders one at a time and lifted them to the rope rung over her head. She grasped it, and her feet started up. He went up right behind her, his arms bracketing her lest she should lose her grip. (He prayed the ladder was strong enough to support their double weight.)

When she got to the top, he boosted her out. She crouched under the torch, hugging herself again. She was shaking violently now. He had no cloak to give her, so he pulled her up against him. She didn't release her cross-armed hold of her breasts. He lifted her and went out the door and started up the stairs.

He burst in on Theresa and the babe's night nurse, a gaunt woman with a bitter expression, and the *damosel*, Wulfa. They had made a pap and were all three trying to cajole it into the fretful infant. Wulfa was older than Jervais had realized. Her skin was beginning to crack into little spiderwebs of wrinkles. Could she have any milk in those sagging breasts? She and the other two stared blank-faced at the sight of him with Kate against his chest, her hair spilling over his arm. By morning the tale would be on every tongue in the castle, but he dismissed that thought as he started across the chamber for the bed.

He noted as he passed the women that Roger's color was a startling, mottled purple. As he cried, he tossed his limbs. Jervais's heart went out to him. For the first time he felt a purely paternal response.

He started giving orders. He wanted hot wine, and a hot stone, well-wrapped, to put at Kate's feet. Theresa and the nurse left Wulfa to contend with the fussing child as they scurried to do as they were told.

Jervais laid Kate on the bed. He tugged the boy's hose down her legs, and pulled the tunic and shirt over her head. A little riot of desire broke out in him. At any other moment, at any other time . . .

He thrust her beneath the bed clothes. Theresa had wrapped a stone and was shoving it under the sheets where Kate's feet were. Jervais called her attention to Kate's swollen breasts. "What can we do about that?"

He'd told Yves to pick a girl to be Kate's maid. Jervais had never detected a trace of warmth in this string-haired Theresa. Certainly she never laughed, and as for making a jest—it seemed it was not in her. She made a sound of embarrassed surprise now as he showed her Kate's naked breasts, then she said, "I suppose the best thing is for her to feed the little one—if she still can, if it's not too late."

"Bring him."

Wulfa didn't want to give the child over. Jervais heard her hiss something about "That one's in a pact with the devil!" Several more snappish words passed betwixt her and the maid. Jervais lost patience. "Bring him here!" The whiplash authority in his tone acted like a handslap across the old woman's mouth, and made her give the child to Theresa.

The hot wine arrived. Jervais stepped back as the babe's nurse and Theresa used pillows to prop Kate onto her side so that Roger could relieve her of some of the pressure in her breasts.

The child quieted immediately and went to his work. Kate groaned. The other women were silent. Jervais felt their disapproval for this wife of his. Theresa began to spoon the hot wine into her. Jervais backed away and stood feeling useless by the fire. He twisted the garnet ring on his middle finger. A voice seemed to sneer, *Jervais Le Strand, such a gentle knight!*

The babe fell asleep at Kate's breast, sated and exhausted. The nurse put him back in his cradle. The women one by one gave Jervais a curtsy and left.

He went to the bedside. He watched Kate with a sense of wonder, and even awe, for despite her ordeal she was bewitching. She had the perfidious beauty of a water undine who lured unwary men to destruction. The color was coming back to her cheeks, a most delicate pink—or was that sunburn?

Yes, bending nearer, he saw that she'd gotten sunburned, on her nose and cheeks and chin. Beneath it her complexion was as white as white cow's milk, however, and hence her long lashes seemed all the darker. Her lips were slightly parted, giving her expression a look of madonna-like innocence. She seemed young and fresh. Perhaps she was a sorceress, but she wasn't evil. In her sleep there was a serene artlessness about her. He knew he had never seen anyone as lovely in all his life. Not even Eleanor.

He straightened away from her.

The scarlet coverlet was pulled up to her shoulders. Candles stood in the holders above the pillows. Red candles. Had she done that, ordered special candles in his color? When? A goodish while ago it seemed, now that he considered it. He looked about and saw that there was a tapestry in the chamber that hadn't been there before, hung on the wall opposite the bed. Here and there were other touches, feminine changes that made the room seem more cheerful.

He realized for the first time how important this room was in his life. He'd been born here, it had been his home for his first years, and it was here that he'd brought his own son.

He glanced back down at the shimmering woman in his bed. Who was she and what did she want from him? And what did he want from her?

In the night, Kate began to move in her sleep. Jervais was awake in an instant. He turned toward her, touched her shoulder. She cried, "Don't . . . don't bury me! I'm not dead! Father, I'm not dead!"

"*Shhh*, you're safe."

She twisted toward him and wrapped her arms about him—with more strength than he'd thought she owned. He stroked her silken hair, suffered her desperate embrace, and after a moment she was deeply asleep again.

The second time she woke him that night, she only wept fitfully. She turned and held him again. Did she know who he was? Or was he the only person near enough to cling to?

In her third nightmare, her hand fretted at her hair.

"I'm sorry . . . sorry I'm not pretty."

That struck him as familiar. He'd heard her say that before, though he couldn't recall when—or why she would ever have occasion to say such a thing, considering her beauty. Yet it seemed so familiar. He cast back, trying to recall, and realized with a dull sense of wonder that he could remember every word that had passed between them since their first meeting in the circle of Satan's Arrows. And as far as he knew, she'd never apologized for not being pretty.

Yet he felt sure he'd heard her say that—when?

Norah woke to find the darkness fading and morning nigh. Jervais was dressed already, sitting at the end of the bed. His eyes seemed to bore into her. Without prelude, he said, "I'm going to have a bed put in my office today. I'll sleep there from now on." He seemed changed in some way she didn't understand. He didn't seem angry anymore—it was as if he shared her utterly drained state of being, as if he were sad, utterly wearied and saddened.

She said listlessly, "This is your chamber. I should be the one to move. Surely there is some other I could move into."

"Roger must remain here, and he needs you. Besides, I can't trust you too far out of my sight."

Her heart clenched hard. "Will I be locked in now?"

"Will there be a need?"

She closed her eyes. "Why didn't you just let me go?"

"Even if I wanted to, there is Henry to be considered. He warned me that he wouldn't accept any excuses if you were to disappear. Frankly, he'd suspect me of murder.''

She sighed. "But if you have an out of the way croft where you could send me, where I could make my own living, perhaps with Dick to help me, I give you my word I would stay there. If I weren't near, you would be able to forget me.''

"Would I?" It seemed the emptiness of the ages was in his face.

"Yes. There is a spell at work, as you have guessed, but it is on me, my lord, not on you. Let me go, stay out of sight of me, and you will soon be at peace again.''

His eyes narrowed. "So you are a sorceress.''

"I don't know what I am." She looked away from him. "Send me away."

"Even assuming that I could trust you not to disappear, what about Roger? He could very well sicken and die without you. I can't take that risk, any more than I could have him reared in a peasant's croft." He leaned a trifle nearer. "Why don't you just banish the spell?"

She looked him full in the eye. "I can't.''

"Well then, it seems we are caught in this together. You'll stay where you are. I'll do my best to avoid you, and all I ask is that you afford me the same courtesy.''

He seemed intently watchful of her through the following week, while at the same time he kept his distance. She did her best to help him. She kept to herself. She knew without a doubt that she was a curse on his life. The castle-folk knew it, too. Dick was gone, and though he'd never been a companion, she felt his absence keenly, for now she was surrounded by strangers and enemies. She had even become an incomprehensible enemy to herself.

A month passed. May became June and summer arrived. Norah more often than not took her meals alone in her chamber, but with the arrival of a visitor, Jervais sent word that he expected her attendance at the noon meal one day.

The guest seemed a man of high breeding. He carried himself as though the very space he occupied was important. Though he was bald, he was hardly older than Jervais. He was Martin of Daigh Lott, most lately from Roecester Castle. Over the smoking platters of venison and the great pots of spicy ale and the cheerful din and clatter in the hall, he told Jervais, "I am but an errant knight, Lord Conniebrook. As you see, I employ only an armor-bearer, because I can't afford to maintain a squire. My father had too many sons, and I am the youngest of all of them. Hence I'm a cavalier without a fief, or even a fitting residence."

"You must be seeking your fortune," Jervais said cautiously.

"I'm hoping that my fortune is seeking me," he answered with a lift of dark strong eyebrows over hard blue eyes. His looks were striking, if not handsome.

Jervais drained his wine cup. "Then you are at leisure to allow us to constrain you long enough to go hawking or to chase down a deer or two before you move on?"

"It would be most ungentle of me to refuse." Sir

Martin reached to help himself from a dish of duck eggs.

As the meal continued, it came out that he was a soldier of fortune indeed, the fourth son of a minor baron with little behind him to help him make his mark in the world. Last year he'd attended tournaments throughout northern France. He claimed that in ten months he'd captured and raised ransoms on more than one hundred knights.

The day after his arrival, in the drowsy afternoon, he found Norah playing a game of dice with Lloyd in a little used recess of the stairs of the chapel tower. It was a place she'd found that Jervais seldom frequented. When Sir Martin appeared, he was wearing a tunic of handsome blue cloth, slit to the waist in front for convenience in riding. His gold-colored hose were made of fine wool, cut on the bias and fitted to his leg. In greeting Norah, he took her hand as if to kiss it, but instead turned it over and pressed his lips into her palm—and sucked on the soft skin. She snatched it away as if he'd bitten her. She flushed, and had to rein in her immediate anger. Without the slightest change in his expression, he turned to Lloyd and asked, "And who are you, young sir?"

"Lloyd of Clarence," the page piped uneasily, confused by the interaction between this stranger and his lady.

"Sir Lloyd, it's a hot day. Will you fetch me a goblet of cool water?" As the youngster rose, Martin pinched his pink cheek. "He's a cute tyke," he said to Kate.

Lloyd looked back at them as he started down the stairs. Martin laughed. "Look at him staring after us as though he thinks I'll steal you."

Lloyd disappeared in the turning of the stairs. Sir Martin immediately leaned nearer; his eyes shone with unvarnished lust. "I *would* like to steal you."

He seemed to enjoy this teasing immensely, but at six feet tall, all of it well-muscled, he was intimidating to Norah. She instinctively disliked him. Seeking for a way to disarm the situation, she asked him politely, "How do you like Conniebrook?"

He winked one blazing blue eye at her and ran his tongue all around his lips before he replied. "I can tolerate the drone of country bees as well as any man, I suppose. Provided there are entertainments."

She struck around for another politeness. "You are most lately from Roecester?"

"I was banished from Roecester—for employing certain skills I have. Certain amorous skills. I succeeded a little too well with Lord Roecester's chatelaine."

Norah considered him. He was no golden-haired youth like Andrew. This was a man in his full powers. And she was alone with him.

He preened a false modesty. "It was a thing of the heart, you understand. She had blue eyes, and I'm very partial to blue eyes."

"Lord Roecester banished you?" She hoped her bland tone gave no hint of the dashing of her mind. Where was Lloyd? Could she rise casually from her seat and start down the stairs? Would he try to stop her?

Martin shrugged. "Roecester's an old man with a young and pretty wife. He has to expect her to take lovers." He eyed Norah. "It's said that you and Lord

Conniebrook are not exactly a love match."

"I can imagine what is said. However, that is no concern of yours."

"I would dearly like to make it my concern. An astonishing beauty such as yourself deserves a man who appreciates her. I know how to appreciate a woman. I am a lover of women."

The time for politeness had passed. She rose and looked him full in the eye. "Stay away from me, sir."

He caught her wrist as she started up the stairs. "Why, you're as pale as bone china. Are you afraid of Conniebrook?"

"Anyone who is wise is afraid of him. He can be a ruthless man. Pair that with a strong sense of possessiveness, and you have a danger that wisdom avoids."

He seemed all concerned. "If you need a champion, I should be happy to serve you—for a small price, of course. Nothing you can't afford. Nothing you'll miss."

"Let go of me."

He grinned. Still grasping her wrist, he pulled her hand forward and down to his crotch. "Meet me where we can be alone for an hour."

She was trying to pull away; he tightened his hold on her wrist mercilessly, so that she was forced to feel him intimately. "Stop it!" she said. Using the full weight of her body, she pulled back, wrenching her wrist from his bruising grip. She lost her balance and almost fell against the rising stairs.

"Of course." He gave her an amused look. "For now."

She glared at him, and rubbed her hand in the fold

of her skirts as if it were soiled. Her heart pounded. "I'm going to tell Jervais—my lord—what you have proposed the minute I see him. I suggest you leave the castle while you can."

He chuckled. "Just as you please. But methinks you're not going to tell him anything. After all, you're naught but a peasant, begot out of wedlock, no doubt, a whore forced on Le Strand by Henry as a lesson in humiliation. He's already had to throw you in his dungeon for fornicating with a common jongleur. Come, *my lady*," his voice was cracked and threaded with dreadful laughter, "promise to meet me, or I shall tell him that you've been trying to seduce me here in this lonely alcove."

A chill pierced her, turning her heart to ice.

"Ah, so you know full true that he would believe me."

As he took a step toward her, she turned and fled up the stairs. She heard him laughing behind her. "*Au revoir* then, my lady—for now."

He didn't follow her up onto the wall walk. She looked left and right to make sure no one had noticed the swiftness with which she'd emerged from the chapel tower. Her wrist hurt. It was marked by his grip and would show bruises by the morrow.

Twilight was descending. The sky was a muddy red and purple, and the edges of the scattered clouds seemed aflame. From the kitchen chimney, smoke rose blue and laden with the smells of supper. As she made her way to the safety of her own tower, she felt eyes watching her. Brilliant, intensely silver, unblinking eyes. But that was impossible. Jervais had ridden out with several of his men right after break-

363

fast. He couldn't know—and *wouldn't* know, for as Sir Martin had shrewdly guessed, Norah would never tell him.

All she could do was try her best to avoid the knight errant. To accomplish this, she stayed in her chamber for the next two days, not even going to chapel for mass. On the third day, Jervais found her sitting at her embroidery frame. As he came into the chamber, she didn't give him a smile. She'd learned to guard her heart at last. She only looked up questioningly when he said, "I'd like to talk with you."

"Of course." She gave Theresa a look, and the girl went out. But Jervais didn't go on right away. Norah said, "Do you mind if I continue?"

"As you wish."

She bent back to her embroidery. She was sitting before a window where the light fell on what she was doing. She'd plaited her hair into braids to keep it out of her way. Jervais came to the side of the frame. She felt shy of having him see what she'd done. In the center of the work was a crowned monarch at a table surrounded by men-at-arms. Along the edge she was depicting scenes of battle, women dancing, a castle, a feast, men hunting. The colors were clear, and she felt she was setting them well; she liked the faces especially. But it was one thing to like them herself, and another to have them looked upon critically by Jervais.

He said finally, "This is skillfully done." There was a hint of surprise in his voice.

"Thank you." She moved a little on her stool. "I find the work pleasant." After the journeys they had made, through the nights and through the days of their tormented relationship, it seemed odd to try to be merely social with him. She snipped her thread, selected another and began to work it carefully into a tree in the corner. He reached for her hand, and took it in both of his, and for an instant she was thrilled, until she belatedly recalled the bruises Sir Martin had left on her wrist. Quickly she said, "I pulled the door shut on myself. It was a silly thing—stupid really." She eased her hand away from his touch. "What was it you wanted to talk about?"

He seemed to come back to his purpose slowly. "I'm thinking of knighting Charles."

That seemed straightforward enough. She waited, and realized that he meant for her to comment. She searched for something to say. "He's certainly old enough."

"Clearly so. A man with his own mind now. There isn't much more for him to learn from me—except a habit of bad temper and actions that lead to regrets."

She didn't dare look at him. "If he is a man with his own mind, then you must feel you have done your duty well. Beyond a doubt, since you're an honorable and able knight, he has received training of enormous value."

"You think me honorable?" Not waiting for her answer, he went on, "I took him when his first master died. He has no father, only an elderly uncle on his mother's side. He was rather fractious at first, and tended to idolize me. He doesn't idolize me now."

"No one deserves to be idolized. Meanwhile you have versed him in all the customary occasions of a nobleman—"

"And some uncustomary ones."

"You will have to find a new squire."

"Yes. There was a boy with the royal court, Nigel of Stanmar. I know his father."

"Well then."

There was an uncomfortable silence. She glanced at him, and saw that he was staring at the bed. She busied herself in searching for another color, which conveniently kept her face bent over her thread basket.

Suddenly he asked, "Will you walk with me around the walls? You've hardly been out of this chamber for days."

Now she did look at him. What did he want? She snipped off her thread and set her scissors down.

At the door he said, "You may need a cloak."

She flushed. "I'll be fine."

He tilted his head to one side. "You have no cloak." His gaze took in her blue dress, which was one of the two he'd had Charles purchase for her in London—one of the two which she'd worn continually ever since.

She said, to cover her embarrassment, "It's a warm day. I'll be fine."

They went up into the sunlight, the soft wind, and the blue sky. Smoke, like tall grey plumes, rose and leaned away from the castle chimneys. As they strolled, he said, "I shall speak to Yves about providing you with things you need. I should have seen to it before this."

They were on the northern wall, and he pointed out this and that bit of work on the new construction. If the laborers noticed them, they certainly didn't stop to stare. Jervais commanded their respect, even if she didn't.

He spoke further of knighting Charles. He would need her cooperation, he said.

"Of course," she said, veiling her pain. "I will keep to my chamber. None of your guests will even know I'm here."

He looked at her sharply. "That's not what I meant. Whatever else you are, you are the countess of Conniebrook."

That was galling. "No," she shook her head, giving him a smile such as she'd never felt on her face before, an acrid little half-smile, "no, I am the peasant whore thrust upon you by the king to teach you humility. To teach you that you must not reach too high in love—a lesson I've learned far better than you," she added more softly.

He stopped. He said nothing, only stared down at her. It was the first time she had intimated that she knew of his feelings for Eleanor.

She said, "For Charles's sake, I will make one suggestion—in my vast capacity as your 'countess.'" She looked up at him sidelong. "Your steward is remiss, my lord. He should be retired."

"Yves?"

"Yes, Yves. Look about you while you are at your supper tonight. The floor of your hall is hardly covered with rushes, and those that are there are sour and soiled by the dogs and untold months of food scraps and bones. The smell is indecent. The shutters on the windows should have been opened as soon as the frosts were over. The host of underlings Yves oversees are lazy and uncaring, your butler and chandler among them, and no wonder, since Yves

367

terrorizes them one and all until they haven't the slightest sense of dignity in their work. It is only because of your master cook's pride in his skill that you eat as well as you do. Otherwise, your castle would be no more pleasantly fed than King Henry's court."

"Retire Yves," he said softly, but he commented no further.

They continued their turn of the castle wall. Down in the courtyard, men were at their various jobs. A smith was preparing to shoe a horse. A cooper was busy with his casks, along with his partner, the hooper. Norah and Jervais arrived back at the wall overlooking the sea. Jervais leaned his forearms on the stone and looked down at the beach below. Norah studied his handsome profile, and her heart throbbed with grief for what might have been.

He said, "I admired your courage in standing up for your page that night." They both knew which night he meant. "And though I can't say I care much for your peasant friend, I approve of your loyalty toward him. Which is why I still can't understand—" He straightened and shifted his gaze further out to the horizon where distant clouds stood like lofty snow mountains. There was a small change in his face. "Where was your loyalty to Roger when you left him behind to fend as he might? I had believed you loved him. You were like a mother to him. Was all that seeming care for him false?"

"I do love Roger!" Her face was suddenly hot.

"Then why did you leave him to the mercy of mere servants? That seems a most curious kind of love to me."

"I ran madly. I knew you would not neglect him and I . . . I ran madly."

"Why?"

One of her braids hung over her shoulder, and she wound its end furiously with her fingers. "Because I bring evil to those I love."

He seemed to think about this, then said quietly, "I wish I knew what manner of woman you are."

The urge to tell him the truth was so strong that her lips fell open, her tongue moved—yet she couldn't say it: *I am Norah.* A selfish fear paralyzed her. He needed to be saved from her, but she couldn't risk breaking the spell and perhaps changing into a monster before his eyes.

Roger! she thought defensively, *I must consider Roger, too, mustn't I?*

But it wasn't for Roger that she kept up this lie. It was for herself; it was out of fear for herself. She knew what was done to girls who were different, who had visions, who were protected by wild boars. They were exiled, entombed in nunneries, despised, starved. How much more vicious would be the treatment for a freak, something ugly and unnatural—which was what she might well become should her identity be revealed.

Words blazed up in her—not the full truth, but all she dared to tell of it: "I never intended to be what I am! I never wanted to bring unhappiness to anyone. I only wanted to—to *belong.* You can't know how maddening it is to live in darkness when you know that just beyond the walls separating you is all the light in the world." She glanced at him, then away again. "I never meant to do you harm, my lord.

But I have. And I will. You should have let me go.
You should cast me out now, today."

"What harm you have done me has seemed all pre-
meditated." There was not a trace of enmity in his
voice, though his pale eyes were cold.

"No. I am loyal to you in my heart. I pray for you,"
she whispered.

He turned from the sea. Together they looked
down into the castle court. The smith was still trying
to shoe a horse. The horse was fighting. It was Sir
Martin's war horse. The knight himself came out of
the hall. The smith shouted at him, and he shouted
back, and laughed. Norah felt as if a vague veil was
suddenly pulled back in her mind, and she got a
powerful feeling of dread, a low, thumping feeling
that rolled through her like nausea. "My lord, that
man," she said breathlessly, "he's not to be trusted."

The horse was kicking out at the smith. Norah
flinched and closed her eyes as if the hoof were about
to strike her.

"I marked that," Jervais said, without explaining.

The smith's hammer rang out. The horse, who had
calmed down, shuddered luxuriously. When Norah
looked up, she found Jervais giving her a questioning look.

"You always want to know about me," she said
savagely. "I can tell you this: I'm strange, different. I
have dreams. I get feelings about things, feelings
other people don't have. I don't understand it, I've
never understood it, but the things I see in my dreams
and the things I feel . . . happen. And just now I feel
very strongly that Sir Martin of Daigh Lott is—" Her
hand went to her head. "I feel some curse." The

370

feeling was building, building. Her head hurt. She felt faint. Her voice fell to a fierce whisper. "He's not to be trusted! Jervais, you must believe me!"

"Stop that!" The sound of his voice boomed around her like a bursting sea. He took hold of her arms and gave her a shake. It seemed the day had darkened, or was it only her sight? He started to pull her toward the chamber tower, searing under his breath, "You're not so much strange as just a plain *lunatique!*"

She stumbled along after him, half-blind, weak, sick to her soul with fear.

Chapter 23

Martin of Daigh Lott lingered at Conniebrook. Norah felt like a prisoner in her chamber, though she was confined by her own fear and not by locks or walls. She was not completely idle, however; she was taking certain steps: she was weaning Roger, and she was praying for strength. Hence it was when she was alone in the chapel one morning that the knight errant finally caught her again.

The few candles left from the morning mass were guttering, their flames almost lost in the sunlight pouring red and blue through the stained and patterned windows. From beyond the glass came the whispering lap of waves. Norah had made it her habit to come and pray after the others had left. She was knelt in the balcony reserved for Jervais, praying ardently for her wickedness to be forgiven, and yes, even for the evil spell to be lifted. *I am weak, I am vain. Lord, you must do it. You must let Jervais see me as I really am, no matter what that might be now. Let him be free of me.*

When she heard a step and looked over her shoulder, it was to find Sir Martin behind her. He stepped out of the shadows of the stairs. He leered and slapped his empty gloves against his thigh. He crooked a finger, beckoning her almost larkishly. "You've been avoiding me, Kate."

She pretended to finish her prayer in order to gain a moment to think. But her mind was so full of dread that thought was impossible. When finally she rose, she said crisply, "Sir," and attempted to go around him.

He blocked her way, of course. He leaned forward, huge and strong, his eyes glittering, his bald head boiled-looking and naked in the dramatic chapel light. "Come, my lady, it's quite taken my heart to see you with your head bowed down, your little neck bent, praying so busily and looking so nunnish and pious. I must insist."

"Insist on what?"

He raised one thick brow. "Why, a kiss will do for a start. It becomes a knight who practices courtesy to claim a kiss of any beautiful woman. If I didn't, you might think I don't recognize what a treasure you are."

"Let me pass."

"Or you will tell your lord?"

"I will this time; I swear it."

"Oh, I tremble, fair one. You will tattle to the great, the only Jervais Le Strand. Ha! The devil fly away with him! Lord Beta, I call him—the second letter of the Greek alphabet—because methinks Jervais of Conniebrook must be second best at everything. If you were mine, you wouldn't tell my rivals that I was 'dangerous.' You would tell them that I am the *best.*" He caught her in his arms. "As you shall soon see, sweet one."

His mouth came down. She turned her head; his wet lips slid over her cheek. He chuckled and fastened his hand in her hair. "Don't be coy, Kate." She felt his fingers against her scalp as he dragged her head back and arched her spine. She struggled.

"Don't take on so. You're soon to be granted a glimpse of paradise on earth. Have you ever seen how greedily a calf nuzzles into its mother's udders? How the first bees scramble into the flowers? That's how I'm going to nuzzle into you."

She mewed with pain as he forced her to the floor. When she tried to call out, he stuffed his leather gloves in her mouth. His lips found her throat and sucked. She could get no leverage to throw him off. His hands were bunching her skirts up her legs. He pressed himself between her bared knees.

Be ready, she told herself; *be strong enough to bear it.* But who could be that strong?

Suddenly his hold on her slackened. As she pushed away from him and spit the gagging gloves from her mouth, she saw a tall cloaked figure—Jervais. The point of his dagger was embedded in the side of Martin's throat, not quite cutting into his flesh.

"Beta?" Jervais said, oh so quietly. "That we must test."

Bracing herself against the railing of the balcony, Norah whispered, "My lord—"

"I would love to test it." Martin slowly got to his feet. He stood stiffly, facing Norah, with Jervais's dagger still at his throat.

"But not with my wife. No, on the jousting field."
Jervais stepped back, removing his dagger.

"Joute à outrance?"

Martin managed an aristocratic half-smile as he
turned to face his challenger. The glances they
exchanged were like edges of ice rubbing together.

"A fight to the death."

Martin gathered himself and bowed. "Be it as you
like."

"In one hour."

"One hour." Martin nodded and started to go.

He turned at the door and glared at Norah. "She's
been begging me with winsome looks for days. She
led me here with a gesture, no doubt knowing you
would come upon us—which was why she was
playing at resisting me. I see it now." He gave Jervais
a glance which ruled a straight line from blue eye to
silver. "She's only a common whore, Le Strand."

Jervais transferred his stare to Norah. She rubbed
her mouth, which was still full of the taste of the
knight's foul gloves. "You aren't really going to fight
him?" she said. She trembled before the determination in his face. "He told the truth; I invited him."

"You haven't been out of your chamber for nigh a
week, except to come here. Yes, I've had you watched.
You've kept yourself like a nun, talking to no one,
not since the day he accosted you in the alcove on the
stairs—and left his marks on your wrist."

"He couldn't help himself! It's the spell! It gives
me a fearful power. It seduces and lures and forces a
man to act against his will. If you can't help yourself
against it, how could he? Cast me out! I'm not worth

this trouble you take."

He stepped forward and took her arms in an iron grip. "Tell me the truth for once!"

When she didn't answer, he swore under his breath and turned to go.

"Jervais! Don't fight him. It is pointless."

"The man has dishonored my wife, and thereby dishonored me. And my honor is not pointless."

She heard his steps clatter down the stone stairs. A man would die today because of her. She felt ill. "Jervais, forgive me, forgive me, I never meant to bring you harm."

She started after him, but she had to slow on the stairs, for a heat focused on her: her body was sprinkled with sparks, the edges of her vision charred. She saw, not the spiraling stone staircase, but a horse, gleaming and foam-flecked, a war horse. It was rearing madly, about to come down upon . . . upon Jervais! Jervais was about to die!

Charles handed Jervais his lance. Scarlet ribbons streamed from its tip. Norah stood wringing her hands. Flickers of intuition still shivered up and down her spine: this was going to be a day of disaster.

It was the hour of noon, and the three of them were under a tree outside the town's wooden palisade. Onlookers had gathered along the side on the knights' training field—groups of peasants and shepherds, castle folk and village people. Most of the masons had come as well, so that the perpetual clamor of their building activities had for the time being fallen silent.

The quintains had been hastily removed from the field. Some eighty of Jervais's knights stood in tense impatience, watching their lord, watching Sir Martin of Daigh Lott.

The knight errant's armor-bearer attended him at the far end of the field. He pulled his war horse's head up, and the animal reared. It was hung with little bells at the breastband. Charles paused to watch. Jervais said, "Even his horse has ugly manners." Charles grinned, but his face was pale.

Norah felt sick in her soul. Fear lay in her stomach like a leaden ball. Jervais mounted his own horse and hung his shield from his neck. His armor was beautifully burnished but completely plain. He was prepared as for regular battle.

He folded the mail mittens of his hauberk down from his wrists until they covered the backs of his hands, leaving only his palms bare to take his lance from Charles. He braced it in its rest, upright like a flag pole. His back was as straight as a wall as his horse curveted. The stallion's hoofs danced, and his heavy neck arched. Jervais leaned forward to scratch it along the base of its mane. He handled both weapon and horse expertly.

His eyelids were narrowed; beneath them his eyes were the same burnished grey as his armor. There was a look of desperation as well as iron decision in them. He leaned low to let Charles put his helmet on his head. When he straightened, his nose had disappeared behind the iron nasal. His voice sounded hollow as he said, "I'm ready."

"My lord," Norah implored, "you are a fool."

He turned his horse so that he faced away from the

noontime sun. With the light on his brilliant helmet and his chestnut horse gathered like a knot, he pierced her with a look. "Yes," he said, "let the sinful truth be told: I am a fool."

A pang of guilt twisted her stomach.

Sir Martin put his helmet on his head. It was crested with a monstrous figure, the head of an ogre of some kind. He threw out his chest like a rooster. He had complete mail leggings and wore a sleeveless cloth surcoat of brilliant white over his hauberk. His sword scabbard was brightly painted, as was his shield and lance butt.

They were both ready now. Neither was a weakling nor a pretend gallant. And this was no joust for mere amusement or for the prize of a lady's smile. The sequence was already agreed upon: lances, until they broke, and then swords. They would continue the battle afoot should either be unhorsed. They would continue the battle until one or the other of them was dead.

The field ran north and south. The sun shone across it. Behind Sir Martin, the River Barset gleamed like dull pewter. Jervais backed his chestnut abruptly, as if cocking a crossbow. The horse tucked its chin to its chest. And then he let the charger go.

Sir Martin gripped his upright lance, set his shield, and put his satin-black horse straight at the chestnut. Two shadows of fused man-and-beast swept over the tall grass. Norah's heart slammed painfully within her breast.

Jervais was a fighter of battles rather than jousts, yet he hoped to unhorse his opponent in this first charge. He encouraged his horse with, "Forth . . .

forth!'' as he put his left arm through the straps on his shield and reached for his lance.

When he was about fifty paces from his enemy he spurred his destrier into a harder gallop and lowered the weapon. He positioned it close against his right side and slanted it across his body so that it projected beyond the left side of his horse's head. He consciously lifted his fingers, one by one, off on the butt, taming his tension.

Martin also took aim. They met at a headlong gallop, each with his lance poised to knock the other out of the saddle. Just at the instant of impact, Jervais thrust his legs out before him and jammed his feet into his stirrups; he braced himself against the high back of his saddle. But he knew a heartbeat beforehand that he'd misjudged his angle. His lance struck off center and merely glanced off Martin's brightly painted shield. He braced his legs all the harder to meet Martin's strike.

The knight's blue eyes were like hard pebbles in the shadow of his helm. His face was sullen but unwavering. The tremendous thrust of his lance smashed into Jervais's shield. The padding for Jervais's arm, meant to help take up the shock, seemed nonexistent. He was slammed into the cantle of his saddle, his breath was knocked out of him. He felt the shock of Martin's lance splintering with the impact. He ducked his head instinctively. Those splinters could be as dangerous as anything. More than one man had been killed or badly wounded by them.

Jervais was not injured, however, and with an oath—"Breath of Christ!" he recovered his seat.

Martin's horse had sped by, and as the man dropped his now useless lance, Jervais heard him shout, "Thus the sheep are separated from the goats!" Jervais tossed away his own lance and hauled his chestnut around after the braggart. He discarded his scarred shield, dropped his reins, and commenced to control his war horse by his knees alone as he reached into his saddle scabbard and flourished his great, heavy sword.

Norah stood frozen, fighting wave after wave of nausea. Jervais's blade swung above his head like a stream of light. The two cavaliers hacked at one another until blood was streaming down their arms. The crest of Sir Martin's helmet was reshaped with dents. Their frantic horses were barely kept under control. About the field, men were shouting, but Norah heard nothing but the rushing of the blood through her head. She made low sounds in her throat.

Dick Jackson was frightened because he could see that Sister Katharine was frightened. After being ousted from the castle, he'd hidden in the area but kept a watch on the place. Sheltered now between the field and the palisade, where there was a dip in the ground screened by brambles, he watched the contestants dealing one another great blows with their two-handed broadswords, five feet long and *sharp*. Wounds were being given. There was blood. Dick repeated two words as if they had some magic power: "Sister Katharine . . ."

Martin swung his sword, and Jervais ducked yet again. He registered what he'd often thought during the hot forays of the war: that the hiss of a blade cutting through the air is louder than any other noise in the world. In the heat of battle, Martin conveyed an animal hunger for violence as strong as the hunger for life that seemed to seethe from deep inside of him. Jervais, on the other hand, was less than completely certain he wanted to survive this challenge. But habits are hard to break, and his sword continued to counterattack. He felt it make contact and cut through the man's armor. It was only a thigh wound, but he knew he had driven several links of the man's own chain mail into his leg. *Beta!* he thought, *fie!* as he regained some of his old confidence.

Norah's vision faded to the queer, phosphorescent darkness of a snowy night. In the dungeon beneath Conniebrook her mind had learned how to simply detach itself from this unsympathetic and unrewarding world, and for a while the grueling occasion went on without her. A pair of the most pitiful screams she'd ever heard was all that recalled her. She forced her eyes to focus—and shouted wordlessly at what she saw:

Reduced to savagery, both horses had collided with a tremendous shock. Men and mounts had all four gone down near Norah's end of the field. Sir Martin lay unmoving, his head twisted at an impossible angle. His horse, however, was struggling to rise, neighing and showing its teeth like something gone mad. Jervais's horse lay thrashing only twenty paces from Norah. Jervais lay half beneath it as the animal kicked and tossed atop him, its wide, pale underbelly heaving and bouncing across Jervais's thighs. Through the horse's left foreleg the bone showed, ragged-edged. It struggled to stand, and fell again, and Jervais yelled.

.Charles rushed out to take the horse's head and to help it stand. After a second mighty lunge, it rose onto three legs, but then it just stood, coated with dust and sweat, shaking violently, balanced precariously right above Jervais.

Sir Martin's horse, now also on its feet, charged at the injured chestnut, ready to continue the fight even without its rider. Charles held onto the chestnut's bridle with all his strength, for if the animal moved, it would surely trample Jervais.

A castle knight, a hale man, short and thickset, ran out to try to divert Martin's horse, but the animal was wild. Jervais's chestnut lifted its head and screamed as the black horse—terrifyingly close to Jervais—reared. The thickset knight was forced to duck aside. The war horse's hoofs came down not a foot from Jervais's head. And it reared again.

Grief like a fearful flash of lightning swept through Norah. She glimpsed Jervais's death, and the revelation was so stark, so dreadful, that she burst from her shocked stance. She ran directly for the snorting, plunging destrier, directly under its great pawing hoofs. Waving her arms, she pitted her fury against the war horse's.

The wild animal was snorting. Part of its long mane hung over its bulging eyes. It swiveled a little on its back legs. She heard the little bells of its breastband just before its left hoof struck her along the left side of her head. She took three stumbling steps to the right; her strength faded; her knees folded; darkness pulsed at the edges of her vision. Her throat made the oddest sound. She felt herself falling, and had not even the strength to put out her arms. Yet, instead of feeling the ground, she suddenly felt herself rushing through a tunnel toward a dazzling light.

On the ground, Jervais shook off his dazing pain. He saw his horse standing spraddle-legged above him, holding its broken foreleg carefully. He saw the danger that it might fall back on him—and he saw Charles's white face, his straining effort to keep the animal upright. Jervais strove with all his will and all his soul to rise, but he couldn't; his legs felt as if they'd been mashed to pulp; the muscles simply wouldn't respond. He swore furiously and tore up hunks of grass with his fists, doing what he could to drag himself to safety. Meanwhile, Martin's black horse reared above him. His sense of danger grew more acute.

And then there was Kate, screaming at the animal, putting herself between it and Jervais.

And then she was falling, collapsing, as if every bone in her body had suddenly become liquid.

A strong sense of wrongness overcame him. *It can't happen this way. It isn't fair.*

Men were frantically shouting at Martin's horse now. They backed it away with prods of their swords. The war horse, trained to charge straight and without flinching, to bite and lash out savagely at the enemy with front and hind hoofs, continued to resist all attempts to capture it.

Kate lay in a heap of dusty salt-green. The sight of her made Jervais's heart flinch. He felt tears—unshed tears, which are the most painful variety. He tried to get up yet again. His mouth contorted with effort, with agony, as he tried to use his arms to pull himself over to her.

From the tall grass at the edge of the field a lopsided figure emerged in an ungainly, crippled, step-slide run. He was headed directly for Kate. "Sister!" he yelled, "Sister Katharine!"

"Charles!" Jervais shouted. "Stop him!"

The squire turned but could not release the chestnut war horse. Jervais saw his squire's utterly bloodless face and the hard edge of terror in his eyes—for Dick Jackson looked so startling—but there was nothing Charles could do.

The peasant stopped over Kate, and knelt beside her.

"Don't touch her!" Jervais shouted. His voice cracked in his throat.

The man paid him no heed. He was straightening Kate's limbs with his one good arm, touching her, "arranging" her with an exquisite tenderness. Her body, as he moved it, seemed too soft, too strength-less, too limp; her face was too white. Jervais knew she was dead, and a terrible bleakness came over him.

Finally, Martin's maddened war horse veered off into a run-away gallop. Jervais's men-at-arms turned to help Charles with the crippled chestnut. Others had arrived and several of them bent over Jervais. "My lady . . . Kate . . . see to her," he insisted.

Several of the knights shouldered Dick aside. Jervais willed himself not to scream with the pain in his legs as four strong men lifted him and began to carry him toward the castle. "Is she alive?" he asked, twisting to see Dick standing in dumb resignation as two men lifted Kate between them. One of her arms escaped them and flopped without life. "Is she alive?" But if his question was answered he did not hear it, for he lost consciousness.

Jervais heard things as through a muffling mist—the sea, the gulls, the hollow wind, voices: "He's been sorely bruised, but the bones held, praise God." He somehow knew this was said by a physician, a cadaverous individual with long locks. In this state, he submitted to being bled, and after that the mist got thicker, and he seemed to sleep for an unknown time.

When he woke, his legs hurt like the devil, but he'd known pain before, and like many a battle-scarred veteran, he stood it. He knew he wouldn't be getting very far from the castle for a while, however.

He tried to piece together what had happened. When everything started to come clear, he realized he'd been feverishly dreaming for days. Now he could go through the joust completely in his mind, and the last thing he saw was Kate—her white face, the pure fear in her eyes.

He opened his own eyes and saw his office. The room was warm, full of firelight. On the floor near his bed was a carpet he'd brought back from the East. Against the wall leaned a knight's battle sword—Martin of Daigh Lott's.

So the man had died.

Charles came into his line of vision. "My lord? Can you hear me? Can you speak?"

These words were like silver dice rolled from a shining cup; they bounced in his thoughts; he couldn't gather them together. He let them scatter, and bent his concentration on voicing the question that had gone unanswered for too long: "Is she alive?" His voice came out sounding raw and weak.

"My lord?" said Charles, bending nearer. Jervais noted his exhausted pallor.

"Is she alive?"

"Lady Kate? She's upstairs in your chamber. Let me get you something to drink."

Charles returned with a goblet that gleamed as he lifted Jervais's head to help him drink of the blood-dark wine within. He swallowed, then repeated, "She's alive."

"Yes, my lord."

Jervais didn't like the compressed silence that surrounded this answer. It said that something was wrong.

His stiff, sore legs were wrapped in cloths beneath which the physician had spread an ointment greener than grass and ranker to smell than any hound. He stayed abed another day, then said, "I want to see her."

The physician fretted, "You can't, my lord. You'll never make the stairs."

He gave the man a grim smile. "If you put me in a chair and carry me up, I will."

"My lord—"

"If you don't do as I say, I'll crawl up the stairs on my own."

Gian arrived just then, blustering. (Charles must have summoned him from Lesterhouse.) "Will you tell me what you're up to?"

"Good. You're here. You can help carry me."

"Great God, you must be raving! Another week abed at least, the physician says."

Jervais felt his vulnerability—and hated it. "I'm going upstairs, with your help or without."

"The physician—"

"Aye, the physician." Jervais muttered a curse. "He seems unduly fond of blood-letting. Don't we have murderers enough in this country without such as him to slay honest folk?"

"Have your wits strayed? You won't fight on a horse again till Christmas as it is."

Jervais made it clear he was not listening. Indeed, he'd thrown back the coverlet and was about to tumble himself onto the floor. He was determined to crawl to the stairs if necessary. Gian's hands on his shoulders stayed him. Jervais looked into his target-like eyes.

"Friend, she is unconscious. There is no point in doing yourself harm just to see that what I'm telling you is true. She wouldn't even know you were there."

The words penetrated like lance-splinters. Jervais fell back against his bed, limp. "I saw her fall." He fought his attention back to his knight. "If she is dead, and you think that by not telling me—"

"I swear to you that she is alive. She was knocked unconscious and has not wakened."

There was that tone again, that same tone that Charles had used, which concealed something. "What is it you're not telling me? I swear to you, Gian, if you don't tell me all, I'll drag myself up those stairs somehow."

Gian straightened. "The physician says . . . he says she may never waken. She may lay there in that state, alive but not alive . . ." he shrugged, "maybe for weeks." His look was steady. "Maybe for years."

Jervais was kept to his bed for another week. Within that time came the day when he could insist upon being carried in a chair to Kate's bedside. But he didn't insist. He didn't even ask.

She'd risked her life—perhaps *given* her life—to save his. Why?

He pondered this question in his sickbed, pondered it through day after day, pondered it through every night. He began to have restless dreams in which he was pinned beneath his destrier, helpless. Sir Martin's horse rose above him—then there was Kate. She was struck down, she looked broken, and then the peasant, Dick Jackson, came onto the field, crabbed and crippled, his head tilted to one side in its perpetual twist. He was shouting . . . something.

The dream always woke him; he came awake with his heart pounding, his every instinct and curiosity alert. Hence he woke from dreaming it again on the tenth day of his bed rest. A night fog was giving way to a dawn of thin rain. The rising sun lifted briefly into an open space between sea and cloud, and the air outside the narrow windows of his office was turned to pale gold, for the rain caught this light and became a visible veil. Its hushed whisper was like the whisper from the interior of a shell; it sighed into the delicatest ear of his memory: *Sister Katharine.*

The rain whispered, *Sister Katharine.*

Chapter 24

Dick Jackson had shouted, "Sister Katharine!"

Jervais shifted his weight painfully in his bed. "Charles!" His squire's sleepy face appeared. "Take me upstairs—now!"

And so a chair with pillows to cushion his bruised legs was quickly prepared to take him whither he was bound. As he was lifted into it, he saw out the narrow windows that the tower was still wrapped in that golden veil of rain. It was still whispering, *Sister* . . . *Sister* . . .

He was carried up the steep, spiraling tower stairs to the bedchamber. Theresa and one of the babe's nurses were talking there, gentle and soft, to baby Roger. The child was weaned at last, and at the moment was being coaxed to eat a pap of mashed food. The women idled near the hearth. Neither of them seemed even aware of the big bed. The only one near it was the pageboy, Lloyd of Clarence, who sat on a stool outside the tightly closed curtains.

Jervais gritted his teeth with pain as his chair was

put down. Theresa came hastily to tie back the curtains for him. "Begone," he said when she was finished. He wanted everyone out. Even the cooing babe was gathered and taken.

Jervais sat and looked at the form of his wife. All he could see from his chair was her profile on the pillow. Clenching his jaw, blinking hard, he rose and maneuvered himself onto the side of the bed. He was clumsy, but the movement of the mattress under his weight had no effect on her. She didn't rouse; she didn't move.

Now he could see her face. Ten days of coma seemed to have melted every ounce of excess flesh from her. Her body, once so lush and full, was reduced to the barest essentials. Her dark hair was drawn back from her smooth brow, and her head was swathed in bandages. A bandage even passed beneath her chin. Her eyes were closed, and those amazingly long, black lashes lay on her high, colorless cheekbones.

She looked frozen. She looked as if she were covered by a sudden hoarfrost, the kind that lies on spring grapes and wild flowers after an unexpectedly cold night. He reached out and touched her lips. Her flesh was cool—cold, so cold it frightened him. He drew his hand back.

There was nothing of her love-philtre, her spell— whatever magic she had used—left to protect her. She lay there as defenseless as a soft-bellied insect in the spider's gossamer. The swathing bandages were like a nun's wimple. They hid her hair and left her face starkly revealed. A face that was as thin as Jervais's child-wife's had been. Like a distant horn calling, realization came. Seeing her thus, in her deep sleep, in her nearness to death, he knew.

He'd almost guessed once. He recalled her dream-fretting: *I'm sorry I'm not pretty.* Now he remembered where he'd first heard her say that. He also recalled how she'd pleaded in her sleep to her father not to bury her alive. Why hadn't he known? He had to surmise that the nature of her magic had caused him to dismiss his own instincts. He'd been like a boy playing on the shore, so absorbed in finding pretty shells that the great ocean of truth had lain all undiscovered, all unseen by him.

He took her hand, which lay over the coverlet. It was white and cold; he could feel every small bone. There was barely a pulse in her wrist. Fear brushed the walls of his chest. He got a grip on it. He looked about. Was nothing being done for her? Was it their thought to let her languish away, and as quickly as possible? Weren't they even feeding her? Was that "physician" bleeding her to death? Did they keep the curtains closed all the time? Did they keep her in the dark as if she were already dead and buried?

A pang of guilt tore through him. Hadn't he lain downstairs content to let others care for her? Hadn't he half-hoped that she might just fade from his life? The servants had taken their cue from him.

Now he was afraid to even let go of her hand. She was barely breathing. It seemed she might die at any moment. He leaned forward, ignoring the pain of his own injuries, to put his ear to her chest. He detected only the softest beat.

He sat up with a groan. "Charles!"

The chamber door opened instantly. "My lord?"

"Get that cadaverous scoundrel of a physician up here!" He felt a flush of fury in his face. "Where is that maid? Yes, you—Theresa! Get some food, some of that pap you've been giving the babe."

As he gave these orders he was at the same time distracted by an interior clamor of connections and speculations that were vying for his consideration: why had she run away from him into the forest in the first place? Why had she come back with her identity concealed?

Why, Norah? You can't die without explaining this! Don't you dare die!

Please, God, I don't want her to die.

She lay silent and white, like a folded swan, her gliding, opalescent beauty faded somehow, so that it seemed she might dissolve into mere mist and moonbeams. He leaned forward, his hands on either side of her head, and he muttered fiercely: "You will not die. Do you hear me? You will *not* die."

The silence, at first, was perfect, like the silence in a church, or on a high peak, the complete hush of such echoing, remote, separate places. Norah couldn't hear the wind, or the sea, or even her son's babyish prattle, not at first. But gradually the silence eroded, and sounds began to fall against her ears. And when she opened her eyes, and blinked, and blinked again, her first thought was: *Jervais.* It was as if he'd just been speaking to her. She opened her eyes—and there he was.

Actually, she saw only dark clothes on a seated male figure—but she knew it was him. He leaned forward, and she saw that he seemed to have aged. But he was still amazingly handsome. Just the sight of him filled her with content.

"You're alive," she said, surprised at the amount of strength this required.

"So are you."

Something in his voice wrapped itself about her like a shawl. "Yes," she said, but warily—with the vigilance of a dog who has been whipped on occasion.

She couldn't understand how he could be sitting there. She recalled so vividly the sight of his screaming horse writhing on the lower half of his body, his yells of pain, his seeming helplessness as Sir Martin's horse reared over him. Those images had been enameled in fire in her memory.

The curtains of the bed were open. The afternoon was ebbing; its light was like a gentle, golden wine dwindling from the room. She said, "I've . . ." she looked for a word for her stay in that place of silence, "slept all day."

"Slept. Yes. All day." He sat there, unimpatient, looking as though he might hang about forever. "Actually," he said, lazily gathering himself, "it's been several days." He lifted his brows. A slight, ironic line came to the corner of his mouth. "Twenty-four to be exact."

"How . . . I . . . I don't remember."

"I don't suppose you do. In twenty-four days, one's very blood falls asleep, I suspect."

Something was changed about him. He was more relaxed than she'd ever seen him, and beneath his easy pose she sensed some subtle difference which made him seem a new man, with new understandings, and new and keener purposes.

Norah recovered her strength and rose from her bed, first just to take a few steps, and then a few more. She was again and again surprised by Jervais's consideration of her. He sent her a heavy, deep green velvet dressing gown that had been his mother's. He visited her often, even helped her to while away the hours by teaching her to play chess. ("The game of chess," he began as he set up the board, "tests one's abilities and character. It dismays many a man-of-arms unused to long concentration.") She did her best at the game, and sometimes glanced up to find him studying her with a look that seemed to see the core of her.

His motives remained shadowy, elusive, but he patiently coaxed her to take in all the terrible concoctions his physician made for her, which covered the ground from shavings of ivory soaked in wine to an "ale" brewed of borage roots and saffron. She soon learned to hate that elderly and cadaverous man, with his fluting voice and outdated views.

While in her presence, Jervais pretended to be in strict accord with Master Payen, as the man called himself, but once Norah overheard them arguing outside her door. Master Payen was talking pedantically of "febrifuges" and "humors," and Jervais suddenly asked, "Where did you learn such nonsense?"

"I learned my craft by travel among the medical schools in Sicily, and even from the Infidels," the old man sniffed.

Jervais swore irately, "May I suffer the horrors of damnation if you've ever been closer to any of those places than London!"

When the physician brought her a bowl of boiled insect wings and hedgehog feet, Jervais at last dismissed him. "She would do better to take her meals with me in the hall, where she can eat well of Master Villhard's rabbit pie and stewed sheep and baked eggs."

She was full of relief for this, until she learned that he truly meant for her to *eat well*. He pressed her to stuff herself, scolded, "Eat your bread, drink your wine." Again she did her best, for her dresses, both the salt-green and the blue, were frighteningly loose on her. She had no mirror, but she was certain her face must be pallid—she could tell by the way the castle folk looked at her, and then looked again, sometimes with small frowns of uncertainty. There was even some whispering, though she could not quite catch what was being said.

Dick was the most open in studying her. His wall-eyes made her uncomfortable. She said, to ease the stiffness of their meeting, "You look as if you've been out in the sun."

He nodded; a huge grin suffused his face. "He . . . uh, the earl has made me a varlet . . . for the castle."

It was late August, and warm, and the garrison knights spent their days in violent exercise. These vigorous, unpolished men hardly ever stayed indoors on a fair day. They rode, hunted stag and boar, and satisfied their passion for falconry, or they worked off their aggressions at gymnastics and foot races.

Jervais took exercise, too, though his legs were not ready for tilting at quintains just yet. He kept himself to daily walks of inspection about his building sites, and short rides on his palfrey to check the greening of the *desmesne's* wheat. He was once gone for three days, to visit the quarry at Ramsay he said. Norah believed the trip was too much for him, for when he returned he was irritable.

Norah, as before, confined herself to her chamber. However, she climbed to the top of the tower sometimes. One afternoon in early June, when she was there, listening to the gulls calling and to the sea washing gently onto the strand far below, she fell into her old habit of daydreaming. Far, far out were a few silver and mauve thunderheads. She was gazing at them when she heard footsteps approach, and she made a wish straight out of her childhood: *Let it be him!* As the footsteps grew nearer, she knew the sound of them, which was different from any other, and when they stopped behind her, she turned.

She caught Jervais with a haunted expression that deepened the silver of his eyes. He said, "I see you've finished your embroidery."

"Yes, I finished it this morning."

He came nearer, and seemed to be searching for something more to say to her. "I wonder—would you like to go down there?" He nodded over the ramparts. "It's not much of a beach, but we could ride down together."

And so, for the first time ever she got her feet wetted by the sea. Her tower seemed far above. Its weathered stone glowed in the afternoon light. The castle seemed a mass of turrets and walls, grey and brown, with here and there a little green where moss had grown.

Jervais helped her off her horse at one end of the cove, and offered her his hand as he led the way down the rocks to the beach. Gulls rose before them in a cloud of snowy wings, outraged at being intruded upon. The surf seemed much louder when it was near. It was a little frightening. But Jervais kept her hand as they began to stroll the packed sand above the waves.

It was a leathery hand, calloused and very powerful, with large, rough knuckles. His handsome features were composed. As they walked, he reached into his wallet with his free hand and pulled out something that glittered. Casually, he turned her palm over and dropped the heavy thing into it. "That's for you."

He walked on, slowly, his hands clasped behind his back now, while she remained where she was, silent, shocked.

A necklace. Sapphires. She was struck by their magnificence. Then she was gripped by curiosity. She caught up with him, dared to catch his sleeve. He didn't stop walking, but looked down at her with a bemused expression. She said, "Why are you being so kind to me?"

He shaded his eyes and looked out at the glittering, heaving expanse, at the towering thunderheads. "Because you saved my life."

They passed a pool filled with shimmering reflections of blue-and-grey sky. What pleasure she'd felt melted from her heart. His answer made everything simple and clear: he felt indebted to her now. That was the reason for all this consideration. And for these jewels. She arranged her features. "You needn't give me a present for that."

He was squinting at the wind, so that his eyes were silver slits. "But I can if I want to." His voice was low and porous. "I've never given you anything. It's time you had some clothes suited to your position. There are some bolts of cloth in storage. I have a new steward as of today—Mark Dolgolvin. He's a bit choleric and has an awful wart on the bridge of his nose, but he comes highly recommended by a widow woman I know. I'll have him bring you the bolts so you can choose from them."

They walked for a time without speaking. The wind blew her hair back from her face, and she said softly, "I've seen the wind."

She'd meant to stun him, but he only looked down at her with an amused expression. "What does it look like?"

"It's rather like a rainbow, only the colors are streaming."

He regarded her with obvious unease. "Is it frightening to see the things you see?"

"It depends on the vision."

After a moment he said, as if to himself, "Perchance it is only the heart that can see rightly. Perchance what is essential is invisible to the eye." Still seemingly apprehensive, he asked, "How did you make me want you? Were you born with a knowledge of spells?"

"I lived with a witch. She helped me." She met his gaze. "If I had the choice, I wouldn't do it again. It became a curse. I should never have played with such arts."

"No, you shouldn't have." Then he added, "But we often do things in the unripeness of youth that bring us regrets later." He smiled uncertainly. "I say this as a man somewhat advanced in age, able to enjoy only a limited amount of deviltry anymore."

When she smiled back at him, his own grin cleared—and transformed him. It was bright and broad, warm and generous. Under its impact, she stopped walking. So did he. He stood looking down at her. A sudden small gust lifted strands of her hair across her cheek. She grew aware of their solitude on this small crescent of sand. She heard the breakers and felt the wind pulling at her skirt and blowing her hair. He was going to kiss her. She knew it before he took her shoulders in his hands. He bent his head down. She saw his eyes plainly, and felt the force of his desire emanating from him. And felt that within his desire was a new and mysterious pity.

She turned away from his lowering mouth. "You must send me away. Surely you see that now—now that I've nearly killed you."

His mouth had found her throat, her earlobe, and then, insistently, her lips. "Right this minute I must kiss you," he whispered wryly into her half-opened mouth.

It was one of the sweetest kisses he'd ever given her. She lost herself in the enchantment of it. She softened all over and became infinitely more pliable, allowing him to mold her against him. When he lifted his head, he was smiling again. He continued to hold her. He stroked a tress of her hair out of her eyes.

"You must send me away, Jervais," she said again.

"That's out of the question."

"Why? Because you mistakenly feel grateful to me?

Roger is weaned; he will do fine without me."

"And you? Would you do fine without him?"

"That's not important."

"Isn't it?" He blinked slowly at her, then took her face in his fingers and kissed her again. Kissed her in a soft, dreamy, mellow way, without urgency.

When he ended it, she realized that her hand was on his chest, her weight was leaning into him. She made the effort to straighten herself.

As she'd known he'd meant to kiss her, she now knew he wanted to tell her something. In fact, it seemed he had several things to say and must choose between them. At last he said, "A man spurred up from Tedlow early today with a message that Henry's going to pay us a visit. They're coming up the coast by ship in nine days. I thought we might schedule Charles's addubment for the same time. Henry isn't a great lover of the ceremonial side of kingship, but it would be an honor for Charles to have him present."

"And . . . and the queen? Is she coming?"

"Yes," he said briskly, unwilling to meet her eyes suddenly. "Yes, Eleanor is coming."

She felt as if she'd taken a quick, hard punch. A gull screamed thinly, giving voice to her own in-held frustration.

Jervais walked on. She made no effort to remain apace with him. Watching him, she realized she'd envisioned this scene—it seemed ages ago, back in Bermondsey Castle. In her vision there had been a sea-mist curling over the beach like smoke. There was no such mist today—except the mist in her eyes. All else was the same: he was walking away from her, and seeing him thus brought her an immense feeling of sorrow and regret.

The day of Henry and Eleanor's arrival was warm but overcast. Butterflies glistened silver in the sultry air. All the shops of the castle town were closed; the entire population lined the bay, waiting to catch a glimpse of the royal ships. Owing to a choppy sea, it was after noon before these were spotted—two high-pooped sailing vessels with supplementary oars. They were a long time tacking about before their boats could finally be lowered. The sun slipped into a crack in the clouds and looked down upon the scene, making a slanting column of bright, rosy-colored light. The hauberks and helms of Jervais's knights suddenly threw off flames, and their shields blazed.

The sailors grunted and floundered in the shallows near the shore, but at last pulled the first boat up onto the shore, and Henry stepped onto the strand. The shrill sound of clarions filled the air and echoed into the distance.

More grunting and loud breathing brought the second boat ashore. Norah had thoughts of flight, but it was too late: Eleanor was already setting foot upon Conniebrook soil.

She shone like a sunstone; she was so slender, so *present* in every way. Norah glanced at Jervais. He was clothed in green velvet and soft leather chamlet, and his eyes glowed like an opalescent, twilit sea. He bowed, and his hand on Norah's arm, cool and competent, reminded her to curtsey.

She too was dressed for this momentous visit.

Though her hair was plain and undressed, she wore a new gown made from a length of Italian silk, blue woven with gold. The glittering necklace of sapphires circled her throat. From her girdle hung another gift from Jervais, a little dagger of silver gilt.

"Le Strand!" Henry slapped Jervais on the back. "And Lady Kate," he added, with less heartiness and more speculation. (There was that frown again, as if there might be something changed about her, but . . . what?)

"Lord Conniebrook," Eleanor murmured as Jervais kissed her hand. She ignored Norah.

It had been arranged that the king and Jervais would ride to the castle, while a horse-litter was at hand for Eleanor and Norah's use. This was the moment Norah dreaded the most, when she would be virtually alone with her rival. Before taking her seat, she whispered, "Almighty God, have mercy upon me."

The people of Conniebrook flocked to watch them pass—the king and queen and all their knights and waiting women and squires. Eleanor waved and nodded and smiled as they made their way to the castle's postern gate. There was hardly a chance for Norah to make any more conversation than, "I hope your journey was smooth."

Eleanor stiffened, as if to say, *Please, don't speak to me,* and at the same time she smiled and waved at a peasant woman holding a baby. Without the slightest word she had communicated that Norah did not exist for her, she had never existed, and would never exist in the future. Eleanor didn't *see* her.

The low, stone-colored clouds tumbled back across

the hole in the sky, and the sun disappeared. The banners and pennons on the walls of the castle snapped in the sultry wind. Since no rain had appeared, however, the first order of business was for Jervais to show Henry what he had accomplished on the new castle walls. Next, Eleanor insisted on seeing little Roger. She smiled and cooed and chucked her godson beneath the chin.

During the final hours of the afternoon, the villeins had arranged a pageant in the royal couple's honor. Mostly this consisted of exhibitions of rough sports: wrestling, archery, cockfighting. In the last event, two men, both broad and powerful with big loose hands, were armed with cudgels. They were to try to kill a goose that was set free in an enclosure. The townspeople roared as the two men began to belabor each other, hitting so hard that blood soon ran down their faces. Norah saw Dick across the enclosure. He was as white as linen. She touched Jervais's arm. He put his hand on her shoulder—but it was Eleanor to whom he put the question, "Would you like me to stop it?"

Before she could answer, one of the men fell almost dead. The goose became the prize of the other, and he promptly, exultantly, pounded the life out of the creature. At least it was over.

The town's most prominent merchants and residents were summoned by a loud blast on trumpets that evening. The castle's great hall had been transformed by the new steward into a place of delights. The walls were hung with colorful scarlet banners, and fresh reeds were spread over the floor. Twisting, heavy torchfires spread a festival light. Three pages wearing matching red and black stood at a cupboard filled with cups and jars of wine and kegs of ale. The king and queen entered to another blare of trumpets. Pages escorted them and Jervais and Norah to the high table at the head of the hall.

Amid good-natured jostling, the king's ministers, the queen's ladies, the servants and residents of Conniebrook found seats at the heavy oak-plank tables fixed in rows close to the walls.

Jervais sat on Eleanor's right, and Norah sat on Henry's left. Hence she could not monitor the conversation between her husband and his lover. Instead, she somehow had to make conversation with this formidable, restless, broad-chested king. All her worrying over this visit had concerned Eleanor; she'd never stopped to think that she might have to sit near enough Henry to hear him eat and drink. He seemed to emanate some primitive force. She could *feel* him.

Master Villhard had been in a frenzy of preparation for days. Many a party of hunters had gone out with falcons to catch small game, and varlets like Dick had hunted with bows or snares, bringing in as many as possible of starlings and blackbirds, quail and partridges.

The master cook, with his sleeves rolled up his fat forearms, came into the hall at the head of a procession which included four swarthy kitchen naves bearing a huge platter on which a whole roasted ox lay with its head braced up, complete with parchment horns and apple eyes, all in a lake of sauce. After this magnificent beginning, food and drink flowed continually out of the kitchen: soups spiced with sage and sweet basil and Jervais's favorite condiment, pepper; large platters of meats; peacocks; great golden fish; vegetables; and a plethora of breads— soft breads made of milk and butter, "dog breads," even a two-color-bread of alternating layers of wheat and rye. Norah watched Jervais select a table loaf of this latter and slice all the crust away with his knife. He passed the tender center to his companion, to soak up her soup.

Eleanor, Norah realized, had two auras. She could be regal and cold or, when around a man, she could emit an aura of feminine tenderness. Jervais seemed vulnerable to the soft glow that was spread over her features now. He was giving her his most winning smile, and when she praised a dish-pastry, he immediately sent word for Master Villhard to come out once more and accept his earned applause.

The feast went on, extremely loudly. Everybody talked at once. A roast stag started innumerable stories, and Jervais was prevailed upon to tell how he'd once killed a bear. Two dogs got into a fight and almost upset Eleanor's chair. She laughed the incident off as Jervais kicked the animals away. Everything was very loud and very merry, everything and everybody except Norah.

Amidst all this, she felt miserable with loneliness. She had the feeling she was being watched by Henry. A page held up a bowl of walnuts, and he took a handful and cracked one in his fingers. She met his glance as he put the nutmeat into his mouth and began to chew. He said, "What do you think of my queen?" Before Norah could form an answer, he gave one himself: "She is incomparably beautiful, strong, and sharp-witted. Qualities rare in a woman. And she uses all of them. Unusual circumstances have given her power far beyond that normally permitted a female. God knows I have little enough influence on her."

Eleanor, at that moment, laughed light-heartedly at something Jervais had said.

Norah said nothing, only took up her cup, swallowed. When a page held a bowl of sugar lumps, she took a small piece to nibble on.

A twinkle appeared in Henry's eye. "You aren't going to console me?"

"What could I say—especially as God himself knows about your situation and clearly does naught?"

Henry chuckled. "Indeed. But it's a terrible thing when a man can scarcely know his own wife's purposes." He shot her a meaningful look, which she was careful not to intercept. "Eleanor encourages what she calls 'courtly love.' Do you know how it works?" He gave Norah no time to answer. "First, secrecy is the essence of the liaison. With extreme caution, lest she betray herself to the world, a lady whets her cavalier's ardor with enticing advances, then with cruel retreats. She encourages him with gifts, then puts him off with frowns. Her caprice is designed to disturb his wakeful hours and assail his dreams. Now she is fond, now mysteriously aloof. Her lover exists in an alternation of hope and despondency, a sweet torment."

"Men seem to like it," Norah said.

"Not all men. Some know the value of a straightforward declaration, a simple 'I love you.'" He added without pause, "I hear you saved Le Strand's life at the risk of your own."

"Some gaudy idea of fidelity blinded me for a moment."

"You have earned respect for it here, though."

She almost laughed, then considered what he'd said: was it possible? Those odd looks she'd been getting didn't feel like respect, but they had aught of scorn in them.

Their conversation was disturbed by the interruption of a variety of musicians, acrobats, and jugglers who came flooding through the doors just then to provide entertainment. A bear rose up among them and began to dance heavily to the music. With a look like a leer, he pranced in a little circle. The attending children screamed with pleasure. Another particular favorite was a ridiculous little bird-faced man who balanced a stick on his nose with a ball atop the stick, and at the same time twirled hoops on his arms, one thigh, and an ankle. The crowd cheered.

Charles attended Jervais at the table until midnight. At that time, he was given leave to officially begin his initiation into knighthood. It was customary for a squire to spend the night before his addubment on his knees in church.

He'd maintained a careful, closed face for days, and bade the company farewell with it now. It was clear to Norah that something was troubling him.

The festivities in the hall went on. The guests grew drunk. Food fell from their mouths as they talked and ate at the same time. They dipped their fingers deep into Master Villhard's sauces, and drops fell on their breasts on the way to their lips. A troubadour, a youth in a saffron tunic, thrummed a harp and recounted the pain and platonic pleasures of love when Norah finally caught Jervais's eye. He correctly interpreted her look, and said to Henry, "Please excuse my lady, Sire. She has been ill and needs her rest."

"Of course," the king said, smiling. "Good night, Lady Kate."

Eleanor did not give her even the briefest upward inclination of the corners of her lips.

The silence of the tower was a relief such as Norah had seldom known. She stood absolutely passive as Theresa undressed her. She kissed her sleeping son, and then said to the maid, "You may go on back downstairs if you like."

Theresa quickly exited, eager not to miss anything.

Norah's thoughts were a wooly tumble: Jervais. In love with a woman other than herself. The queen. How her senses ached at it! She wished she had a spear, a helmet, a hauberk—garments of iron against this pain. But she didn't, and so she could only throw herself upon the bed and seek the oblivion of sleep.

Chapter 25

Candles flickered on the night-shadowed altar. The chapel was silent, yet Charles could feel that the whole castle was in a great, merry stir. Everyone was comfortably replete and in the best of humors. Everyone but Charles. (And perhaps Lady Kate. She couldn't possibly be happy about Queen Eleanor's presence.)

As for himself, he could not feel happy about the great ceremony planned in his honor tomorrow. How could he let it take place when he was so unworthy? If he accepted knighthood with the secret he harbored, his entire life hence would be a lie. As the hours passed, and he went over and over the facts, he felt as if a screw was twisting up his belly. At last he sent a page with a message for Lord Jervais, asking him to come at once.

In time, the chapel door opened, and the earl came through it. Charles could face him only obliquely. The earl frowned at this. "What is it?"

Their relationship was worse than it had ever been

since he'd openly taken Lady Kate's side the night the earl had cast her into the dungeon. In truth, it hadn't been a close relationship for a long while. But clearly the earl was frustrated by Charles's hesitation to even look him in the eye, on this night of all nights.

"My lord," he began haltingly, "I once did something, and it has sat heavily upon my soul ever since. I've struggled, and I believe the only thing to do is tell you and leave it to your judgment whether I am worthy to become a knight on the morrow. Or on any morrow."

He could feel Lord Jervais's sharpening perturbation, and went on hastily: "My lord, I caused your Lady Norah's death."

The earl seemed to stop breathing.

"Do you recall the night before she disappeared?"

"The night we had to turn out of our beds and chase after the outlaws," he ground out.

Charles swallowed. "Yes." He could envision that night so well; he could see little Norah. Time touched her not in his memory, where she was still a pitifully thin girl dressed in a nun's habit. "While you were gone that night, Lady Norah came out of your tent and asked for a cup of hot wine. I was most ungracious." He clenched his hands. "I acted a stranger to all kindness, my lord. I heated the wine for her, but—she was very young—"

"So were you."

"Yes, but I believed myself infinitely older than her, infinitely wiser. I could see she was infatuated by you. At the time I was infatuated with the queen. Not for myself, no! but I took a vain pleasure and pride in knowing that she loved my liegelord. And that he loved her. It seemed the most romantic thing possible, that hopeless love you shared. And I saw Lady Norah as an interloper. I felt outraged that she, so homely—if you'll pardon me for saying so, my lord—so homely and thin and, well, simple. A dolt, I thought, as blind as a kitten, and—"

He paused, then somehow found the courage to look the earl straight in the face. "I told her, my lord."

The earl's brows lifted in surprise. "Told her what?"

"That you loved someone else, that you had loved her for years and that you would always love her. That Norah, being so plain, could never hope to win your heart. I was cruel." His voice dropped to a whisper. "I hurt her. And I didn't even feel a pang of guilt for it—not then, leastways. 'Twas an evil thing to do." He lowered his head. "It was because of me that she ran away from you, that she suffered, that she died. It was all because of me."

Lord Jervais turned to face the altar lights. Charles didn't expect a challenge from him, for a knight could not honorably challenge a mere squire. Still, he fully expected to be banished from the castle. And if he happened to be set upon by men on his way hence, well, he would understand who had sent them, and why.

The earl was silent for so long that at last Charles whispered, "My lord, what will you do with me?"

Lord Jervais, who had been standing absolutely still, now lifted his hands and rubbed his face, as if he had just awakened from a light drowse. He turned so that Charles could see his profile, dark against the

411

glowing candleflames. He said, in a voice charged with emotion, "How can I blame you when you only told her the truth? Had she not learned about me that night, she would have learned soon enough. Her heart was bound to be broken."

He stepped closer. "This explains much. More than you can know." He placed a hand on Charles's shoulder. "A numbness had been falling over me for some time before I wed Lady Norah, and when I thought she'd been murdered, I stopped feeling altogether for a while. Even so, I noticed the change in you. I had no idea why you had suddenly become such a solemn young man. I thought, cynically, that you were maturing and learning early that life is all promise and no fulfillment. I see now that you had this sin, *my* sin—and Eleanor's—on your conscience all the time. We have done great harm, the queen and I, and inciting a bit of viciousness in a loyal young squire is not the least of it."

He took Charles's shoulders in both his hands and gave him a manly shake. "You were kind to Lady Kate from the first. I mistook that kindness; I saw it as a sort of betrayal, not as compassion learned through remorse. I beg your pardon for that."

"My lord, you must not beg my pardon for anything. Lady Kate, if she were evil—she doesn't seem evil, my lord. She seems, well, she has a streak of willfulness, but she seems—if I may speak plainly—to love you."

"You think so? Truly?" The earl regarded him.

Charles lowered his head. "How can you ask? She placed herself before Sir Martin's horse—my lord, she was willing to die for you!"

412

He dared not look at the earl's face. He sensed the expression there would be ravaging, and he dared not look upon it.

"Charles, what you did to Lady Norah was wrong, but more my wrong than yours. On the morrow you—"

"No," Charles said quietly. He felt tears in his eyes, heard his breath catch, as if in a shameful sob. "How can I become a knight when I have her unhappiness, her death in a poor hut in a forest on my conscience? I am unworthy, my lord."

The earl stepped back. "Do you believe that there's a knight alive who doesn't carry the weight of some act of cruelty on his back? One sign that a boy has become a man is that he can shoulder his mistakes and go on, using the weight as a reminder to do better in the future. You can only right your wrongs through action. . . ."

His voice trailed off, and he seemed to fall into thought. His head turned as if in a listening pose. "Through action," he repeated to himself. He looked about him, gazed up at the balcony where he worshipped, glanced at the chapel door. Charles hesitated at the odd smile that softened his face. What did it mean?

Jervais seemed to shake himself. His face was grave again as he turned back to Charles. *"Nil desperandum."* The Latin crunched between his teeth like sugar. "'Despair of nothing.' Have the courage to accept knighthood tomorrow for Lady Norah's sake. Spend the remainder of your vigil here dedicating yourself to her."

Charles felt a splinter of light dawn through his

413

bleakness. "Yes," he said slowly. The light grew, like the first sunrise of spring, and finally the sun broke into his mind as with a salute of trumpets. "Yes!" he said, grasping what the earl was trying to say. "I will live well in order to make her death meaningful!" He was struck with love for his lord who in one stroke had made all he so desperately wanted not only possible, but right, even necessary.

The earl's expression was odd, as if he'd not expected quite such an enthusiastic response. "Well, not her death, mayhap, but if you dedicate yourself to her I can almost promise you that you will gain her forgiveness—more directly than you can suppose just now. So stop thinking of what you can't do and begin praying for the strength to do what you must, which is to mount your horse and behold your enemies, strike your spurs into your steed, and go and break into their midst."

As the new day dawned, Charles prepared for his solemn cleansing, the custom demanded of a man about to be knighted. He was attended by several older cavaliers and with considerable ceremony. There was no boisterous splashing or bantering words or making merry as he sat in the wooden bathtub. The act's general significance meant more to him than his attendants could suppose, since it was meant to symbolically erase all villainies of his past that he might enter into knighthood blameless.

The stripling, Lloyd of Clarence, reported from the window that a favoring wind was blowing yesterday's clouds out to sea. He also reported that a host of beggars were swarming the courtyard, called by the occasion's traditional almsgiving. Charles could imagine well their quavers, "Alms, fine sir!" which was the professional whine of beggars everywhere as they held out their wooden clackdishes. "Even the king and queen are throwing coins," Lloyd piped.

"That's how they prove their nobility," Charles told him patiently. Lloyd was going to act his squire today. It was a new experience to be the master; Charles believed he was going to like it.

Lady Kate, as substitute for Charles's mother, brought to the door of his chamber the costume in which he would assume his new position. The clothing had been selected as carefully as for a bridal. As Lloyd took it from her, Charles got a glimpse of her. She was somehow changed, not as beautiful as before her accident, yet, with her sable hair falling straight over her lovely shoulders and back, she was still fair beyond question. What was the difference then? Neither Charles nor anyone else in the castle could say, yet they all had noted it.

After bathing, he was dressed in a crisp white linen shirt, hose of brown silk, and a ceremonial tunic that was interwoven with gold. Finally, he was draped with a cloak of costly white ermine. His feet were shod in silken shoes Lady Kate had personally embroidered.

Friends of his own and of Lord Jervais's came to witness his dressing and to flatter him on the breadth of his shoulders and his height. (At five foot six, he was a little taller than the average man, though not nearly so tall as his liegelord.) He was glad of the unusually robust breakfast Master Villhard sent up to him. He was ferociously hungry after his wearying night's vigil, and he would need all his strength for the trials of the day.

Finally everything was ready. Decked out in this finery, he strode into the courtyard, consciously trying to move with the same big easy strides that Lord Jervais took.

Two loud trumpets blazed into sound. The courtyard was crammed with knights and ladies, old and not so old, all in their full finery. The scene was alive with color and brilliantly spectacular with flags and pennons. He didn't see the queen, but there was Lady Kate again, in a dress he'd never seen before. It was the purple color of ripening figs. The knights wore tunics of yellow, blue, or red, or chain mail of dazzling brightness. Several priests were there in their finest robes. It would be many a day before Charles would again see such an exhibit of martin, ermine, and vair, sendel and samite, gold and pearls.

Everyone shouted, "How proud your mother would have been!" "A true Silda!" "Right worthy of your father!" as he threaded his way through them and set out through the still-early sunlight for the exercise grounds.

There a platform had been covered with fine Saracen carpets. The king stood upon it, majestic in a gilded hauberk. Charles stepped up beside him. His white cloak furled. He felt so shy he could not look at Henry directly.

Behind him came the crowd. He spotted the queen now, riding side-saddle on a white mule.

Immediately his first sponsor came up onto the platform, the elderly, white-headed knight who had been his mother's uncle and was Charles's only living relative. Deliberately he kissed Charles; then, kneeling, he put two golden spurs on his nephew's feet.

Lord Jervais presented himself as second sponsor. He removed Charles's flake-white ermine cloak and pulled a dazzling steel hauberk over his head. The castle armorer had been a month at the laborious work of making this mail. Lord Jervais's frosty eyes took on a gimlet stare. "Feel the weight? Welcome it! 'Tis your reminder." Before Charles could answer, the earl set an equally brilliant helmet, studded with semi-precious stones, upon his head.

Next, a stately Sir Gian girded him with a sword, saying in gruff admonition: "Use this worthily." Charles heard the break in his voice. He feared his own voice would do worse, and so he replied by wordlessly pressing his lips to the weapon's hilt.

His sponsors stepped back. The trumpets gave out a mighty crash of song. The king, who had been standing to the side with his arms folded, now lifted his clenched fist. "Bow," he ordered "and I will give you the blow."

Charles bowed meekly to his greater lord. His meekness was tested by the tremendous stroke of Henry's fist, which sent him reeling.

But the instant he recovered and gained his feet, Henry seized him in a manly embrace. "Be brave, Sir Charles. Remember that your line is famous, both as lords and as vassals. What God has given as an inheritance, let a man work with all eagerness to retain. Do nothing ignoble. Honor all knights. Give to the poor. Love God."

Charles replied, "I thank you, Sire, and may God let me serve and love him for as long as I live."

He stepped down from the platform. The crowd had followed the ceremony with utmost interest, and had joined in a shout as the blow of honor was dealt. Now they backed away from him. The trumpets were silent, allowing the sweet music from a thousand invisible birds to be heard. He stood like a statue. He still felt the effects of Henry's fist, and that, combined with his excitement, seemed to make the air itself iridescent, as if it were spangling delicately. In truth, it was the most evanescent moment of his life.

Lord Jervais waved to a groom. "Bring the destrier!"

Immediately Lloyd appeared leading a white steed, perfectly groomed and in beautiful harness. For a moment the horse waited in front of the platform, striking at the turf with its shapely hoofs. Then Charles broke from his statue-like stance. Clothed as he was now, in weighty hauberk and helmet, he must run to the steed and leap onto its back in one bound, without touching a stirrup. This was an anxious moment for him.

From the time a young nobleman was in his cradle, his mother discussed with his father, "Will he make the leap?" It was a great test of his martial education, and one that must be taken in full public view. Charles had practiced it with desperate energy for the last month. Would he . . . ?

Done! He'd mounted fairly! He couldn't help grinning amidst the salvo of applause. He had the strongest, sweetest sensation of triumph and relief.

The destrier snuffled and snorted softly, tossing its

white mane. Charles held it motionless for an instant while Lloyd ran to him with a triangular shield and a lance tied with bright pennons that floated down upon his helm.

He put his steed through all manner of gallops and caracoles, and then away they went, flying toward a quintain that had been readied. The wooden figure, suspended on a pivot, was shaped like a man holding a sword. The object was to strike it between the eyes with his lance; any deviation of his aim would cause the target to spin and clout him or his horse as they passed.

Sweat broke out all over him. To smash the target and fling it to the ground with one lance thrust was another test.

And when this ordeal was also passed with tolerable glory, the newest knight of Conniebrook was eligible to indulge in his first tournament.

Squires ran to and fro. A great saddling and girdling took place, amidst much whinnying and stamping. A few pious knights had hurried back to the castle to pray hastily in the chapel, but the bulk of the company merely crossed themselves and muttered, "Blessed saints, take pity!"

By the time the sun was straight overhead, those who were going to participate in Charles's tournament were all wearing their armor and mounted on their battle-horses. They wielded lances and swords and, except for the presence of the ladies and the omission of the usual military precautions, the event looked like a regular muster for battle.

Henry had elected to take part, and was mounted upon a horse with silk trappings. Over his gilded armor he now wore a long surcoat, a beautiful garment, embroidered front and back with his coat of arms. It was meant both to identify him when his face was concealed by his helmet, and to shelter him from the direct sunlight. On a hot day, armor could become an oven and warriors had been known to collapse and even die of heat exhaustion or sunstroke. Several other knights wore such surcoats, and a few wore adaptations of the Saracen burnoose.

Jervais had not fully recovered the strength in his legs yet, and had to remain a spectator. Hence, while the rustic folk arrayed themselves about the edges of the field, he led Eleanor to the gallery he'd had built for the ladies. He and the queen took the most prominent seats and became the tournament's ruling couple. Norah, coming behind on Charles's elderly uncle's arm, felt a keen sense of displacement. Her new dress of purple silk was overshadowed by Eleanor's red brocade embroidered with gold. The queen also wore a golden circlet about her brow, beneath which her hair was neatly plaited.

Norah had never attended a tournament before, and she found it difficult to distinguish it from real warfare. No rules were to be enforced, the victors would strip the conquered of their armor and horses, and prisoners would be captured for ransom. She felt uneasy about it, for she knew that whenever men's blood rose high anything could happen, and this seemed a particularly foolhardy event.

Women had no place here except as admiring onlookers, as the givers of favors to the victors and of

420

soothing words to the defeated. Bold and beautiful Eleanor fulfilled her part as the reigning queen. Many gallants came to the gallery to beg her favors. She honored four knights with her tokens. The king came up to the railing, too, but he surprised Norah by asking, "Lady Kate, may I have a riband to distinguish my lance?"

Flushed and pleased, she stepped down from her second-row seat to tie a purple ribbon from her waist to the shaft of his weapon.

He kept his eyes on her face with a frank, unsmiling curiosity that disconcerted her until, abruptly, he wheeled his horse and galloped away. She turned back for her seat. Eleanor's expression seemed condescending. It altered slightly, however, when Norah heard behind her, "My lady!" She looked over her shoulder to see Charles—*Sir* Charles. She thought surely he was speaking to Eleanor, but no, he was looking directly at her from beneath his jeweled helm. And it was toward her that he leaned his lance. "May I have the honor of displaying your color?"

"And may I, Lady Kate?" This from a third knight who had also galloped to the gallery railing.

Norah was completely flustered, completely surprised by, filled by, a reasonless happiness. She tied on Charles's ribbon, and turned to the other knight. She'd known the king by the gilding of his armor, and Sir Charles by the shiny newness of his, but this third man was not at first recognizable to her. His armor was so covering she could only distinguish him by the boldly colored heraldric device depicted on his shield, which told her he was one of Jervais's men-at-arms. Her face flooded with color as she said,

"Sir, but I cannot favor you if I cannot first know who you are."

He lifted his gauntleted hand and pushed back his helmet, revealing the familiar face of Sir Gian of Lesterhouse. He asked again, "May I wear your color, lady?"

Sir Gian, who had always treated her with such reserve! What could this mean? Swallowing hard against the tears in her throat, she parted with a third ribbon. As she did, Gian called to Jervais, "It's as well you're not competing today. 'Twill keep your lady off the field and out from under the horses."

"Indeed," came Jervais's voice from behind her—in a tone she couldn't quite define.

Gian lowered his helmet. "She is brave, but brave is not always wise."

"No, not always," Jervais answered.

Norah looked into his deep silver eyes and felt herself drowning in them.

Eleanor meanwhile had her eyes cast down, her golden lashes lay together like iridescent fans. What was it about the woman that she could always look as if she were graced by the soft light of candle flames? She showed no interest in the exchange between Gian and Jervais.

From where Norah sat, she could hear the queen conversing with Jervais. Was it foolish hopefulness that made her think Eleanor's chatter limped a little?

"How you must miss being out there on the field," she said to him. "I know how you love war."

Jervais regarded her. "I hate war." His tone indicated surprise that she would think otherwise.

Eleanor glanced at him, and Norah caught the uncertainty on her face. That was like a sip of triumph to Norah; true, the draught was small, but it was pure and unmixed.

"But you were most eager to fight against the Saracens."

Jervais smiled at her. (Was there a trace of pity in that smile?) "I was but a boy then; I didn't know any better. Over the years I've fought . . ." he shrugged, "countless battles. I've fought ham-high in mud, in snow, and in choking dust, and now that I'm old and weighted with repentance what I remember most about war is the sight of men dying and the heart-rending wails of children driven from their homes."

Eleanor lifted a brow and murmured something that Norah couldn't catch, for just then the trumpets shrilled. She felt a pang of jealousy as Jervais responded to the remark by tipping his head back and giving the queen a deep rich laugh.

The knights had divided into two lines of twenty men each at opposite ends of the tourney field. Encased in their iron armor, mounted on their mighty chargers, bracing their cruelly pointed lances, they heard the trumpets and suddenly hurled themselves across the battleground. The two flashing squadrons rushed at each other like thunderbolts. The ground shook, sod flew, as they hurried forward with irresistible strength.

As they galloped, each man ducked down in his saddle and covered his body with his shield, each lowered his helmet nigh to the top of his shield; and kneed his horse so it would pass a chosen foe, and with a sure grip, aimed his lance point before him. As the great rush of men and mounts met and engaged, the splintering shock of their collision resounded. Many a war horse was thrown upon its hind legs so fiercely their riders could hardly force them back to their feet. Many a knight flourished a broken lance, and across almost every shield was a long jagged mark.

They dissolved into a single writhing line. Norah and several other ladies gave cries of distress. Others cried for blood: "Fairly broken!" "A noble course!" Of them all, Eleanor showed the least emotion.

The sole allowance to safety today was an agreement to aim one's lance at an enemy's body and not his head. Ransoms, after all, were better than corpses. Even so, the game was played robustly.

A well-aimed, powerful thrust by Charles transformed the spectacle of one of Eleanor's favored knights into a bruised, half-conscious, helpless man, blinded by his rammed helmet and ripe for capture and ransom.

A moment later, Sir Gian wheeled his destrier gracefully in the rising dust to attack a knight in Eleanor's Aquitaine armor. He held his lance so true that the queen's man took it dead-center on his shield and shot backwards out of his saddle. He seemed to hang an instant on the end of Gian's lance, then fell head over heels. Gian rode him down, whooping at his capture.

If Eleanor saw either of these defeats, she pretended not to and said nothing. Norah didn't know if her own champions were actually set upon defeating the queen's in particular or if this was only a coincidence, but she was inordinately pleased.

At first the fighting was good-natured, but as the men discarded their lances and shields and began to attack one another with swords, the contest became more desperate. An awful cloud of dust rose. All across the field, metal swords clanged like bells. The *mêlée* became nothing less than a pitched battle on a small scale.

Charles had somehow been unhorsed, and was now amidst a clutch of men fighting on their feet. His opponent was evidently determined to increase his wealth with the ransom of the day's honored knight, for he flung all his strength into his swing. The sheer weight of his stroke descended like a sledgehammer onto Charles's helmet. The new knight toppled like a log.

A great shout went through the crowd: "Dead!" Norah rose to her feet in a rustle of silk. Jervais did the same, and half turned to reach for her hand.

Chapter 26

It soon became clear that Charles was only soundly stunned. Captured he was, but he insisted on walking from the field on his own two legs. Jervais gave Norah a smile that reached into her and warmed her. Without a word, they took their seats again.

She was left utterly confused. How natural it had been to turn to him for consolation. And clearly he had felt the same. Was it possible that some sort of uneasy peace had emerged between them? It was like the view from a plateau of a painfully climbed mountain, and it seemed unreasonable to Norah that, having come so far, she could not enjoy it. Then again, maybe it was just as well, for she shouldn't let her imagination get carried away. Looking at her life, it was like a swift stream, satin smooth on its surface, but rushing headlong to one sheer drop of tragedy after another.

In the gallery and on the field the sun was hot and bright. Less venturesome knights began to drop out. Dust rose beneath the thrashing hoofs of the remaining horses. Squires dove into the murk of men and horses to drag out now this, now another stunned cavalier. The number of captives mounted, until only the most exceptional knights were left. These included Gian and Henry.

Norah could hardly make out what was happening anymore. From the thick cloud of dust that hung over everything came shouts and the clang of swords and the cries of horses. She could see only dim shapes twisting and plunging back and forth. Now and then a knight burst from the cloud, grabbed a new sword from his armorer, and turned to fling himself back into the battle again. She grew tired of the dusty sunlight and the heat and the smell. Her heavy hair felt like a blanket hanging down her back. The fighting surged back and forth until, finally, mercifully, Jervais had the horns sounded once more.

It was over. With their helmets hanging from their weary hands, the last warriors walked or cantered from the field. A few servants were left to pick up a combatant who had been tossed off his horse in the final moments. No one was dead, although several bones were broken, thigh bones, collar bones, and ribs. Doubtless the affair had brought honor to the men, though Norah could not quite appreciate how. Henry, his dusty face marked by rivulets of sweat, rode to the gallery to congratulate his vassal. "A very *gentle* passage at arms, Le Strand."

The men washed at the trough of cold water in the castle's inner ward. They were as hungry as hunters and ready for another round of gorging and guzzling. The smell of roasting venison and sauces flavored with rosewater filled the great hall. Servants set about immediately to bring food to the tables.

Norah excused herself to visit Charles in his chamber. Lloyd and another knight were with him. He was conscious, but his face was ashen; his eyes were like dark holes, and he complained of a terrific headache. "It feels swollen, ready to burst, like a melon in July." He wanted badly to join the feast, but Norah insisted he lay still. She went to the kitchen herself to make an herbal compress for his head. He was in too much discomfort to thank her, however.

When she rejoined the hospitality, the second course was being served: a thick French pottage, mallard pheasants and roast chickens, pasties of small birds, and a sweet *blanc mange* made with minced capon, cream, and sugar. A midget troubadour was extolling the glory of battle and retelling the great deeds of Charlemagne's paladins. When he finished, Eleanor was persuaded to sing for the company. With her harp, she produced several songs of her own composing, songs of romantic heroes. The names of Lanval and Tristan and Roland tumbled off her tongue.

When she fell silent, all the dames and nobles and villeins rose as one and shouted together. A jongleur tossed a sword high in the air and caught it as it whirled downward.

Just then, three squires tugged in an enormous pie. Amid an expectant hush, Jervais rose from his seat and went to slash it open with his dagger. Out fluttered a score of little birds. They began to dash about. Immediately a dozen falconers stood up, grinning. They were prepared, and now unhooded and loosed a score of hawks which pounced after the wretched birds and killed them, right above the feasters' heads. Inevitably there was confusion, a great rustling and a merry scrambling before the screeching hawks could be caught again, and hooded and taken away.

The visiting, eating, sporting, and minstrelsy went on into the evening, the whole characterized by bagpipe "music" that became deafening to Norah. Jervais left the hall, giving no explanation. When he showed no sign of returning, she excused herself as well. She was reeling from the din, yet she felt she should look in on Charles once more before she retired to her chamber.

He was better. She could tell by the strength of his humiliation. He was sitting up in bed, gloomily studying the misshapen wreck of his jeweled helmet. Hearing her entrance, he quickly tossed it aside. She smiled. "One day you will display that proudly, sir."

He turned his head and shut his eyes in an eloquent call for silence. But he was so obviously miserable that she couldn't help but try to comfort him. Hence she sat on a footstool near his bed and reached for his hand. He didn't want to give it, but was not so surly as to jerk away. She said, firmly, "I heard Lord Ravenford congratulate Lord Conniebrook on your training. He said he was impressed by the way you fought him and that he was not at all sure he was going to be able to set an example of valor for his little son seated in the gallery."

Charles grumped, "He wouldn't take my armor—or my horse."

"Your addubment armor? Your first war horse?

But of course he wouldn't! No more than he would do you the condescension of fighting against you with less than his full strength. He's a man of honor." She gave his hand a squeeze. "You'll show that helmet off one day, Charles, and tell how you were among the last of the day's warriors, and that it took a veteran of many battles and many wars to best you, though you were only newly knighted, a cavalier of just twenty years."

He looked at her sidelong. And finally gave her a slow, meditative, half-grin. "You and the earl are well-matched in your talents for giving misery a semblance of glory."

He wouldn't explain what that meant. He wasn't exactly cheered when she left him a few minutes later, but he was certainly less morose. She was starting back across the courtyard with a night candle to light her way, thinking of the acrobats beyond the blazing windows of the hall, turning themselves inside out—and thinking of her own bed, for she was exhausted and had had all she wanted of entertainment and ceremonies—when a page stopped her.

"A message from the king, my lady. He asks if you will most generously agree to meet him in your chapel, in your lord's balcony, alone."

Her heart thudded. What could Henry want?

She dismissed the boy. For a moment she looked up at the pacing sentinels on the rugged walls of the fortress. One of the queen's ladies-in-waiting flitted out of the hall, and before the bronze doors swung closed, Norah saw a man tossing a meat bone to the hounds prowling about the tables. Behind her in the courtyard, a young squire and a younger page

430

bustled about their evening duties. Through the portcullis of the gate she saw a group of villeins clapping and singing and dancing a homely round about a bonfire. She looked up again, and saw the evening star in the intensifying blue of the sky. With heavy trepidation, she started for the chapel. She felt as if she were being pushed, like a cart with frozen wheels.

Stillness met her inside the thick-walled tower. She lit her way up the stairs to the balcony. At the door, Henry ran into her on his way out. He kept her from stumbling backwards with his hands on her shoulders, saying, "There you are. I was about to give up on you."

She was held so close she felt his ornate dress sword pressing into her side. Somehow she kept her hold on her night candle. She felt the warmth of its flame beneath her chin. The light it threw up onto their faces made Henry look dangerous. She said nothing, only looked up at him warily.

"Well," he said, "what is it? If you're going to complain to me about Le Strand, don't say I didn't warn you. You wanted this, and now you've got it. I know all about his tossing you in his dungeon—yet it seems to me you're gaining ground here. Gian of Lesterhouse is a good man to have as a supporter, and—"

He paused, noting that she was not responding to his flood of justification. "What do you want? Is this what happened to Martin of Daigh Lott? Did you ask him to meet you here? Is it your intent to torment Le Strand, to get him killed, if not by one man then by another?"

Unease stirred in her stomach. This was all awry

somehow. "I came because I got a message that *you* wanted to meet *me*."

His eyebrows came down in an instant. He opened his mouth to speak, then closed it, for he'd heard what Norah had heard—a feminine voice in the lower part of the chapel: "Jervais?" it said softly.

Henry pinched her candle out. "Come, Katie," he whispered, "let's go and see whatever it is we were brought here to see."

Her mind strove to come to grips with this, even as she let him lead her through the door into the balcony. The chapel was dark except for a few candles burning on the altar. Henry's hand kept Norah from going forward to the balcony rail; they stayed in the black shadows toward the back as Norah made out the woman who paced below them.

She was alone. Her hands were clasped nervously. She was very French in her dress, and no other woman could be so straight-backed and formidable. It was Eleanor. As Norah's eyes adjusted to the dim light, the faint candleflicker playing on the faultless bones of the queen's face revealed her great beauty.

The outer door opened and shut with a thud. The queen turned quickly to the sound, her red skirts swishing out in a silken gleam. She arranged her features into a smile and said, "I came, but I can't stay long."

She held her hands out, and Jervais came forward to take them into his own long-fingered, capable hands. The ring on his middle finger flashed blood red in the candlelight. "Eleanor," he said. The name was an endearment the way he said it.

Norah felt Henry's hand tighten on her arm.

Random thoughts took shape in her mind and fluttered about aimlessly in all directions, like the startled birds out of Jervais's giant pastry. She'd suspected that Jervais and Eleanor must be finding moments to meet during this visit, and all along she'd prevented herself from thinking about it, for it was simply too terrible. She would have left the balcony that instant, but Henry held her arm tightly, as if he knew her will and was determined to make her stay.

Below them Eleanor murmured, "What is it, my poor darling? You look so solemn."

Norah glanced slant-wise at Henry. His bright, unblinking eyes gleamed in the dark. She felt alarmed for Jervais. Choked with cares as she was, an instictive loyalty gathered in her. She looked back down at the pair in the chapel. The candlelight fell softly on Jervais's hair, but left his face in shadow. He said, "I asked you to come so that I could thank you."

"For what?" Eleanor smiled at him tenderly.

"For your love, such as you could give me, such as it was." His tone seemed tinged with regret.

Eleanor's face lifted in a half-smile. "Was? I don't understand."

"I think it only honorable to tell that I'm in love with someone else now."

As Norah jerked involuntarily in the darkened balcony with Henry, Eleanor pulled back a little from Jervais. "You mock me! That . . . no! Not that *woman?*"

Norah winced. The word was full of spite, like saying "slut" or "whore."

"She's young and pretty—though somehow hardly

433

so pretty as I remembered her. She's no doubt lively in bed—no doubt a woman capable of corrupting an entire monastery! But she's a demon, Jervais!"

"She's not. She's been ill-regarded all her life, and couldn't help believing what she'd been told. But I've been looking into her background, and I don't think she's a demon at all. If anything, I believe she may be strangely blessed."

"Oh, Jervais, I've heard many stories of your determined little beauty since I've come here—how she led a troubador astray, and how, when you banished him, she ran off and had to be hunted down and disciplined. And how she tempted a knight and put your very life in danger. She is a sorceress, my darling, a witch!"

He took a deep breath, like a man whose chest was full of pent-up feeling which he was finding hard to express. "Eleanor, it will all be explained in the fullness of time, and when it is, knowing you, I think you will call it romance, not sorcery." His mouth moved in a slight, forebearing smile. "Romantic enough to be worthy of one of your composings. Suffice it to say for now," he went on quickly, "that she is Roger's true mother and my true wife. She has won her rightful place with me: she has become the center mark around which my life revolves. I can't imagine living without her. Whatever I do, I want her beside me. And whatever good befalls me, I want it to befall her as well."

Norah's legs felt weak; she locked her knees. Henry whispered, as if to himself, "Saint Michael be praised."

Eleanor disengaged her hands from Jervais's. Her

434

smile had faded into something else. Meeting his eyes squarely, the two contemplated one another for a long moment. Her voice was small and cold when it came out. "I can't believe this. She's enchanted you entirely."

He moved restlessly. "Listen to me. From the moment I met her there was something happening, something I couldn't quite unravel. Every detail of her seemed to affect me. Her simplest words seemed to contain enormous significance. The feeling was so strong that, being the man I am, I naturally interpreted it as dangerous.

"But some time ago I realized what was going on, what had struck me as so mysterious. Very simply, it was merely love. Love, Eleanor! So unusual, so almost magical—I'd traveled so long and so far from such a simple feeling that I scarcely recognized it even as I felt it."

Norah felt something open in her, like a flower.

"Dearest," he went on with quiet intensity, "I'd simply fallen in love with her. And I've loved her ever since. She means everything to me that love should mean."

Eleanor's reaction came slowly, and did not reflect any part of his obvious exultation. "You are lost to me."

"I can hardly expect you to accept a secondary position in my heart when you've refused to do so everywhere else. You are Eleanor. You are a great queen. You will always command first place or nothing, and that is your due. It might have been useful for me to lie to you, but we never once tarnished the love we shared, and I cannot tarnish it now with anything less than honor and truth. And the truth is," he finished soberly, "that we two loved ourselves to a checkmate, to a standstill, long ago."

"A standstill!" she hissed. "I have intervened on your behalf on more than one occasion! I've fought for you despite your blunders and your defiance of Henry."

"Indeed, my lady," he said more formally, even giving her a small bow, "and I will never cease being grateful for those good acts. To your kindness I owe everything. And I entrust myself to that kindness now."

They regarded one another suspiciously. At last he bent toward her, becoming more intimate again, as if to force her to feel his intensity. "Eleanor, all my life I've looked for someone. You know that's true, don't you? Someone I could spend my days with—and my nights. I *need* someone. Be happy for me that I've found her at last. Rejoice for me, if you ever loved me, and release me."

After a moment, holding herself stiffly erect, she said, "Very well. You're—" She stopped. It was as though she didn't trust her voice and must wait to mask some elemental emotion. "You're right. There is no point in tarnishing what was once so bright. I release you of your vow to me, Jervais. And I wish you well."

He pulled the garnet ring off his finger. "You must take this back."

If nothing that had been said seemed more than a dream to Norah, the significance of this act was utterly apparent. Relief washed through her, body and soul. She felt a need to weep.

Eleanor's smile returned Jervais's fleetingly as she accepted the ring. Looking at it, she said, "This caused you grief once, when it angered Henry."

"But more often it caused me joy."

Her smile gained strength, became a poignant grin. "He was jealous, my young king."

Beside Norah, Henry made a small sound of irritation.

Eleanor glanced about her, as if becoming aware of the passage of time. "I must go." She hesitated, and reached up to cup Jervais's cheek. "Goodbye, my darling."

Then with a rustle of silk, she was gone. As the door opened and closed, the candles on the altar shuddered. Jervais stood alone in the dimly lit chapel. Henry took a deep breath, let it out, then whispered in Norah's ear, "One thing I've always admired about your husband—whatever he sets himself to do, he succeeds, even if the task is the graceful rejection of a queen." His hand left her arm and she felt, rather than saw, him leave the balcony.

She stood alone now, too.

How deathly still everything had become. Norah heard the murmur of the sea, and felt the beat of her own heart. Jervais was looking up, watching for her when she took a faltering step forward. She peered over the balcony rail as if over the edge of an abyss that was as beautiful as it was dangerous.

His eyes were like a silver twilight, and as full of stars. So incandescent were those eyes that they threw light wherever they looked. And at the moment they were looking at her. He said, "Norah?"

Her heartbeat slowed from a gallop to a dreadful

halt. She'd come, finally, to the blade's edge of it. She could scarcely believe any of this. She couldn't speak. She yearned to, the urge swept through her again and again, and yet she couldn't. It seemed it was someone else who at last answered—and with such calm!—"How did you guess?"

"It wasn't necessary to guess. I simply looked at you and saw."

"You couldn't have, unless—" Her hands gripped the railing. She had to pull them free; they moved slowly to her face.

"The spell is broken, Norah."

Now came her gasp of terror. With her hands still covering her face, she stepped back from the railing. And then she fled.

In a moment she was on the open wall walk, running instinctively for the chamber tower which had become her place of refuge. She heard steps behind her. Jervais caught her arm, and when she pulled against his grip, his other arm circled her waist.

"Are you crazy? Running up here in the dark? Have you ever seen a man who's fallen—"

"Let me go!" She wasn't listening. She was huddling away from him, keeping her face hidden in her hands.

"Norah!" He tried to lift her chin.

"Don't look at me!"

"Norah, what's the matter with you! Stop this!"

But she wouldn't stop. At last he freed her enough to push her along before him toward the chamber tower.

The chamber was dimly lit by a fire. Roger was

downstairs with his night nurse. Norah crossed to the bed and hid her face in the tied-back draperies.

"Will you tell me what this is all about?" Jervais snapped.

"When was it broken?" she whispered.

"When you were lying in that bed near death."

So long ago! How could that be? "But I've been about the castle—no one noticed."

"They noticed. No one has said aught, but they've all noticed."

She recalled the way people had looked at her, as if something were changed about her, but they couldn't place just what it was.

She made her fingers search her face. It seemed she was no gargoyle. There were two eyes, a regular nose, lips, a chin. She let her hands fall, and slowly she turned. She felt exposed, as if she were utterly naked—but the fine edge of her dread had by now been blunted. And Jervais's expression was not one of horror.

"I'm not ugly?"

He closed his eyes and muttered a blasphemy.

"Sidella, the witch who helped me with the spell, warned me that she didn't know what the consequences would be if it were ever broken. She was very worried about it, and I imagined . . . I imagined I would become a monster."

Jervais came forward now, and took her into a huge embrace. "You're not a monster."

At first she went limp against him, groaning out loud. Then she leaned back, in order to see his face as she said, "But I'm not beautiful anymore, am I?"

He was cautious. "You're not as you were." He

laughed without humor. "I can hold you like this and not feel like ravishing you."

"You don't want me."

This time his laugh was less grim. "I didn't say that."

She hid her face in his shoulder. "I don't understand."

He led her to the hearth, where he sat facing her on the two stools there. The fire made his eyes shine like fine-gilt steel. "I think your playing with spells was unnecessary. I think you simply grew up, Norah. Grew up into a lovely woman."

"My hair would never have grown so fast," she argued.

"But did it grow any longer or thicker than before the nuns cut it?"

She ran her fingers through it. "Well, no—it was always my best feature."

He smiled down at his boots, then looked up again, and leaned forward and took her hand onto his knee. She felt the warmth of his flesh beneath her palm. He said, "I believe the spell wasn't nearly so magical as you and your Sidella thought. It was like a gloss, an aura that turned your natural prettiness—which you would have grown into anyway—into an unnatural, unholy beauty."

"It was strong enough that you couldn't pass me by without wanting to make love to me."

He frowned.

Her emotions felt flat. "You don't feel that way anymore, do you?"

He shifted on his stool, then said in a voice that melted over her skin like dark, warm honey, "If you're wondering if I want to make love to you, the answer is yes. Would you like me to prove it?"

Hot tears were building in her throat. She answered solemnly, "I would like you to hold me."

Her heart beat once, twice, and then he was rising, urging her up with him. He didn't just embrace her, however, but swept her into his arms and carried her to the bed. There he did hold her.

She snuggled against him, absorbing his smell, the warmth of his body, the security she felt just being with him. "Was it true," she asked shyly, "what you told Eleanor?"

"That I love you? Do you think I would be lying here doing nothing more than this, if it weren't true?"

"When did you first love me?"

He sighed. "I see this is going to be a long night."

Chapter 27

The morrow came. The fires in the hall had sunk, the torches smoldered in their sconces; the jongleurs' music had fallen silent, there was no more story-telling; the whole company of celebrants was either abed or departed. After two days of ever-intensifying gaiety, Conniebrook was suddenly returned to sobriety. Even the king and queen were gone—Eleanor, with her slanting eyes and her binding smile; Henry, with his uncertain temper. The sun was rising on the sea, a lemon-yellow orb. Birds looped above the surf. The water was the most wonderful blue, a green-blue near the shore, and a very dark blue out where the sails of the two royal ships were just disappearing.

Norah felt a new life beginning with that sunrise. She felt *she* was new. A change was happening in her, some painful growth. It was going to be hard, because she was not the child she had been, nor the sorceress Kate, and not yet the new Norah.

From the ramparts above the chamber tower, she

442

watched Jervais, in a grey cloak, ride up the path running between the castle and the sun-spangled bay to the postern gatehouse. He'd been to see the ships off, and now he was coming home.

A quarter of an hour passed, and then he joined her. He came out of the tower onto the wall walk saying, "Well, they're off. Of them all, only the king seemed to have any energy left. But that's the way he always is." He leaned his arms on the rampart and looked away, out to the horizon. His face took on an expression of remembering something far, far off and long ago.

He'd rejected a queen for her. It was all so neat, so cut and dried, such a *fait accompli* that she couldn't realize it. She studied him. He was bathed in brilliant sealight, yet there seemed to be something dark about him yet, some sadness. Was he grieving for the lost love he'd felt for the queen? Eleanor had held him enchanted, magnetized, spellbound for nigh a third of his life. It was hard to give up dreams, Norah knew—that was one fact of life in which she'd had much experience. She longed to embrace him, to solace him, but she couldn't seem to do either of those things.

They had neither one had any sleep. During the few hours between Jervais's meeting with Eleanor in the chapel and the extremely early hour at which the royal pair had risen to prepare to board their ships, they had talked—talked of this incident and that, of things which had never been talked of before, such as when she'd given birth to Roger, and Jervais's journey to Compostella, and of incidents which they had both seen but from opposite points of view, such as the episode with Andrew Pastor. Jervais confessed he had never known jealousy before that moment when it had wrung him so viciously. They had talked without even once kissing. There had seemed to be a subtle, invisible boundary between them, which neither knew exactly how to cross, a hesitancy that even now held them in thrall.

Gulls filled the sky with screams; the wind smelled salty. The silence between them went on. Had they worn out all their emotions in talking?

At last, turning from his absorbed examination of the sea, Jervais said abruptly, "I love you."

She stood there, incapable of responding, her heart as wordless as a bird in flight. She waited for several breaths before saying, "But part of you still loves Eleanor as well."

"A part of me."

Her soul was singed.

"That part always will love her," he went on, unmercifully bent on the truth. "It's a boyish part. But that love is so far away and long past it's like—" he searched for an analogy "—like a star, a dim sparkle with no fire to warm me." His face changed; he gave her a little cat's grin. "And if Eleanor loves anything it is to be queen."

The smile faded. "From this moment on, I swear that I am yours alone." He held out his hand, at long last bare of the garnet ring. "I know we have been wed twice, but I feel neither ceremony was proper or true, for in neither did I commit my heart to you. Hence," he said formally, "in the sight of God I hereby give you myself. I love you, Norah of Ramsay. You are the only woman I love absolutely, with my complete heart, with all my flesh and mind and soul."

There was a divinity in that moment. She took his hand, and at the touch of him felt faint. She squeezed her eyes shut, trying to force a firmer grip on herself. When she opened them again, it seemed a glass sphere had materialized around them, and the day within was incandescent.

Wordlessly he led her down to their bedchamber. She noted how deserted the tower was. No pages, no servants. The chamber was bright with the glare off the sea, but it too was empty. Theresa was gone, and the nurse, along with Roger. The revelations of the night had dazzled her and kept her from thinking about anything else, but now she seemed to wake from the trance which had bound her, and she fretted for her son.

"Where is everyone?"

"I sent them all away. Roger is fine, with that whole throng of women to look after him. I told them that you and I were going to sleep all day to make up for the sleep we've lost these past two nights—and that I would be very unhappy at any disturbance." He gave her a look. "I would be, too. I want you to myself."

On the table was a covered dish. He crossed to it and removed the lid, releasing a savory billow of steam. Some of Master Villhard's oven-fresh bread. He raised his eyebrows at her. "Are you hungry?"

She shook her head.

He put the cover back. "Neither am I." He came to her. "Not for bread anyway." His long, sensitive fingers began to untie her girdle. She saw in his face a proprietary look. She responded to it with a delicious shiver of belonging.

He slipped her gown and chemise from her shoulders, and she stood naked before him. He lifted her breasts with his hands and seemed to marvel at their pale roundness, their strawberry-pink tips. He said musingly, "You were such a skinny little thing. Your breasts were like two water-flower buds. And I assumed you were as much a full-grown woman as you would ever be. I was mistaken."

Blood was pounding in her head, and in several other places. "Jervais, I feel so unsure now, with the spell broken."

He tilted his head; his eyes were full of laughter. He put back her hair to uncurtain her entire pale nakedness. "*Is* the spell completely broken?"

She shuddered. "It must be! I can't bear to think that what you love may only be an illusion, not me at all."

"Ah, now you feel the scorpion's tail of your own magic." He moved in cautiously, smoothing his hands around her bare waist. "Darling, I love *you*. Now I'm going to kiss you," he whispered, "and you are to be still for it." He slipped an arm around her and lifted her toward his mouth. She revelled in the feel of his embroidered tunic against her naked skin, his hands on her bare back. She moaned and pressed herself against him.

His hands were moving on her when he let her mouth go. His arms crushed her to him with something akin to despair. "I've never known such a love before; I didn't believe it was possible; when I first felt it, I was afraid it would burn me to cinders."

446

She pushed out of his hands and went to the bed. In a moment he was undressed and reclining beside her with one arm bent and his head propped on his hand. It had been so long since they'd lain together naked that she'd almost forgotten the impact of his physical presence. He was a very big man indeed, all muscle, and very broad in the shoulders. And he was about to make love to her. His face was shadowed by his beard, since he had not shaved since yestermorn, yet he seemed mellow and washed of all darkness. While his free hand made signs and secret patterns on her flesh, he said, "You look frightened."

She gathered her courage and turned into him, and pressed her lips against his throat. "I want another child. I'm not afraid. I want—" Her brave speech was spoiled by the unstoppable yawn that overtook her.

He grinned. "Not afraid, only exhausted. Shall we sleep first?"

She leaned up over him. Her hair hung about them, enclosing them. "My lord, you must learn to gather your water-flowers afore they become too blowsy."

He rolled, placing her half beneath him. His mouth was at her throat. He nibbled the skin. His lips trailed to the pink nipples of her breasts, taking one and then the other between his teeth.

"I thought you weren't hungry," she murmured.

He squinted the way he always did when he was serious, making his eyes narrower and brighter. "Not for bread." He took her lips with his own, gently, then kissed her harder, opening her mouth. His hand ran down between her thighs, cradling her. His touch entered her, stirred the sleeping embers of her desire. The chamber seemed to fill with molten light which flowed liquidly over her skin. Her blood rose and sang like the surf: yes . . . yes. . . .

Lifting his head, he studied her even as he continued to caress her. "I love the way you look now, sort of vague and softened, your mouth pouting and soft and so luscious."

She felt a sudden, swollen, and almost irrational need of deliverance. "Jervais." Her eyes were stung with tears. "It's too much," she cried softly, "too much. Please don't be slow."

"No," he soothed, "no, I won't, no, my darling, my beloved. And may we have a child to show for this nine months hence, a little daughter with the smile of a female born to the uses of magic."

Norah felt that inexpressible sensation of being spread and the lovely pang of pleasure as he came into her.

"Je t'aime," he said, and "je t'aime . . . je t'aime," over and over.

"Je t'aime . . ." she whispered, picking up his rhythm, "je t'aime. . . ." She wound her arms around his shoulders, and her body moved with his. "Je t'aime. . . ."